Port Call to the Future

Port Call to the Future
©2012 Janet Elaine Smith

ALL RIGHTS RESERVED
No part of this book may be reproduced in any form, by photocopying or by any electronic or mechanical means, including information storage or retrieval systems, without permission in writing from both the copyright owner and the publisher of this book, except for the minimum words needed for review.

Port Call to the Future is a work of fiction.
Any similarities to real places, events, or persons living or dead is coincidental or used fictitiously and not to be construed as real. The exceptions are that both Maria Hallett (and her family) and Black Sam Bellamy were real historical figures, and the Whydah Museum is operational today. Barry Clifford and Ken Kinkor were members of the Whydah Expedition, which located the *Whydah*, and are affiliated with the Whydah Museum. They are used with their permission.

ISBN:978-1-935188-46-9

Edited by Star Publish LLC
Cover by Richard Stroud from strouddigitals@aol.com
Interior design by Star Publish LLC

A Star Publish LLC Publication
www.starpublishllc.com
Published in 2012
Printed in the United States of America

Port Call to the Future

Sequel to House Call to the Past

Janet Elaine Smith

SP
A Star Publish LLC Book

Dedication

To Maria Hallett and Black Sam Bellamy,
Who would not let me sleep until their tale was told.
May you finally rest in peace.

And to Dorothy Suggs, who gave me the great "cat line"
At the end of the book.

CHAPTER I

Yarmouth, Massachusetts, 1717

The handsome, black-haired sailor clung to the mast. The ship yawed, veering from one side to the other in the wind. The life of a privateer had seemed so exciting, but he had never seen the sea as ugly and mean as it was today. For the first time since he had left his home in England, he wished he was back there.

"Sam!" a fellow crewman bellowed, causing him to jump. He was not expecting anyone to call him. After all, he was the newest member of the crew. He hoped they would not miss him, as his stomach felt like it was in his throat.

"Sam!" the man called again. "Get on deck and give us a hand. We need everybody topside to bend the ship."

Sam Bellamy wondered how he would find the strength to move his feet up to the top deck, much less help secure the sails and ropes, but if he was going to continue on the trip once the storm abated, he knew he had to do whatever was asked of him now.

Sam wandered about, forcing himself to do what was necessary in spite of his own yens. He toppled about like a bloody drunkard.

"Whatcha need?" he asked the captain.

"It's all I can do to try to keep her on course. We've got to get the bower down as soon as we are close enough to land to let down the pinnace."

Sam smiled. It had taken some work, but he had kept his ear tuned to the men's conversations. He knew, now, that the captain wanted to set the anchor down off the coast and get the men to shore in the little boat.

"Aye, aye, Cap'n," Sam said. "You want me to fit the pinnace for shore?"

"Go to it," the captain said. He turned to face Sam. The water, which was spraying him in the face, came spouting back out as fast as he could get rid of it. Between the whale-like shots of water he said, "You've turned out all right, Bellamy. Glad to have you aboard."

"Thank you, sir," Sam said. He knew he didn't need his approval, as long as he did his job well, but he was glad to have it nonetheless.

❋ ❋ ❋

The men trudged through the muddy trails of Yarmouth, Massachusetts to Crosby's Tavern. They knew there would be a roaring fire to warm them on the outside and plenty of black rum flowing to warm them from the inside out.

"Where we headin'?" Sam asked. "Someplace dry, I hope."

The two men behind Sam grinned broadly at each other.

"Betcha Maria's out tonight," one of them said.

Sam wondered who Maria was. He couldn't imagine any woman being out in weather such as this. And, he wondered, *why* would she be meandering about? What could she possibly hope to find on a night like this?

❋ ❋ ❋

Soon the men had shed their wool coats and were sitting around, exchanging stories of days gone by and storms which "were far worse than the likes of this." Sam enjoyed listening to the tales of the sea. There was something about the water that made his skin crawl. He dreamed about the day he would have such stories to tell as well. *Tonight will be the start of my own collection of memories. Something,* he thought, *is going to change my life.* He could feel it in the air. Something more than high winds, thunder and lightening. He had never known such a feeling before, yet there was no denying it.

※ ※ ※

The door burst open and a young girl, her hair as black as his own, clad in a bright red cape and with red slippers on her lovely feet nearly fell into the tavern.

"Wondered how long it'd be 'ere you got here," Mr. Crosby, the tavern proprietor, said. "The men have all been asking after Maria. They all figured you'd be here."

Maria shook her cape as she dropped it and found an empty table where she could perch herself.

The men crowded around her, casting longing glances in her direction as they talked of life in Yarmouth since they had last struck anchor there.

Sam, his gaze intently set on the beautiful young woman, wondered at her presence in such a place as this. He had known more than his share of women in the few months since he had joined on with the crew of the *Maid Marian*, but none held the fascination he felt for this one.

"Who's the dame?" he asked Mr. Crosby, who filled his mug with more rum as they talked.

"Maria," he said simply, as if that would explain everything. Like Sam should know Maria. Of course Sam could tell by watching the men with her that *everybody* knew Maria! Everybody except him. But the more he studied her, the more he was determined to remedy that situation before the night was over.

Mr. Crosby went to Maria and spoke to her, motioning towards Sam. In return, Maria smiled warmly, enticingly, at him. She lifted her glass in the air, as if to propose a toast to the stranger.

When Sam had enough rum under his black leather belt to make his confidence as bold as his voice, he wandered to Maria's table. The other men who were sitting with her moved aside, almost as if she held a magical power over them.

The two young people exchanged idle chit-chat for what seemed like minutes, but had in reality turned into hours. The storm was still raging outside, the rain and hail pelting the roof, the wind howling through the cracks in the building. Sam shivered from time to time as he heard timbers breaking and crashing to the ground.

"I've got to go!" Maria exclaimed, jumping to her feet and wrapping herself in her red cape. She pulled the hood securely up over her head, but wisps of the curly black hair disobediently popped out here and there, defying any semblance of order.

"Let me accompany you home," Sam said.

"No!" Maria protested. "You can't! You mustn't!"

Sam sat and watched as she hurried out the door, nearly running down the muddy streets to her home.

Sam's head told him to do as Maria said, but his heart told him to go after her. Never had he known such a feeling. nor such a woman. She was barely past childhood, he mused, yet she knew how to handle herself like a professional.

The thought frightened Sam. Was it possible? Could such a young woman as Maria possibly be... No, he decided, shaking his head to clear it of such nonsense. Still, the men did all know her. He wondered how many of them had actually *known* her. The thought was more than he could bear.

Sam got up and pulled his own navy wool pea coat about himself and went out to brave the storm. It didn't matter how wet he got. Suddenly nothing mattered. Nothing but Maria. He had to catch up with her. He had to find her. He had to make her understand.

When Maria heard the footsteps behind her, she quickened her own pace, trying desperately to keep ahead of him. Instinct told her it was Sam Bellamy. She knew if she allowed him to catch up with her she could not be trusted as to what action she might take. He was so infuriating. So forceful. Yet beneath it all there was a tenderness she felt which defied explanations or logic.

"Maria!" the voice called out to her. "Maria! Wait! I must see you!"

Maria did not turn to look at him. She did not answer him. She fled to the safety of her father's house, pushing hard to get in. She had left the iron across the door ajar when she had gone out earlier so she could get back in easily. The wood chink she had wedged between the door and the frame fell to the ground and lay floating in the puddle at Sam's feet.

Sam watched as the tiny swatch of red wool from her cape which had caught in the doorway disappeared inside. He heard the *clunk* of the iron rod as it was set in place to hold the door securely in place against the winds—and against the onslaughts of Sam Bellamy.

"Maria!" Sam bellowed, banging on the door with tightly clenched fists. "Maria! Open up!"

Maria stood inside the house, leaning against the door. She gasped for breath, as the race home had taken its toll on her.

"Maria!" Sam yelled. "If you don't open this door—right now—I'll break it down!"

Maria could hear the desperation in Sam's voice. Afraid her father would hear him, she pulled the security bar back just enough to allow the door to open a crack.

"Go away!" she hissed at him. "If you wake my pa, he'll kill you!"

"I'm not scared o' yer pa, nor nobody else, 'cept you."

Maria began to laugh. It was the strangest laugh Sam had ever heard. It was not a normal, soft laugh, but a cackle, much as he imagined a witch would laugh.

"You're scared of me?" Maria asked. "Why? I ain't got no way to hurt the likes of you."

"You've already hurt me," Sam said through the crack in the door.

"Me? Hurt you? But how?"

"You went and stole me heart away," Sam said. "I've got a hole clear through where it oughtta be."

"That's nonsense!" Maria said. "But, well, if you insist, meet me tomorrow at the Inn. You'll just have to wait 'til then." Her statement was followed by more of that same hollow laughter, then the door clicked shut and the iron bar went back in place with the dead sound of finality.

❄ ❄ ❄

The morning of the second day in Yarmouth brought only more of the same. The wind still howled as it blew the rain and the trees out of control. Most everyone stayed in their own homes, afraid to venture out.

Sam Bellamy had found a room at the Inn, and he arose early in the morning, wondering what time Maria would come, or *if* she would come.

The men gathered around the table, waiting as Mrs. Clark served them venison sausage, corn cakes and coffee. They ate greedily, as if it was the first and last meal they would ever have.

Sam listened as the others jabbered away gaily. They all loved the sea, as any sailor does, but they welcomed a few days inland too. As Sam tried to see out the window he wondered if this town would ever be land-locked again. Everything seemed to be drowning.

"How'd it go with Maria last night?" the captain asked Sam, his eyes glistening mischievously.

"Whadya mean?" Sam asked innocently. "I didn't do nothin' with Maria."

"Well, that's good to know," the captain said. "Least you ain't no better than the rest of us."

The men began to explain their plot to Sam.

"Now you take Maria," Briny said. "She's a woman what likes a man who's rough an' tumble. Sam, if'n you wants to win her heart, you best be set to show her who's the boss. Be hard on her! She'll thank ye fer it later."

"Don't drop yer guard fer a minute," the captain warned Sam. "If ye do, she's sure to run away 'fore ye get a chance to do what you want to do to her."

Sam could hardly believe his ears. Here were these men, all giving him advice on how to win Maria. He wondered how many of them had already "had their way" with her.

Sam's mind wandered back to the girl who had sat and drunk with the best of the men last night. Why were they all so concerned about his victory or loss of Maria?

She seems so innocent, Sam thought, *but I'll bet she's been laid by every last one of them.* The idea made him cringe. He wanted her desperately. He would have her, if it was the last thing he ever did.

❋❋❋

It was much later when Maria rushed into the Inn, her cape dripping wet. The rain fell gently from the black curls which still hung loosely around her face.

"Ye came," Sam said.

Maria looked around the Inn. She noticed that they were alone, save for Mrs. Clark, whom she could hear clanking pots and pans in the kitchen while she prepared another meal for the men.

They would return, Maria knew. Then what would she do? No, what would she do if they *didn't* return? Oh, she was so confused. She had never felt like this before. One part of her cried out for Sam Bellamy to love her. The other side panicked at the thought of his trying to possess her.

"Let nature take its course," she said, too softly for Sam to hear.

Sam began to talk to her. His voice was soft, tender, not that of the rough sailors Maria was used to. It made her uncomfortable.

Sam sensed her uneasiness. He recalled the words of his shipmates. Could it be that they were right? They had obviously known Maria far longer than he had. Well, it was worth a try. He certainly wasn't making any headway like this.

Mrs. Clark served them a big steaming bowl of fish stew, which Sam ate with gusto. When he saw that Maria had nearly finished her bowl as well, he leaned across the table, his face so near hers Maria felt his hot, steamy breath full in her face.

"Come upstairs with me," he said. It was not an invitation, but rather an order.

Maria hesitated. Sam rose and grabbed her by the hand.

"I told you to come upstairs with me!" he growled, appearing to be a completely different person than the man who had been sitting there just moments earlier.

Maria could not explain her actions, but she willingly—no, gladly—followed along with him. She gave no thought now to her father, nor to her sister-in-law who was ready to deliver her baby at any time and whom she had been sent to help in the midst of this storm. Maria had her own storm to try to calm, the storm that ravaged within her heart, which tore at the very core of her being.

"I'm ready for you," Sam said, securing the door behind them and then tossing the key into the window box just outside the window.

Maria went to the window and leaned outside. The shutters flapped violently in the wind, hitting her on the head and nearly knocking her unconscious. Besides, her arms were far too short to reach the box or the key.

Sam fell onto the bed and began to laugh, a deep, hearty laugh. He would play his role to the fullest. He found his new character a most pleasing one. The best part of it was he could see that Maria enjoyed it as well.

"What's so funny?" Maria asked, putting on a pouty, little-girl look.

My God! Sam thought. *She is no more than a child. I must be mad!* Yet he could not stop himself, even if he wanted to. And he didn't.

To his surprise, when she had the shutters closed, Maria came over and stood at the side of the bed. She began to unfasten her jumper and soon it fell to the floor.

Sam gasped as he took in the fullness of the lovely young body before him. It had been disguised, oh so well, in her shapeless frock. But now, as Maria stood before him, he knew she was far more than a child. She was the most beautiful woman he had ever laid eyes on, and in the past few months that was a fair number. Suddenly she jumped.

So she wanted to play hard-to-get! Well, he would give her a run for her money.

Sam jumped up from the bed and began to chase Maria about the room. She jumped onto the bed and ran across it. He grabbed for her and she jumped to the side, then she turned on him and pushed him hard onto the feather mattress.

Maria laughed. Again it was that inhuman, cackling laugh.

"Try to get me if you can," she teased.

Sam easily rolled over on top of her and began to tear the rest of her clothes away.

The rest of their time together was lost in history. When they finished their playful romp, Maria quickly got up and dressed.

"I have to get to Mehitable's," she said, running out the door. She did not know, nor care, if Sam knew who Mehitable was or that she had to go help her in case her baby came in the storm. No, Sam Bellamy had given her more than she had asked for. More than she had dared to hope for. And judging by the look on Sam's face, he had gotten all he hoped for as well.

❋ ❋ ❋

On the fourth day the storm cleared and the men were ready to set sail once more. The captain, as always, was the first one on board. The men had made the necessary repairs and it was ready to cast off. He sounded the fog horn, calling the crew from the Inn, the tavern, from all corners of the village.

The sound shook Maria Hallett to the very core of her being. Soon she was on her way to the shore. She knew that sound all too well. It meant that the sailors would be going out to sea. Sam would be leaving. Her heart sank at the emptiness she felt within her very being. She longed for him to stay, yet she knew that could never be. He was a sailor—a privateer. Nothing, she knew, could keep a man of the sea on dry land. She was lucky the storm had lasted as long as it did. At least they had their few days together. She would hold them close within her heart until he returned.

As if he was reading her mind, Sam walked up behind her and swung her around to face him.

"Don't worry, my lovely," he said, again seeming to have changed like a chameleon back to his original self. "I'll not forget ye. I must go out to the sea. The water is calling me. I'll make my fortune on the waters. When I do, I promise I'll come sailin' back to you. Mark my words, Maria, I'll be back fer ye. Just hang a lantern out to sea and let me know you're still here, waitin' fer me, too."

Maria laughed. "And just where am I supposed to hang these lanterns?" she asked. "On a wave?"

"Why no, my little witch," he said, joining her in the laughter. "You'll hang them on the tail of a whale."

The horn sounded again. The men passed them by, one and all calling their goodbyes to Maria but not daring to interfere any more than that.

"I've got to go," Sam said, kissing her so hard she nearly lost her breath. She responded warmly to his passion. She clung to him fiercely.

"Don't go!" she begged. "Please don't leave me here alone."

"I have to," Sam said. "Try to understand. But I'll be back. Wait for me."

❈ ❈ ❈

Maria stood on the shore, the tears streaming down her cheeks, as she watched her true love, her first love, set out to sea. He promised to come back for her, but she had a sinking feeling in the pit of her stomach that she would never see Sam Bellamy again.

CHAPTER II

As the months wore on, Maria Hallett waited for Sam Bellamy to return. She longed for him, ached for him. One day, as she sat moping in the house of John and Mary Hallett, her ma and pa, she noticed a strange sensation in her stomach.

"Ma," she said, getting up from her loom where she was working her magic to create the finest fabrics in all of Cape Cod.

"What is it?" her mother asked. "What's wrong?"

Maria described her feeling to her mother.

"Does it mean that Sam is coming back for me?" she asked innocently. "Is this what love feels like?"

"No," Mary said to her daughter, speaking softly. Maria caught a glimpse of a tear in her mother's eye.

"Ma," Maria said, "what is it? Did I say something wrong?"

"No," Mary said. "Well, yes. Your pa, he's gonna be furious."

"Ma!" Maria shouted. "What did I do?"

"It's not what you did," Mary said. "At least not just you. You and Sam," Mary asked, knowing the answer all too well, "Did you—you know, did he make love to you?"

"Oh, Ma!" Maria exclaimed. "I wanted to tell you, but I was so scared. Ma, it was the most wonderful thing in the world."

"But Maria, how could you? He's the devil incarnate! Everybody knows him for what he is."

Maria's eyes dropped to the floor. She felt such shame, yet the joy of the moments they had spent together far outweighed anything else.

The rumors had flown fast and furiously since the day Sam Bellamy had sailed off with the crew on the *Maid Marian*. The fishermen from Yarmouth and other Cape Cod towns all bore witness to the same facts. Only Maria clung to the memory of the handsome, dashing young Sam Bellamy who had set foot on Yarmouth sod just a few weeks ago.

"Maria, don't you see? You are going to have a baby!" her mother shrieked at her. "Sam Bellamy's baby! The devil's baby! Oh, Maria, whatever is to become of you?"

❈ ❈ ❈

Sam Bellamy, following the cue of his crewmates, had become what people made him. He was no longer Sam Bellamy, the English privateer. No, now he was Black Sam Bellamy, pirate of the seas, captain of his own ship, the *Whydah*, which he had stolen from its captain. The crew, frightened of the fierce man, joined on with him and soon they were as loyal to Black Sam as they had been to its original owner.

Black Sam roamed the seas by day and by night, often attacking ships much bigger than the *Whydah*. Beneath it all was the reason which made it all perfectly legal for him to pursue such a course of action.

"It's for Maria," he would say, smuggling the treasures onto the land at Hyannis, where he had found a friend to sympathize with his exploits. Ironic, it was, that his friend just happened to be another Hallett.

❈ ❈ ❈

"Another load?" Thomas Hallett asked Sam as he stood at the front door, awaiting an invitation in.

"Yes," Sam replied. "Can we bury it in the same place?"

"Sure," Thomas Hallett replied. He was a man of honor; he would never steal from Sam Bellamy, but if something should happen to Sam there would be nothing to stop him from claiming the treasures as his own.

"We'll be back shortly," Sam said, then disappeared.

Soon Sam was back, dragging a huge trunk along behind him. It made a deep rut in the sand, which he stopped every so often to cover by brushing his foot back and forth over it.

"What is it this time?" Thomas Hallett's wife, Sarah, asked him as they sat at the table eating the evening meal.

"Emeralds," Sam said. "Some of the finest I've ever seen."

Neither Thomas nor Sarah asked about the jewels. They had discussed this matter many times and Thomas had finally succeeded in convincing Sarah that if they knew nothing about where it came from they could not be found guilty of any wrongdoing if Sam was ever caught and tried as a pirate.

Before long the conversation shifted.

"Maria?" Sam asked simply.

Thomas and Sarah looked at each other. Their eyes seemed to be filled with fear. They had not talked about what they would tell Sam if he asked about her, as he always did. Now, the matter was before them.

"I..." Thomas hesitated, thumping his fingers nervously and rhythmically on the table. "I think you'd better tell him."

"Me?" Sarah shouted at her husband. "Why me? She's *your* kin!"

"Will somebody please tell me what has happened to Maria?" Sam pleaded, fearing the worst possible news.

"She—she had a baby," Sarah finally said.

Sam could hardly believe his ears. She had played so innocent with him. Here she was sleeping with every sailor who set into port. Of all the nerve! And he was out risking his very life to gather enough treasures and goods to her to feel worthy of her hand in marriage.

Worthy! he thought. *I'm far better than she is.*

When Sam finally got enough courage mustered up he asked, "But the father... Who?"

Thomas and Sarah looked at each other in total shock. Surely, if what Maria said was true, he of all people would now who the bastard's father was.

"Maria," Thomas said, "she claims it's yours."

Sam rolled his eyes heavenward, threw his head back and laughed hysterically.

"You mean Maria had my kid?" he asked. Suddenly his face grew serious and he asked, "Was it a boy or a girl?"

"A boy," Sarah said, then added, "He looks just like you, he does."

"A wee pirate Sam!" Sam exclaimed, obviously delighted with such news. "I've got to go to her. If she's there alone, with me baby, I've got to go and see her."

"There's more," Thomas said. "I think you're best to stay away from her."

"Stay away from me own flesh and blood?" Sam bellowed. "Over me own mother's grave, I'll leave her there alone."

"You see," Thomas continued, relating the tale of Maria Hallett to Sam Bellamy for the very first time, "the whole town council set about to lock her up in jail."

"But why?" Sam asked. "With a new baby to tend, they couldn't do such a thing!"

"They said the baby died," Sarah said. Her mind went back over the babies she had lost. She knew the hurt Maria would feel if the baby had died.

"Who killed him?" Sam yelled, pounding his fists on the table. "Who killed me own son?"

"No," Thomas explained. "He didn't really die. Only Jonathon—you know, my brother, Jonathan—he said it was so."

"Go on," Sam said, sensing there was much more to this story than he had heard so far.

"A stranger appeared in town," Thomas said. "He seemed to be able to work miracles. They said he breathed into the little Sam's mouth and he began to cry."

"Little Sam?" Sam asked. "Maria named the baby Little Sam?"

"Yes sir. After you, Maria claimed. She's one mighty fine little mother, too. Takes care of him real good."

"Then I've got to go to her," Sam insisted again.

"There's still more," Thomas said. "Jonathan claimed Maria was a witch and that she'd had the baby by bein' in league with the devil."

"He called me a devil, did he?" Sam yelled. "I'll show him the devil in me! Let me at him!"

It took all the strength Thomas could find to stop Sam Bellamy from going to kill Jonathan. He knew he couldn't let him anywhere near Yarmouth.

"They were going to throw her in jail," Sarah said, "but then that stranger— you know, the one who saved little Sam's life—he did a very brave thing."

"Wha'd he do?" Sam asked.

"He married Maria," Thomas said.

Sam jumped to his feet and again began to run for the door. "There's not a man alive who can marry me Maria! I won't hear of it! I'll put an end to this, if I have to put an end to *him*!"

❈ ❈ ❈

"Let him go," Sarah said as they watched Sam head back to the *Whydah*. "Just pray that he'll come to his senses before he docks at Yarmouth."

❈ ❈ ❈

With no warning and the town of Yarmouth in view, a terrible gale arose. It was a storm as fierce as the one that had sent him ashore the first day he had met Maria.

"Hold the masts tight!" Sam bellowed to the crew. "We're gonna put in to shore at Yarmouth."

With the wind the way it was, it was no surprise to any of the men that their captain gave such an order. None of them had any idea of what lay behind his order.

Sam checked around town, asking person after person about Maria. He learned that her husband was a doctor, and "a fine one at that." He was also threatened by the townsmen to stay away from Maria.

Finally, in sheer desperation, Sam saw that it was hopeless to try to get to Maria. The best he could do was to take a token of his love to Maria and leave it at her doorstep. He had been told which house was theirs, and he waited until it was dark before he took a basket filled with fish, pearls and a fine linen hand-embroidered handkerchief he'd gotten in France for his love. He hoped she would know who had left the gifts there for her. Both items came from the sea, and she just had to know it was from Sam.

❀ ❀ ❀

Before he left town he made one final visit. He called on Jonathan Hallett and beat him to a pulp. He was careful not to kill him, but he came as close as he dared before he fled and boarded the *Whydah*.

❀ ❀ ❀

Only one more time did Black Sam Bellamy venture back to the town of Yarmouth. It was a day he would never forget.

It was another storm, which should have been a clue by now that even the gods did not want him to see Maria.

Sam pulled the *Whydah* up off shore and dropped anchor. He released the men for the duration of the storm, then walked slowly along with Ahab, his first mate.

"I've got a tall order for ya," Sam said to Ahab. "It's one I'd rather do meself, but I know the doc would never hear of it. Not from what I hear tell."

"What is it?" Ahab asked.

Sam told Ahab about Maria and his son, Little Sam. He laid out a plan for Ahab to kidnap the child.

"Let me see if I've got this straight," Ahab said. "You're scared to go in after him, but you want me to do it. Is that it?"

"Aye!" Sam said.

"You're mad!" Ahab shouted. "I'll have no part of it. You do it yourself!"

Sam pulled his dagger from its sheath and swung it through the air, whistling as it whizzed past his ears.

"And I'll have yer bloody head!" Sam shouted.

"I'll be back inside an hour," Ahab said, hurrying away from his captain, hoping to escape his wrath.

Port Call to the Future

※ ※ ※

Black Sam Bellamy sat at Crosby's Tavern, belting one mug of sweet black rum after another. The more he drank, the bolder and more brazen he became. When enough time had passed that he figured Ahab should have returned, he became nearly uncontrollable. He had no way of knowing that at that very instant John Hallett, Jonathan Hallett and Dr. Angus McPherson were carrying Ahab off to the sea, where they would cast him to fend for himself in the troubled waters.

※ ※ ※

With that task behind them, the three men headed for Crosby's Tavern in search of Black Sam. On Maria's behalf, they were determined to put an end to Black Sam Bellamy.

Sam recognized John Hallett immediately. He was not any fonder of him than Maria's father was.

With the look of a most determined man, John headed fearlessly towards Sam.

"You've ruined my daughter's life," John yelled at him. "Now it's time you pay the piper. Draw your weapon!"

Sam went to reach for his dagger when...

Black Sam Bellamy dropped to the floor. It was the biggest bee sting or mosquito bite he had ever felt. He did not see Dr. Angus McPherson, Maria's husband, behind him, nor know that he held the most dangerous weapon any of the people of Yarmouth had ever seen.

Doc Angus grinned, blew on the needle of the hypodermic needle, filled with a powerful knock-out medicine that he'd brought across the field of poverty grass—and across time—with him.

He joined the others as they hoisted Black Sam by the arms and feet and carried him off to the jail.

It was April, 2008. Blair Smythe was sitting at her kitchen table, the papers and books spread out over its entire surface.

"I wish I had known you," she said, running her fingers over the yellowed pages of an old personal journal. "Maria Hallett, you must have been quite a woman."

CHAPTER III

Hyannis, Massachusetts, April, 2008

Blair's eyes wandered from one document to another, finally focusing on a file folder marked "Andrew Hallett, Jr." She took the folder and began examining its contents.

As a recent college graduate with a master's degree in history, she was enthusiastic about all she had learned, but the most exciting part was her own heritage.

"Hallett," she mused aloud. "I'm proud to be one of the earliest families of Cape Cod."

She lifted her eyes heavenward and said, "Thank you, Grandfather Smythe." It was because of his generosity and the trust fund he had established for her that she had been able to attend college and she would never have to worry about money again. She was only twenty-six years old, and already she was a wealthy woman.

She set the file for Andrew aside and grabbed a huge pile of papers instead. It told the tale of Maria Hallett, who had been accused of witchcraft, and Black Sam Bellamy, the pirate who had wooed her, won her and given her a baby, all in one short stay at Yarmouth during a storm.

"Must have been some storm," she said aloud, laughing at how much could happen in just four days. Blair could not explain it, but she always felt a mysterious, eerie closeness to Maria Hallett. It was more than their natural relationship. They were distant cousins, umpteen times removed, since Blair's grandmother Smythe was a Hallett by birth. It was more than living in the Hallett house, which originally belonged to Thomas and Sarah Hallett, in Yarmouth.

Blair had fought so hard when her parents had announced that they were moving to a condominium. Blair and her brother were both out on their own, and they said they didn't need that much room. Finally, to prevent any other family from moving into the Hallett house, Blair had purchased it from her parents.

The renovation was nearly completed, Blair realized as she looked around her. She closed her eyes and imagined Thomas and Sarah sitting at the same table where she was now seated, entertaining Black Sam Bellamy.

In amongst all the papers she had gathered on Maria Hallett and Black Sam there had been one extremely small notice in the "town gossip" column: *Much to everyone's chagrin, Black Sam Bellamy was again entertained at the home of Thomas and Sarah Hallett.*

"Why didn't you leave me some clues?" Blair asked aloud. She sat and waited for an answer, as if she expected Black Sam's very ghost to reply.

Blair continued poring through the pages of documents she had collected about the infamous Maria Hallett. At last her eyelids grew heavy and her head dropped onto her arms on the table. As she slept, she dreamed of pirates sailing the wild seas, treasures hidden on the shore and witches being burned at the stake or hanged. She awoke in a sweat, shaking from the sense of reality she felt.

She shook her head, her long, blonde hair flying from side to side, trying to rid herself of the images she had seen. They would not leave; she was their captive.

"I know what I'll do," she said, though no one was there to hear her. "I'll revenge Maria's fate and Black Sam Bellamy's demise."

She rushed to the phone and began to call friends and influential people on Cape Cod, from Hyannis to Yarmouth and everywhere in between.

"It will be fabulous!" she exclaimed to Edith Hallett, the curator of the Yarmouth Historical Society Museum. "Just think, it is almost three hundred years since they disappeared. It was in April, 1717. This is April, 2008. We can celebrate their love with the gala right here in Hyannis. Oh, won't it be wonderful? We'll all come in costume, and it will be just like we were living back then."

Blair's enthusiasm was contagious and soon all of Cape Cod was looking forward to the event. The publicity was spread far and wide and relatives of the Hallett clan began to arrive in droves.

❇ ❇ ❇

Black Sam Bellamy, in Yarmouth, Massachusetts, in April, 1717, was carried by John Hallett, Jonathan Hallett, Dr. Angus McPherson and numerous other men to the brig, where he was placed for safekeeping, with Jonathan Hallett standing guard over him. Outside the jail, the storm raged on and on, with the streets being nearly empty.

As Jonathan Hallett napped, leaving Black Sam Bellamy unattended, the pirate pulled the sash from about his waist, formed it into a loop and managed to put the loop about the key to the cell. He pulled it to the bars, reached down and retrieved it and unlocked the great iron door, hitting Jonathan on the head to be sure he had plenty of time to make a getaway.

Black Sam let out a shrill whistle, the call to his crew, and together they ran through the mud and rain to the shore, where they quickly boarded the Whydah.

The anchor was hoisted and the schooner set sail, despite the weather.

The townsmen, hearing the commotion outside, raced to the shore to try to foil Black Sam's escape, but they were too late. There was naught they could do but stand and watch the devil, Black Sam Bellamy, and his crew pull away from them, knowing that one day he would return to haunt them.

As they watched, helpless, it seemed that the gods of the sea were in harmony with them. A bolt of lightening flashed from the heavens and struck the Whydah. *They heard the cries from the crew as the ship split in half, then sank into the depths of the ocean.*

They were the screams of death. The men were plunged to their eternal doom. Twelve men survived and made their way to shore, then were nabbed and dragged to jail to await their hanging.

When the storm lifted, the men from the village began to search for the bodies, continuing until they had located one hundred and seventeen bodies. The entire crew was accounted for—all except Black Sam Bellamy, who had disappeared.

❄ ❄ ❄

As the ship split in the middle, Black Sam felt himself sliding downward, into the water, away from the light, away from humanity, away from life. He was a strong man—a strong swimmer—yet he was unable to save himself.

He felt the forces pulling at him from within the water. Perhaps the people of Yarmouth were right after all. Maybe he had turned into the devil's adversary. Was Lucifer coming to claim his soul for the ills he had wrought on others? If only he had another chance. Some way that he could right the wrongs he had committed. He had only done what he did for Maria's sake. Maybe she was a witch, like they said. If it had not been for her, he would have spent his entire life as any normal sailor. Were it not for her, he would not be afraid to die. His soul would be at peace, not in the turmoil it was enduring at this moment.

The eddy sucked him farther and farther down, into the darkness of the turbulent waters. He closed his eyes, praying that it would end.

❄ ❄ ❄

Suddenly he felt himself being cast upwards. The sea vomited him out, as the whale must have done to Jonah centuries earlier.

Strange, Sam thought, *having such a thought at a time like this*. His mind wandered back to the woman, Susannah Wesley, who had taken him in after his mother died. She taught him the ways of God when he was but a lad. He had gone so far astray. Had she been praying for his soul all these years? Was she even alive? He had lost all contact with the Wesley family, putting them out of his mind, lest they should learn of his life and what he had become. How long had he been in the deep waters of the ocean? He had no idea.

Sam felt solid ground beneath his body, which lay sprawled in a heap on the shore. He wondered if he was dead. He sat up and rubbed the water and sand from his eyes. He looked around and found himself right in the center of a huge circle of—*pirates!*

Sam knew now that he must be dead. There couldn't possibly be any other explanation for it. *So all pirates die and go to hell,* he thought. *At least I'll have company.*

❅ ❅ ❅

A beautiful young woman walked over to Sam. She laughed as she greeted him.

"Welcome to the festival of Maria Hallett and Black Sam Bellamy. You went all out portraying a pirate, didn't you? You only forgot one thing. Where's the *Whydah*?"

Sam gasped in disbelief. It couldn't be! But it was, he was sure. There, right before his eyes, was Maria Hallett, complete in the jumper he had seen her in when he first saw her at Crosby's Tavern. The only difference was that his Maria had coal black hair, and *this* Maria had hair the color of summer flax.

Sam studied her carefully, causing Blair a great deal of discomfort. Her dress was identical in every way to Maria's, except that the fine embroidery from her petticoat which showed through in the front lacked the colorful red flowers.

"Your garb," Sam said. "Where are the flowers on your petticoat?"

Blair chuckled. She had read about the incident in Maria's journal, right down to the last detail, even to the fact that when Maria and Sam Bellamy had their rendezvous at the Inn Maria had donned her petticoat backwards.

Blair gave a flip of the back of her jumper, just as Maria had done when she and Sam were alone. There, beneath the jumper in the back were the flowers, all hand done by Maria herself.

Blair grinned. Yes, her costume was truly authentic. She had persuaded Edith Hallett, the curator of the Yarmouth Museum, to let her copy Maria's actual costume for the day's festivities.

But who, where and what was this strange pirate? Blair wondered. *And why did he give her such an unsettled feeling, as if he was from another time, another era?*

CHAPTER IV

Sam was soon drawn up into the gala occasion. He grinned widely through his sharp black beard. *If this is hell,* he thought, *it won't be so bad after all.* He never thought there would be such revelry, such joy, such gaiety. *And best of all, Maria is here!*

Sam stuck to Blair like glue during the whole day. He would have to ask her, later, how her hair had changed color. He supposed he could grow accustomed to it, with time. If they were in hell, that was one thing they would certainly have plenty of—time.

As the sun began to set and the bonfire burned brightly on the sandy shore, there seemed to be a crisp chill in the air. It was not the chill of a falling temperature, Sam realized, but a chill which came from within himself.

His blonde Maria was up in front of everyone, speaking into a blowhorn, much like Sam had used when he was out at sea, but hers seemed much more powerful than anything he had ever seen before. He was amazed that such at tiny creature as this new Maria could speak loudly enough for all the people—and there must have been hundreds there—to hear her. But they did, as cheers went up from the very front of the crowd to those who were the farthest back.

"Thank you all for coming to the first annual celebration of Maria Hallett and Sam Bellamy Day!" the young woman bellowed. "I trust you have all enjoyed yourselves."

Again, there was a cheer from all corners of the group.

"We have only one activity remaining," she said. "It is time for the reenactment of the demise of Black Sam Bellamy, the devilish pirate who caused Maria so much grief."

Sam looked around. None of this made any sense at all. How could they reenact his demise? He was standing right here in their midst. What had become of him? Where was he?

"We want to take this opportunity to extend an invitation to all of you for this year's remembrance of this solemn occasion here in Hyannis."

Well, Sam thought, *at least I know one thing. I am in Hyannis.*

Thomas Hallett's house! It was the one place he was sure would be safe.

Sam wove his way in and out of the crowd, trying to escape being noticed by anyone, and headed for the house he knew so well. As he wandered through the streets, he recognized some of the houses, but other buildings looked very strange. It had not been that long since he had visited Hyannis, but there had certainly been a lot of changes.

After he had traveled the full length of the main street, he spotted Thomas Hallett's house near the end of the street. He went up to the door and found it tightly locked. He tried pushing it and shaking it, hoping to jar the iron rod loose. The door did not budge, and Sam reasoned that if the rod was secure someone must be inside.

"Thomas!" he called out. "Sarah! Is anyone home?"

There was no reply, so Sam tried the door again. Still no luck; it was as tight as ever.

The root cellar! Sam knew he could get in there. There was no way to lock it. He made his way around to the back of the house and located the knoll which hid the root cellar. He knew he would be safe there until the Halletts came home.

Sam ran his foot over the ground, searching for the wooden door which lifted up to reveal the ladder inside. He found no sign of it, so he got down on his hands and knees to try to locate it. His hand hit something hard and began to pull the sod away from it. There, beneath the grass, was the old, rusty handle to the door.

He pulled and tugged at the iron rung until it finally began to give way, ever so slightly. Once he saw the outline of the door, he took his dagger and cut a line all the way around it. He pulled and tugged some more until slowly it surrendered to his force and opened, creaking at first, then bits and pieces of the rotten wood falling into the hole until it finally opened enough for him to slide down into safety.

Sam hurried below into the cold, musty darkness. It was miserable, but at least he was safe. No siree, if somebody was going to act out his death he certainly wanted no part of it. He would stay down here until he knew it was safe to come out.

❋ ❋ ❋

Blair Smythe looked around at the crowd by the beach. She wanted desperately to find the pirate who had made such a splash when he arrived. She saw no sign of him and she wondered if he had disappeared into the ocean the same way he had appeared. There was something very mysterious about the man.

She hoped that after the busyness of the day she would have an opportunity to sit down with the stranger and find out more about him. There was something which aroused curiosity, as well as a multitude of other feelings, about him. It was difficult to put her finger on it, but he gave her the same sensation that reading Maria's journal did.

Blair could find no sign of him, and she looked down at her own costume. She brushed a fleck of something gold off her skirt, only to find it stuck to her fingers. She shook it to get rid of it, but it clung to her like ivy to a wall.

"It's just the costume and all the excitement of the day," she said quietly. "Tomorrow the stranger will be gone and everything will be back to normal."

"What did you say?" a man standing nearby asked. "Have you chosen the man who will play the role of Black Sam Bellamy?"

"Yes," Blair said, looking around one last time. Since he was not there, she chose another pirate, not as authentic appearing as the missing one, but still a dapper young man.

"You," she said, pointing to a red-headed, bearded fellow who was dressed in much the same costume as the one the stranger had worn. "You will be Black Sam Bellamy."

Dr. Angus McPherson, a promising young obstetrician from Brewster, made his way to Blair.

"I'll get you for this!" he quipped. "Some day, when you need me the worst, I'll make you pay for what you are doing to me."

His impish grin told Blair that he was enjoying this challenge as much as anyone.

"If our paths ever cross again," Blair said, "I will be sure to be wary of the dapper young Scottish pirate."

"Cast the devil out to the sea!" Blair called out.

"To the sea!" a rush of men cried out, running towards the phony Black Sam Bellamy.

The men grabbed him and swung him back and forth until they felt they had enough momentum built up to get him as far from the shore as possible. Then they released him, sending the *pirate* out into the depths of the ocean.

The crowd stood and cheered, waiting and watching for him to surface. When they felt too much time had lapsed, everyone grew silent.

"Someone get the boat!" John Bacon called out. "We'd better go in after him!"

Blair's heart sank. Was the curse of Black Sam Bellamy still around, even after almost three hundred years? It had been such fun. She never meant for it to end in tragedy.

"Over this way!" John Bacon ordered. "I think I saw some rings in the water."

"With any luck he's still alive," one of the men in the boat remarked.

"Don't say such things!" John Bacon said. "Just pray!"

"Pray for the soul of Black Sam Bellamy!" one of the other men scoffed. "Humph! Even St. Peter himself couldn't have saved that man's soul!"

The men felt the boat rock slightly from behind them.

"Looking for something?" Dr. Angus McPherson asked.

The men let out a united cheer for their pirate.

"We got him!" John Bacon bellowed to the crowd on the shore. "He's fine."

Again there was one tremendous cheer from the group. Black Sam Bellamy, a.k.a. Dr. Angus McPherson, was alive and well.

❋ ❋ ❋

The noise from the crowd echoed through the air for miles around. Even in his hole in the ground, Black Sam Bellamy heard the cry of victory.

When the noise had subsided and the crowd had broken up, Blair headed for home.

"Mind if a pirate accompanies a beautiful young witch to her home?"

Blair jumped in surprise. She had not realized anyone was following her. She turned to face Dr. Angus McPherson.

"I'm sorry," he said. "I didn't mean to startle you."

"It's okay," Blair said. "Actually, I would welcome the company."

They made their way down Main Street to Blair's home—the Hallett House of Hyannis. As they strode together in the moonlight they talked and laughed about the events of the day.

"You did a fine job," Dr. McPherson said. "I'm told you did most of the planning yourself."

"Oh," Blair said modestly, "I had lots of help."

"But the idea was yours alone?" he asked.

Blair's face turned beet red, causing it to nearly glow in the brightness of the full moon. She had never liked compliments. They always made her nervous.

"You gave everyone a start yourself," Blair said, anxious to steer the conversation in a different direction. "I thought sure you had drowned."

Dr. McPherson laughed loudly. "I didn't mean to give anyone heart failure. Fine doctor that would be, wouldn't it?"

"You're a doctor?" Blair asked, intrigued that a doctor would be so taken up with a celebration the likes that they had seen today.

"Yes," he replied. "Does that surprise you?"

Blair snickered. "I guess I find it a little disappointing," she said, smiling at him.

"Well!" he huffed, feigning hurt feelings. "I'm sure my mother would be delighted to know that all the time and money she spent on medical school was a complete and utter waste of time and money."

"No," Blair said. "I think the medical profession is a wonderful one. One of the finest. It's just that I thought you were a pirate."

"And you'd like that better?" he asked.

"Well, lots of people know a doctor," Blair said, "but how many people can say they know a real pirate?"

"I'm sorry to be such a failure," Dr. McPherson said, faking a pout that made him look like an impish little boy. "If I had only known sooner, I could have taken some steps to correct it, but it's too late now. You see, I've already taken the Hippocratic oath. I'm afraid I'm stuck being a doctor for the rest of my life. I'll have to leave the pirating to someone else."

They were both laughing when they reached Blair's house.

"Would you like to come in for a cup of tea after a *very* long day?" Blair asked.

"Your parents won't mind?" Dr. McPherson asked.

"I live alone," Blair said.

"Me too," Dr. McPherson said. "Awful, isn't it?"

Blair unlocked the door and they went in together.

"I think if we are going to have tea together we should at least strike up a few rules," he said.

"Are you planning on getting so fresh that we need guidelines?" Blair asked. "Maybe you'd better leave."

Dr. McPherson grinned at her through his bushy red beard. "Nothing as exciting as all that," he said. "I just thought we should at least be on a first-name basis. Blair, I would be delighted to have tea with you."

"I'd truly enjoy your company, Angus," she replied.

❋ ❋ ❋

Outside, Sam heard people talking. He listened as the key turned in the lock and the door opened. He opened the door of the root cellar a crack and poked his head up, studying the house. He blinked his eyes, trying to adjust to any light which seemed unbearably bright after the darkness of his "hole in the ground." He stared at the window of the house in utter amazement. He had never seen a place with so much light in it. He wondered how many candles or lanterns Thomas and Sarah had lit inside. And why?

He crawled up onto the ground and went to the window. He carefully looked in and saw...not Thomas and Sarah Hallett, but the blonde young Maria from the party at the shore.

He looked more closely and saw a dashing young man there with her. Was this the man he heard about when he anchored at the port in Yarmouth? And if so, how did he get here? Was this Maria's husband? And why were they at Thomas and Sarah Hallett's house? Was this the doctor who was supposed to be in Yarmouth? And where was Little Sam? Something about the man sent a shiver up and down Sam's spine. So many things seemed fuzzy in his mind, but he knew he had seen this man before. Something warned him to beware of him.

Sam found the whole thing too confusing to deal with tonight. He would try to catch Maria alone tomorrow and ask her all about it. Meanwhile, he made his way quietly to the back door, which he saw was open a crack, and climbed down the narrow steps to the basement. Spending the night there was a much better option than sleeping in the root cellar.

As he went downstairs, he purposely left the door slightly ajar, as it was dark down there. Maybe their conversation would shed some light on this most confusing life.

CHAPTER V

Sam stayed in the basement, listening for what seemed like hours, to the strange Maria and that man talking upstairs. His mind was whirling about in circles faster than the eddy he had survived in the ocean.

Why did those two people act like they were total strangers? And why did he call her—what was it, Blair? What a strange sounding name. In all of his travels around the world, he had never met a "Blair."

Sam finally drifted off to sleep, slouched in the big old overstuffed chair he found covered in cobwebs in a dark corner. He brushed it off and curled up in it the best he could, and he slept.

When he awoke in the morning, he could see a beam of light pushing its way through the tiny windows, which were hardly more than slits above the ground.

Sam got up and stretched, stomping his foot to try to wake it up to match the rest of his body. He longed for his bunk on the *Whydah*.

He tuned his ear to the upstairs, trying to hear who all was there. After some time, he heard footsteps. One person, he assumed, paying close attention. So Maria, or Blair, or whoever this strange young woman was, was apparently alone.

Music! The house was filled with the sound of it. This made no sense at all. Where was it coming from? It was not just one person singing; it was instruments—hoards of them.

Sam sensed that Blair was nowhere near the back door, at least not at the moment, so he crept up the stairs and made his way outside. He hid in the bushes beside the house and peeked in the window.

He gasped. There was a box sitting on a table. In the middle of the box was a white space, and there were tiny little people sitting on stools inside the box.

Sam rubbed his eyes and stared in disbelief. Who were these people, and how did they get into the box? Why were they so small? They were smaller than the pygmies he had seen in Africa.

"Welcome to *Live With Regis and Kelly,*" a voice informed him.

Sam caught a glimpse of Maria, or Blair, or whoever she was, as she came into the room. She walked over to the box, reached down and turned some sort of black knob on the front of it. The voices of the people in the box grew louder. Sam squinted, trying to see what she was doing. She turned toward the window and he ducked down, lest she spot him.

When he heard footsteps, he thought she must have left the room, so he raised up again and looked inside.

"Are you lookin' at me?" the little man in the box bellowed in his infamous Robert DeNiro impersonation. "'Cuz if you're lookin' at me..."

Sam disappeared into the bushes again, shaking in his black pirate boots at the thought of this little man threatening him. The fact that Sam was at least a hundred times bigger than the little man who was yelling at him didn't seem to penetrate his consciousness. He had faced fierce foes on the seas many a time, but none had the impact this tiny man possessed. His voice was that of a bull elephant on the rampage.

From somewhere off in the distance, Sam heard bells ringing. They were not the bells of a church steeple, nor were they the tones of a ship's horns. It was unlike anything he had ever heard before. They were coming from inside the house.

Sam again crept up to the window and looked in, just in time to see Blair walk back into the room and turn the knob on the box, and suddenly the people inside it totally disappeared. It was the craziest thing he had ever seen.

Blair was carrying some small thing in her hand, and in the quietness of the moment she began talking into the little gizmo she was holding. She paused, then began to speak again. No one answered her, but it seemed as if she was hearing voices.

"Whew!" Sam said. "I think they were right when they said Maria was a witch. That is, if this is Maria. The poor girl must have gone completely mad."

Sam thought about the treasure he had gathered from all corners of the world, including the last great conquest he made when he successfully pillaged the loot from the Spanish galleon that was on its way back to Spain from Colombia. Too bad it all sank off the coast when the *Whydah* went down. Still, he had hidden some of it... Wait! He was practically sitting on top of what treasures he had dropped off on that one fateful visit to the Cape. He didn't know how he would manage to do it, but someway he had to get out to the old barn out behind Thomas Hallett's house, the very house he was in this very moment. He licked his lips as he thought about the barrel of the finest Jamaican rum he had hidden out there.

Sam scratched his head, trying to collect his thoughts. He hadn't taken close notice of the surroundings, afraid of being discovered, but he didn't remember seeing a barn out back. Still, he knew this had to be the very same house.

The memory of that horrendous event caused Sam to shiver uncontrollably. He seemed to relive the whole episode, including the feelings and thoughts he had as he spun around in that awful whirlpool.

"Good," he heard Blair say. "You'll be here in about an hour then?"

No one answered her, but Sam watched as she went out of the room, tossing her shiny blonde hair from side to side, just as he had seen Maria do with her long black hair.

"I've got to get out of here before somebody spots me," he muttered as he slithered along the ground to the root cellar. He opened the door, climbed slowly down the ladder, then felt himself fall part way down as the old, rotten rung gave way beneath his weight, leaving him in a pile on the cold wet ground of the hole.

"Drat the luck!" he sputtered, rubbing his ankle where it had twisted. "Now what will I do?" Reflecting on the overgrown grass that he had had to cut through to get to the door, he wondered how long it had been since anybody had been down here, or if anyone even knew the root cellar existed.

"Nothing," he replied to himself. "There's not a whole lot you can do. Just sit here and wait for nightfall and try to pull yourself up so you can get back into the cellar and try to learn more about the crazy lady."

"Egad!" he nearly shouted. "Sam, me boy, you've become quite as daft as the witch herself. Here ye are, talkin' to yourself like you enjoyed your own company."

Sam rested his elbows on his knees and put his head in his hands. "Oh, that tomorrow will be a better day," he said softly. "I don't know if I can survive another like today."

❄ ❄ ❄

"Hi. Come on in," Blair greeted Jennifer Wentworth, her best friend, warmly at the door.

"I just couldn't wait to talk to you," Jenny said anxiously, panting for breath. "The car is being repaired so I ran all the way over."

"What's so important?" Blair asked. "You sounded so excited, I hardly had a chance to say anything."

"Sorry," Jenny said. "I didn't mean to sound pushy. It's just—that pirate. Wasn't he just to die for?"

"He sure was," Blair quickly agreed. "The way he came up out of the water, it was so..."

"Theatrical!" Jenny said, finishing the sentence for Blair. To Jenny, *everything* was connected to the theater. While Blair had worked away at getting a degree in history, Jenny had concentrated on theatrical arts.

Blair smiled as she looked at her friend.

"A penny for your thoughts," Jenny challenged.

"It's nothing," Blair said. "I was just thinking that we both probably wasted all those years in college and will never do anything with our educations."

"Who, me?" Jenny asked. "Why, have you forgotten? I intend to be the next Marilyn Monroe."

"Yeah," Blair teased. "A dumb blonde."

Jenny jabbed her fist into Blair's arm playfully.

"Anyway," Jenny continued, "getting back to yesterday's pirate..."

"Yesterday's pirate," Blair said, staring up into space. "I like that. He did seem sort of like a pirate out of yesterday—or yesteryear. He seemed so *real*, like he really could really be Sam Bellamy."

"Oh, you and your history. You just let your imagination run away from you all the time."

"But didn't you see his get-up? It looked so authentic. And that gold chain he had around his neck. I've read all about chains like that. The sailors of old used them to buy things. They would unfasten one link, and it was worth a small fortune."

"Sure, and like that guy's was real 22-carat gold," Jenny said.

"Actually, if it was the real thing, they were 28-carat," Blair said. "Did you see the way his shoulders stooped forward? Like it was real heavy?"

Blair was tempted to tell Jenny about the gold dust she had found after the pirate had disappeared, but she thought better of it. The whole thing seemed so surreal, she didn't need to add more fuel to the fire of her insanity.

"Hey," Jenny said, "I think we've got something mixed up. Are you talking about the good looking red headed guy they threw in the ocean?"

"No," Blair exclaimed. "I'm talking about the one the ocean blew up onto the shore. You know, early in the day."

"Yeah, he was strange all right," Jenny conceded, "but he wasn't nearly as handsome as the redhead."

"Okay, so you take the redhead and I'll go after the black bearded one. He looked more adventurous anyway."

"Suits me fine," Jenny said. "I'd hate to fight with my best friend over something as stupid as a man."

Both girls laughed. Men—that was definitely a priority on their list of "must haves." They had discussed the matter countless times, and the available bachelors had been scrutinized, debated and cast aside, waiting for the "right one" to appear.

"Well, we have to find them first," Jenny said. "Do you have any idea who either of them were?"

"Just your redhead," Blair said. "The other one disappeared as mysteriously as he came. I know who your redhead is," Blair chanted teasingly.

"Don't keep me in suspense," Jenny shouted. "Come on, spill!"

"You haven't read this morning's paper yet?" Blair asked.

"No, I called you as soon as I got up, then I came straight over. What's the paper have to do with it?"

Blair handed the society section to Jenny.

"Wow!" Jenny said as she opened the pages. "Look at these pictures."

"Let me see that," Blair said, grabbing for the paper. It ripped in two, leaving each of them holding a section as it flopped downward towards the floor. "I didn't see that."

"Here you are in your witch's costume," Jenny said, laughing. "Pretty cute little witch, if you ask me."

Blair scooted over closer to Jenny to see the picture.

"Look!" Blair shouted. "There he is!"

"Who? My redhead?"

"No, silly. My black-bearded pirate."

"Make up your mind," Jenny said. "First you think he is Black Sam Bellamy, and now you say he's Blackbeard. Really!" She sighed in exasperation. "And you're supposed to be the history expert."

"Forget about him," Jenny said. "Where's my pirate?"

"You looked right past him," Blair said, turning the torn paper back to the picture on the front page. "Here." She pointed to a tiny dot out in the ocean, clinging to the rescue boat for dear life.

"Boy, like you can really see him," Jenny said.

"Sure, it doesn't show much, but look what it says about him."

Jenny read the article about the festivities of the day. There, giving a complete description of the "castoff" of the pirate into the water was his name. "Dr. Angus McPherson, prominent young obstetrician from Brewster."

"All right!" Jenny yelled, jumping up into the air. "He's not only beautiful; he's rich too!"

"Sure," Blair said. "He's probably still paying off his loans from med school."

"Are you trying to tell me that he's poor? You can tell he's a Scotsman. You know how tight they are."

"I just hate it when your prejudices show through," Blair said. "Besides, he didn't seem like the tight non-caring type."

"What do you mean, he didn't seem like…"

"Last night," Blair said, grinning at her friend, "he seemed quite nice."

"You talked to him last night?" Jenny asked.

"He, um, sort of walked me home last night, after most everyone else had gone home."

"He walked you home? And you didn't tell me?" Jenny thrust her hands around Blair's throat, pretending to choke her. "How could you?"

"You didn't ask," Blair said, grinning.

"Well…" Jenny said, waiting for Blair to explain.

"Well what?" Blair asked.

"Do you know how exasperating you can be?" Jenny asked. "Sometimes I don't know why I put up with you."

❄ ❄ ❄

"Yeeeowch!"

Blair and Jenny raced to the window. The yell came from out behind the house. It was a man's voice, but when they looked around there was no sign of anyone there.

"Come on," Blair said, running to the door. "Let's go see if we can find out who or what that was."

Jenny anxiously followed her. There was nothing she loved better than a good mystery, unless it was a stage play.

Old Mr. Davis's dogs had apparently heard the yell from next door. In no time at all they were over in Blair's yard, barking up a storm and sniffing all around.

"Go get him!" Blair ordered the dogs.

They soon found a strange scent and followed it, their noses close to the ground, heading right for the little knoll in the yard.

"There's nothing there," Blair said.

The dogs, however, had other ideas. They set up a howl worse than any wolf's cry. One of them began to claw at the ground, uncovering the rusty handle to the root cellar door.

"What's that?" Jenny asked.

"I don't know," Blair said, shrugging her shoulders. "I never saw it before."

"Looks like somebody did," Jenny said, tracing the shape of the door with her eyes. "Wonder who's down there?"

"No time like the present," Blair said. She began pulling at the handle, the old wood breaking off here and there and falling down into the hole. "Better be careful."

Jenny helped her pull, and soon the door was wide open.

"Go in the kitchen and get the flashlight on the counter," Blair said to Jenny.

Jenny ran to the house and was back in a moment.

"Here," she said, handing the flashlight to Blair.

Blair shined the light into the hole and there, lying on the ground, staring up at her, was her mysterious pirate—the black-bearded one. Now she could find out who he was.

"Come on up from there!" she ordered.

Sam stared up at her. Again, he was stunned by how much she looked like Maria, but he knew this was the one he had heard that other man call "Blair" last night.

His head began to spin again. This whole mess sure didn't make any sense. And this Dr. Angus McPherson. How did he get there as fast as he did last night? Why, he was sure he had seen him back in Yarmouth. Down there with nothing but time on his hands, he finally put the pieces together. He remembered the man attacking him and getting others to help throw him into the sea. Yet here he was in Hyannis today. At least he assumed he wasn't in hell. Maybe that would make more sense than all of this did.

"I told you to come up here!" Blair ordered again.

"Sorry," Sam said. "I seem to have hurt my ankle."

"Fine," Blair said. "Come on, Jenny. Let's go down after him."

Blair climbed down the ladder, followed by Jenny.

"Careful," Sam said. "One of the rungs is missing."

He no sooner said that than Blair fell on top of him.

CHAPTER VI

Jenny screamed as she watched Blair tumble down into the hole. She stopped dead in her tracks without going down the ladder, afraid she would join them in the heap that lay before her eyes.

"Blair!" she yelled. "Are you okay?"

"I'm fine," Blair called back up to Jenny, breaking up into fits of laughter.

Jenny stared, the flashlight hitting them directly in their faces. She couldn't help herself. She began to laugh too.

Sam looked at the two women quizzically. He couldn't see one single thing funny about any of this. First of all, he had lost his hiding place. Secondly, he had no more idea now of what was going on around him than he had when he first landed on the coast. And last but not least, he did not like the feelings this strange version of Maria brought about in him—feelings he had not known since that day when he and Maria had first loved each other.

"Blair, give me your hand and I'll help you out," Jenny called down to her.

"No," Blair said. "I'm going to get behind our friendly neighborhood pirate and try to help him up first. His foot is hurt, not mine."

"No!" Sam protested. "I don't want to leave. I'm perfectly happy here."

"You can't live here forever," Blair said. "I wanted to ask you, where did you come from anyway? I mean, the way you blew in from the ocean. It was like you were some sort of mysterious sea creature."

Now it was Sam's turn to laugh. "Maybe I am," he said. The deep, gruff laugh made Jenny cringe, but it didn't seem to bother Blair in the least.

"Come on," Blair said. "Up on your feet, pirate. You've got a lot of explaining to do."

Sam wondered how he would explain what had happened to him. He couldn't even explain it to himself, let alone to strangers.

Sam tried to stand up, but the pain wrenched his ankle and he yelled.

Blair chuckled. "For a big tough pirate you're really a baby at heart."

Fire raged in Sam's eyes. Nobody had ever called him a "baby." He had conquered the fiercest opponents on the seas. No, he would not take that from anyone, not even from a woman like Blair.

"I am not a baby!" Sam bellowed. "And don't you dare talk to me like that. I'm..."

He stopped. He knew he couldn't tell anyone who he really was. He was a wanted man, and he knew that a revelation of the truth would seal his doom.

"You're who?" Blair asked. "That's part of what I want to know. Who are you? What is your name?"

Sam hesitated a bit, then answered, "Sam. Sam Black. That's me name."

Blair smiled at him. Her mind was really playing tricks on her. For a moment, one brief moment, she could have sworn he said he was "Black Sam."

"Who did you say?" she asked, hoping he would repeat his name.

"Sam."

"Sam what?"

"Sam—Black. Would you prefer Sam White? I could always change it—for you."

He flashed an evil sneer at her. Blair was suddenly afraid of him. Then his eyes filled with warmth and humor and she knew she had to find out more about him.

"Come on," she said, getting behind him in the small hole they were confined to. "You get up on the first rung—well, the first *solid* rung—and I will boost you from behind. That way you shouldn't have to put too much weight on that foot."

Sam stood up and hobbled towards the ladder. He put one foot up, placing all of his weight on the injured one, and fell backwards from the pain.

"Blair?" Jenny called out. "Are you okay? Did he fall on you?"

"No," Blair answered her. "I got out of his way. I'm fine, but I don't know how we are going to get him out of here. If that ladder gets another jolt like that we'll likely lose another rung. Then another and another..."

"Then you better get up here so I know you're safe. We can figure out what to do with him after you're safe. Two heads are better than one, you know."

"Depends on the heads," Sam teased.

"Hey!" Blair barked, slapping Sam on the behind. "You better watch what you say. Your destiny is in our hands, you know."

"Your wish is my command," Sam said sarcastically.

"Humph!" Jenny grumbled. "Now he thinks he's a genie. Sure wish he'd make up his mind."

Blair climbed up the ladder, slowly and carefully, not trusting the wood beneath her feet as she went. When she was almost at the top, Jenny grabbed her hand to help her up, just as another rung gave way.

"That was a close call," Blair said. "Why don't you run in and call the fire department? They've got ladders—good ones."

"What do I tell them? Jenny asked.

"I don't know," Blair said. "Tell them we've got a strange man trapped down in a hole behind the house. Tell them we've got a runaway pirate. Tell them we've got a genie but he's lost his bottle."

They both laughed. "No matter what we tell them," Jenny said, "they'll never believe it when they see him."

Sam wondered why they would call the fire department. The fire brigade had buckets, but he didn't know why they would have ladders. And why would they come when there was no fire? Surely this "fire department" must be the same thing as the "bucket brigades" he knew so well.

Before he could ponder the matter any more there was the most horrible din he had ever heard. There were high, shrill whistles. He could see some sort of flashing red lights above him; people were running around all over the place, and soon he had a whole group of men wearing funny black hats staring down at him from above the hole.

"There's no way out of this mess," Sam told himself. "I'll just have to let them do whatever they want to do to me. They'll probably take me and throw me in the brig—or maybe worse. What if they hang me? That's what they usually do to pirates when they capture them. Or maybe they'll toss me back in the sea and I'll be right back where I started."

Two of the men lowered a ladder into the hole for Sam to climb up. When it was secure, he tried to obey their orders to surface. With his sore ankle, there was no way he could put enough weight on it to climb even a solid ladder. After a brief exchange of words with the men in their funny hats, one of the men lowered a rope down into the hole. They instructed him to secure it around his armpits, and soon they hoisted him up out of the hole. He was prepared for them to grab him, lock him in irons and haul him off. Much to his surprise, Blair spoke to one of the men.

"No, he is fine here. I'm not worried about him. With that ankle the way it is I could easily outrun him. If you will just help me get him inside the house to the sofa, I can handle him fine."

Sam hobbled into the house, supported by a fireman on each side of him, knowing it was futile to protest. Blasted foot! He wanted to figure things out for himself. Well, maybe this strange Maria would prove helpful after all if he handled the situation carefully.

"You sure you'll be okay?" the fire chief asked Blair again. "We can call for the Rescue Squad to come and check his foot out."

"No, I'm fine," Blair answered. "And thanks. Thank you so much."

"Don't mention it," the chief said, waving as he went out the door. "It isn't every day we get to rescue a pirate. Wait till I tell my wife about this one."

He was laughing as he left, waving again to Blair.

❈ ❈ ❈

"Well," Sam said, grinning through his gold teeth at Blair and Jenny. "You've got me at your mercy. What do you intend to do with me? Are ye goin' to hang me yourselves to save the town council the trouble of a trial?"

"What are you talking about?" Blair asked.

"Isn't that what they do with the likes of me? I reckon I'll like it much better with just the two of you fair maidens to try me."

"We have no intention of trying you," Blair insisted. "What century did you come out of, anyway? They haven't hanged pirates for nearly two hundred years."

"Just joshin'," Sam said, confused. He wondered what century he was in. Everything was so strange. And how did he get here? Was he swirling around in that eddy for hundreds of years? Granted, it had seemed like an eternity, but he didn't believe such things were possible.

"I'm glad to see that at least I'm not in hell," Sam remarked.

"Why would you say that?" Blair asked.

She struggled to try to get his black leather boot off his swollen foot, but she couldn't budge it.

"Ouch!" Sam hollered. "Careful, lassie!"

"I can't get it off, but I know it has to come off so we can get some ice on that ankle. I hope it's just a sprain, not a broken bone."

"I've had me share o' breaks, and they've often said that a sprain can hurt worse than a break," Sam said. "I never thought they knew what they were talkin' about, but they sure 'nuf did."

"Come on, Jenny," Blair said. "Give me a hand with this."

Jenny went over beside Blair and together they pulled as hard as they could, but it still wouldn't budge.

"I'm going to call Angus," Blair said.

Sam jumped. "Angus? Angus who?"

"Angus McPherson," Blair said. "He's a doctor. He will know what to do."

"No!" Sam yelled. "He can't come here! Not while I'm here!"

"What gives?" Blair asked. "You know Angus McPherson?"

"No," Sam said. "I mean yes. I mean, I don't know if I do or not. But if I do, and if he knows me, I can't let him see me here."

"And just why not?" Blair asked.

"Because he—he'll kill me!"

Blair laughed. "Angus? Kill you? Why, he wouldn't hurt a flea. There's no need to be afraid of him."

Blair looked at Jenny. "What do you make of him?" she asked.

"Like nothing I ever saw," Jenny said. "Boy, would this make a great play! This story line is better than the 'Pirates of Penzance.' What do you want me to do?"

"Call Angus," Blair said. "Tell him... Oh, you watch Sam here and let me call him."

"Good," Jenny said, breathing a sigh of relief. "I don't even know your Dr. McPherson. I couldn't call him."

Blair smiled at her friend. She had forgotten how awestruck she was with the young Dr. McPherson. Well, this might work out well for both of them. She would have to get Dr. McPherson over here while Jenny was still here so she could meet him too.

Sam watched Blair as she picked up that small thing he had seen her talking to earlier. She began to poke at it. Soon she was talking to it again.

"Dr. Angus McPherson, please," she said to the box.

"Blair Smythe."

Well, Sam thought, *at least now I have a last name. I'm glad it really isn't Maria. I thought I was plumb insane there for a while.*

"No, I'll hold. It is quite important."

She paused. It was obvious that this thing talked back to her, Sam reasoned, but no one else seemed to be able to hear what it said.

"Yes!" Blair snapped. "No, I won't tell you what it is about. It's personal and highly confidential."

Blair put her hands over half the little box she held and said to Sam and Jenny, "Don't you just hate nosey nurses?"

"Yeah," Jenny said, "and nosey secretaries too."

Sam didn't say anything, but he wondered if maybe his earlier assessment of himself had perhaps been right after all. Maybe he was insane.

Soon Blair began talking to the little box again.

"Angus? It's Blair."

Silence.

"I didn't think you would mind. After all, it is the twenty-first century."

The twenty-first century, Sam thought. *So somehow I have jumped ahead in time from 1717 to the twenty-first century. So that's why things seemed so different. But what happened to the missing years? Surely I couldn't have been in the ocean for that long.* Well, one thing he would have to figure out—he would have to compensate for the missing time some way to Blair.

"Well, first off," Blair said to the box again, "I wanted to thank you for the lovely time last night. It was great. Let's do it again some time."

"You know, you should have been a psychiatrist," Blair said, laughing. "What makes you think I had some ulterior motive for calling?"

Again, a pause.

"Okay, I'll tell you, but you have to promise not to laugh at me. A friend of mine, Jenny Wentworth, is here with me and we just rescued a pirate from a hole in the back yard."

"You *what*?"

Sam sat up straight. The little box was talking to all of them now. This Dr. Angus McPherson had yelled so loud that even he heard what he said.

"That's right," Blair said. "We captured him."

Sam waited, crooking his ear to try to hear the man's response, but he couldn't hear anything again.

"No," Blair said. "I'm not kidding. He's here on my sofa. That's why I called you. I need a doctor. He hurt his ankle and I can't get his boot off."

More silence.

"No, I don't think anything's broken."

More waiting.

"Sure, we can keep him here until then. With that foot like it is I don't think he'll get very far if he does try to leave."

Pause.

"Okay, we'll see you around five."

Blair set the little box down on the table, then she turned to face Sam and Jenny.

"He has to finish up at the office first, so he can't make it over until around five o'clock. Hope you don't mind sticking around here for the rest of the day, Jenny."

"Are you kidding?" Jenny said excitedly. "For a chance to meet him? I'd spend the week. The month!"

Sam watched the two of them as they talked and giggled together. So that was it; Jenny had her sights set on the strange young Dr. McPherson. Well, that left Blair free for him. He could handle that.

Sam shook his head, trying to come back to reality. Somehow he couldn't get rid of the feeling that he had heard that name before—Dr. Angus McPherson. And it wasn't a good feeling. Could it be the one he'd heard of the last time he'd been in Hyannis? The one Thomas and Sarah Hallett claimed had married Maria? And if it was, would he be an old man, or would he have skipped over time like Sam had?

Reality! What a funny thing, Sam thought. He had no idea what reality was. Maybe this whole thing was some sort of a weird dream. Or was it a nightmare? Would he ever figure it all out? Did he really want to know?

Blair and Jenny left the room. When Sam was sure the coast was clear, he got up and tried to walk to the door. His ankle hurt, but he was determined to get away before the doctor appeared.

Sam nearly lost his balance. He grabbed hold of a small

table, causing a large crash when it toppled over.

"What are you doing?" Blair screamed at him. "Did you think you could get away?"

Blair motioned to Jenny. The two of them grabbed him and steered him back to the couch. "No, sir," Blair said. "You are here for the duration. You're not going anywhere."

She reached into the drawer and took out a funny looking black cord. She tied each of his hands to the legs of the sofa.

"Don't have to worry about your feet," Blair said. "You can't do much of anything with that one anyway."

Sam struggled, trying to free himself, but it was useless. He was "stuck" here, as Blair had said, "for the duration."

"You stand guard," Blair instructed Jenny. "I'll go get something to eat. I don't know about you guys, but I'm starved."

Blair disappeared into the other room. As she went, she laughed. The sound of that laugh sent shivers through Sam's entire being. He had heard that laugh before. Where? Suddenly he knew! Maria!

CHAPTER VII

Sam lay on the sofa all day, watching the world go by him. He wondered at many of the things the two women who were his captors discussed. From his position he could see out the window. There were strange looking boxy things that whizzed past faster than lightning.

Lightning! He felt the *Whydah* split in two as he stood on it. In his mind, he relived the whole ordeal over again and again. He felt himself plummeting down—down—down into the depths of the ocean. The swirling, around and around, his head twisting and turning like it would never stop.

Sam looked for people to go past on their horses and in their carriages, but there were none in sight. Once in a while he would see people get out of those weird things that went by so fast.

Blair had tried to pry into Sam's past. Where had he come from? Who was he *really*? How did he get here? Why was he out in the ocean? Why did he seem so odd? Why did she get such strange vibrations when she was near him? She decided to pursue this route again.

Sam wished he could answer all of her questions. He wished he knew the answers himself.

Finally, Sam tried to tell her about himself and his past. He grinned from time to time, proud of the yarns he was spinning. Pirates were known as tale-tellers, and he was certainly holding true to that reputation.

"Wait!" Blare shouted, just after he got started with another story. "I hate to have you tell this whole thing twice. You'd better just wait until Angus gets here. He won't want to miss this."

❈ ❈ ❈

The subject was not brought up again. They talked of many things, waiting for Dr. Angus McPherson to arrive.

One of those strange things pulled up in front of the house and a man got out and walked towards the door.

"Come on in," Blair called out.

The man entered.

"Hi, girls," he said, then turned to face Sam. He was tied to the legs of the sofa. Angus broke into peals of laughter. "Boy!" he exclaimed. "If I was going to be captured, I'd sure like to do it your way."

Sam laughed at him. He had not seen him close enough yet to tell...

"Let's take a look at that ankle," Angus said, lifting it slightly and turning it from side to side.

"Ouch!" Sam shouted. "That hurts, man!"

Angus turned to look at Sam. For the first time, Sam got a good look at Angus McPherson face on. Yes, he was sure of it. There, right before his very eyes, was the same man he had seen running through the field, hand in hand with Maria, the day of that awful storm. The day the *Whydah* sank. The day he had been thrown in the ocean—by this very same man. The day he disappeared from Yarmouth.

"You really are Dr. Angus McPherson!" Sam said, his voice filled with obvious surprise.

"Of course," Angus said, "but I don't remember our having met. You are..." He paused a few moments, then continued. "I told you I don't remember meeting you. I've always been terrible with faces. Names I do better with. I guess it's...the first signs of Alzheimer's."

Blair, Jenny and Angus laughed at this. Trying no to appear too dumb, Sam laughed with them, even though he had no idea who or what *Alzheimer's* was.

"Your name?" Angus asked again.

"Sam," he replied. "Sam Black."

"Pleased to know you, Sam Black," Angus said, extending his hand in friendship. "Hate to tell you this, Sam, but we are going to have to cut that boot off."

"Cut me boot off?" Sam shrieked. "Never, lacky! It's the only pair I've got."

"I'm sure Blair here will be glad to see that you get a new pair of boots. You see, in case you haven't discovered it, Blair here is one of the richest young women in Hyannis."

Sam stared at her in surprise. Here she was, living in Thomas Hallett's house. Had she found the rum he had buried in the barn? Or maybe even the gems he had hidden in the root cellar? Sam knew he had to find a way to get out there, soon, to see if he could unearth the barrel. It was so dark and his ankle hurt so badly when he fell down into the root cellar he hadn't given it a second's thought. But now... After that, he would have to figure out some way to get back down to the root cellar to try to find the treasures he had put in the hollowed out hole he built in behind the regular wall. Surely they were still there. He knew those treasures could buy him anything he wanted. Far more than the gold links from his pirate's necklace he had draped around his neck.

"It's not my fault," Blair said almost apologetically. "I owe it all to my grandfather."

"And who was your grandfather?" Sam asked.

Blair laughed. "I did have two grandfathers," she said, "but it sure wasn't my great grandfather Hallett! Though I loved him dearly, no Hallett ever gave anything to anyone else, not even after they died."

The color drained from Sam's ruddy, rough-hewn face.

"Your great-grandfather was a Hallett?" he asked.

"Yes," Blair replied. "Did you know him?"

"I don't know," Sam said. "Maybe. Which Hallett was he?"

"John Hallett," Blair answered. "Well, actually, it was Jonathan, but everybody called him John. It was a long-standing family tradition to have both a John and Jonathan in the same family. Been that way for generations."

Sam paled even more, if that was possible. Yes, he knew John Hallett. For that matter, he also knew Jonathan Hallett. But why would anybody think they were the same person? Of course they were brothers, but they were as different as black and white. As different as day and night. Why, they couldn't stand the sight of each other!

Oh, the tales I could tell you about John Hallett—and Jonathan Hallett, Sam thought.

"Enough about me," Blair said suddenly. "Now, to get back to you, Sam. We want to know all about you."

"You bet we do," Angus said. He looked at Jenny, who had hardly said a word since he had arrived.

"Blair told me her best friend, Jenny Wentworth, was here with her. I presume that's you."

Blair stammered a bit. She was always the perfect picture of good manners. She could hardly believe that she had not even introduced the two of them, and when Jenny was already so smitten with the doctor, even before she met him.

"I'm sorry," Blair apologized. "It's just that this whole day has been so confusing."

You think it's confusing! Sam thought. *You should be in my shoes—or my boots.*

He rubbed his boots subconsciously. He hated to lose his boots. They were too good to just toss away, but he knew he didn't have any choice.

"Jennifer Wentworth, meet Dr. Angus McPherson," Blair said, watching Jenny for her reaction. She soon got it.

"I'm meased to pleat you," she said, her words forming into spoonerisms. "I mean, I'm pleased to meet you."

Jenny felt her cheeks turn fiery red. She hated it when she did that, but when she was nervous it always happened, just when she didn't want it to the most. *Some actress you'll make,* she thought. *You can't even talk straight.*

"The pleasure is all mine, I'm sure," Angus said, trying to put her at ease.

"I don't mean to slight two such lovely young women," Angus said, "but I do want to get at poor Sam's foot. Blair, do you have a real strong butcher knife?"

Sam reached down beside him and pulled his dagger from its sheath.

"This do?" he asked Angus.

Angus gulped. For a phony costume, this thing sure looked real.

"Umm, well, yeah, sure." He took it from Sam and began to try to cut the boot away. It was a most awkward job, as the blade seemed about four times too long.

"Blair, do you have that knife? I think it would work better. This thing is pretty unwieldy."

"You ought to let me show you how to use it," Sam said. "It is really a tool of many uses."

"And I suppose you use it when you are out at sea?" Angus asked.

"Why, of course," Sam replied. Suddenly, he knew the story he could tell them about his past, which they seemed so curious about. "You wanted to know about me past?" Sam volunteered now quite freely. "Well, I might as well tell you now. It will help keep me mind off what the doc's doin' with me foot."

Angus continued working on the boot, having much better success with the shorter blade, as they all listened to Sam Black's incredible story.

"Years ago, it seems that it must be," Sam began, "I set sail with me pa."

"Where were you headed?" Jenny asked.

"Quiet!" Angus commanded. "Let him do the talking."

"Aye aye, Cap'n McPherson," Jenny said.

"Actually, 'tis a fair question," Sam said, continuing with his made-up tale. "We were headed for Jamaica. We were in search of rum. We'd heard they had the finest in the world. We were going to take it back to England, where we knew we would get a good price for it."

Sam stopped. He remembered his stopover right here in Hyannis, when he had visited this very house, only Thomas and Sarah Hallett lived here, not Blair Smythe.

No, he thought, *that tale will have to wait for another time—not today.*

"We were in a horrible storm," Sam continued. *Sure, that was likely! Seemed every time he came near Cape Cod there was a terrible turmoil in the air, like fate itself was looking out for Maria, trying to keep them apart.*

"We were tossed to and fro like a leaf in the autumn wind."

Sam studied the faces of each of his listeners to see if they were swallowing his line. Satisfied that they were—hook, line and sinker—he continued.

"The ship broke right in two when a bolt of lightning hit it."

"Just like the *Whydah!*" Blair exclaimed excitedly.

Sam's mouth dropped open. What could she possibly know about the Whydah? He had to find out before he went on with his story.

Seeing his confused expression, Blair asked, "You don't know about the *Whydah*? What kind of a pirate are you? *Everybody* around here knows about the *Whydah*. You must be a phony."

"I've heard the tale," Sam said cautiously, "but I'd like to hear your version of it."

"All right," Blair said and proceeded to tell him the story of the demise of the *Whydah*.

"And that's why you celebrated the demise of Black Sam Bellamy yesterday?" Sam asked.

"I've always been fascinated by history," Blair said, "especially the history of my own family. You see, Maria Hallett, the witch of Yarmouth, was a distant cousin of mine. I always thought she and Black Sam were treated unfairly, so I decided to set the record straight—to avenge their deaths."

"*Their* deaths?" Sam gasped. "Do you mean to tell me that Maria died too?"

"Of course," Blair explained. "When she heard of the death of Black Sam, who had finally come back for her, she took off her red slippers and left them on the shore. Then she dove into the ocean and drowned herself, hopefully to be with her beloved Black Sam Bellamy for eternity."

"And they found their bodies?" Sam asked. This was too much! Here he was, in a strange place, at a strange time, with strange people, listening to them tell him of his own death.

"Never!" Blair said, filled with enthusiasm. "But maybe we are near some answers at last. After all these years, a diving team went down to search for the remains of the *Whydah*."

"And what happened?" Sam asked, sitting on the edge of the sofa.

"They found it!" Jenny jumped in. "And millions of dollars worth of treasures."

"It was rumored that there were emerald aboard but they never found them," Blair said. "They were supposed to be bigger than anything any that had ever been seen before. They said they came from Colombia, South America. That was the last vessel Black Sam was supposed to have pillaged. The way I have it figured, he thought he finally had enough treasure to offer Maria, and he thought he would take them back to her and ask her to marry him."

"Pretty story," Angus said. "Too bad you don't know whether it's true or not."

"I think it's true," Blair said. "What else matters?"

"What else indeed?" Sam agreed. "But you," and he pointed an accusing finger at Dr. Angus McPherson. "Where do you fit into this whole thing?"

Angus shrugged his shoulders. "No place, as far as I know, except that my great-great-great-great-great-great grandfather was also a Dr. Angus McPherson. It has been said that he doctored the Hallett family several times."

"Yer grandfather was Dr. Angus McPherson, the same as you?" Sam asked.

"My great-great-great-great-great-great grandfather," Angus corrected. "That he was."

"And did he look just like you?" Sam asked.

What a strange question, Angus thought. How would he know? They didn't have cameras back then, and he had never seen a painting of him. Besides, what difference would it make?

"I don't rightly know," Angus confessed. "Why?"

"Just wonderin'," Sam said.

"Go on with your story," Blair pleaded. "What happened after the shipwreck?"

"Well, for a long time, I don't rightly know. I woke up one bright, sunshiny morning on some deserted island. There was no one else there. I guess Pa must have died in the wreck. I searched and searched for him, but there was no sign of anybody else, dead or alive."

Blair had a weird sensation, listening to Sam's tale. If she didn't know better, she would think this man was Black Sam Bellamy himself, that somehow he had fallen asleep like Rip Van Winkle, only for a couple of hundred years, and had just come back to life.

"Get a grip on yourself!" she told herself silently. "You are just letting your imagination run away from you. You know such a thing is impossible."

"Anyway," Sam continued, "I stayed on the island for—I don't know, I guess years—until I finally got a raft built that I trusted to take me to shore."

"And you made it?" Blair asked.

"Well, I'm here," Sam said. "The raft didn't make it quite all the way. It broke up just a ways off shore."

"And that's how you got here yesterday?" Angus asked.

"Yup," Sam said, "and now it's a closed subject. I don't want to talk about it no more. Not ever."

And they all knew that to Sam Black it was a closed book, never to be opened again.

CHAPTER VIII

Angus and Jenny had both left. Blair sat in the chair opposite Sam Black, studying him intently.

Sam fidgeted about nervously. He didn't like it when she stared at him this way. His uneasiness came from the feeling that she could see right through him. She had called him a "phony."

He had a million and one questions in his head, but he was not sure exactly how to ask them without giving away all of his secrets. Still, he thought that he had managed to persuade them of the veracity of his escapade at sea and on the island. It sounded perfectly plausible. He grinned at Blair, wishing he knew more about his lovely captress.

God, he thought, *she looks so like Maria!*

"A penny for your thoughts," Blair said.

"I was just thinking how lovely you look," he said.

"That's easy for you to say," Blair said, laughing at him. "You have been marooned on an island for who knows how long. Any woman would look good to you!"

"Some more than others," Sam said, winking teasingly at her. "I may have lost consciousness on the island, but I didn't lose my memory. I still know a pretty woman when I see one."

"In that case," Blair said, "thank you."

Sam rubbed his ankle. It had helped when Dr. McPherson put the ice on it, and the bandage he had tightly wrapped around it made it feel much better.

"I know you will think this strange," Sam said, "but there are so many things I want to ask you."

"I already think you're strange," Blair said, "so you might as well ask anything you want to."

"Humph!" Sam grunted. "Ye think I'm strange, do ye?"

"Just a wee bit," Blair said, "but I like the unusual, the unpredictable." She looked down at the floor. "I like you," she added. Subtlety had never been one of her strong suits.

"I like you too," Sam said. "Ye can't imagine how much I like ye." *Or why*, his mind teased him.

Blair smiled. She could just hear her mother. She was such a prude! She would never understand Blair letting a complete stranger stay with her, not even one who was injured and who could not escape because of his sprained ankle. No, Blair was not worried about him "coming on" to her. She could take care of herself under normal circumstances, and Sam Black was certainly anything but normal.

"What was it you wanted to ask me?" Blair inquired.

"Well, I told you I've been on that island for a long time. Would you mind telling me what the date is?"

"April 18th," Blair answered.

"And the year?" he asked, finally, realizing that she wasn't going to volunteer any more information without his prying it out of her.

"Oh, sorry," Blair said. "Guess I wasn't thinking—2008."

Sam swallowed hard. The day he had disappeared from the deck of the *Whydah* had been April 17th, 1717! He had somehow missed a whole—his mind tried to perform the calculations—*almost three hundred years!* One thing he knew for sure was that he couldn't tell Blair, or anyone else, that the last day he remembered was April 17th, 1717. No one would understand that. *He* couldn't understand it. It was impossible. Yet here he was. No wonder things were so different. He had a whole lifetime worth of changes to settle in his mind. No, he had about *seven* lifetimes to try to figure out.

"Next question?" Blair asked, snapping Sam back to reality.

"This house," Sam said. "Isn't it a Hallett house?"

Blair laughed. "And I thought I had done such a good job on the remodeling. I could write a book about the Hallett houses. Hey, Sam, that's a wonderful idea! Thanks."

"Sure, but for what?"

"Why, for the idea," Blair said excitedly. "There is such a great bunch of stories about the early Hallett houses. You should have seen them. Why, Maria's father, John, was a wonderful carpenter, but his own house was a disgrace."

"A disgrace?" Sam asked. "Why?"

Sam's mind wandered back to the house he had gone to the first time he tried to see Maria. He had never actually seen the inside of the house, but from the outside it appeared quite respectable.

"Oh, John built wonderful houses for all the people of Cape Cod. He built *this* house. But when it came to his own house, why it had originally belonged to Andrew Hallett, his grandfather."

"Andrew Hallett?" Sam asked innocently, trying not to let the familiarity these names brought back to him show.

"Yes," Blair said. "Andrew Hallett, at least the senior one, was the first Hallett to come to America from England. He tried to tell everyone he came over on the Mayflower, but I found out that wasn't true."

"He didn't come from England?" Sam asked. He knew nothing about the first Halletts, those who came before Maria and her immediate family. He found these stories completely fascinating.

"Oh, yes," Blair said, "Andrew Hallett—and his wife and children—they all came from England. It was sometime around 1635. At least his name appears on a number of Yarmouth records as early as 1636."

"But not on the Mayflower?" Sam asked.

Blair laughed again. "No. In fact, Andrew Hallett came over as an indentured servant."

"A servant?" Sam nearly shouted. "But the Halletts were all rich!"

Blair looked at Sam in surprise.

"How do you know that?" she asked.

Sam thought quickly, then replied, "Well, I remembered that Angus said earlier that you were rich. It just seemed like all the Halletts before you..." His voice drifted off, leaving the sentence unfinished.

Blair seemed satisfied with the answer and continued talking.

Whew! Sam sighed in relief. *That was a close call.* He would have to watch what he said more carefully.

"Anyway, like I was saying before I was so rudely interrupted, Andrew Hallett came over as an indentured servant."

"But why?" Sam asked.

Blair laughed loudly. "He made a deal with a friend of his, it seems."

"What kind of a deal?" Sam asked.

"Well, indentured servants didn't have to pay any fares for their passage over to the new country—'New England,' they called it."

Sam caught himself just in time. He almost said, "I know," but he bit his lip instead.

"He agreed to pay half of his friend's fare. You see, he was a bachelor, so he only had to pay for one passenger. By signing on with him as his servant, Andrew Hallett got to bring his whole family for nothing. Well, almost nothing. He paid half of his friend's fare so his whole kit and caboodle could come on that half fare."

"If that isn't just like a Hallett!" Sam exclaimed.

Blair looked at him closely. "So you do know something about the Halletts."

"Yes," Sam admitted, moving about nervously. "I do have to admit that I do know a little. Me—pa and me—we set down anchor several times along Cape Cod. Why, everybody knew a tale of some kind about at least one Hallett."

"I guess that's true," Blair said, seeming to accept his explanation. Still, she felt she had to keep an eye on Sam Black. There was definitely something unusual about him. She wished she could put her finger on it, but it continued to elude her.

"You were telling me about the Hallett houses," Sam said. "What about them?"

"Oh, yeah," Blair said, twisting her foot up under her and scooting over closer to Sam. "Well," she continued, "Andrew Hallett's house had a lot of holes in the walls. You know, between the boards. Whenever his wife complained about them he just said, 'That's so you don't have to kill yourself doing housework. While all the other women are dusting the furniture, one good Cape Cod wind and the dust in here all blows right on through."

"What a nice man," Sam said sarcastically. "Such concern."

"Yeah," Blair said. "I'll bet you would be the same way to a woman."

"Hey, that's not fair!" Sam snapped.

"You're right," Blair said. "Sorry."

"For generations later, whatever Hallett lived in Andrew's house, they all used the same excuses when their wives complained about it."

"And this John Hallett, Maria's father," Sam asked, "they lived in the Andrew Hallett house?"

"They sure did," Blair said. "Maria lived there too, at least until Black Sam Bellamy came into her life."

Sam pulled away from Blair. He knew the people of Yarmouth never liked him, but he didn't realize just how bad his reputation was, but he was about to learn.

"What happened to Maria then?" he asked. He could hardly wait for the answer. There were so many strange things that had happened in his life, but Maria was the most important part of that life. *Everything* he ever did had been for Maria. Couldn't people understand that? Would Blair understand, if he could tell her? He knew he couldn't.

"She was accused of being a witch," Blair said.

Sam nodded. Yes, he had heard that tale countless times, but he wasn't prepared for what followed.

"She had a baby. They said it was Black Sam's child. The baby died the same night he was born."

"Whoa!" Sam wanted to shout. He had heard about Maria's baby. He had even seen the child on one occasion, the night he had left the gift basket for her. How could the baby have died, when he saw it when he peeked in the window at the infant, sound asleep in an elaborate cradle? Nothing was making any sense.

"No!" he screamed, unable to stop himself. "It can't be! The child didn't die. I saw…"

"Calm down," Blair warned. "The neighbors will hear you. There will be such gossip about my having a man living with me..."

"Sorry," Sam said. "It is just so sad. If Black Sam left her and all she had was his child, it shouldn't have died."

"Perhaps not," Blair said. "I always thought they loved each other so much, nothing should have kept them apart."

"And did they ever get together?" Sam asked. "Black Sam Bellamy and Maria Hallett?"

"No," Blair said, her eyes suddenly filling with tears. "Honestly, I think their love story is far more tragic than Romeo and Juliet. At least the two of them died together."

"Black Sam and Maria?" Sam asked.

"No, silly!" Blair said, punching him playfully on the arm. "Romeo and Juliet."

"What happened with them in the end?"

"Well, I told you about the storm that destroyed the *Whydah*, Black Sam's ship."

Sam nodded and waited for Blair to continue.

"It seems that Black Sam had finally gotten enough treasure together to ask Maria to wed him."

"And did she?" Sam asked, knowing the answer full well.

"Why no. When the *Whydah* sank, it was rumored that Maria drowned herself. I thought I told you that earlier. Still other accounts say that she was outcast from the town and lived out her life in a tiny thatched roof shanty, watching for the return of Black Sam for many years."

"It's just all so puzzling," Sam said. "Are you sure?"

"Positive," Blair said. "History never lies."

Sam tried to clear his brain of all of this. It just didn't make any sense to him—none of it. If what Blair said was true, how could anyone explain that he had seen Maria and Dr. Angus McPherson, *with little Sam, his son*, running through the poverty grass the night the *Whydah* sank? Where did they go? What happened to them? And how did Little Sam survive, if he had died like Blair said? And why did everyone insist that she had married Dr. Angus McPherson the last time he visited Crosby's Tavern?

And if she did marry him, why didn't that Dr. Angus McPherson that he had met the other day know that Blair's great-great-great-great-great grandmother was really Maria Hallett?

Sam was stymied. Perhaps he would never figure it out. "You can't change history," Blair had said. Still, if what he saw on his last day in Yarmouth was the truth, someway, somehow, someone had succeeded in doing exactly that.

❋ ❋ ❋

"I think we've both had an incredibly long day," Blair said abruptly. "I don't think you've heard a word I said. You look like you are living in some other world."

"Oh, yes, I have," Sam argued. "I've heard every single word." He had definitely heard all of it.

"I'll help you get into the downstairs bedroom," she said. "I wouldn't want you to have to go upstairs with that ankle. How does it feel?"

"It's much better, thanks," Sam said. "Your Dr. Angus McPherson is pretty good." He cringed at the mere sound of the man's name.

"Yeah, he sure is," Blair agreed, "especially since he usually just delivers babies."

Sam looked at her blankly. Somehow, he felt that Dr. Angus McPherson—this one or that other one years ago—had delivered Little Sam—and *he did not die!*

Sam grinned at Blair. "You trust me enough to stay downstairs with the likes of you up there all alone?"

"Until your ankle is better," Blair said, laughing and tossing her hair from one side to the other. "Then we'll have to make some other arrangements."

Sam shivered. She was so much like Maria.

"It will be the slowest healing ankle anyone ever saw," Sam mumbled, too low for Blair to hear.

CHAPTER IX

Sam watched from his perch on the sofa, trying to absorb all the modern gadgets he had never seen before. He watched Blair look in a book, find something, then punch some buttons on the phone. He looked carefully at the way she did it. He studied the way she pushed the tiny switch on the wall and the whole room lit up like the Aurora Borealis in the northern sky. He saw her, through the doorway into the kitchen, open a door on a big white box and come out with a cold can that she opened and told him to drink. The can said "beer." When he tasted it, he recognized it as ale. He was learning quickly, by simple observation, and he was glad that he did not have to ask a lot of questions as long as he watched her every move.

From time to time he heard her talking to someone in the kitchen, but there was no sign of anyone there except Blair. He assumed there must be another telephone in that room too.

❈ ❈ ❈

"Jenny is stopping by later," Blair informed Sam one day. "We are going out shopping. Will you be okay alone for a while?"

"Sure," Sam said. *Actually*, he thought, *it will be good to be alone for a while. Maybe then I can figure things out. Know where to go. I can't stay here forever.*

"Good," Blair said, tripping about like a little elf. Sam realized that she was as excited about going "shopping" as he was about being alone.

"Take your time," Sam said. "It will do you good."

"I didn't think you cared," Blair said.

"About what?" Sam asked.

"About me," she replied simply.

"Of course I care," Sam said. "If it wasn't for you, I'd probably be layin' at the bottom of the root cellar floor—dead by now, no doubt."

"And I would be accused of murder when they found you," Blair said. "Then I would be put on trial, and I would be found guilty and I would go to jail and you would have to come and set me free."

"Just like Maria," Sam said softly.

"What did you say?" Blair asked.

"Nothing," Sam answered. "Nothing important."

"Well, ta-ta," Blair said, waving gaily at Sam as she skipped through the front door. "See you in a bit."

"Have fun," Sam said, waving back at her.

❈ ❈ ❈

As soon as he was certain that she was *really* gone, Sam got up from the sofa. Dr. McPherson had told him he should stay off his foot as much as possible, but surely it had been long enough that it wouldn't hurt it now.

Sam put his weight down carefully at first, just in case it still hurt to walk on it. No, it felt fine. *Well,* he thought, *I won't let Blair know that—at least not yet.*

He walked over to the table that held the telephone. He took the book that Blair always looked in before she punched the tiny buttons, and he found a long list of names. He leafed through it until he found a listing for Halletts.

"Wow!" he cried out, although there was no one there to hear him. "There must be dozens of Halletts in here. No, way more than that. Maybe even hundreds."

He smiled as he remembered his mother. She had taught him to read when he was but a wee lad and Mother Wesley had continued with his education, as well as with that of all her other children, and now he was very grateful to both of them.

"M. Hallett," one name on the page said.

"I wonder," Sam said, scratching his head in bewilderment. "No, it couldn't be." Still, he figured it wouldn't hurt to find out.

He looked at the numbers which followed "M. Hallett" and began to poke the corresponding buttons, one by one, until he had pushed all seven of them. He lifted the little thing to his ear, just as he had seen Blair do. He heard a funny b-r-r-r-r sound, then a woman's voice say, "Hello."

Sam was shocked. He knew Blair heard people talk on here someway, but he still wasn't totally prepared for the actual sound of a human voice.

"Hello," the voice said again.

Still no response from Sam.

"Hello! Is anybody there? Hello!"

Again, more silence.

"If there is somebody there, please say something. If you don't answer me I'll call the police."

Slow, almost shyly, Sam asked, "Who is this?"

"This is Maria Hallett," the voice said, "but who are you? And what do you want?"

Sam set the phone down on the table. He had heard enough—more than enough. When Blair came back he would have to ask her about the Maria Hallett who talked to him in that little box. Was that thing full of ghosts?

Sam wished he was back on the high seas. He felt safe there. Here, he didn't know what he felt. Fear! And for a pirate to admit he is scared, that takes some doing.

Sam wandered out into the kitchen, where he opened the refrigerator door. He couldn't believe his eyes. It was filled with wonderful, delicious food of every description imaginable.

"No wonder she has fixed such good food," he said. "I wonder if this is some sort of a garden." He laughed. No, it couldn't be. You can't grow meat in a garden. Even an "old-timer" like him knew that.

Sam went to the cupboard doors next. He opened them and found round containers with pictures of food on them, packages you could *see through* of rice, pastas, and all sorts of other things.

This was just unbelievable. He could never have imagined such a thing as this. So this was what 2008 was like.

"Well, Black Sam Bellamy," he said, grinning broadly, the gold on his front teeth shining, "welcome to 2008. You've done okay, matey."

Sam walked to the basement door. He opened it and looked down. It looked pretty steep, and his ankle had been okay so far, but he thought he ought to wait a little longer before he tackled the steps under his own power. He had leaned heavily on Blair when he had gone down there at night.

"You'll just have to wait," he said. "As soon as I can, I'll try to find my way down to you."

❈ ❈ ❈

Sam was so engrossed in whoever or whatever was in the basement that he didn't hear the intruders who had come in through the front door.

He jumped when someone—a woman—called out, "Blair! Blair, dear. Are you home?"

It was followed by a gruff, deep man's voice. "How many times have I told you to keep that door locked? You never know who's lurking about these days. A person's not safe in their own home any more. Why, did you hear what happened to poor old Grandma Clark?"

The couple came into the kitchen together, and Sam stood there, frozen, facing them.

"Who in blazes are you?" the pudgy, balding man bellowed.

"Martin!" the woman said, placing her hand on his arm. "Don't you remember that Blair said she had a house guest? This must be—oh, dear, I forgot your name. How awful of me!"

"That can't be him!" the man barked. "Blair said he had an injured ankle. She also said he was handsome. Why, he's the scraggliest, ugliest man I've ever seen."

"Martin!" the woman said again, rolling her eyes around in exasperation and embarrassment. "Mind your manners."

She was begging with more than her voice. Her eyes pleaded

for him to be silent. Her hands squeezed his arm, trying to get him to stop.

"I knew I should have married Eunice Kennedy," the man grumbled. "She never would have let the likes of *him* in her house."

"Martin!"

"It's all right, ma'am," Sam said finally. "I imagine it is quite a shock for you to come callin' on Blair and findin' the likes of me here. Let me explain."

Sam wondered what Blair had told them about him. He didn't want to make matters worse if what she told him wasn't *exactly* the truth.

"I should have known," the man said. "He must be one of Jenny's friends. Nobody else would be caught dead in a get-up like that. Those theater people—you can't trust a one of them. And he's sure no exception. Made up like a pirate."

"Maybe I'm the one who should be asking the questions," Sam said, turning the tables on the man. "Blair asked me to keep an eye on the place while she and Jenny went shopping. I'm just doing a friend a favor. But you, sir—I haven't a clue who you might be. Why, you could be the police, coming to drag her off to jail."

Now it was the woman who screamed. "Jail!" she shouted. "Why would they take her off to jail? What has she done this time? Oh, I knew she would get herself into trouble some day. I think I'd better sit down. Martin, help me."

The man forgot about Sam for the moment and helped his wife to a chair by the kitchen table. Sam had not planned it quite this way, but at least it got the man's mind on something besides him for a while.

"Are you okay, Maggie?" he asked. His concern, in spite of his harshness a few moments earlier, seemed genuine.

"Yes, I'm fine," the woman said. "But please, what did you mean about Blair going off to jail?"

Sam went over and sat on the chair opposite her. His piercing, black eyes penetrated her very being as he stared directly at her. "I didn't mean anythin' by it, ma'am. Honest, I didn't. I just meant that I didn't know whether I could trust you any more than your husband knew if he could trust me. Blair just went shopping with Jenny. They should be home any..."

"Come on out into the kitchen," Blair called to Jenny as she pushed the door open with her foot. Her hands were loaded to the limit with bags and packages. She dropped them onto the sofa, and soon Jenny followed suit.

"Sam! Sam, are you there?" When he didn't answer, she yelled at Jenny. "Oh, Jenny! What if he has gone? I told him to wait here and he said he would. Oh, Jenny, I don't know what I'll do if he's walked out on me. I—I really need him. No, I want him. Oh, I don't know what I want."

Blair ran out into the kitchen, where she saw Sam sitting at the table with her parents.

"Oh, Mom, Dad! I guess you've met Sam, huh?"

CHAPTER X

This was not the way Blair had planned it at all. She had gone shopping for the express purpose of buying Sam new clothes, hoping to make him presentable before she introduced him to her parents.

"Blair Maria Smythe!" Martin Smythe yelled at his daughter. "How could you possibly have brought this—this *creep* into your house?"

Blair laughed. She knew her father was upset. He never called her Blair *Maria* Smythe unless he was really mad about something. There was no need for Blair to ask what it was that upset him. It could be only one thing: Sam Black.

"Don't you laugh at me!" he ordered. "I will have respect from you, and I don't care how much past twenty-one you are."

"I wasn't going to say anything about being an adult," Blair said. "It is just 'creep' is so outdated. Really, Daddy, you ought to get with the times, for your own sake, if nothing else. People will begin to think you are *old*."

Blair and Martin were so busy in their own battle of words, they did not notice the look that spread across Sam's face. *Why*, he wondered, *didn't she tell me her middle name was Maria?* It sent shivers up and down his spine, just as it had done when he talked on that telephone and had some strange old lady tell him her name was Maria Hallett. Could it possibly be... Was Blair a transplant just like he was? Was she Blair Smythe? Or was she really Maria Hallett, in some sort of a disguise?

Margaret Smythe saw Sam's hands shaking.

"Psst, Sam. Are you all right?"

"Yes," he whispered back, glad that Blair and her father were still yelling at each other. "I just wasn't expecting your husband to be so upset."

"Daddy," they heard Blair say, "if you will just sit down for a few minutes, I will explain all about Sam. Or better yet, he can explain things himself. I'm sure once you hear all he has been through, you will feel sorry for him too."

Feel sorry for him? Was that all it was? Pity? He had never had anyone's pity before, and he didn't need it now. Especially not Blair Smythe's pity. He had made mistakes once before in his life—his other life—and it had cost him Maria. Now, finding Blair, he felt like he had found Maria again, and that maybe he had a second chance. At what? Love? Could it be? Whatever it was, he had the same feeling about Blair that he'd had for Maria that first night when he set eyes on her in Crosby's Tavern. He wasn't about to risk losing it again. What he wanted from Blair was her respect, her love, but certainly not her pity.

Sam's mind wandered briefly, just for a moment, back to the whirlpool. He had made a vow. A vow with God. A vow with his mother, wherever she might be. In heaven? He could only hope so. He would keep that vow. He would right the wrongs he had done in the past. At the very least, he would pay for the evils he had wrought on innocent people. All he needed was the opportunity.

"Well," Martin said, "we are waiting." Softly, almost inaudibly, he added, "And it better be good."

Blair grinned from ear to ear. They had no idea how good Sam's story was. They were in for the treat of a lifetime. No TV show could come close to Sam's story.

"It started several years ago. In fact, I was only a teenage lad when it all began. My pa, he was a mariner, one of the best on the seas. Well, when he figured I was old enough, he took me with him."

Blair rested her elbows on the table, then she put her head in her hands. Sam's strong English accent fascinated her. In fact, everything about Sam fascinated her.

"And your mother let you go?" Blair's mother asked. "Why, if...if Brian had tried to pull a stunt like that..."

"Brian?" Sam asked. "Who is Brian?"

"Blair didn't tell you?" her mother asked.

Sam shook his head.

"Brian is Blair's brother," Martin explained. "He's the exact opposite of Missy here."

Sam saw that he smiled warmly at his daughter, in spite of the argument they had just had. One thing was sure; Martin Smythe was out to protect his daughter, and he knew it was because he loved her. That would make Sam's job that much harder. If he was going to win Blair for himself, he knew he would have to win her father as well. They went hand-in-hand.

Sam continued his tale, telling them of the shipwreck and of the years he had spent on some deserted island, "God knows where."

"How did you ever get here?" Margaret asked. "Did some ship finally rescue you?"

"Nothing as wonderful as that, Mrs. S," he said. Sam threw his head back and laughed, that deep, throaty laugh. "Actually, for a man who prided himself on bein' the best-fitted man on the seas, I failed a few more times than I care to recount."

"Failed at what?" Martin asked, finding himself caught up in the story, whether he wanted to admit it or not.

Sam could hardly believe his ears. He had never in his entire life—however long that had been—admitted failure to anyone—about anything. Was this the beginning of a *new him*? He couldn't decide if it made him feel good, or if that was what was making him so miserably uncomfortable. He knew he was lying through his gold-crowned teeth, but he'd never had a conscience before.

When it hit him, like a bolt out of the blue, that he was lying and that made him feel almost sick to his stomach, he couldn't find the words to describe it, not even to himself. Truth had never been one of his strong suits, and he had never known the feeling of guilt. So that was what it was. Now, though, he was too far in to back out. Besides, he couldn't tell them the truth, even if he knew and understood it. *No one* would believe him, and who could blame them?

"Well, I tried making a raft. The first one I made sank as soon as it got in the water."

"Some sailor!" Martin huffed. "Huck Finn did better than that."

Sam shrugged his shoulders. *Huck Finn?* He'd have to try to find out who Huck Finn was. Must be some guy from Finland, he deduced.

"Over the years they gradually got better and better. Finally, I got one done that took me out so far that I couldn't see the island anymore. Then I got scared. What would happen if the raft sank out in the middle of the ocean? I searched and searched for land, but there was none in sight. Not for days and days. Weeks and weeks. I ate the berries I had brought along from the island. I ate what fish I could catch with my hands. Ate 'em raw, I did."

"Yech!" Jenny said. Blair had almost forgotten that Jenny was there. It was strange for her to be quiet. She'd been taken in by Sam Black and his story too.

"It wasn't so bad," Sam said. "The worst part was the water. The supply I'd brought from the stream on the island was gone in the first few days. I tried drinking the briny salt water, but it made me thirstier than if I didn't drink anything. Made your throat feel all parched and dry, it did."

"How could you survive that long without water?" Martin asked. "That must have been awful."

"Awful ain't the word for it," Sam said, pleased to see that even Blair's father was enjoying the tale. He was actually believing it.

Again, Sam felt that twinge. *A conscience!* What a strange sensation it gave him. He didn't even know, before this time, that he possessed such a thing.

Beads of sweat broke out on Sam's forehead. His hands shook nervously. His throat was dry, and he found it hard to talk. Still, he knew he had to go on.

Maggie reached over and took one of Sam's hands in hers.

"It's okay," she said reassuringly. "It's all over now. It's behind you. You can make a new beginning."

"I'd—like to tell you the rest of it," Sam said. "I have to get it out."

"Go ahead," Martin said. "We're all ears."

"I managed to get some fresh water when it rained," Sam said, speaking much more slowly now than he had been. "I let it fall into the bucket I had brought the berries in."

They all stared at Sam like they had been hypnotized. Never had they seen such a man or heard such a story. He was a mystery, to be sure, yet there was something that fascinated them—each one for their own reasons.

It was Martin who finally spoke. "And what do you intend to do now?"

"I—I don't rightly know, sir," Sam said. "I haven't given it much thought. The only thing I know is the sea. That and precious gems." He grinned at all of them.

"Don't tell me you really were a pirate!" Jenny exclaimed excitedly. "Oh, this is just too much!"

"Jenny! Really!" Blair said, patting her on the back. "You are letting your imagination run wild again. There is no such a thing as piracy anymore. That's a thing of the past."

"So am I," Sam wanted to say. "If you only knew."

"I guess you could set sail again," Martin said. "There's always a need for good men on the schooners off the coast. We do have a very lucrative tourist business, and some of the men would be glad to hire on a man of your experience and character."

Character! Blair thought. *Sam Black is definitely that—a character.*

Jenny picked up on the same word: character. What a fascinating character Sam Black would make in a Broadway play. She could just see him. Sam would play himself, and she would play... Well, that didn't matter. She would have to track down that producer she had met and see what he thought of the whole idea.

"One thing is sure," Martin said, "he can't continue to stay here with you, Blair. People are already talking. Why, we have always been more than respectable people. I won't have our daughter in the middle of a nasty scandal."

"Why, no!" Blair said sarcastically, smirking. "We haven't had a scandal in the family since Maria Hallett's affair with that pirate way back when."

"That was years ago," Martin bellowed, "and I'll thank you not to mention her again."

Margaret laughed. "Yes, you know your father forbid me to go to the celebration the other day. Why, I think it would have been just oodles of fun."

"I hear they got that handsome new young doctor from Brewster to play Sam Bellamy. Why, the society pages were full of pictures of him. They even said for a while they thought maybe he had disappeared, just like the real Sam Bellamy did. They couldn't find him, but I guess he finally surfaced."

"Too bad you weren't there," Martin said, looking at Sam.

"Oh, but he was there," Blair said. "At least at the beginning. After his dramatic entrance from the water, I figured he would be perfect to play Sam Bellamy, but when I tried to find him, he had disappeared."

"Where had you gone?" Margaret asked.

"I wanted to get away from that big crowd of people," Sam said. "After being alone on the island, and then on the water, it was more than I could manage all at once."

"Well, I can certainly understand that," Martin said, "but that still doesn't solve the problem of where you are going to stay. I presume you don't have any money."

"Just this," Sam said, tugging at the gold chain around his neck. "I will be glad to unscrew a few links to pay for what I have eaten and used of your daughter's."

As if seeing it for the first time, Margaret gasped at the sight of the gold around Sam's neck. Martin had given her more than her share of jewelry in the past, but it paled in comparison to the gold Sam had on.

"Where did you get that?" she asked, nearly choking at the size of it.

"This?" Sam asked. "Why, me pa gave it to me. That was just about the last thing he did before he..." Same lowered his head reverently. "Before he—went under."

"What do you mean, unscrew it?" Martin asked.

"Like this," Sam said, loosening three links and separating them. "They come from Colombia. And Barbados. And Jamaica.

Sailors often use them for currency, since it's not the same in every land."

Blair gazed intently at Sam. She had read all about "money chains." They were widely used, just like Sam said, but that was in the eighteenth century. They had not been used in over two hundred years.

"We still have to find a place for you," Martin said. "I won't leave here until that is settled. Maggie, what is old Mrs. Clark's phone number?"

He turned to Sam to explain. "She's a widow here in Hyannis. She runs a boarding house. She almost always has a room available, especially this time of the year."

Sam thought of the Widow Clark he knew. She certainly wouldn't be around now. She would be—*ancient*! Of course, she wouldn't be all that much older than he was.

Martin went to the phone and punched in the numbers Margaret told him.

"Mrs. Clark?" Martin asked. "This is Martin Smythe."

"Yes, I am just fine, thanks. Maggie too."

"Yes, it was quite a show Blair put on, wasn't it?"

Sam noticed that he didn't admit to Mrs. Clark that he had not attended the event.

"Yes, I did have something in mind. I heard about your—trouble—the other day. I may have a way to help you out."

Martin's face reddened. "You've heard about Blair's guest? Well, I suppose I shouldn't be surprised. I'm sure everyone on the Cape has heard about it by now."

He glared sternly at Blair as he spoke, his disapproval obvious.

"Yes, what I have to say has everything to do with him. He needs a place to stay. Do you have a room available?"

"But just think about it. If someone tries to break in again, it would be so much better if there was a big strong man like Sam Black to protect you."

There was a long silence while Martin simply listened to Mrs. Clark ramble on and on about the youth of today, then she finally admitted that maybe it was a good idea after all.

"I'm sure you won't be sorry," Martin said. "He is a most interesting man. He should be able to keep you entertained for hours with his tales of the sea."

"I'll bring him by shortly," Martin said in closing. "Oh, and as far as the rent goes, I'll cover it for the first month."

He hung the phone up and turned to Sam.

"It's all settled," he said, "and like I told Mrs. Clark, I'll cover the first month's rent..." He held his hand out to Sam and took the three gold links from the table in front of him. "In exchange for these," he said with a wide grin.

Sam pondered the statement Martin had made on the phone. There had obviously been some "trouble" at the Widow Clark's house. He wondered what it was, then decided to wait until he was settled in at her boarding house to ask. He was sure they would have plenty of time on their hands—to discuss "whatever."

CHAPTER XI

Sam stood beside the strange rig. He had watched them come and go for days now, seeing people climb in and out, suffering no apparent ill effects. Still, he was quite apprehensive about getting in with Martin Smythe, who had insisted that it was better if he took Sam to Mrs. Clark's than if Blair drove them there. Sam tried to talk Martin into letting him walk, but it didn't work.

Finally, slowly, Sam got in and sat on the passenger side of the car. Martin pulled a belt from the side of the car and wrapped it around himself. "Better buckle up," Martin said, and Sam did as Martin had done with the belt on his side of the car. Martin pulled away from the curb, and Sam reached out in front of him, bracing himself by putting his hands firmly against the dashboard. He inched forward, watching out the window as things seemed to whiz by.

"You might be a wonderful sailor," Martin said, laughing at Sam, "but you're not much of a landlubber, are you?"

"N-n-no, sir," Sam said, his voice suddenly sounding like a soprano in a church choir.

"When's the last time you had a car ride?" Margaret asked from the back seat?"

"C-c-car?" Sam stammered.

"I swear," Martin said, clucking his tongue between his teeth, "if I didn't know better, I'd think you got amnesia while you were on that island. You don't remember cars?"

"Sure," Sam said, assuming that this *thing* he was in was a car. "It's just, I never did spend much time in them. Why, back home in Dorchester, we always walked. Ma and me, that is. Pa, he was pretty near always gone out to sea. So, when I was old enough, like I said, he took me out on the water with him. Didn't leave much time for such things as cars."

"Makes perfect sense to me," Maggie said. "I keep telling Martin we should walk more. It is good for the heart, you know."

"Yeah, but works havoc on your legs," Martin grumbled.

"Well," Margaret said, "here we are. This is Mrs. Clark's boarding house. Your new home, Sam. I'm sure you'll like it. Mrs. Clark, she's a real story teller. You might find a lot to talk about. You see, her husband, God rest his soul, died while he was at sea. The Clark men have all been mariners for generations. You should feel right at home."

Sam shivered, listening to Maggie talk. He had known a Seaman Clark one time. Indeed, he had been the cause of his death. And the widow Clark—well, he had plenty of memories of her too.

Sam sat with his eyes glued on Martin. He had to figure out how to open the door so he could get out of this contraption. He sure didn't want to be stuck in here alone. That would be a fate far worse than facing another Widow Clark.

Sam watched Martin open his door, and he successfully got his door open too. He followed Martin and Maggie up the walk to the front door. Martin lifted the heavy old brass door knocker and let it bang several times, announcing their arrival.

"Door's open," a voice from inside called out. "Come on in."

The threesome entered and there, seated on an old leather-cushioned sofa, sat Mrs. Clark. She didn't look like the Mrs. Clark Sam had known—before. But as soon as she spoke, he could have sworn the two Clark women were one in the same. Their voices sounded identical.

"Your room's upstairs, second door on your left," she said. "You want to go up and take a look at it to see if it meets with your approval?"

Sam laughed. "Don't rightly know what I'd do if it didn't," he said. "You see, I'm sort of at the mercy of those around me at the moment."

"That so?" Mrs. Clark asked.

"I'm sure Sam here will tell you all about his exciting adventures at sea, given the time. Mrs. Clark, she has a myriad of tales of her own to tell. Her husband used to spin a pretty yarn when he'd come back to shore," Martin said.

Mrs. Clark offered them all a cup of tea, which they drank as they sat around the old oak kitchen table. Sam looked around, trying to digest everything he saw. There were the same bright lights up in the ceiling as there were at Blair's house, even though it was the middle of the day. Suddenly, he shivered. He didn't know what there was about this place, but it gave him an eerie feeling. It was as if he'd been there before. He blinked his eyes and studied his surroundings more closely. Yes! It didn't make any sense, but he could swear this was the same house where he had stayed with the Widow Clark. But that was in Yarmouth, and this was Hyannis. It was impossible.

He heard the Smythes and Mrs. Clark talking, but it was like they were far away. Maybe this Widow Clark's husband had built an exact replica of the earlier Mariner Clark's house. Yes, that had to be it. It would make perfect sense. Most of the people he knew from the Cape weren't all that independent. They seemed to cling to tradition and family like the barnacles on the bottom of a sailing vessel.

Sam saw Martin's hand come towards him and he instinctively ducked. Was he going to take a swing at him? If so, why? He hadn't done anything.

"You off on that island again?" Martin asked.

"Sorry," Sam said. "I guess I was sort of daydreaming. What did I miss?"

"Not much," Martin said. "I just said that Maggie and I were going to head on home if there wasn't anything else you needed us for."

"You've been very kind," Sam said. "Thank you."

Martin and Maggie stood up and headed for the door. "If you think of anything, just give us a call," Maggie said.

"Yeah, sure," Sam said, figuring they meant that strange machine that he had talked to Maria Hallett on.

❈ ❈ ❈

"So, do you want to go on up to your room for a bit?" Mrs. Clark asked. "It sounds like you've been through quite an ordeal."

Sam wished he had paid more attention to the conversation. He wasn't sure what the Smythes might have told her about him. He'd have to watch what he said until he could figure it out.

"That might be good," Sam said. "The second door on the left you said?"

"That's right. I'll call up to you when it's time for chow. Meanwhile, make yourself at home. I might put you to work some once that ankle's healed up. It's been a mighty piece since I've had a man around the house for more than a day or two."

"Be glad to help," Sam said, sounding sincere enough, she thought.

❈ ❈ ❈

Sam made his way up the curved stairway, limping on his tender ankle. When he got to the landing, he stopped to catch his breath. After a few moments, he continued on the climb.

When he got to the hallway, he looked down towards the door to his room. He gasped. It looked exactly like the room he had stayed in in Yarmouth. The room where he and Maria…

He carefully turned the knob and pushed the door open. It was indeed identical, right down to the wallpaper and the curtains on the windows. The bed coverings were different, if he remembered right, but it was like he was looking at a ghost. He shut his eyes tightly and he could have sworn that he saw Maria standing there, flipping her jumper up in the air so he could see the embroidery on her petticoat.

"Ye gods!" he nearly screamed, then clapped his hand over his mouth. He didn't want to alarm the Widow Clark. He would have to deal with her later. Right now, though, he was not about to stay in that room. Not until he had some sort of an explanation.

He walked down the stairs again and quietly headed out the door. He had taken careful note of the way they had come. He had to get back to Maria—er, Blair—and find out what was going on. If she had any answers, that was.

He dragged his lame foot along as he tried to go as fast as he could. At this point, he wouldn't have been at all surprised if she admitted to him that she was indeed Maria Hallett, and that this whole thing had been some sort of a cruel game the people of Cape Cod were playing on Black Sam Bellamy. Did she really know who he was, or had his phony name convinced her that he was somebody completely different? If only he had been a bit more creative. Black Sam Bellamy—Sam Black. Didn't take a genius to figure that one out.

He hoped, as he walked, that Blair's parents had gone to their home, and not back to Blair's house. It would be a lot easier to pose his questions to Blair if Jenny was gone too. He would have to deal with one person and one issue at a time, and he wasn't sure he could trust Blair, but she was his best bet for now at figuring this whole mess out.

Sam rubbed his head, which had suddenly developed a throbbing pain in it. "Just how long was I out there whirling around in that eddy?" he asked.

❄ ❄ ❄

Behind a tree, a young boy watched and listened to the strange-looking man. He was intrigued, and followed along behind the bushes where he couldn't be seen.

Sam jumped as a whole group of cars began honking their horns at him. He looked at them, puzzled.

"Hey, idiot!" a man inside one of the cars yelled at him. "Can't you see there's a red light?" The man pointed at a light that was on the other side of the street Sam was crossing.

"Yes, I see it," Sam hollered back. "It's right pretty, isn't it?" He continued his slow stroll across the street, with all the cars still honking at him. When he got across and they all began to move, he wondered what power he had that he could make all of these cars stop and wait for him. He flashed a sinister grin at them and waved.

"Another question to ask Blair," he said to himself. "Why are those red lights there?"

CHAPTER XII

Sam went around to the back door, hoping nobody would see him. He rapped loudly enough to raise the dead, then wished he had been more quiet, or perhaps he should have just walked in.

"I'm coming," Blair called out, racing to the door. She smiled at Sam. She had hoped he might return, but she hadn't dared to count on it. She wanted to quiz him some more about this island he'd been stranded on. Somehow, she didn't believe his story any more than she figured the soap operas on TV were true. Of course, she reasoned, it was not unusual on them to have somebody return from the dead. A strange clammy feeling crept up and down her body.

"Come in," she invited. Sam vaguely remembered some story his mother used to tell him about a spider inviting a fly into its cobweb. He felt like he was walking into the same kind of a trap.

Sam stepped slowly inside.

"So your ankle is all better?" Blair asked, a know-it-all smirk sneaking across her face.

"No," Sam said, sitting down on one of the chairs at the kitchen table. "I hobbled all the way over here."

"Couldn't resist me, huh?" Blair countered.

"I, um, er, I have a few questions," Sam said. "Things don't seem to be quite the way I remember them the last time I was—on the Cape."

"So you've been here before? When?"

"It's been a long time," Sam replied.

※ ※ ※

Something crashed outside the window, and Blair got up to see what it was. She giggled as she watched a black cat race out into the bushes in the back yard.

"Just a pesky cat," she said, returning to the table and sitting down across from Sam. "Stupid thing always seems to show up at the worst times. It's like an omen or something."

The little boy who had followed Sam curled up closer to the house so he wouldn't get caught eavesdropping.

※ ※ ※

"So how do you remember things?" Blair asked, her curiosity piqued to the ultimate level.

Sam rubbed his beard, a habit she had noticed before. It seemed to be when he got that really puzzled look on his face.

"Well, for starters, your house..."

"What about it?" Blair asked.

"Is—is it—a *Hallett house*?"

Blair laughed. "Of course it is. I told you that I am related to the Halletts. They were going to tear it down and I couldn't stand the idea of losing a part of history. *My* history." She paused. "Now you'd better tell me, what do you know about the Halletts?"

"It seems that everybody who ever sets foot on the Cape knows the Hallett family. Their reputation has spread far and wide. So which Hallett did it belong to?" He already knew the answer. Of course it was Thomas Hallett's house. He had been there many times, in *that other life* he had lived.

"It was originally Thomas Hallett's house," Blair said. "Oh, the tales that were spun about this house. It was the only way they could get both John and Jonathan together. They tricked them. They convinced both of them, after Thomas had a heart attack—or something like that—that he needed help to put the siding on the house. They invited both of them to come and help, but they didn't tell either of them that the other one was coming."

"Why wouldn't they both come if their brother needed help?" Sam asked.

Blair flinched. She was sure she hadn't said anything about the three of them being brothers. She tucked it back in her memory, along with several other things Sam had said in the past few days that didn't quite add up. He remembered, not too fondly, how the one thing both John and Jonathan Hallett had in common was their hatred for him.

"Okay, now it's my turn for a question," Blair said.

"Go ahead," Sam said, twisting nervously on his chair.

"How did you know about the root cellar?"

Sam shivered. How was he going to explain this one?

"I don't, um, know, really. I guess I must have heard someplace that most of the homes on the Cape had one."

Check two, Blair thought. She had never heard that, but it sounded fairly plausible.

"But I didn't even know it was there," she admitted.

"Drastic circumstances call for drastic measures," Sam said quickly. "I had to find someplace to hide, and I noticed that there was a slight mound of dirt there. I just took a chance."

"Okay," Blair said, winking at him. "If we are playing 20 Questions, it's your turn."

Sam didn't know what "20 Questions" was and he wondered if he should mentally count how many he asked before he ran out of his turn.

"That little box," Sam said, pointing to the TV. "How do those little people get inside of it?"

Blair laughed. "You're joking, right?"

"No, I'm dead serious." Sam laughed that throaty roar again, thinking, *Or am I just dead?*

"It's called a 'television,'" Blair explained, "but I know they have them in England. Of course over there they call them a 'telly.' Where did you say you lived in England?"

"Dorchester," Sam replied.

"But isn't that a pretty big city?" Blair asked.

Sam shrugged his shoulders. "I guess so."

"It is all about electronics," she continued. "Technology."

These words were all about as foreign to Sam as if she were speaking to him in Greek. He tilted his head a bit, rubbed his beard, and said, "I still don't understand."

Suddenly, something popped into Blair's mind. There was something definitely odd—off, perhaps?—about this man. *No!* she thought, shaking her head about to try to discard such weird thoughts. *It is impossible. Still...*

"When was the last time you were on the Cape?" she asked. "I mean, *exactly* when?"

"Um, it was April 17th, I think. Yes, that was it. I remember it all too well."

He shivered as his mind went back to the men who were chasing him, trying to get rid of him. He could feel the cold water as they tossed him into the ocean. Then there was that dreadful storm, as he climbed aboard the *Whydah*, along with his crew, hoping to get out of town before somebody killed him. And then that dreadful crash of thunder and the lightning that split his ship right down the middle. Then that awful, dreadful feeling as he felt himself going down to the depths of the ocean floor, and the time that seemed like an eternity until, like Jonah from the belly of the whale, even the ocean could not stomach him any longer and he was cast out into the middle of the celebration when he first laid eyes on Blair.

Blair knew that date all too well. In her studies of the infamous pair of Maria and Black Sam, she knew it was his last day on earth—unless he somehow managed to escape and went into hiding.

"What year was that?" Blair asked, leaning forward to listen intently to his answer.

"It was..." Sam hesitated. Oh well, he might as well get it over with. He knew that he had lost many lifetimes to the water, but he couldn't explain it to Blair. He couldn't even explain it to himself. "It was, I think, in 1717."

Blair's mouth gaped. She gasped. When she was finally able to speak, she exclaimed, "My God! You *are* Black Sam Bellamy. But how..."

"I have no idea," he said, and he began to recount that awful day, the last day of his life, or whatever that had been.

"How have you lived all these years? You are a scientific wonder! Oh, how people would love to get their hands on you."

"No!" Sam yelled. "I don't want anybody to know. I shouldn't even be telling you. I just know that I ended up in the water when that storm hit, and I've been down there, swirling around in a stupid eddy, ever since, until the day I blew up on shore here."

"Nobody is going to believe this," Blair said, her eyes growing bigger by the second. "Nobody, but nobody."

"I told you, you can't tell anybody," Sam warned. "I shouldn't even be telling you. I know it makes no sense. It doesn't make any sense to me either." Again, he stopped momentarily, wondering how to continue. "I've never heard of such a thing, but I know who I am and what I've been through. And that Dr. Angus that was here—he was there, too. Again, I don't know how, but he was one of the men that ran me off and threw me into the ocean that day—April 17th, 1717."

"Dr. Angus was there?" Blair asked. "But how..."

"I told you, I don't know. I just know that he had up and married Maria after the baby died... At least that's what they claimed. But I saw the baby. My baby! I should have been there with them, not him!"

"But the baby did die," Blair insisted. "The history books all tell the tale of the demise of Black Sam Bellamy and the baby that died soon after his birth, and that Maria was outcast for the rest of her life when they accused her of witchcraft."

"This might be a long day," Blair said, "but I have to know the rest of the story. *All* of it. I don't care if it takes several days. I have to figure this whole thing out. And as for Doc Angus, well, he isn't even married, and he certainly doesn't have a baby. He just delivers babies."

❊ ❊ ❊

Outside, the little boy who had been listening slinked away on his belly until he reached the bushes and then took off running.

"Ma! Ma! You're never gonna believe this!" he said, panting

and out-of-breath. "That crazy man I told you about? He's Black Sam! Black Sam Bellamy! I heard it myself."

The boy's mother came over and felt his forehead. It wasn't hot. No fever. Still, he must be delirious. Black Sam Bellamy had lived over two hundred years earlier. Whatever kind of games the man was playing, she didn't want her son to have any part in it.

"Stay away from him," his mother cautioned. "He's obviously crazy. You don't know what he might do to you. There are all kinds of loonies in the world anymore. You can't trust any of them."

But the boy continued on, recounting to his mother everything he had heard Blair and Sam discuss. With no explanation, his mother began to sweat profusely. Soon she fainted dead away, leaving the boy alone. He dialed 911.

"My mama is layin' on the floor," he said to the emergency dispatch lady. "I don't know what happened. I was just tellin' her what I heard at a neighbor's house and she got real hot and then she got all white, and... Well, now she's layin' out cold on the floor. Come fix my mama, please."

CHAPTER XIII

Blair could hardly believe her ears. Was this man crazy? Did he actually believe he was Black Sam Bellamy? The original one? Her mind twirled like the eddy he claimed he'd been locked in for all those years. She struggled to remember the things she had read about him and Maria. Could she find some questions in the recesses of her brain that would trick him up if this was some far-fetched game he was playing?

"Why did you go ashore the night you first met Maria?"

"It was a dreadful nor'easter," he quickly replied. "The worst I'd ever seen."

Blair studied him, trying to catch something in his eyes or his actions that would give him away. This one was too easy. Anybody who had read the story from the history books would know that one.

Before she could ask the next question, he continued. "We were there for several days. I didn't want to leave her, but I promised her that I would be back for her as soon as I made my fortune at sea."

Again, an easy answer, Blair thought.

"How did you meet Maria?"

"She showed up at Crosby's Tavern." He grinned, the gold in his teeth nearly blinding Blair. "It was late at night, and it was pouring down rain like cats and dogs." He hesitated, nervously rubbing his hands over his knee. "Her cape—oh, that red wool cape—it was soppin' wet. She hung it on that hook and started flirting with every man in the Inn."

Blair decided that she would just let him carry on, without asking him anything further, hoping that he would trip himself up sooner or later.

"All the men, the old-timers, they all seemed to know her. I had to go ask the owner who she was. Next thing I knew, she was sitting with me at my table."

He stared at Blair, realizing once again how much she resembled Maria. Was this some sort of trick? Had Maria somehow escaped from the past too? Could it be possible that they might be reunited? Or would he once again be snatched up by some unknown source that was far bigger than he was and he would find this blonde version of Maria gone too? Could fate be so cruel that it would take her from him twice?

Sam sat there, silent, until Blair finally asked, "So did you—you know—did you fall in love with her right then and there?"

"Ah, yes, lassie, t'would be a cold-hearted man who could withstand the temptation of Maria Hallett. I was in love with her the moment I laid eyes on her."

Blair wondered what it would be like to fall in love as soon as you met somebody. She had never felt a strong attraction like that to anybody.

Her head jerked as she suddenly realized that she had fallen in love with Black Sam Bellamy—or whoever he really was—the second he had washed up on the beach at the celebration. Oh, no, she hadn't admitted it to herself. Maybe it was just all the mystery and intrigue that surrounded him. She knew nothing about the man, even now, and his story made less sense than if she had read a fairy tale or watched another Johnny Depp movie about some unknown pirate.

Blair sat, her eyes glued to Black Sam's face. Somehow, no matter how preposterous it sounded, she believed him. Time travel—it was impossible—until now. She knew that whatever had caused the pirate to spiral through time, it had nothing to do with science. It had to be something much more—or less—complicated than that. There was no logical explanation for it. Since Black Sam seemed as puzzled about the whole mess as she was, she knew he couldn't have manipulated his own fate.

"How—how did Maria get pregnant?" she finally asked.

Black Sam threw his head back and roared with laughter. "Surely someone as smart as you knows the answer to that one," he said.

"I know how a woman gets pregnant," Blair said, frustrated at his insensitivity in such an important matter. "I meant Maria, specifically. Tell me about it."

To her surprise, Black Sam actually blushed. He didn't answer, so she repeated the question. "I asked you to tell me about how Maria got pregnant."

Again, this was a matter of record in countless history books. She knew the tale so well. She had actually dreamed, on several occasions, that she was Maria and that Black Sam had made love to her that night at Widow Clark's Inn. She had awakened, feeling more loved than she had ever felt in her life. As she stared at him, she wondered if he would be as good in bed as he was in her dreams.

"We rendezvoused at Widow Clark's Inn," he said softly.

Blair waited for him to continue, but she wasn't sure he would. Finally, he said, "I chased her around the bed." He laughed. "What a sprite she was. 'Tis no wonder they all claimed she was a witch. When she went to the window, I would have jumped after her had she tried to escape. Perhaps it would have been my demise, long before it finally came in the storm."

Blair giggled. She had read about the petticoat and the way she had put it on backwards and that was how her father knew she'd been out and about the night she and Black Sam made love. She wondered now if he even knew about it. She reached into the recesses of her mind, trying to recall if Maria and Black Sam had seen one another after that night that changed their lives. Or was that a part of history that he never learned about?

"Did you see her petticoat?" Blair finally asked.

"Her petticoat?" Sam asked. "Of course I saw it—that and a whole lot more."

"What can you tell me about it?" Blair asked.

"The petticoat? Not much to tell, as I recall. I know it had a tie around the waist, and I thought she would never get it undone."

"That's all?"

Black Sam sat, pondering that night. A light twinkled in his eyes as he said, "It had some kind of flowers on it. Pretty, as I recall. Why do you ask?"

Blair grinned. As Black Sam watched her, he once again thought that she looked exactly like Maria, except for the flaxen hair. He waited to hear her bewitching cackle, but there was none. Surely if she was *his* Maria, it would be there.

"'Twas the petticoat that gave her away," Blair said.

Sam waited for her to continue. How could that be? He was sure she had donned it when she fled from the room at the Inn.

"Her father, he saw when she returned home, that the flowers were not visible. He discovered that she was wearing it backwards. There was no explanation for it other than..."

"Her damned petticoat gave her away? From such a simple thing he demised that Maria had been—*taken*?"

"That and the fact that before too long her mother figured out that Maria was pregnant."

"So what did they do with her? I only returned to the Cape once after that, and I heard rumors..."

"They kept her hidden at home," Blair explained. "At least until after the baby was born. And the baby died shortly after his birth. That's when they declared her a witch. They said she'd been 'cavorting with the devil.' That would have been you, I assume."

Blair shook her head. She couldn't believe that she was actually buying the tall tale this stranger was telling her. Could it be possible? Was he truly some sort of modern scientific wonder? Had he somehow or other survived for almost three hundred years?

"But—but I saw him," Sam insisted. "He was almost two years old. He was there, in their home."

"Whose home?" Blair asked, getting more confused by the moment.

"Maria's and that doctor—the one you call Doc Angus. He was there with her. They were married. He stole my Maria. I know I left her, but I promised her I'd return. Why couldn't she wait for me? And where did he come from? And how could the baby have died, like you say, and still be alive?"

Sam grabbed his head and massaged it. "I feel like I'm going to explode!" he yelled. "Oh, why have I come here? And how did I come here? And why did you rescue me? I would have been better off if I had just stayed at the bottom of the ocean for eternity. I can't take any more of this."

He looked up at Blair and asked, "Do you have any rum? I could sure as the devil use a good stiff drink."

Blair went to a cupboard and took out a bottle of wine. "I don't have any rum," she said as she poured a small glass of cooking wine, the only alcohol she kept in the house. "Maybe this will help."

"The barn..." Sam said again.

"You've asked about the barn before. I told you, there is no barn. What is so important about the barn?"

"There used to be a barn," Sam said. "I hid—*things* in there. If only I could find the barn."

Blair got up and went to a desk in the living room. She opened a drawer and pulled out a big thick wad of papers.

"What's that?" Sam asked.

"An abstract," Blair said. "It tells everything that has happened on the property here. If there was a barn, it will tell us exactly where it was and what happened to it."

"I can tell you where it was," Sam said. "It was just behind the house, about 80 paces back. I can show you where it was." He grabbed Blair by the hand and headed out the back door in the direction of where the barn had once stood.

"What did you hide there?" Blair asked.

"The best damn rum anybody's ever tasted," Sam said. "It came straight from Jamaica. I hid it there so I could share it with Maria when I returned for her." Suddenly, the big burly pirate sobbed. "Now she's gone, and so is the rum. I can't live without her. I *won't* live without her. You have to help me."

"Help you what?" Blair asked, suddenly nearly frozen with fear. She had just met this strange man, and he was holding her captive. His stories of his past, his apparent fear of the present, and his lack of comprehension of whatever the future might hold.

"Help me join Maria," he said, his piercing black eyes shooting daggers at her. "Surely by now she is dead. There is no reason for me to live."

Blair reached across the table and tenderly took his hand. "I will not help you die," she said, "but I will try to help you live."

Sam put his head on his arms and shook, crying like a baby. "I can't do it," he said. "I just can't do it."

CHAPTER XIV

Little Jason sat in the hospital waiting room while they examined his mother. He was so scared, but he was determined not to cry. She had to be all right. He had lost his father less than a year earlier, and he knew he couldn't survive without his mother. She was his strength, his rock. Maybe he shouldn't have told her about the strange man who claimed to be Black Sam Bellamy. What was it about him that made her so upset?

"You can go in and see her now if you'd like," the short, round nurse said to him. Her face was kind, and he found comfort in the extended hand she shoved towards him.

"Is—is she going to…" He couldn't bring himself to finish the question.

"She is going to be just fine," the nurse assured him. "Something apparently put her into a bit of shock, but the doctor has her all fixed up now. She will be here for a few hours so we can keep an eye on her. Do you have anybody you could stay with?"

"Not really," he said, a tear breaking through his tough exterior.

"Then you will go home with me," the nurse said. "I am due to get off work in about an hour. You can stay with your mother until then."

Jason tried to smile, and he tilted his head to look up at his new friend.

"But you don't even know me," he said.

"I'm Sally," she said. "And you are Jason, right?"

"How did you know my name?"

"Your mother told me. Just as soon as she was conscious—awake. The first thing she asked about was where you were. I told her you were here and that I would keep an eye on you. Now that we know each other's names, we aren't strangers anymore. Guess that makes it okay for you to go home with me, doesn't it?"

Jason simply nodded his head and smiled again. She did make him feel better.

"Did you know that I rode in the ambulance with my mama?" he asked Sally.

"No, but I'll bet that was exciting, wasn't it?"

Again, Jason nodded. "They had the sirens on and everything. I was so scared. Not from the sirens, but that my mama was going to die." He hesitated, then added softly, "just like my daddy did."

"If you can wait until I'm done with work, I'd like to hear about your daddy," Sally said, patting him on the head. "I'll bet he was a very special man, wasn't he?"

"He was the best!" Jason exclaimed, his face beaming with pride. "Just like Black Sam Bellamy. My daddy said he was a good man too, but people didn't understand him. That's what got him shot."

Sally couldn't explain it, but the hair on the back of her neck bristled at the mere mention of Black Sam Bellamy. How could he have such an effect on people after so many years? Yes, Cape Cod was filled with the legends of Black Sam Bellamy and his young lover, Maria Hallett, but that had all happened over two centuries ago. Still, they seemed to have an eternal hold on the minds of the people on the Cape.

"What did your daddy know about Black Sam?" she asked.

"You told me we could talk after you get off work," Jason said as he peeked inside the door at his mother lying in the bed, looking so fragile. "Mama?" he asked quietly.

"Oh, Jason! Thank God you are here and you are all right. I've been so worried about you. The nurse told me she would take care of you."

"Her?" he asked, pointing to Sally. "She's not a nurse. She's Sally. She's my friend. She's going to take me home with her until you are all better." The worry caused his little brow to wrinkle. "You will get better, won't you, Mama?"

"Yes," she assured him. "I will be better in no time at all. I really don't know what happened to me. Do you remember?"

"You were just fine until I told you that I had seen Blair talking to Black Sam. The *real* Black Sam! He said so himself."

Jason's mother's face went ashen. Sally hurried to calm her down. For some unexplainable reason Sally's hands were shaking like a leaf. Whatever it was about the old lost pirate, it seemed to do the same thing to both of the women. Sally continued talking to her patient until her pulse rate leveled out and she was breathing normally again.

"What made that happen?" Jason's mother asked Sally.

"The old pirate," Sally said, shaking her head in disbelief. "He caused problems when he was alive, and now he seems to have somehow been resurrected. No matter where his name is mentioned, he has this ill effect on everybody. That stupid Smythe woman! She should never have had that stupid celebration to remember the demise of Black Sam Bellamy and his ship, the *Whydah*. It all started with that big bash."

"I think you are right," Jason's mother said. "It doesn't make any sense, but it's almost like he is moving around here on the Cape, casting his evil spell over all of us."

"I'm sure it's just overactive imaginations," Sally said. "It should be behind us in a few days."

"Unless he's really here," Jason whispered. "I have to find out." He was more determined than ever to go back over to Blair's house to see if he could learn any more about the stranger who had washed up from the ocean that fateful day.

❋ ❋ ❋

Blair spread the abstract out in front of her. She studied it carefully, working her way backwards until she came to an entry for 1942.

Barn demolished. Hole filled in. No remains.

"*Voila!*" Blair shouted. "Here it is. It was torn down in 1942."

"Does it say anything about what was left in it?" Sam asked, his eyes squinting as he tried to envision the building.

"It just says that there was nothing remaining," Blair said.

"Do you think we could find exactly where it was?" Sam asked.

"I'm sure we could. The legal description, telling how many feet it was from the house, is right here." She pointed to the figures and Sam stood up, heading for the door.

"Where are you going?"

"I'm going out to find the barn—or where it used to be," Sam replied.

"What is so important about it?" Blair asked. "It says the basement was filled in and nothing remained. What do you think you could find out there?"

"A barrel," Sam said, a gleam in his eye.

"A barrel?" Blair asked. "What is so special about a barrel?"

"It is not just any barrel," Sam said. "It contains the very best rum in the entire world. I brought it from Jamaica on one of my trips."

"But why would it be in Thomas Hallett's barn? I don't understand."

"Most of the Halletts hated me," Sam said, "but not Thomas. He was different. Both John and Jonathan, they would just as soon have killed me as anything, especially after Maria..."

"*After Maria what*?" Blair shouted at him accusingly. "She didn't do anything. It was you who attacked her."

Sam laughed. "Ah, if you could have seen her, running around the bed, jumping onto the bed, causing me to nearly pass out from exhaustion from trying to conquer her..."

"*Conquer her*? You thought she was a mere plaything that you could claim as your own? She was a woman—in her own right."

Blair snickered when she realized that the Maria she was talking about and the era she was retracing was eons before the days of women's liberation. Yes, in those days getting the woman you wanted as your own was truly a conquest. Oh, but she was going to have a field day teaching Black Sam Bellamy a thing or two about how the world had evolved since 1717.

"I can't believe I'm almost believing you," she said suddenly.

"This has to be a trick of some kind. You can't possibly be here from 1717. It is impossible. Now, tell me who you really are."

"I told you, I'm Black Sam Bellamy. And you have to know that this is just as hard for me to understand as it is for you. I have no concept of time. I just know that it seemed like an eternity down there in the bottom of the ocean. I don't know what kind of witchcraft you worked to bring me up, but I am most grateful to you for doing so. I don't know how much longer I could have stayed down there."

"Most likely forever," Blair said, "but you have to know that when I planned that celebration of your demise, the last thing in the world that I expected to see was you."

"Then why..."

"I did it because I have been captivated by Maria and Black Sam's love story. It is more romantic than Romeo and Juliet." She glanced at Sam. "You do know who they are, don't you?"

"Aye, I've read Shakespeare's works."

Blair was surprised by his declaration. She wondered if Johnny Depp, that *other pirate*, had read any of Shakespeare's actual writings.

"So the barn," Sam said, rubbing his beard as he spoke, "was about there?" He pointed to a blank spot in the back yard. "Do ye have a shovel?"

"Of course I have a shovel," she said. She didn't ask the obvious, but waited for his explanation.

"I'm going to go dig up that barrel of rum," he said, heading for the door. "So where's the shovel?"

"In the basement," she said, pointing toward the door that would lead him there. "The light switch is on the left."

She saw the puzzled look on his face. "Just push the doohickus on that little white box down and it will turn on."

Sam did as she said, and he jumped back when the stairwell filled with light. "Never will get used to that," he muttered as he went down the steps. He spotted the shovel over to the right of the steps and turned and headed back upstairs as fast as he could. All these things made him feel stranger than the sense that had overtaken him the night he made love with Maria. He shook his head, sure that Blair was as bewitching as people claimed Maria was.

"What do I tell people if they ask me what you are doing?" Maria asked before he got out the back door.

"Tell them whatever you want to," Sam said. "Whatever it is, they won't believe you anyway." His throaty laugh filled the air as Blair watched him walk back to the spot where he was sure the barn had once stood.

❋ ❋ ❋

When she was sure that she was going to be alone for a while, Blair hurried into her study and took down a thick notebook. She ran her fingers slowly along the edges, wondering if she had courage enough to open it and try to unlock the mysteries that she had read over and over again, countless times.

It was the scrapbook she had compiled over the years of every piece of information she could find about Maria and Black Sam. The tales had sadly brought more questions than answers. Was it possible that she would finally be able to close the book, after getting all the answers from Black Sam Bellamy himself?

She shivered, realizing that she probably knew more about the rest of the story than he did. After all, he had been gone for several years, and during that time Maria had had the baby—Sam's son, had lost the baby, had been cast into prison after being accused of witchcraft, been bailed out by her father, been outcast from the town and lived in a tiny little cottage by the coast. Alone, so alone. Sam had no idea of the lonely life she had lived, nor that she had gone to the water's edge every night to watch for his return. He did not know that a crew had raised the *Whydah*, nor that just a few miles down the coast from them was a museum that housed all of the jewels and treasures he had collected so he could return to claim his ultimate prize—Maria herself.

Blair reached up and took a copy of a *National Geographic* magazine off a shelf. The pages opened immediately to the article about Black Sam Bellamy, Maria Hallett, and the discovery of the *Whydah*. She knew the passage by heart, but she still reread the words carefully, describing Maria, the bewitching young woman, who was purported to "hang a lantern to the tail of a whale off the coast of Cape Cod to alert her beloved Black Sam Bellamy that she was still waiting for him."

She closed the magazine and rested her head on the scrapbook. Soon she dozed off, for how long was anybody's guess. She was awakened by a large rumble out in the back yard.

CHAPTER XV

Blair ran to the window of her study and gazed out into the back yard. There was Sam, tossing one shovel after another of dirt into a big pile. A crowd had gathered to watch him.

I'm sure glad we got him some decent clothes, Blair reflected, *or they would really wonder who he was and what he is up to.*

She giggled like a little school girl. He couldn't have created more interest in what he was doing if he had set up a bullhorn to announce that he was looking for buried treasure—pirate style. She thought about the studies that had been done many times, placing one person out on a sidewalk, gazing up at the sky, and before long a big crowd would assemble, looking up with the person, not having any idea what they were supposed to be seeing.

She went to the back door and joined the group of people.

"What's happening?" she asked an observer.

"I have no idea," the woman replied, "but this man seems to think there is something valuable buried down there."

"What?" Blair asked.

"I don't know," the woman replied, shrugging her shoulders. "I just saw the crowd gathering, so I came to watch too."

Sam had been digging long enough that he was only visible from the shoulders up. Blair wondered how long she had been asleep. The rest of him was in the hole he had dug for himself. Blair chuckled as she wondered if he had any idea that he really was digging himself into a hole. How on earth was he going to explain to these people what he was doing, or what he was looking for?

Suddenly the sound of a deep melodic voice echoed from the depths of his soul. His voice was like that of an opera singer, deep and mellow at the same time. He was singing some tune that, Blair reasoned, must have been something they sang when they were sailing the high seas, declaring his power and might.

Fifteen men on a dead man's chest
Yo ho ho and a bottle of rum
Drink and the devil had done for the rest
Yo ho ho and a bottle of rum.
The mate was fixed by the bosun's pike
The bosun brained with a marlinspike
And cookey's throat was marked belike
It had been gripped by fingers ten;
And there they lay, all good dead men
Like break o'day in a boozing ken
Yo ho ho and a bottle of rum...

Listening to the words as they resonated throughout the entire area, she knew that nobody would dare question anything he said. It could be mighty dangerous, especially for Sam, if they did. Would he be declared an imposter? Of course he would. Nobody would believe the truth. She hoped he had enough sense to make up a really good sounding, yet plausible tale. Ah, yes, she had heard so many times that truth is stranger than fiction. In Black Sam's case that was exceptionally true.

An SUV pulled up in front of the house and parked. Blair immediately recognized the woman who got out. The local TV affiliate logo on the side of the vehicle confirmed her fears. This was certainly fodder for a news story, but she wished it had come before the big celebration. What great publicity it would have been. Several thousand people had gathered for the festivities as it was, but if they had a real live pirate digging for buried treasure, it would have created even more interest in the events.

The woman was followed by a cameraman, and Blair watched

as the news team began to shoot the scene. Blair got a little closer so she could hear what the woman was saying.

"At the recent festivities that were held to commemorate the demise of the *Whydah*, a pirate-like person washed up on shore, as if he had come out of nowhere. As soon as he appeared, he vanished. Now we have received a tip from an anonymous source that informed us that he could be found at the home of Ms. Blair Smythe, the organizer of the festivities. The tipster insisted that he heard the man tell Ms. Smythe that he is Black Sam Bellamy. As impossible as it sounds, since almost three hundred years have passed since anyone saw the infamous pirate, one must pause to wonder if some scientific miracle has occurred and this truly is Black Sam Bellamy. Remember, he was the only member of the crew of the *Whydah* that fateful night in April, 1717 that was never found."

"That's her over there," someone said, pointing to Blair. The camera turned toward Blair and the woman approached her.

"Ms. Smythe, can you tell us, please, who this man is that seems bent on digging a huge hole in your back yard."

Blair felt her hands chill and the hair on the back of her neck rise up like a cat that is ready to attack its prey.

"He is a stranger in town," Blair said, her voice trembling. "I felt sorry for him, so I offered to help him until he decides to move on."

"So he's basically your every-day indigent guy?" the reporter asked.

"Something like that," Blair said.

"And what do you know about him?" the reporter continued. She shifted from one foot to the other, wondering if she even dared to delve into the tip they had received.

"Not much," Blair said. Then, to dispel her mother's fears—and the gossip that was sure to ensue, she added, "He is staying over at Widow Clark's Inn."

"What is he digging for?" the reporter queried.

"I'm not sure," Blair said. "He seems to think there used to be a barn back there. He said something about some old rum."

"Sounds to me like he's nothin' but an old drunk himself," an old man yelled from the crowd.

"'Tis true there was once a barn there," another old-timer hollered back. "My pa, he told me about it many a time. It was said that Black Sam Bellamy himself had buried something there, way back when he was sailin' the seas, before his ship split right in two."

The curator of the local historical society in nearby Yarmouth felt a cold chill blow past her. She knew the tale of Black Sam Bellamy and Maria Hallett forward and backwards. She had read every scrap of paper she could get her hands on over the years. *Is it the ghost of Black Sam?* she wondered. She slapped her cheek, thinking how utterly absurd that sounded. She certainly knew better than to believe in ghosts. It didn't matter; the cold chill hung in the air like a heavy rain-filled cloud just before a strong nor'easter hit, the kind they told about the day Black Sam disappeared.

"Is your stranger really Black Sam himself, come back from the dead?" the reporter asked Blair.

"Don't be ridiculous!" Blair snapped. "He would have to be over three hundred years old. He's not like Methuselah."

"But the tip we got..." the reporter said. "He insisted that he heard the man tell you, in no uncertain terms, that he really is Black Sam Bellamy."

"Then he needs to be locked in an institution someplace," Blair suggested. "He's obviously delusional if he honestly believes that."

They were interrupted by a loud shout from down in the hole. It was hard, Blair thought, to tell if it was a cry of glee, or one of despair. At any rate, it seemed like it rocked the earth beneath her feet. Soon there was a bellowing "Arrrgh!" She knew that whatever Sam was looking for, he hadn't found it.

The reporter dropped her microphone and raced to the open hole, staring down into it to see if the strange man she had come to find out about was hurt.

"You okay down there?" she hollered.

"Yeah, just great," Sam called back. "But somebody stole my damn stash."

The reporter chuckled. "Stash? What stash? Surely you don't expect us to believe there was buried treasure down there."

"Somebody throw me down a rope," Sam yelled. "I want to get out of this hole. No damn sense stayin' here when it's gone. Gone! All gone!"

"What's gone?" the reporter asked. "We all want to know what you expected to find down there. Diamonds? Gold? Silver? Like a pirate's booty?"

The crowd roared at the reporter's taunts directed at the stranger. They had all heard her say that he had claimed to be the real Black Sam Bellamy. It was anybody's guess who the informant had been, but it didn't matter.

Blair cringed as she came running from the house with a long rope she had found in the basement. A man came over and took it from her, securing it around a nearby tree. He threw it down into the hole, and Sam grabbed hold of it and hoisted himself up until he was near the top. The man grabbed his hand and helped him up onto solid ground.

Blair wondered what he would say about what he was after, how he knew something that was there, and—God forbid—who he claimed to be. Would he be stupid enough to actually follow through with this impossible idea that he truly believed that he *was* Black Sam Bellamy?

Blair decided that when she was alone she would call the neighboring mental institutions to see if there were any escapees. At this point, anything was possible. Anything, that is, except his *being* Black Sam Bellamy. She couldn't believe that she had almost fallen for his line. She'd had a lot of guys use pick-up lines on her, but that had to be the most creative one yet.

She watched as the reporter approached Sam and began to question him.

"Someone called and said they heard you tell Ms. Smythe that you are Black Sam Bellamy. Surely you know that he disappeared over 250 years ago."

"So I've been told," Sam said, scratching his head like he was as puzzled over that fact as the reporter was.

"If you want us to believe you, where were you all that time?"

"Lost on the bottom of the ocean," he said.

Port Call to the Future

Blair felt faint as she listened. Was it possible that he was going to play this game of charades with the whole world? Why didn't he just tell them the story he'd told her at first? It was much easier to believe that he had been shipwrecked for a few years on some deserted island than to try to swallow the idea of him whirling around in an eddy for more than two centuries.

Blair grinned broadly. Whether it was true or not, the mere fact that this stranger in town who had blown up out of the ocean on the day they were celebrating Black Sam's demise claimed to be the missing pirate—up close and personal. *What a movie this would make,* she mused. Names of directors who would bite on this danced through her head like the leaves blowing on a tree in a stiff autumn wind. One thing she was certain of: Jenny would insist on playing Maria. Oh, what a field day she would have with that role. For some unexplained reason, an image of a field of poverty grass popped into her mind. She shook her head, trying to erase the image. It was disturbing.

Blair laughed. She had many more things to disrupt her thoughts than a stupid field of grass. It held no meaning for her, or at least it should not have.

She listened as Sam droned on about a fantasy that would have made Isaac Asimov proud. *Science fiction at its finest,* she thought.

"I have no explanation," he continued, "for how I survived so long. Nor why." He threw his head back and laughed. His laugh was almost infectious, and others joined in, without knowing why. Perhaps because it was so preposterous?

"Can anyone tell me what became of my crew? Did they survive as well? Were they doomed to an eternity in the sea, as was I?"

The curator of the Yarmouth Historical Society stepped forward. "They all perished," she said. "'Tis an important part of our history. There were only a couple of them that lived to tell about it." She chuckled. "Not that it did them any good. The townsmen made sure that they met their own ends. Hanging, it seems to me. At any rate, the only one that apparently survived was Black Sam himself. Nobody ever saw or heard anything from him again."

Sam continued to laugh. "You mean they were lookin' fer me...er, him?"

"For decades people were hunting him down. Him and his treasure. There were people that wanted his loot more than they wanted him."

"Did they ever find any of it?" Sam asked.

"A few gold coins here and there along the coast when they would wash up," the curator said. "Governor Samuel Shute hired a salvor by the name of Cyprien Southeck to try to find more of it, but he failed."

Sam sighed deeply. At least the treasures he had pilfered were still there for the taking. All he had to do was figure out exactly where he was when the ship broke asunder. And then there was always the part of his findings that he had hidden right where they were standing. He roared again, realizing that the people who were talking to him, so rapt in his tale, were standing almost on top of that. Forget the rum. He had more important things to deal with. *At night,* he thought, *lest they try to rob them from me. They are mine! Rightfully mine!* The fact that he came by all of them illegally, no matter how long ago it was, certainly didn't bother him. They were his.

CHAPTER XVI

Pandemonium set in as the word spread throughout all Hyannis that Black Sam Bellamy had somehow been resurrected. For some odd reason, Sam recalled another story from his childhood. First he felt like Jonah, who had been spit up from the belly of the whale onto the beach. Now, he thought, he knew how Jesus must have felt when He walked along the road to Emmaus and His own friends and closest confidantes didn't even recognize Him.

Odd to think of these things now. He hadn't given a thought to the training his Mother Wesley had given him all those years ago, after his mother died. How many years? Ah, yes, according to the figures Blair had given him, almost three hundred years had lapsed.

Suddenly, he realized how absurd it must have sounded to that reporter, as well as the rest of the people who had gathered to watch him try to unearth the barrel of rum, for him to tell the truth. It made no sense to him whatsoever, but he didn't think he could lie about his past, even if he tried. What had happened to him? He was like a stranger to himself.

His mind went back to the first tale he had spun to Blair. How much simpler it would have been to have followed through with that story. So much more believable than the truth. In all of his life as a pirate, telling the truth was not his normal practice. He could spin the best yarns of anyone who sailed the seas. He had entertained his men many a night while they moved over the waters.

The truth! Whatever had possessed him to get a... His mind struggled for the word to describe what had forced his hand in what he related to the reporter.

Conscience! The word appeared like it was written on a ledger. He jumped at the mere idea of it. He knew what it was, but he knew full well that he'd never had one before. Was it some inherent part of the eddy he'd been in? He felt like he had acquired it by sheer osmosis. Like he breathed in one day, and *voila*! It was a part of his being. It was an idea as foreign as the distant lands he had visited when he was the commander of the *Whydah*. It was like trying to understand French, or Spanish, or Portuguese when all he knew was English, and he usually butchered that. Granted, he was from England, and this was America, but they claimed what they spoke was English too. Still, it had a strange lilt to it that was so different he had to strain his ears to understand what they were saying. And the words! They spoke of things he had never heard of. Things he could not have imagined in a million years. Big machines that flew like birds, carrying hundreds of people inside them. Little boxes with tiny people moving around inside of them, yelling at you. Strange little things in your hands that would let you talk to people miles away. Switches that lit up the whole room... Why, they even talked about men on the moon.

Sam breathed a deep sigh of relief as he watched the woman who had been questioning him get into that contraption they called a "van" and disappear down the road. He'd had enough of people trying to pry into his background for the rest of his life. He knew, though, that this wouldn't be the end of it. Everybody seemed to be fascinated with him. All he wanted was to be left alone for long enough that he could get back down into the root cellar and find his stash of loot, then take it and head for...where?

❈ ❈ ❈

He looked around, hoping to spot Blair. The crowd broke up and headed for parts unknown. She was nowhere to be found. He looked toward the house and saw her standing in front of the kitchen window. When she spotted him looking at her, she waved and grinned, motioning for him to come inside.

He sat down on the back steps and pulled his shoes off. They slid off much easier than his pirate boots, and he was thankful that Blair had gotten some soft shoes for him. His foot was still a bit swollen from his fall down into the root cellar. He banged one against the other to try to loosen the dirt from the hole where he'd been looking for the barrel of rum.

He'd found the spot in the side where it must have been, and he wondered if whoever had found it had enjoyed it as much as he would have. The mere thought of it made his mouth water and he licked his lips in anticipation of what might have been, but now would never be.

"You look like the cat that swallowed the canary," Blair said as he came into the kitchen and sat down.

"Why?" he asked, trying to appear innocent.

"Whatever it is you are thinking about, you had better stop it before you get yourself into trouble."

"I don't know what you're talking about," he said, the grin on his face broadening even more.

"What did you find down under where the barn was?" Blair asked.

"Dirt," Sam replied. "Just damn pure dirt."

"And you expected to find—your rum? And you thought it would still be fit to drink?"

"Hey, like a good woman, booze gets better with age."

"Sorry to disappoint you," Blair said, a gleam in her eye.

"Huh?" Sam asked. "How did you disappoint me?"

"I'm pretty young stuff, all things considered," she said. "I mean, considering your age."

"I like them young and sassy," Sam snapped back, "just like Maria was."

Blair winced at the impossible thought that she almost believed he was who he said he was. *Boy, would my Psych 101 prof have a picnic with this one,* she mused. *This could be the best test of any textbook that's ever been printed.*

Suddenly, Blair turned on her heel and headed out of the kitchen.

"What are you doing?" Sam asked.

"Just be patient. I'll be right back."

Sam waited, thumping his fingers nervously on the table and tapping his foot on the hardwood floor. Finally, he heard Blair coming back towards him. He gasped when he saw her.

Blair had studied every inch of the tale of what happened that fateful night in the past when Black Sam Bellamy and Maria Hallett made love. She knew exactly what she had worn. She had related the story of Maria's embroidered petticoat to Sam, and now, here she was, looking for all the world like Maria had looked when Sam chased her around the bed.

"What the..."

"Do you like it?" Blair asked, winking playfully at him. "Does it make you think of anything else? Or *anybody* else?"

"My God, woman! You *are* her! You are Maria!"

Blair watched as the big hunk of a pirate collapsed and fell to the floor. She should have known better than to tempt him with such tomfoolery. She hadn't thought rationally about the effect such a trick might have on him. She wasn't sure what she had expected, or what she wanted, but it wasn't this.

Blair rushed to the sink and filled a glass with cold water. She knelt beside Sam, then dipped her fingers in the water and sprinkled it on his face. In just a few moments he began to come to, much to her relief. She couldn't kill him. Not after he'd waited this long to put an end to—whatever it was he hoped to gain by resurfacing after all this time.

"What happened?" Sam asked as he slowly opened his eyes. He closed them quickly, shaking his head to rid him of the image of Maria that was crouched over him.

"I don't know," Blair said. "You just passed out. I have no idea why."

The thoughts and images whirled around in his head like the waters in the eddy he had gotten to know so well during all the years he was lost at sea. Now, they almost made him feel comfortable. They had become like the water in a mother's womb to an unborn baby. They were peace. They were solace. They were all he knew. The water—and his thoughts.

"Who—who are you?" he finally managed to ask.

"You know who I am. I'm Blair Smythe. I've been taking care of you since you…" She hesitated, not knowing quite what to call his "surfacing" the day of the gala affair to recall his demise.

"But…" Sam opened his eyes again, slowly, staring at her. "Your clothes. They are *her* clothes."

"You mean I really did a good job of duplicating them?" Blair asked, smiling at the success of her research into Maria.

"Good job?" Sam said, rubbing his head. "You—you look exactly like her. All except the hair, that is."

"What was her hair like?"

"It was like the black shiny feathers of a raven," Sam said. "If you had her hair, you would not be able to tell one of you from the other." He paused again, then asked, "Are—are you a witch too?"

Blair laughed. Now it was that same cackle he had heard Maria do so many times in the few days they had spent together.

"Do you think I am a witch? More importantly, do you think Maria really was a witch?"

"I don't know," Sam admitted. "It's possible, I guess." He smiled and said, "She sure got me under her spell."

"You couldn't resist her?" Blair asked.

"Oh, from all I heard tell, thar wasn't nobody who could resist the charms of Maria Hallett. I don't know why I was the lucky one, but I was, and I've spent all those years not knowing whether to thank God above that He blessed me with her love in return, or whether to curse Him for what she did to me."

"What she did to you?" Blair shouted. "You're the one that got her pregnant! What did she do to you?"

"She sent me to the depths of the ocean for, well, for what was almost an eternity. I never thought I would see the light of day again. I knew I wasn't in hell, because hell is supposed to be hot, and it was cold down there. So cold. I knew if I was in hell, even the water would not have been able to survive. It's a wonder I didn't freeze to death."

"What do you know about hell?" Blair asked, intrigued by his reference to spiritual matters. She never imagined that a pirate the likes of Black Sam Bellamy would give such things a moment's notice. Still, she supposed that spending all that time in limbo would certainly give a man time to think. Time to contemplate all the ills they had cast on the world.

"I don't rightly know," Sam replied. "I do remember me aunty draggin' me to the church when I was but a wee lad. I didn't think any of it stuck in me head, but it must have. And then there was that other woman, Mother Wesley, who took me in." He threw his head back and laughed until Blair felt like the whole house would shake. "Guess I didn't rightly have much else to put me mind to while I was whirlin' around down below. Such tales as I'd heard spun and taught they were the truth, that and thinkin' about Maria and wonderin' what she was doin' and if she ever knew I tried to get back to her. And about the baby—me wee bairn—that was supposed to have died, yet I saw him…"

"Your head must have been one royal mess," Blair teased.

"Tain't never been no royal blood coursin' through a Bellamy's veins," Sam said, wondering why she would think such a thing might be possible. Surely she knew better than that. After all, she did seem to know a lot about the whole Hallett clan, as well as Black Sam Bellamy. He never imagined that he would end up as a part of history.

Suddenly, Blair shifted the direction of the conversation, once again causing Sam to turn wan and nearly faint away anew.

"I forgot to tell you, but there were a bunch of men up in Provincetown that found the remains of the *Whydah*."

"You forgot to tell me?" Sam bellowed. "How can it be? Where? When? How? What was in it?"

Blair grinned. "Well, they were hoping to find your remains, since nobody ever found them after the shipwreck. For that matter, they looked for you for years after the accident, but nobody ever even claimed to have seen any signs of you."

"'Tis no wonder," Sam said, rubbing his hand over his beard like he did when he was either nervous or puzzled about something. "They were obviously looking in the wrong place."

"It is the biggest pirate treasure they've ever found," Blair explained. "The group of men that had been looking for it for years, they brought it up a bit at a time."

"I told her I'd come back for her when I had something to offer her," Sam said, standing and stomping his foot, causing him to wince from the pain in his ankle. "She should have listened to me. She should have believed me."

"Maria?" Blair asked, and Sam merely nodded his head.

"Oh, but she did believe you," Blair said, reaching over to try to calm him down as he sat back down in the chair and rested his head in his hands at the table. "I told you, they said she went down to the water every day to watch for you."

Blair chuckled. "It was rumored that she hung lanterns on the tails of the whales to let you know that she was there, awaiting your return."

"That's impossible," Sam said. "How could she have... Where did you hear such a tale?"

Blair got up and headed to a bookcase in the living room. She carefully pulled a copy of a *National Geographic* magazine and turned to a page that opened automatically, since she had read it so many times. She set it in front of Sam and waited, watching him carefully, as he read the story.

CHAPTER XVII

Sam read the entire article with great interest. Not only did it tell about the discovery of the *Whydah* off the coast of Cape Cod, right near Provincetown, but it related the whole sordid tale of the short romance of Maria and Black Sam Bellamy. He was amazed at how accurate the account was—until he got to the part about Maria indeed hanging the lanterns on the tails of the whales.

"Don't they know that is impossible?" he bellowed. "Even Maria could not accomplish such a thing."

Blair laughed, then asked him, "But if the rest of the things they say are true, how do you know she couldn't do that? After all, they said she was a witch, and witches can do many strange things."

Sam studied Blair carefully. *Was she a witch too? Was it something that passed down from one generation to another? Could he resist her wiles better than he had done with Maria? Was he being drawn in, enticed, by another witch from the Halletts?*

Sam quickly changed the subject, hoping to erase such thoughts of flirtation from his mind.

"You said they found the ship? *My* ship? The *Whydah*? How did they know it was the *Whydah*? What did they do with the booty they found?"

"Slow down," Blair said. "There were a lot of skeptics who said it could have been any ship. The men who found it set up a museum in Provincetown. All of the treasures are there. There was a ton of information flying around about the ship. Like this..." Blair pointed to the magazine that was still lying open on the table in front of Sam. "Then they found something that removed any doubt about what ship it was."

"What did they find?" Sam asked, trying his best to comprehend all of the information Blair was firing at him.

"They found the bell," Blair said. "It had the name of the Whydah engraved on it. There was no longer any question. Everybody had to admit that it was indeed the Whydah."

"So the bell is at this museum?"

"The bell, and a whole lot more."

Sam rubbed his beard, waiting for Blair to continue. When she didn't, he cleared his throat and asked, "What else?"

"There was a lot of gold and silver, silverware like knives and spoons and forks, some tin dishes, cannons, cannonballs, and your gun."

"My gun?" Sam asked. "How did they know it was mine? All of the men had a gun of their own."

"I don't remember, but I think it was attached to the cannon that had your name on it. I can call them and find out for sure."

"No!" Sam shouted. "They can't know I'm here."

Blair laughed. "Can you imagine what the men from the Expedition Whydah would say if they knew you were within shouting distance from them?"

Again, Sam insisted, even more vehemently than before, "They can't know I'm here."

Blair grinned as she watched him squirm. Oh, what a field day she could have if she played her cards right. This would be better publicity than any history buff could ever hope for. Of course there was always the possibility that people might consider her crazy and lock her up, or at least run her out of town like they did Maria.

Once Sam calmed down a bit he asked her, "So what else is at this museum?"

"I have been there several times," Blair said. "There are cannonballs, cannons—oh, and some pearls."

"Pearls?"

"Yes, pearls." She hesitated a few moments, then added,

"There has been a lot of talk about some emeralds that were supposed to be on the ship. Black Sam, er, you were supposed to have gotten a lot of emeralds from Colombia. I have looked every time I have been there, but I've never seen them. I even asked Ken Kinkor—he's one of the men who was in on the recovery of the *Whydah*—about them. He said it's purely a rumor. They found pretty much everything that was on the ship, and there was no sign of any emeralds."

Black Sam threw his head back and howled with laughter.

"What's so funny?" Blair asked.

"Of course there weren't any emeralds on the ship. I had gotten rid of them a long time before the ship sank."

"So there were emeralds?" Blair asked. "What did you do with them?"

"I buried them," Sam said. He rubbed his beard and chuckled. "But I'm not going to tell you where."

"So you expect me to believe that someplace there is an honest-to-goodness pirate's treasure that you buried," Blair said, a puzzled look on her face. "You aren't going to tell me where it is?" She smiled. "Or do you need a pirate's map to remember where you put them?"

"Oh, I remember quite well where they are. But no, I won't tell you. Why, God knows what you would do with them if you found them. I might only be worth something to you as long as I know where they are—and you don't."

"You don't trust me at all, do you?" Blair asked, looking disappointed.

"About as much as you trust me," Sam replied.

"What would I have to do for you to get you to tell me where the emeralds are hidden?"

"I suppose we could play your game of 20-Questions again," Sam suggested. "You get one question a day. If you guess where they are... Well, we can cross that bridge when—or if—we get to it." He winked at her, and Blair laughed as she tried to picture him with a patch over one eye.

"Wrong eye," she said, causing him to shake his head, not understanding what she was talking about.

"What?" Sam asked.

"You winked with the wrong eye," Blair said, still not making any sense to him about what she meant.

"You are crazy," Sam said.

Blair looked at him, her eyes traveling up and down his body. "You blow into port like a ghost from the past, try to convince me that you have been whirling away at the bottom of the ocean for nearly three hundred years, and I am the one who's crazy? Tell that to your local shrink."

"Shrink?" Sam asked.

"Psychiatrist," Blair tried to explain. *Nope, try again,* she thought. That concept is as foreign to Sam as he was to the rest of the modern world.

"Head doctor," she said, trying again. 1

"My head is just fine," Sam said.

"If you say so. A psychiatrist is a doctor who studies a person's brain to determine if they are sane or not." She tried to think of what vernacular from the past he might understand. "As in gone mad," she said.

A light registered in Sam's eyes, indicating that he did understand that.

"You think I'm mad?" he asked.

"No. Yes. I don't know."

With no warning at all, Sam stood up and walked over beside Blair. He leaned forward and kissed her, madly, passionately. To his delight, she did not try to fight him off, but returned the kiss with the same feelings he had put into it. Finally, he pulled back and walked back to his chair and sat down, as if nothing had happened.

"What was that all about?" Blair asked.

"I—I'm not completely sure," Sam said. "It is just, for a minute, every once in a while, I think you are Maria. Perhaps you are, and you have come back to haunt me instead of my haunting you."

"You believe in reincarnation?" Blair asked.

"What is that?" Sam asked.

"It is when a person dies, then they come back at a later time as a different person."

"That's just insane," Sam said. "I don't know if I died or not. Sometimes I felt like I was dead. Then I would feel something, or think something, and I would realize that I wasn't. Sometimes I wished I was! Oh, God, how I prayed to be delivered from that terrible swirling water!"

"And finally you were," Blair stated, matter-of-factly, like it was the most natural thing on the face of the earth for someone to disappear for an eternity, or what must have seemed like an eternity, and then suddenly surface in a completely different world. *At least,* she reasoned, *if a person were reincarnated they would start out at the base of the chain in which they resurfaced. That would no doubt be easier to accept than what Sam had been through.*

"But if you were Maria in another life," Sam said, "why would you come back now as Maria?"

Blair laughed. "You think I am Maria?"

"You look just like her," Sam said. "When I first saw you, I thought it was Maria, only your hair... Your hair is a different color. If your hair was darker, I would swear you are Maria."

Blair skipped across the kitchen and went to a cabinet in the living room where she kept her family photo albums. She took it back out to the kitchen and set it down in front of Sam. She began turning the pages until she came to her high school graduation picture. There she was, in all her glory—and her dark brown hair.

"What the..." Sam paled as he stared at—*Maria*? "How did you get this—this image of Maria?"

"It's called a photograph, or a picture," Blair explained. "And it is not Maria. It is me."

"But your hair..." Sam managed to choke out.

"Thanks to L'Oreal," Blair said. She got up again and this time she went into the bathroom and got a bottle of her latest hair dye.

"What is this?"

"It is hair dye. It will change the color of your hair."

"But why would you want to do that?" Sam asked. It was beyond his comprehension.

"Because I've heard that blondes have more fun," Blair answered. "I was tired of always being *the good girl*. I was a good student in school. I never caused my parents any trouble. When they said to be home at 11 o'clock, I would come at 10. I always obeyed what they told me. I was tired of it. Sick and tired of it. I wanted some fun out of life. I thought if I could change my hair color, it would change my personality too."

"And did it?" Sam asked, cocking a quizzical eye at her.

"No. The only difference was that I was a boring—and bored—blonde instead of a boring and bored brunette." She looked at him as she spoke. "But then you came along. Suddenly I am the center of everybody's attention. Of course it is not because of me, but because of you. Everybody wants to know about you. Some people actually believe that you are Black Sam Bellamy, and others think you are an imposter that has a hidden agenda."

"Hidden agenda?" Sam asked. "I have hidden treasures that they have not yet unearthed, but I have nothing else hidden."

Suddenly, in a manner most unlike her, she began to kiss Sam, and then she was teasing him. She could sense his passion rising, and she knew that if she would just allow herself to let go, she could be taken in by Black Sam's—or Sam Black's—love, just as Maria had been. *Would that be so bad?* she wondered. She could just imagine what his body would feel like, pressed against hers.

❊ ❊ ❊

Blair's parents came into the kitchen. They didn't knock. They never knocked. It was their daughter's home. You don't have to announce yourself to your own child. It was a law—unwritten, surely, but a law nevertheless.

"What the hell?" Martin shouted. "What are you doing to my daughter? You might not be Black Sam Bellamy personified, but you sure as the devil act just like him. Get out of this house. *Now!*"

CHAPTER XVIII

Blair jumped, surprised by the sudden intrusion of her parents. Sam slumped in his chair, looking for all the world like he wished the ocean would swallow him up again. He had bested more than his share of seamen, but he was not prepared to take on the parents of a forward, brazen hussy. Not since he had been threatened by Maria's father had he felt so helpless.

"He did nothing wrong," Blair said softly in Sam's defense.

"I saw what I saw," Martin insisted.

"What you saw was *me* kissing *him*, not the other way around. I am a grown woman, and if I choose to kiss a man, it's *my* business, not yours."

"You are still my daughter," Martin said, banging his fist on the table, "and you will conduct yourself with decency."

"We were not doing anything indecent, Dad," Blair said, running her hand across Sam's back, almost like you would do to a youngster who was in trouble, not some big strong pirate.

"That's not the way it looked to me," her father said.

Maria turned to her mother and asked, "Mom, did you and Dad kiss before you were married?"

Her mother fidgeted nervously. Oh yes, they had kissed—and a whole lot more. She tried to imagine her own father if he had caught them in the back seat of the car, or under that apple tree in the dark of the night...

"That's not the point!" Martin shouted. "What were your intentions towards my daughter?" His eyes looked like they could bore holes right through Sam.

"Beggin' yer pardon, sir," Sam said, his voice deep, yet soft. "I did nothin' to yer daughter." He paused, looking at Blair helplessly. "She—she came after me, sir. I was just sittin' here, mindin' me own business, listening to her tell me about the museum, when she..."

"She *what*?" Martin bellowed.

"She kissed me, sir," Sam said, lowering his eyes toward the floor, looking like a whipped puppy dog that had been caught chewing his master's best slippers.

"And then..." Martin asked.

"And then you came in, sir." Sam grinned, baring his gold tooth so it sparkled in the sunlight that shone in through the kitchen window. "And that was the end of that."

"Well, it's a damn good thing we came in when we did then," Martin said. "See that it doesn't happen again." His command was directed at Sam, not at Blair.

"I can't guarantee that, sir," Sam said. "You probably know that your daughter does what she pleases."

"And it pleased you just a bit too much," Martin said. He turned to Blair now as he admonished her. "You make sure that you don't ever do that again, or I'll..."

"You'll what, Dad? Spank me like you did when I was a little girl?" Blair giggled as she tried to picture her dad spanking her, now that she was all grown up.

"I swear, if I didn't know better I'd think that he brought Maria's spirit with him when he came back out of the ocean." He shook his head, not believing that he was admitting—almost—that Sam Black was who he said he was. It was such a farfetched tale that he'd be as crazy as the rest of the populace that seemed to be buying into his fantasy of trying to re-create the ghost of Black Sam Bellamy actually coming back to life.

❈ ❈ ❈

Maggie motioned with her finger for Martin to follow her. "I want to speak to you outside," she told him.

Like a marionette whose strings were being pulled, Martin obediently went outside with his wife.

"You are acting like a..."

"Like a what?" Martin boomed.

"Like a jealous lover," Maggie said. "She is right, Martin. Blair is a grown woman, and we can't dictate what she does."

"But she would choose to be with the likes of that—that *shyster*!"

"Maybe he isn't so bad, if we would just give him half a chance." She paused. "Granted, he is a bit strange, and it does take a lot to swallow his tale of how he got here. Why, it's all over the news, not just here in Hyannis, but all over the country, that the ghost of Black Sam Bellamy has somehow resurfaced."

"He's not to be trusted," Martin insisted. "Even without his wild tale of who he is, he's not to be trusted."

"And just why not?" Maggie asked.

"Because he's—he's a *man*!"

Maggie laughed. They were both oblivious to the fact that Blair and Sam were watching them through the kitchen window. They strained to hear what they were saying, but they could only catch a couple of words here and there. There was no mistaking Maggie's laugh though.

"What's so blasted funny?" Martin asked.

"Are you forgetting that you are also a man?"

"Of course I haven't forgotten! That's why it worries me so much. I know what a man is capable of."

"Ah, yes," Maggie said, smiling impishly. "I remember it too, my dear. If my father had known..."

"Thank the good Lord above he died not knowing."

"And you want to deprive Blair and Sam of such wonderful memories? Remember the old apple tree..."

"Enough!" he said. "I know. I stole your virginity that night. I know it was wrong, but I couldn't help myself."

"You stole more than that that night," Maggie said, running her hands over the shape of his lips.

"What?" Martin asked innocently.

"You stole my heart. I knew from that moment on that I belonged to you. And I suspect that Blair feels that she belongs to Sam."

"You think they have..." Martin asked, his face red with rage.

"I don't think so," Maggie said, "but back in our day, it was almost criminal to do what we did that night. Ah, but it was the most wonderful night of my life. Today, it is almost a requirement for a couple to live together before they get married."

"I'll not have it," Martin said, shaking his finger in the air. "She will never..."

"Never say never," Maggie warned. "It will come back to bite you in the butt." She stood on her tiptoes and kissed her husband. Despite their years together, she still knew exactly how to get to him. He melted under her spell. At moments like this she could have asked him for anything and he would have gladly obliged.

Held in the passionate kiss, they did not see Blair come out and stand, silently, nearby. When they broke from each other, Martin cringed when he espied her.

"What are you doing out here?"

"Taking lessons," Blair said, a twinkle dancing teasingly in her eye. "It seems to me that the two of you are a perfect example of how to do it right."

"Enough!" Martin said. "You were not supposed to see us..."

"Oh, it was precious, Dad," Blair said. She turned towards the window and gave Sam a two-thumbs-up signal, which caused him to shake his head in bewilderment. He wondered if he would ever learn to adjust to this world.

Maggie pulled on Martin's hand. "I think maybe we should go home and leave the two of them alone."

"No, we have some unfinished business to take care of here first."

Blair grinned. The air was almost ablaze with the passion she had just witnessed between her parents. They had never been particularly secret about their love for each other, but somehow today it took on a whole new meaning. Perhaps, Blair mused, it was because she felt some of that love herself, for the first time in her life.

"I think you have a lot of unfinished business," Blair teased, "but I don't think this is the proper place for you to tend to it."

Martin started to protest, but Maggie continued to tug on his hand, and soon they were at the car. Maggie waved to Blair as they pulled out of the driveway. It was more of an "I'll deal with your father" than it was a parting gesture.

❃ ❃ ❃

"What was that all about?" Sam asked when Blair got back inside.

"Marital mishmash," Blair said, grinning broadly.

"What?" Sam said, shaking his head in confusion.

"Never mind. Someday maybe you'll understand." She watched him as he tried to make sense out of what she was saying. "I think Mom is about to give Dad a lesson in—sex."

Blair realized that even if Sam was a "man of the world," talking about such matters was not an easy thing for him to face.

"Show, don't tell," Blair quipped, quoting her favorite old English teacher.

"You aren't making any sense at all," Sam said.

"Well, I'll be," Blair said. "Seems to me when it came to Maria, you understood that saying all too well."

"What exactly do you know—or think you know—about Maria and me?"

"Oh, I know the whole story," Blair said, loving the way he was squirming when he was under the microscope. "From the night you met her at Crosby's Tavern to the day you left port, hoping to find enough treasure to take care of her when you came back to claim her, and everything in between."

"Methinks it's all been greatly exaggerated," Sam protested. "It was a very simple matter. I found her irresistible, and she found me..."

Blair snickered. "She found you what?"

Sam's throaty roar escaped like air from a punctured balloon. "Oh, I found—I found her *everything*. I guess that's how she ended up having my son."

Blair studied him before she asked, "How did you find out about her baby?"

"I came back a couple of times before the shipwreck. I didn't actually see her... Well, I did see her, but I made sure she didn't see me."

"Why?"

"I didn't go back to Crosby's Tavern meself the first time I went back. I sent one of my crew there to see what they could find out instead."

"Why didn't you go yourself?"

"I was afraid the whole Hallett crew would come lookin' fer me head," Sam said, shivering at the mere thought of what they might have done to him.

"But you said you saw the baby once?" Blair asked, getting more confused by the moment. How could it have been, if the baby died soon after his birth? None of this made any sense. None whatsoever.

"I know. It is all very confusing. It is to me too. It is like I lived two different lives there. Or maybe it was Maria who had a double life. In one life she was an outcast, living outside the villages, forbidden to enter the towns. In the other life—the one I saw the last time I was there—she was married and her son—*our* son—was there, living in a house of their own right in Yarmouth." He shook his head, trying to free it of the confusion he felt.

"But if she was married... Who was her husband?"

"They said he was a doctor. They said his name was Angus McPherson, just like your doctor friend." Sam rubbed his beard and squinted. "He did say he had an ancestor who was a doctor in Yarmouth, didn't he? I suppose it must have been him."

"It's funny," Blair said. "He never mentioned that to me until the day he met you."

"How well do you know your Dr. McPherson?" Sam asked.

"I never met him until the day you surfaced." Blair laughed. "I guess that's about the most appropriate word for what happened to you that day, isn't it? You surfaced, quite literally, after spending eons on the ocean floor."

Sam grimaced. "You don't have to remind me. The memory is quite enough to haunt me for the rest of my life."

❊ ❊ ❊

Sam abruptly changed the subject back to the museum Blair had started to tell him about.

"About the museum..."

"What about it?" Blair asked. "You said you didn't want to go there."

"That's not what I said!" Sam bellowed, banging his fist on the table. "I said I don't want them to know I'm here. I want to go see it, but I want to do it—secretly."

"How do you intend to do that?" Blair asked.

"Simple. I'll just go at night. I assume there are windows so I can see what's in there."

"There are a lot of windows. How do you plan to get there?"

"I'll walk," Sam replied matter-of-factly.

"It's a long hike," Blair said. "About thirty miles."

"So?"

"So I will take you. I'll be your 'get-away driver.' It will be just like in the movies." Blair's pulse quickened at the thought of being involved in something so sinister. It was unlike her usual behavior. She giggled as she thought, *I'll bet anything Maria would do that if she was here.* She looked at Sam as she rehashed his accusations that he believed she might well be Maria reincarnated. "What do you hope to find there?"

"How can you ask me that? I expect to find *my* booty! They have no right to it. It's *mine*."

"It might have been yours at one time," Blair argued, "but it belongs to them now. They found it. You—you sort of deserted it. Gave up your rights to any of it."

"Certainly not by choice," Sam insisted. "I didn't choose to spend a lifetime—or as many lifetimes as it was—down at the bottom of the ocean. I would have chosen almost any other life if anybody had bothered to ask me."

"If you had survived," Blair said, "surely you realize that they would have put you to death if they had found you."

"It might have been more pleasant than what I endured."

He hesitated a few moments. "I don't want to get you in trouble. It might be better if I go alone."

There it was again. That damned conscience! Why wouldn't it leave him alone? It made him so uncomfortable. He squirmed in the chair, rubbing his beard.

"Problem?" Blair asked, noticing his uneasiness again. *It's so cute,* she thought, which made her laugh. *Imagine thinking a 300-year-old pirate is cute.*

"No," Sam answered. "I just don't know why I seem to be so nice. It's just not like me."

"Maybe it was all those years you had down under to reflect on your past sins," she suggested. "I suppose it could do strange things to anybody."

"Must be," Sam agreed. "I'll have to see if I can get over it." Under his breath he muttered, "Sin? I'd hardly recognize it if it slapped me in the face."

Blair tried to hear what he said, but it escaped her. *Probably just as well,* she thought.

"I do want to take you there," she said. The tone in her voice didn't allow for any arguments. It was obvious that to her it was a done deal. She had committed herself to do what she could to help the strange man, no matter what the cost to her. Of course she knew better than to tell her parents what they were planning.

❉ ❉ ❉

"I should probably be getting home," Sam said. "I've done enough damage here for one day."

"Probably enough for a year," Blair teased him. "Do you want something to eat first?"

"No. The Widow Clark includes meals in my room and board, and since your father already paid for it, it would be a shame to waste it."

He got up and walked to the door, waving at her and giving her a wink as he left.

Blair stood at the window and watched him as he walked away. His ankle had healed well. There was hardly any trace of his limp.

What have you gotten yourself into? she thought as he disappeared from her sight. *Is it possible he really is Black Sam Bellamy? Or is this the biggest scam job anybody's come up with in almost forever?*

She jumped when she saw a black cat go howling across the yard from a clump of bushes. Something scared it, but what? She wasn't usually so jumpy, but it made her uneasy. No way was she going to go out to investigate. She went into the living room and turned the TV on, missing Jason completely as he crept away from the house, intent on following Sam Black, or Black Sam, or whoever he was. He felt like a spy, but he was determined to figure out what was really going on with the stranger in town.

CHAPTER XIX

"What do you know about some museum over in Provincetown?" Sam asked Mrs. Clark as they sat at the table, eating their evening meal.

"The Whydah one?"

"Of course. How many museums are there in Provincetown?" Sam countered.

"That's the only one people talk about anyway," Mrs. Clark said, studying this strange man she was getting to know, and she realized that she liked him, and she didn't like the fact that she liked him. The admission made her nervous. For starters, he was—she studied him carefully—somewhere in his early thirties, she'd guess, and she was—way older than that. She wondered what he would look like if he shaved off his beard and got a decent haircut. *He might clean up pretty good,* she reflected.

"I'd like to go see what they have there," Sam said.

"You want me to drive you over there?"

"No. I'd rather go when they aren't open."

Mrs. Clark rubbed her forehead, like she was developing another one of her migraines. "Pressure," the doctor told her. "Most migraines are caused by nervous tension. You should try to avoid it as much as possible."

How could she avoid tension when this man was bound to drive her up the wall? She was trying to figure him out. Oh, sure, she'd heard all the rumors and seen the reports on TV that he was supposed to be Black Sam Bellamy somehow brought back to life. That was absurd! It was impossible!

"Mission Impossible," she muttered, not even aware that she had spoken the words aloud.

"What'd you say?" Sam asked her.

"Nothing," she said, putting her hand over her mouth. Whatever she was thinking, she needed to keep it to herself. *Who knows what this lunatic might be capable of, especially if he really is Black Sam?* No, that was crazy. It was something out of a science fiction book. Time travel was a thing of fiction books. Novels.

A novel idea, she mused. She had never thought about writing a book before, but if she could get enough convoluted information out of this nut case, it could make a best-seller. *Maybe even a movie,* she thought, the wheels turning at mach speed in her head. She could just see Johnny Depp playing the role of Black Sam.

"You people all have the funniest habit," Sam said, rubbing his beard like he always did when something puzzled him. "You say things that don't make any sense at all, but when I ask you what you said, you all answer 'Nothing.' You say the biggest bunch of nothings of any people I've ever met, and I've met plenty in me day and in me travels."

Mrs. Clark realized that she was not the only one who couldn't figure this guy out. She snickered as she thought about her husband. Her *dead* husband. The Clark men had all been plagued by the doom of the sea, from the first one that fell prey to Black Sam Bellamy. *The real* Black Sam Bellamy. Her own Seaman Clark must be turning over in his grave at the mere idea that Black Sam Bellamy—whether he was the real one or a fake one—was sitting at her table, supping with her, and sleeping in one of their beds.

"What do you want to know about the museum?" she asked.

"What do they have in there?"

"They have gold chains, silver dishes, coins of all sorts, guns, swords…I don't know. There is a lot of stuff in there." She laughed, then said, "It's been rumored that Black Sam was supposed to have a lot of emeralds—I think from Colombia—but when the crew scoured the ship's remains, there were none to be found."

Sam threw his head back, his long black hair trailing down his back, as he roared.

"What's so funny?" Mrs. Clark asked.

"Emeralds? They honestly thought the emeralds were on the ship?"

"So I've heard. What's so funny about that?"

"There warn't no emeralds on the ship. I'd already got rid of 'em all," Sam said matter-of-factly. "They've never found them, I take it."

"No," Mrs. Clark replied. "You—you really are him?" She could hardly believe that she was almost convinced to believe his wild tale. She thought about a verse from the Bible. She'd taught Sunday School at the local Methodist Church for many years, but never had a verse rung so clearly in her head as it did right now. When Paul was brought before King Agrippa, the king admitted, "Almost thou persuadest me to be a Christian." If she wasn't careful, she would swallow this self-proclaimed pirate's yarn like the king of old.

"I told you I am," Sam said. "Don't ask me how it can be possible. It's as confusin' to me as it is to the rest of you. If some guy washed up on the shore and claimed to be some 300-year-old fellow, I'd think the guy was a lunatic too."

"Anyway," he continued, "getting back to the museum..."

Mrs. Clark got up from the table and headed for the office, where he assumed she did all of her figuring and kept the records for the Inn. She wagged her finger at him, luring him in to share the inner sanctum with him.

Sam got up and followed her. Once inside, he saw the same sort of a machine he had seen over at Blair's. He had no idea what it was, but he felt certain he was about to find out.

Mrs. Clark punched a few buttons on it and there were pictures on it, much like the ones in the television set he had just learned to operate.

"Another kind of television?" he asked.

"No," Mrs. Clark answered. "This is much more complicated than a television." She sat down on the rolling chair in front of the machine and began to type letters onto a little box at the top of the screen.

Sam watched with rapt attention when he saw what she was typing: *Whydah*. In no time flat there was a picture of—his ship! How could it be? It had been missing for—as long as he had been.

"What the hell?" he asked, his face as ashen as the sails on the ship.

"Does it look right?" Mrs. Clark asked.

"Right? It's me bloody ship!" Sam bellowed. "But how? It's been at the bottom of the ocean since that bloody day the lightning split it right down the middle. Nobody can know what it looked like."

"After the crew recovered as much of it as they could," Mrs. Clark explained, "they tried to reconstruct it so they could tell how it looked."

"They did a bloody good job of it," Sam said, rubbing his beard. "A damn bloody good job! I've got to go see it."

"The museum?" Mrs. Clark asked.

"No, not the museum. Well, that too. But where have they got the ship?"

"They couldn't salvage the whole ship," Mrs. Clark said. "They brought up some pieces of it, and they are at the museum. Some people have tried to make models of it."

"Models?" Sam asked.

"Yes," Mrs. Clark said. "They are little sort of patterns of what they thought the big one looked like. That's what you are seeing there."

"But how?"

"This is a computer," Mrs. Clark said, realizing that if this mad man was indeed from the 1700s, the difficulty of explaining a myriad of things was overwhelming. "People can take cameras…" She shook her head. He obviously didn't know what a camera was either.

"Have you ever seen a portrait?" she asked him.

He simply nodded his head, trying to take in everything she was saying.

"There are little boxes that are called cameras. There is a film—a roll of…" She hesitated. "Anyway, a person can push a little button and it puts an image of what the box is pointed at onto that film and it comes out as a picture, like a portrait."

She reached over and took her digital camera and pointed it at Sam. He quickly covered his face, afraid of what the strange thing might do.

"Now you've gone and ruined the picture!" Mrs. Clark shouted at him. "Here, look at this."

She showed the back of the camera to him and he could see his own image on the little box. The color drained from his face. It was doing exactly what Mrs. Clark said it would do, but how?

"Now," Mrs. Clark said, pushing a little button that forced a small blue strip to pop out of the box. She took the strip and inserted it into the front of the thing she had called a computer. Soon the entire screen was filled with the picture of Sam, complete with his hand across his face.

"It's possessed!" Sam shouted, shaking in his boots.

"There is a lot of stuff on the computer about the *Whydah*," Mrs. Clark said, pushing a button on it and it went back to something that said it was "Google." It was the page where they had started when she had found the pictures of the *Whydah*. Now, though, she moved the little arrow and Sam watched closely, like it was a magic wand, and a whole list of things about the *Whydah* showed up on the screen. Mrs. Clark clicked on one that said, "Real pirates at Nauticus." Sam looked over her shoulder, reading the words silently. It described exactly how the storm had struck, what he had done to try to save the ship, then how the cannon crashed across the deck, how the main mast snapped and how the *Whydah* was capsized and how the crew and the entire ship was cast into the depths of the sea.

"By the morning, the bodies of the crew were washed up onto the shore. By all accounts, there should have been one hundred and forty-six men on board. They recovered all of the corpses except three. Thomas Davis, a carpenter, and John Juliet, the pilot of the ship, somehow managed to survive."

Sam was aghast as he read the account. These were not just *bodies*. They were his crew, his friends, the men who had depended on him to keep them safe, the men who had helped him pilfer the wealth that he had been bringing back to Maria, to claim her as his bride.

"But who was the third one they didn't find?" he finally asked Mrs. Clark.

"Why, you, of course! You were never seen or heard from again."

"Until now," Sam said softly.

Mrs. Clark studied him carefully again. He seemed like he really was Black Sam Bellamy. Nobody could fake it this good.

"So after almost three hundred years, it appears that here you are. Safe and sound." She paused, then added, "Well, not sure quite how sound you are. Seems to me a bit of a stretch to believe it could be possible."

"Do you want to see more about the *Whydah* on the computer?" she asked.

"No," Sam said, shaking his head vehemently. "I think I've seen more than enough for one day. I would like to go to the museum some night though."

"I'll see what I can do about that," Mrs. Clark said.

Sam finished eating his meal, then he excused himself to go up to his bed. His head felt like it was swimming in the eddy he'd spent so many years in. He pulled off his shoes and rubbed his feet. He'd worn his boots for so many years, they felt funny after he took off the shoes Blair had gotten for him when his ankle was so swollen.

❈ ❈ ❈

Down below Sam's window, Jason hid in the shadows, hoping to learn more about the mysterious newcomer to town. When he didn't hear any conversation or sounds, he decided he might as well get home. Besides, his mother still didn't seem quite right, so he didn't like leaving her alone for too long.

As he walked along, he kicked at the stones scattered here and there on the sidewalks. He carefully avoided each crack, reciting to himself as he went, "Step on a crack, break your mother's back…"

The image of his mother's face, like she had seen a ghost when he mentioned Black Sam Bellamy, flashed in his mind. He didn't know what he would do if something happened to her. Was this mad man dangerous? Should he desert his efforts to try to figure the whole thing out? Was he putting his mother at risk by sneaking around to follow him?

As he thought about it, he knew the answer. He should leave it alone. Let the police, or whoever needed to deal with it, handle it. Deep inside, though, he knew he was already in too deep and that he had to keep on. Besides, he was the best informant the police—and the media—had. So far, he had just called his information in. They had no idea who their informant was. He would just have to be more careful.

A black cat jumped out from between two parked cars, screaming as it ran out onto the street. That was the second time a cat had nearly scared the pants off him.

"Scram!" he yelled at the cat, throwing a small stone at it. The cat ignored it and just went on running.

"There's something spooky about that damn cat," he muttered as he ran across the front lawn and into his house.

"Jason, is that you?" his mother called out. "Where have you been?"

"I just went out for a walk," he answered.

"I've told you not to go out after dark," his mother scolded. "With that strange guy in town, who knows what could happen?"

"He's home at the Inn," Jason said, slapping his hand over his mouth, but it was too late.

His mother came into the living room and glared at him.

"Young man, I think you'd better sit down. We need to have a talk."

Jason cringed. He hated it when his mother was mad at him. Her talks were far worse punishment than if she'd taken a whip to his backside.

CHAPTER XX

Sam tossed and turned all night. Visions of his ship, sometimes whole and other times split in two as it was by lightning the night he disappeared, invaded his dreams. Even in his sleep, he seemed to be trying to figure things out. He could not remember ever dreaming in the centuries he had been in that black hole. He knew he had thought about things, but no dreams. He was sure of it. He wondered, in his state of stupor, if he had even slept during all that time.

Now he saw Maria in his dreams. It excited him to the point of no return. Then he saw the blonde version of the girl of his dreams—Blair. Were they one and the same? And why hadn't he been able to bring her all the treasures he had promised her? He so wanted to be with her, his entire body ached, longing for her.

Then he caught a vision of the emeralds, buried in the sides of the root cellar in the very home where Blair was living. He tried to get down there, but in his dreams he fell on the broken ladder. He awoke, rubbing his ankle.

They say that if you reach the bottom of a fall in a dream, he reflected, *you will never wake up. You will die when you hit the bottom.* Would that really be so bad? He had endured punishment for an eternity. Could death be any worse?

He decided, as his mind whirled like the eddy he knew so well, that in the next couple of days—or nights—he would try to make a trip to the Whydah Museum. He contemplated how he would get there. He could ask Blair, and he knew she would be delighted to accompany him. Of course Widow Clark had also volunteered, and she probably wouldn't ask as many questions as Blair would.

He finally drifted off to sleep after deciding that he would get Widow Clark to take him the next night. Maybe he could get her to show him how to use that machine that had all those pictures of the loot. His loot! It gnawed at him that he had worked so hard, for so many years, to collect enough treasure to come back and stake his claim for Maria—legitimately, this time. Ha! Fat lot of good that had done him.

Once again in his dreams he was going down into the root cellar. He was sure, even though his barrel of rum was gone from the barn, that the emeralds were right where he had left them. The way the grass was all grown over it, nobody had been down there for—practically forever.

When he woke up, it was still dark, and his ankle was hurting again. It had been doing pretty well, so why should it start acting up now? *Maybe,* he thought, *it was because I fell down into that hole again.*

That's just plain stupid, he reasoned. *You didn't really fall down there again. It was just a dream.*

Day after day, week after week, it was getting harder and harder to tell what was reality and what was a nightmare. He was gradually getting used to all of these newfangled inventions people had. He had even thought about asking Blair if she could teach him to drive.

He also knew that before long the money Blair's father had paid for the room at Widow Clark's Inn was about used up. He had no idea how he would be able to pay for the next month's rent. He didn't think she'd throw him out on his ear, but he couldn't be sure of that. He had tried to help her do odds and ends around the house. He had learned how to use the lawn mower. He chuckled as he thought that it would be a whole lot easier if she would just buy a goat.

Sam decided, somewhere between being awake and drifting off to sleep, that he would try to get Widow Clark to teach him how to find things on that thing they called a "computer." He needed to be armed and informed before he put his plan into action.

Plan! he thought. He didn't have a plan. He was going in as ignorant as he did when he attacked a ship on the high seas. Still, he was always successful in those actions. This one should not be any different.

It seemed like there were all sorts of strange sounds in his mind as he slept fitfully. It was hard for him to sort them all out. He heard the crashing of the *Whydah* as it split in two. He heard Maria's voice—or was it the voice of Blair? It was almost impossible to differentiate one from the other. Some of the images had her with her black locks, while others were with her blonde tresses. He heard the sounds of the huge bell as it rang out to warn others that they were nearby; or was it those incessant alarms for what he had learned were fire trucks, ambulances, and police cars here and now?

He sat up in bed, screaming far too loudly and clapping his hands over his ears, "No! Get out of my head! Leave me alone! Send me back to the ocean!"

He was horrified that he might have awakened Widow Clark, and maybe even frightened her. There were no other guests at the moment. They seemed to come mainly on the weekends. He listened carefully to try to hear her moving around on the main floor. He had no way of knowing that she wore ear plugs at night to keep some of those same noises he hated from invading her head.

He lay in bed, staring out the window at the moon overhead, waiting, wishing for the daylight to arrive. He would ask Widow Clark for help with the computer while they ate breakfast. He had to find out more about what had happened to him. He laughed, burying his head in the pillow so he would not disturb the sleeping innkeeper.

There was a TV in each of the guest rooms at the Inn. He finally got up and turned it on softly. Blair had shown him how to change the channels with the remote, so he began to cruise the channels to see what he might find. He sat bolt upright as he watched the Discovery channel rerun the documentary they had made to showcase the discovery and raising of the *Whydah*. A man they identified as Barry Clifford was telling them how he had found it, after years of searching for any signs of the sunken ship.

Not caring who heard him or who he woke up, he screamed at the TV. "Get him away from there. That is *mine*! All of those coins, and even my bell and my gun—they are *all mine*!"

He continued watching the program, more determined than ever to get to the museum and to stake his own claim. He had pillaged the goods once, when he was at sea. It shouldn't be any harder to get it from the museum at night when there would be no one there. He wouldn't have the crew of some other ship to deal with. It should be...he paused, trying to remember the phrase Blair had used when she said something was very easy..."a piece of cake," he said softly.

Suddenly, his stomach growled at the mere thought of food. He was relieved when he heard the sound of pans banging in the kitchen below. He got up and dressed, then made his way down to join Widow Clark.

"Good morning, ma'am," he said. "Do you need any help?"

She stared at him. He was a conundrum, all by himself. He looked as scruffy as if he had been rolling around on the bottom of the ocean, as he claimed, yet he could be as polite and personable as if he'd been bred to the highest folks Cape Cod had to offer.

"Got along without you before I met you," she sang, flitting about the kitchen, "gonna get along without you now."

Sam grinned, his gold-capped teeth glistening in the light above the table.

"Never heard that one," he quipped. "Or a whole lot of other ones you and Blair sing."

"Oh, I've a wealth of 'em," she remarked. "Some night I'll give you a concert. Now, I reckon as to how you're hungry."

"That I am," Sam admitted. "Me stomach was a howlin' so loud it woke me up."

Sam sat in silence as Widow Clark finished cooking the breakfast and served it to him, then she sat down across from him.

"Mighty quiet this morning," she said as she set her coffee cup back on the table.

"Jist thinkin'," Sam said.

"'Bout anything special?"

"That thing—computer—you have in there. You think you could teach me to use it?"

"Reckon I could," Widow Clark said. "You seem pretty smart. Shouldn't take you too long to learn. Whatcha lookin' for?"

"Me," he answered matter-of-factly. "Me and me ship. I know a few things you've all told me, but I want to know all of it."

"Then you ought to go see Blair," Widow Clark said. "She knows more about it—about you—than anybody else on the Cape."

"Why?"

"She made it her point to find out," Widow Clark explained. "She did her thesis for her degree in history about it. About you and Maria."

"What's a thesis?" Sam asked.

"It's a paper to prove you know what you're supposed to know about what you studied."

"Sounds confusin'."

"She got some sort of honors for it," Widow Clark explained, "so I 'spect she did her homework pretty well. I hear tell she's got a whole room full of what all she found."

Sam tried to think of the different rooms at Blair's house. He had been in every room there except her bedroom. He chuckled as he thought, *You mean she was sleepin' with me the whole time I was there—and I didn't even know it?*

Now he had to figure out which would get him the best information—the computer or Blair. It didn't take more than a couple of minutes to decide to try to learn how to manipulate the computer. He knew that if he got wrapped up in Blair, he'd be apt to do something he'd regret later. He had to find out what kind of a life Maria had. Had he ruined her entire life? He never meant to do that. He just couldn't help himself. Blair said they called her a witch after the baby died. He did hear on that one trip he made back to see her that she'd had a baby, but somehow he knew the baby survived. He'd seen the baby the day he'd perished with the *Whydah*. He could swear somebody said it was his son. How could that be? And why did he keep seeing the men who had nearly killed him? Oh, yes, he'd wanted revenge, but it seemed like they won out in that battle. He'd paid his dues, and then some. All those years at the bottom of the ocean... It was a worse fate than if they had left him in jail to rot. He would never have lasted three hundred years locked behind bars. Try as he might, he could not see all of the faces clearly. He was sure most of them were local residents, but there was one that seemed strange, out of place. Yet the image seemed so haunting. If he ever saw that guy again he vowed that he would kill him.

What a ridiculous idea! The man has to have been dead for centuries. No way I'll ever see him again.

Yes, it was much safer trying to dig out the facts in the computer. Once that was done, then he'd approach Blair and try to pull out the rest of the story from her. Somehow, he was pretty sure what she had in her possession, from her research, was more folklore than facts. Still, it would be interesting.

He was daydreaming when he heard Widow Clark say, "Well, if you want to try to learn to use the computer, let's get to it. I ain't got all day, you know. I'm a workin' woman. Only a couple more days until the weekend is here and then we'll have all the rooms filled up." She got up and started for the office. She turned back and looked at Sam. "Well, whatcha waitin' for? Hop to it."

Sam stood up and began to hop on one leg. He nearly fell over, his ankle still not as sound as it should be.

"At that rate, you'll never get there," Widow Clark taunted. "I could hop better than that myself, and I'm a whole lot older than you are." She began hopping on one foot and was in the office and seated at the computer before Sam could get in the door, and he was walking on both feet.

Hmmm. She thinks she's older than I am. If she only knew! Why, I must be older than Methuselah. He shook his head to try to clear his thoughts. *Who the devil is Methuselah?* he wondered.

❈ ❈ ❈

He took to the computer like a duck to water. Before long Widow Clark decided to leave him to do his own searching. She'd shown him how to Google things.

"Google?" Sam asked. "That sounds strange. It makes me want to giggle."

"No," Widow Clark insisted, "it's Google, not giggle. If you need any help just holler. I'll be out in the kitchen. I have to start baking today for the weekend."

Sam typed "Whydah" into the place where Widow Clark had shown him to type in what he wanted to find. There was a long list of articles about the ship. He clicked on the first few and read about the history of the ship, as well as about the Expedition Whydah that found the first artifacts from the ship on July 20, 1983. According to the things he read, there was still no positive proof that it was the *Whydah*. Then, in November, 1985, they found the bell. There was no doubt that this was indeed the ship Barry Clifford had spent most of his life searching for. There, still readable, on the bell was the word "Whydah."

Sam could not explain it, but he suddenly found himself weeping. He got up and closed the door to the office so Widow Clark would not hear him. He was a pirate. The toughest of the tough! He could not explain, not even to himself, why the sight of the bell should affect him like this. *Maybe*, he thought, *it is not the bell. It is not even the ship. It is the men. My men. I had promised to protect them as long as they obeyed me, yet they all perished with the ship. All of them were gone. All of them but me.*

Sam went back to the computer. He rubbed his beard as he pondered his next move. Widow Clark had said something about some other thing to type in there to get some different articles about him and the Whydah. What was it she said? Bang! That was it. He quickly typed in "bang.com" and a bunch of people, all silhouettes, popped up on the screen. It said something about that site not being reserved yet. At the top of the screen he saw the words that set him into fits of laughter.

Hearing him, Widow Clark came in to see what was so funny. She looked at the computer screen. "Ever feel like you're in the wrong place?" If this really was Black Sam Bellamy—the original one—that was the most understated idea anybody had ever come up with. She couldn't help it. She laughed as hard as he did.

"What were you looking for?" she asked Sam.

"That other place you told me to type in. I did. Bang.com. And this is what showed up. Hell, yeah, I've been in the wrong place most of my life, but this world I'm in now is about as far from the right place as is possible."

"I can't really argue with that," she agreed. "It was bing.com, not bang.com." She paused momentarily, then said, "I think, though, maybe somebody is trying to tell you something."

"Yeah? What's that?"

"Just that if you really are where you shouldn't be, you need to back off a bit. Let the Whydah Museum sit for a bit. It won't go anyplace. Just get your bearings a bit before you go running off half-cocked."

"But it's all my stuff," Sam argued. "My loot. I owned all that stuff fair and square."

"You call stealing it from others getting it fair and square? You robbed it. Pillaged it, I suppose you'd call it. Well, it's not yours any more than it's the property of the U.S. government. Oh, yeah, they tried to say it all belonged to them because the seas are not part of the state of Massachusetts, and they tried their best to keep Barry from having their hooks into it."

"Barry?" Sam asked, puzzled by her casual reference to Mr. Clifford by his first name. "You know him or something'?"

"Sure," Widow Clark answered. "I've done some volunteer work down there when they needed help."

"Volunteer work? What could you do? You don't know anything about that stuff." Sam huffed and puffed, disturbed by everybody under the sun getting their hands on his treasure.

"Sure," she said, grinning at him. "The place was getting pretty messy, so I went down and helped them give it a good cleaning. I am good for something, at least once in a while."

Sam didn't know why, but he felt bad that he had implied that she was inferior to—him?

"I'm sorry," he said. His words surprised him. He wasn't in the habit of begging to be excused by anybody. He was in command. He was the boss. He was the captain of the ship. *Ha! What ship? You don't have a ship. It's busted up into pieces at the bottom of the ocean, with just these remains on display for everybody from little kids to old men and women rubbing their fingers of my possessions.*

❄ ❄ ❄

Sam continued reading the information he found on the computer about him, Maria and the Whydah. The more he read, the more confused he got. Everything seemed to agree that Maria's baby had died as a newborn infant. Had he imagined the whole thing that had happened on that awful night when he was cast into the depths of the sea? He subconsciously rubbed his butt. He could still feel whatever it was that had bitten him that night at Crosby's Tavern. It stung like nothing else he'd ever felt in his life.

He closed his eyes and tried to remember exactly what he had seen when he looked in the window to try to catch a glimpse of Maria. He saw the little toddler as he tottered over to crawl up on his mother's lap. He recalled the people at the Tavern talking about the doctor in town, the one that had married Maria. His Maria. He tried to picture the man, but he didn't think their paths had crossed. He had no right to his woman. He had no right to raise his son as if he were his own flesh and blood.

In a rage, he stormed out of the office and headed outside, slamming the door behind him.

"Wonder what he found," Widow Clark said to herself, continuing to peel the apples for the pies for the weekend guests. "Whatever it was, my guess is that he's heading for Blair's."

CHAPTER XXI

Sam swung his fist at the door, causing it to slam against the cupboard, making a loud crash. He hadn't bothered to knock, like he usually did. He had to try to unravel this puzzle, and he didn't know anybody else who could help him make sense out of it.

"Where are ya?" he bellowed.

"I'm in here," Blair said, her voice coming from the living room. "You get up on the wrong side of the bed, or what?"

Sam rubbed his beard. "Thar's only one side of the bed you can get out on," he said. "You should know that."

"And how should I know that?" Blair asked.

"Surely ye've seen the rooms at the Inn. It's the same bloody room I was in when..."

"When what?" Blair asked, looking up at him.

Sam related the fact that the Inn he was staying in seemed identical to the one he and Maria had rendezvoused in so many years ago.

"How can that be possible?" he asked Blair. "That was in Yarmouth."

"About three generations ago the Clark family had the Inn moved to Hyannis. One of the women they married was from Hyannis and she refused to live in Yarmouth. "Too many ghosts there," she declared. "If only she could see you here, now."

Blair laughed. "There are many things you have missed in all the time you've been gone."

"Never mind," Sam said. He caught a glimpse of her, sitting on the floor, her legs crossed in front of her, surrounded by papers, books, magazines, and pictures. He threw his head back and let loose with that deep throaty laugh she loved so much.

"Something funny?" she asked. "It's all your fault, you know."

"You—you look just like an island out in the sea, only you're lost in a sea of paper instead of water." He paused a few moments, then asked, "What's my fault?"

"It's your fault I had to go digging in these papers to try to figure out when the last time was that anybody saw you. I was sure, or at least I thought that it was right before your ship sank."

"My *Whydah*," Sam said, his voice shaking at the memory of the loss of his beloved ship. He knew he'd been on the ship when he heard that crack as the lightning hit it and divided it right in two. He had no idea, all the time he was missing, if any of his men had survived, but he knew what he had to do. Until you know for sure that everybody is safe and accounted for, the captain never deserts his ship. But how had he managed to survive? And why didn't anybody come looking for him?

He'd seen all sorts of tales on that machine, the computer, over at the Inn, but they hadn't answered his questions. If anything, it had just raised more questions. The same old questions that kept haunting him. The questions that he'd mulled over and over—for three hundred years.

He wasn't sure where to start, but he figured he might as well just plunge in with what he did know.

"So you told me, and that machine said that Maria's baby— me own babe—died the same night it was born?"

"That's what's been reported."

"Where was it reported?"

Maria rifled through her papers. Finding what she was looking for, she began to read.

> *Maria Hallett, along with her father, John Hallett, was summoned to the town council's special session. Word had spread like a wild fire that her baby had not survived the night. Councilman Andrew Thacher and Maria's own uncle, Jonathan Hallett, are accusing her of witchcraft.*

Following the meeting, she was placed in the local gaol, but her father paid for her release. A small thatched-roof hut is being constructed for her. As soon as it is completed, she will be sprung from the prison, but she is nevermore to set foot inside the town proper, no matter how long she shall live. Further, no one shall set foot inside her home, save for her immediate family, no matter how long she shall live.

Sam again rubbed his beard and shook his head. Who was it he saw that day so long ago when he looked in the window at the home where Maria was living. It was in the town of Yarmouth, so how could they say she had been outcast? Were the town records wrong, or had he dreamed he'd been there that day? And what of the day he disappeared and the ship sank? He knew, from what he'd read on the computer, that the ship was wrecked in the storm. He wished he was back in that eddy. Life was much less complicated there.

Finally, he spoke, his words coming haltingly. "I remember things different from what everybody says."

"How are they different?" Blair asked. She placed her elbows on her knees and rested her chin on her hands, giving him her undivided attention. If this truly was Black Sam Bellamy—and she was becoming more and more convinced of it daily—she had to know what his story was. As they say, every coin has two sides to it.

"I went back to Yarmouth twice," he said. "Once I didn't see anybody, but I did leave a gift for her." His eyes filled with wonder. "I wanted so much to see her. I would have given anything to see her again."

"Where did you leave the gift? At her shanty?"

"No. That's part of what doesn't make any sense. She was living in a pretty nice house right in Yarmouth. I stood outside the window at Crosby's Tavern and I heard them talking about her. They said she was married to some doctor."

"She never got married," Blair insisted. "She waited for you, watching every day for you to come back to her like you promised you would do." Blair started fumbling through a bunch of magazines until she found a bright yellow one. *National Geographic* was emblazoned on the front of it.

"That's the place I was looking at on the computer over at the Inn," Sam said. "How does a magazine get into that machine?"

"It doesn't. Well, not really," Blair said, trying to figure out how to explain yet another unknown to Sam. "National Geographic is a company. They publish a magazine, but they also have a website."

"Is that like a spider's web?" Sam asked.

Blair laughed. "Not quite. It is a place on that machine where people can put things for other people to see."

Blair turned to a page in the *National Geographic* magazine that was marked with a little metal thing. She began to read. "Maria was seen at the coast, staring out into the ocean, watching for Black Sam to come back to her. Often it was at dusk. If there was danger onshore because the men of the village were waiting for him too, she would tie a lantern to the tail of a whale to warn him."

"That's impossible!" Sam shouted. "You can't tie a lantern to a whale's tail!"

"The *National Geographic* is known for their research. They never print anything that isn't the truth."

"Humph! 'Tain't the truth. Can't be. Nope. No way. Besides, if they'll lie about that, who knows how much of the rest of the stuff they say is a lie too?"

Sam had read the same article when Blair showed it to him before. He didn't believe it then, and he didn't believe it now.

Blair pulled one article after another from magazines, notebooks, loose papers, and one after another read Sam the stories they all told. They were all pretty much the same. Sam sat, spellbound, listening to complete strangers talking about him. He was surprised by how much they knew about him. For the most part, his capture of different ships, the booty he had stashed on the *Whydah*, his brief affair with Maria, the men on his crew, these things were all eerily accurate, until they got to the part about Maria's baby dying and her being an outcast. He knew that someplace along the line the facts turned into fiction. He had seen the lad. He'd heard that she was married. He struggled to try to remember the name of the doctor she was supposed to have married.

"Dr. Angus McPherson!" he shouted when he remembered.

"What does Dr. McPherson have to do with any of this?" Blair asked.

"I don't know." He looked heavenward, as if he expected the answer to all of his questions to fall out of the sky.

"You met Dr. McPherson," Blair said. "Don't you remember? He fixed your ankle for you after you fell down into the root cellar."

"Yes, I remember *that* Dr. McPherson, but there was another one. There had to be."

"Of course there was," Blair said, trying to put the pieces of the puzzle together for Sam. "He told you he had an ancestor who was a doctor in Yarmouth years ago. There is nothing strange about that."

"But he wouldn't have married Maria!" Sam insisted. "He wouldn't have been allowed to marry a—a witch!"

"Do you mean to tell me that you honestly believe she was a witch?"

"I don't know," Sam admitted. "I do know it was like she cast a spell over me that night when she showed up at Crosby's Tavern. There was no way I could resist her."

"But according to the things people said about that night, it was Maria who was captivated by you. She felt like she was trapped." Blair paused, wondering what would happen if Sam got really upset and... Would he ever attack her? Was she safe with him? She was definitely attracted to him, but could she trust him? If he was who he said he was, maybe he should be committed someplace. An insane asylum? A lab someplace so medical people could examine him to try to figure out how he had escaped from time itself? She knew her mother and father would breathe a lot easier if he was locked up someplace.

Suddenly, Sam walked to the phone and asked Blair, "How do I make this thing work?"

"You want to use the phone?" she asked, surprised.

"Yup. I want to talk to that Doc Angus."

Blair turned abruptly and stared at him. She had done some checking around town to find out more about the doctor who had been at the festivities the day Sam had washed up out of the ocean. In all the inquiries she had made about him, not one person had ever called him "Doc Angus." She wondered where that had come from.

Blair got up and got the phone. She took the phone book and looked up his number. She dialed the number, handed the phone to Sam and said, "Just talk into it and you will hear him answer you."

Sam didn't admit that he had tried to use this thing once before, the day he had spoken to the woman who said she was Maria Hallett.

The phone rang, causing Sam to jump a bit. He waited until he heard Dr. McPherson's voice. It said something about "Not available. Please leave a message at the sound of the beep. If it is an emergency, dial..."

Sam handed the phone to Blair. "What's that?" he asked.

Blair heard the tail end of the message, so when the beep sounded, she said, "This is Blair Smythe. Sam would like to talk to you. When you are free, would you please call me back? He's here now. I'm not sure how long he'll be here."

"Until he answers some questions," Sam said, settling into the recliner and raising the leg rest to take the pressure off his ankle. He wondered how long it would be before it quit hurting. It seemed to him that it should have been better by now. What kind of a doctor was that man anyway? "A baby doctor," he told Sam the night he wrapped his ankle.

Sam stared down at the running shoes he was wearing. If he had his old boots—the ones the doctor had cut off of his foot—he would have some support for that ankle and it would probably be completely better now.

❋ ❋ ❋

"Blair?" Jenny skipped into the living room, where she found Blair still sitting on the floor, and Sam dozing in the recliner.

"Oh, hi!" Blair greeted her warmly. "I'm glad you came."

"Really?" she asked, winking at her as she tipped her head in Sam's direction. "Wore him out, did you? Well, I suppose, considering his age and all, it wouldn't take much. Three hundred and how much?"

Blair picked up a scrap piece of paper and fashioned it into an airplane. She fired it at Jenny. Jenny ducked to avoid the onslaught, sending it right towards Sam. The point of the plane hit Sam right smack dab on the nose, like it was a bulls eye on a giant target. Sam jumped into action, trying to stand up, but his foot caught in the space between the footrest and the main part of the chair, sending him careening to the floor. And that's exactly where he was when Dr. McPherson knocked on the door.

"Come in," Blair called out.

Dr. McPherson came in, and hearing the laughter in the living room, went directly there. He looked at the pirate, lying sprawled on the floor like a giant spider that had been stepped on, his arms and legs outstretched in different directions.

"Seems to me, matey," he said, trying to talk in a vernacular that the pirate would understand, "you're beginning to make it a habit of falling in unforeseen places and in a most unpirate-like fashion."

"I was attacked by a flying object," Sam said by way of an explanation.

"A flying object?" Dr. McPherson asked.

"I think they call it an airplane," Sam said, reaching for the paper airplane. "This," he said, stomping his foot. "It hit me right on me nose."

"Which one of you is the guilty party?" Dr. McPherson inquired.

"Not me," Jenny said, looking accusingly at Blair.

"You attacked me?" Sam shouted. "But why?"

"I wasn't aiming for you," Blair explained. "Honest, I wasn't. I was trying to hit Jenny."

"Some way to treat her best friend, isn't it?" Jenny said, hiding her snickers behind her hand. "Just imagine what she does to her enemies."

"Is your ankle okay?" Dr. McPherson asked Sam. "Maybe I should have a look at it."

Sam pulled himself over to the recliner and managed to get up and back into the chair. He wouldn't admit that his ankle hurt if his life depended on it. He'd been quite humiliated enough in his short time in this modern-day world. He was as tough as they made them. At least that's what people *used to* believe.

"No," Sam grumbled, "but you owe me a new pair of boots, man."

"Done," Dr. McPherson said. "What size do you wear?"

"It's been years since I've bought me a pair of boots," Sam said, laughing. Boy, was that an understatement. He had not thought about it before, but you'd think after all those years down on the ocean floor his clothes and his boots would have disintegrated. He looked down at the running shoes he had on his feet. "Better ask her. She bought these little things."

"Do they fit you okay?" Blair asked. "They aren't too tight, are they?"

"They feel fine," Sam conceded, "but there's not much to them."

"They're a size 13," Blair said to Dr. McPherson.

"I should have guessed as much," Dr. McPherson said. "The unlucky 13. No wonder your feet get you into so much trouble."

Angus headed for the door. "See you in a little bit."

"I'll be right here, Doctor McPherson," Sam said.

"I told Blair before, and I'm going to tell you now, since we seem to be friends, I'll thank you to call me Angus."

Sam wriggled about nervously, rubbing his beard. "Angus it is," he said.

He couldn't figure out why, but the good doctor made him as nervous as a cat's tail that was too close to a rocking chair.

"Blasted cats!" Sam muttered, frustrated at all the black cats that seemed to get in his way. They were as creepy as could be. They made the hair on his neck stand up on end.

"What did you say?" Jenny asked.

Port Call to the Future

"Nothing," Sam said, smiling as he thought that he could play that game as well as the rest of them. When they didn't want somebody to know what they'd said, they all said, "Nothing." Fine, he'd play the "Nothing game" right back at them.

"Damn!" Sam sputtered. "I forgot to ask him about what I wanted to find out about."

"He'll be back as soon as he gets your boots," Blair assured him. "You can ask him then." She studied him carefully. He seemed disturbed about something. Of course that shouldn't surprise her, since there was a whole world of unanswered and misunderstood things since he'd walked into a different life.

❄ ❄ ❄

Angus went into the shoe shop and sat down, waiting for a clerk to come over to help him. He smiled as he thought about the simplicity that remained of some of the old world that still existed on Cape Cod. He liked the personal feeling of sitting on a chair and having somebody come over to wait on him. It was a whole lot better than roaming the aisles of a WalMart or Target store. He fiddled with his wristwatch as he waited for the clerk. It wasn't like they were busy. He was the only customer in the store. When nobody came to assist him, he began whistling.

"Sorry, Doc," a young man said as he came out from behind the curtains where the shoes were kept. "I didn't hear you come in."

"No problem," Angus said. "I've got today off. You know, doctor's hours. We don't work on Wednesdays, not unless there's a baby that won't wait till Thursday to put in an appearance. Otherwise, you know all doctors hit the golf course on Wednesdays."

The clerk blushed slightly. "I guess I should study up on all that stuff," he said.

"You going to change careers?" Angus asked, winking at him.

"No. It's just that I guess Barb is pregnant. We weren't planning on having a family just yet, but...well, you know how things just sort of happen when you're not looking."

"I'm guessing you looked plenty," Angus teased the young man. "Have her call me and set up an appointment, unless you want to see another doctor."

"From what I hear, you're the best one on the Cape. I don't think she'd go to anybody else. We want the best for him." He paused, then added, "Or her."

"Any preferences?" Angus asked.

"Nope. Just a fine healthy baby. But Barb, she says she knows it's a girl."

"No point in arguing with her," Angus said. "Somehow, a mother is usually right about such things." He chuckled and said, "Unless it's twins, of course. Then you could get one of each."

The color drained from the clerk's face. "You think..."

"I don't know," Angus said. "But you can't rule anything out until we run some tests."

Anxious to change the subject, the clerk asked, "So what are you looking for today? You surely haven't worn out that pair of Florsheims you got just a month or so ago. Maybe you want something with some good grip out on the green."

"Not this time," Angus said. "I need some boots. Nice shiny black ones. Something that a pirate would wear."

The clerk laughed. "I heard about you disappearing the day of that big shindig. Glad you didn't drown. You planning on taking up privateering as a second job?" He started to go to the storeroom to see what he had that would fit the bill. Before Angus could say anything, he had disappeared behind the curtains. In just a couple of minutes he was back with three boxes. "Let's see if these will work," he said, setting the boxes down on the floor in front of Angus and sitting down on the little stool in front of him.

"I forgot to tell you, I need them in a size 13."

The clerk looked puzzled. "But you've always worn a size 10."

"These aren't for me," Angus explained. "I ruined the boots of a fellow because I had to cut them off of him to bandage up a sprained ankle."

"Okay," the clerk said, disappearing again. He came back

with two boxes. "Sorry, but it seems that we only have two styles in that size. Here, see what you think?" He opened the boxes, pulled the tissue paper back and let Angus study them.

One of the pairs was a lace up style and he knew that wouldn't work. The other pair was more like the pair he had cut off of Sam. It had the pull on tabs at the top, and even a gold chain on the side.

"Hmmm," Angus said. "A pirate always likes gold. I'll take this pair."

"Are you sure?" the clerk asked. "They're—um, a bit expensive."

"Doesn't matter," Angus replied. "I owe him. I'll take them."

The clerk closed the lid on the box and went to the cash register. Angus reached into his pocket and took out his billfold, then extracted his credit card. He handed it to the clerk without batting an eye.

"Um, they're—two hundred and eighteen dollars," the clerk said softly.

Angus flinched. "They're how much?"

"Two hundred and eighteen dollars," the clerk repeated.

"They should be made out of solid gold for that price, not just have a little gold chain."

"I'm really sorry, Doc. The other pair is cheaper, if you'd rather."

"No way would he settle for them," Angus said, handing the clerk the credit card. "I just have to bite the bullet and let him have them."

"Who is this guy?" the clerk asked. "He must be one heck of a fellow."

"He's a pirate," Angus said, laughing.

"*The* pirate? The one everybody is talking about? The one who claims he is really Black Sam Bellamy?"

"The same."

"You've actually met him?"

"I've not only met him. I've taped up his ankle after he sprained it."

"You think the guy's for real?" the clerk asked. "He says he's—what—over three hundred years old? That's just plain crazy."

"That's what he claims."

"And you buy it?"

"It's hard to argue with all the yarns he spins, yet he does seem to be sincere about it. I'm not sure if he's delusional, or if he had amnesia and when he woke up he read about Black Sam and he just assumed his identity, or if he's just plain crazy."

"Or he really is him?"

Angus shrugged his shoulders, signed the slip, took his copy of the receipt and headed out the door, swinging the boots in a bag to take back to Sam Black, or Black Sam, or whoever the guy was.

Angus got into his car and headed back to Blair's. This guy really was starting to bug him. He made him so uncomfortable, he wished he'd go back into the ocean, or wherever he came from. He was a man of science. He liked to reason everything out. There was no rhyme nor reason to this man. Maybe he should warn Blair to be careful of him. He hardly knew her, but she seemed like a decent sort. He would hate to see the pirate take her for everything she had.

"Yup," he said aloud as he drove along, "I have to get her alone and tell her to stay away from him. He's nothing but bad luck. I can feel it in my bones."

Angus laughed as he heard the oldies station on the car radio play "Bewitched, bothered and bewildered am I." Made perfect sense, under the circumstances.

CHAPTER XXII

Angus heard the threesome laughing inside as he walked up to the back door. He knocked, but they didn't hear him, so he went in and called out, "One pair of black boots coming up!"

Sam reached down and pulled the Velcro fasteners loose on his running shoes. He had one off and one on when Angus walked into the room.

"Diddle diddle dumpling, my son John," Angus recited, causing both Jenny and Blair to snicker.

"Wouldn't he make a great father?" Jenny whispered to Blair.

"Yeah, and he could even deliver his own baby," Blair whispered back.

"Here you go," Angus said, setting the box with the boots on Sam's lap. "Hope you know what you cost me on that one."

"Sorry," Sam said, almost sounding like he meant it. "It was your fault, though. You ruined the old ones."

"The old ones," Angus said. "I wonder how much the museum would give me for the authentic Black Sam Bellamy boots."

"Nothin'," Sam retorted. "You ruined them."

"Yeah, but still..." Angus thought about the possibility of trying to convince the fellows down at the museum that they were really from Black Sam. Surely they had seen the reports on TV and read in the paper that this wacko thought he was the original. It wasn't that he needed the money, but a man could never have too much loot. He wondered where Sam had stashed them.

"What was it you wanted to ask him that you forgot about before?" Blair asked Sam.

"Oh, yeah," Sam said. "You might as well sit a spell, Doc. This might take a while to sort out."

"What's got you so troubled?"

"Are you sure you don't know me?" Sam asked.

"Of course I know you," Angus said. "I've known you from the first day you got washed up from the ocean, during the big shindig down at the coast. Ever since you fell down into that root cellar."

"No," Sam said. "I don't mean from now. I just get this weird feeling that sometime before—a long time ago—our paths crossed. Like you and I both lived in some other world."

Angus scratched his head. This guy really was a nut case. He wondered if he could somehow get him to see a psychiatrist. Maybe they could put his mind at ease. As mixed up as he was, he must be going crazy, if he wasn't already there. He knew, beyond a shadow of a doubt, that he had never met this man before that day at the festival. He had never believed in reincarnation, and he sure wasn't going to start now. Nope, he knew the date, the time of day, the place where he was born. And it was only thirty-seven years ago. He knew his mother and father. They had both been an important part of his life. They both died way too young. Longevity had been a part of his family history for generations before them. His father was killed in that terrible accident, and his mother...she should never have had cancer. If only he had studied something besides obstetrics, maybe he could have done her some good. He still felt guilty over that, but there was nothing he could do to change it now. She was gone.

For some reason, he wanted to get back to his house. He wanted to sit in his dad's recliner, with his feet up, and watch *Brigadoon*. It was his mother's favorite movie. He couldn't count how many times they had watched it together. It was a wonder it wasn't worn out. It was one of the old VCR tapes, not a modern-day DVD version. One day he should break down and buy a newer copy of it. He'd hate to lose out on wanting to watch it when he felt nostalgic.

"What do you know about Maria?" Sam asked Angus.

"About as much as anybody else on the Cape," Angus answered. "If you really want details, you should ask Blair. She's the one that has an obsession about her. It's almost as if she had some sort of a connection to her. You know, of course, that Maria was an ancestor of Blair's."

"You're kinfolk?" Sam asked, looking at Blair.

"Sort of," Blair said. "My mother was a Hallett. She's not a direct descendant of Maria. Maria only had one baby—your baby—and the baby died during its first night. There aren't any direct descendants of Maria. Just collateral ones."

Angus chuckled. Blair was, it seemed, an "almost" everything. He dubbed her, right then and there, "the almost Blair." Little did he know how close to the truth he was on that assumption.

So much of what she said was the same thing Sam had read in everything he'd found on Widow Clark's computer. He shook his head, trying to clear his mind. He didn't understand all this collateral business.

"You think the baby died too?" Sam asked Angus.

"That's what everybody said," Angus said. "There's no reason to think otherwise."

"What if I told you that I saw the baby?" Sam asked.

The three of them—Jenny, Blair and Angus—looked at him suspiciously.

"That's impossible," Blair finally said. "I have read everything that's ever been written about them—about you. Everybody said the baby died. That's why they kicked her out of town. Why do you keep saying that?"

"But what if I told you that she continued to live in Yarmouth?" Sam waited for them to try to digest what he was saying.

After a long silence, Blair said, "That's impossible. How could you know that? You were never there until the day you came back and your ship sank. Everybody knows she was an outcast for the rest of her life."

Angus looked at Blair. *Maybe they both need a shrink,* he thought. *She believes him as much as he believes himself.*

"I came back one other time," Sam insisted. "I left gifts for her. I told you that. I left them on the back stoop of the house where they said she lived. Her and that doctor husband of hers." Sam glared at Angus. "You're sure you weren't there?" he asked in a most demanding voice.

"I am positive that you, my friend, are the only person who has ever even come close to believing that he is over three hundred years old. I make no such boast."

"What kind of a gift was it?" Angus asked.

"It was a basket, with some fish, a hand embroidered handkerchief from France and some pearls in it. I got the pearls in…just off the coast of Margarita. That's a little island off the coast of Venezuela."

Angus's face turned as white as if he'd seen a ghost. Pearls! He got a mental image—out of nowhere—of a bunch of pigs in a yard, and the yard was full of pearls. It was the creepiest feeling he'd ever known. What on earth could it mean?

Suddenly, standing up and changing the subject, Sam asked, "Who is going to take me to the museum tonight? I have to see what's there."

The three others looked at each other, waiting for a response. When none came, Sam said, "Do I have steal a car and get there myself?" He stomped his foot and the gold chain on new boots jangled so loudly it brought Marley's ghost from Dicken's *Christmas Carol* to Jenny's mind.

The thought of Sam behind the steering wheel of a car sent shivers through Angus's entire body. In order to protect the rest of the world from him, he said, reluctantly, "I guess I can take you." He shook his head as he added, "But the museum isn't open at night."

"I know that," Sam said. "That's what I'm counting on. I don't want anybody to see that I'm there."

"Then what's the point?" Angus asked.

"I just want to look in through the windows to see what the stuff—*my stuff*—looks like after all these years."

"You aren't going to try to break in?" Angus asked.

"Nope. Just want to take a look around."

"I guess that can't hurt anything," Angus conceded. He poked Blair in the ribs and said, "Can you come bail us out of the brig if we get caught?"

"Gladly," Blair said. "Maybe I should take some cash out at the ATM just to be sure I can cover it. How much do you think they'd fine you?"

"Hard to tell," Angus said. "I suspect that in a few hours, at the longest, they'd have both of us locked up in the nut house instead of the jail though."

They all laughed. Blair could just picture the whole affair being captured by somebody who saw them there, probably on their phone camera.

❋ ❋ ❋

Jason scooted along the ground, not moving away from the house until he was sure he would not be spotted. Oh, yeah! This was just what he'd been waiting for. He hurried home and called the TV station that he'd talked to before, carefully wrapped the tiny cell phone with a piece of Kleenex to disguise his voice. He'd seen people on TV put a handkerchief over the mouthpiece to change the sound of their voice. He didn't own a handkerchief, so he hoped the Kleenex would do the trick. He knew he'd be in hot water if his mother found out he'd been spying on the pirate. She had given him strict warnings to stay away from him.

"I heard this guy that claims to be Black Sam Bellamy tell somebody that he plans to break into the museum tonight," he told the receptionist at the TV station.

"Just a minute," the woman said. "I'll get a reporter for you."

"Yes?" the woman said. "You said you heard the guy that says he's Black Sam Bellamy say that he was going to break into the museum tonight?"

"That's what I heard," Jason said, wanting them to get the information and let him get off the phone before he got caught.

"Which museum?" the reporter asked.

"Which museum?" Jason shouted. "The Whydah Museum, of course. What other museum would Black Sam be interested in."

It caught the reporter's attention that the caller referred to the imposter, or actor, or whatever he was as simply "Black

Sam," yet on earlier calls he had referred to him as "Black Sam Bellamy." Was this the same caller, or somebody else? If it was the same one...

"Do you know this guy who claims he's the real pirate?" the reporter asked.

"Oh, no, sir," Jason quickly said. "I've just been watching him. You know, sort of like a spy. He doesn't know who I am, and I don't think he knows who I am. I hope he has never seen me." Jason shook from sheer fear that his mother might find out that he was still chasing the crazy man.

"Do you know what time he's planning..."

"All I know is after dark," Jason said, then hit the "End" button on his cell phone. He'd been on the line far too long already.

The reporter sat there, intrigued by the information, yet not sure if she should put any credence into the caller or not. Should she call the police and tip them off? Should she take a cameraman with him when she went to get the story?

She began to assemble her equipment and grabbed one of the cameras, deciding she didn't want to include anybody else, in case it was a phony call. She didn't need anybody else to help her make a fool of herself. She'd missed a couple of good stories lately because she didn't believe the person who had called with a tip. She had proven that she could do the job all by herself—both the job of capturing whatever was about to go down at the museum tonight and the job of making a fool of herself.

❋ ❋ ❋

Sam and Angus stayed at Blair's for several hours, until it was almost dark. Blair filled them with tales of Maria and Black Sam while they waited. Both men listened, enrapt in the stories they had both heard before. Angus watched Sam for his reaction for what Maria had been through. Several times he thought the hardened old pirate was close to tears when he realized what Maria had suffered because of him. Did the man actually have a conscience? Was he indeed the one who had caused all of her problems? It seemed impossible that what the pirate claimed was reality, yet the more he watched him and the more he listened to his side of the story, the more convinced he was that he was Black Sam Bellamy. Of course it was impossible. He was a man of science. He was even a man of faith. He'd been a good church goer all of his life. Yet this was harder to swallow than it was for him to believe that a great fish swallowed Jonah. Or that God spoke a few words and the entire Universe was spoken into being.

Sam asked Angus, "Where did you get those clothes you were wearing at that thing down by the coast?"

"You mean my pirate costume?"

"Yeah, that."

I had a lady, a seamstress, copy the one on the Black Sam statue at the museum. She did a fine job, don't you think?"

"It was pretty good," Sam admitted. "Not quite like I would have worn, but a good job of looking like the one in the museum."

"Then you've already been at the museum?" Angus asked.

"No, but I saw it on that thing—what do you call it?"

"The computer," Blair contributed.

"Yeah, on that."

"Do you still have it?" Sam asked.

"Sure, it's at the house. Why?"

"I'd like to borrow it, if you don't mind."

Blair, Jenny and Angus all looked askance at one another. What was he up to now?

"I suppose, but why?"

"If I'm going to see the treasure—*my* treasure—I'd like to at least feel like I belonged there. My own pants, when I took them off, they just sort of fell to pieces. I had to throw them out."

"A shame," Angus said, clicking his teeth together. "They would have made such a nice addition to the display at the museum. Them and your boots."

"Well, you made sure they weren't any good," Sam grumbled.

"So you have told me before," Angus shot back at him. "I spent almost everything I would have made for delivering a baby to get you those boots. I should have left your own doggone boots on when you hurt your ankle and let you complain about having a bad leg for the rest of your life. Some appreciation!"

"We might as well go back to my place so you can get your duds on and then head over to the museum," Angus said.

Sam got up and went towards the back door. With every step he stopped and jingled the chains on his boots, as if to rub it in to the doctor that he had gotten his own way, no matter how much it had cost.

❈ ❈ ❈

Sam pulled up to the garage door. He got out of the car. Sam didn't move.

"You coming?"

"Yeah, in a minute," Angus called back.

The hair on Angus's neck bristled. What was he doing, anyway? He knew they might get caught, and they could actually end up in jail for—for what? Breaking and entering? Impersonating a pirate? While he wouldn't be guilty of that, he could be charged with aiding and abetting. He always figured that if he ever got accused of anything it would be for malpractice as a doctor. Hanging out with a pirate, especially a three-hundred-year-old pirate, had never crossed his mind. Not until tonight.

It was dusk, and he was sure that Sam didn't intend to go to the museum until it was well past dark. That meant that he would have to entertain the pirate in his home for an hour or so.

"What's the matter?" Angus called back to Sam.

"I don't know," Sam said. "Something just seems... strange."

"Yeah," Angus retorted. "It does to me too. It's you, buddy. You're the thing that's strange."

Angus opened the car door and got out and stretched. He glanced down at his boots.

"Nice," he said. "Thanks, Doc Angus. I guess you're an okay bloke after all, even though there's a part of you that I really don't like. The part I don't trust."

"Can't say why. I've never done anything to you."

"Not yet," Sam said, as if he knew something that even he didn't know. He just couldn't shake the feeling that somehow, somewhere, sometime or other, he knew Doc Angus.

"Why do you call me Doc Angus?" Angus asked. "Nobody else has ever called me that.

"Don't rightly know," Sam admitted. "I think I heard it someplace. You know, back there."

"I told you," Angus said, his voice raised in protest, "I was not back there. I don't know who you knew back there, or what you thought you saw, but you're plum mad, you are. I've only lived once, and you'd be well advised to remember that. You can play whatever little games you want to, trying to convince people that you lived three hundred years ago, but it won't fly with me."

"I have no intention of flying with you," Sam said. "I won't get in one of those big birds. And you sure don't impress me as some angel type that's gonna sprout wings and sail around the heavens like an angel. And God knows I sure nuff ain't no angel. Not with what I did to Maria. And if I had known that she was with child..."

"Would you have done things differently?" Angus asked, suddenly overtaken with the idea that maybe there was a way to change history. Could it be... No. It was too absurd. What if he had been able to transport himself to another time, another place, to change Maria's outcome? Could there be two different scenarios for the little witch? Was she truly a witch?

Angus shook his head. Was Sam making him as crazy as he was himself? He didn't believe in witches, or living more than one life, or even pirates, for that matter. He had to convince people somehow that Sam was really an imposter. He was a con artist. A mighty convincing one, but a con artist nonetheless. He decided at the moment that he had to start by convincing Blair that Sam was a fraud. If he could save her from the so-called pirate, maybe it would be worth his involvement in this whole crazy thing. Yes, as soon as they were finished with this escapade tonight he would head back over to see Blair. He would find the right things to say to her to convince her that just like she was the "Almost Blair," Sam was no more than the "Almost Black Sam Bellamy."

He laughed as he thought that maybe, just maybe, they deserved each other. They were both nothing in and of themselves, yet they were convinced that they were important people. Perhaps people with a mission? But what exactly were they out to prove? And who did they intend to prove it to?

Sam walked slowly across the yard and followed Angus into his home. Angus nodded to a chair and said, "Make yourself at home while I go get the clothes for you." As he left the room, he flipped on the lights.

Sam sat in the chair and looked over beside him. There was a cradle. Not just any cradle. It was, he was certain, the exact same cradle he had seen the baby—*his* baby—sleeping in that house where Maria lived. The house that the other Doc Angus lived with her as his wife. It was overwhelming. At the shock of seeing this cradle here, in Doc Angus's house, he fainted dead away. And that is how Doc Angus found him when he returned with the pirate garb.

CHAPTER XXIII

Angus came back to the living room, his arms laden with the outfit he'd worn for the anniversary of the demise of the *Whydah*. He went toward the chair where Sam was sitting, and jumped a bit when he saw him. Was he asleep? Had he died? His mind went immediately to writing his obituary. How do you tell the world that the man who had died was somewhere between twenty-eight years old and three hundred years old? How do you find a birth certificate for him so you can report his parents' names, his place—and date—of birth, and his next of kin.

Angus dropped the clothes in a heap on the floor at Sam's feet. He took his fingers and placed them on Sam's neck. He breathed a deep sigh of relief to find a pulse. At least he wasn't dead. Was he just sleeping? This whole thing of having to deal with the strangeness of life in a different world, if it was such indeed, must be enough to exhaust anybody. Life today moved at such a fast pace, trying to adapt to it would be more than almost anyone, even a pirate, could accept.

Sam began to stir and he looked up to see Angus standing over him.

"What happened?" Sam asked.

"You either fell asleep or you fainted. I'm not sure which. Do you know what would have caused you to pass out?"

Sam turned and pointed to the cradle, which held untold books and magazines, not a baby.

"That," he said. "Where did it come from?"

"It was in the attic when I bought the house. I thought it would make a very nice magazine rack. Why? What about it?"

"I could swear it is the same cradle I saw the baby in when I looked in the window at Maria's house in Yarmouth." He waited for the idea to sink into Angus's mind. "Do you know anything about it?"

"Like I said, it was in the attic. I did study it pretty closely when I brought it down. I am sure it is an antique, but I haven't checked to see if anybody has any information about it. There are specialists who can trace almost any antique to its general age." Angus stopped a moment, trying to remember if there was anything else about it that might be helpful. "It does have a couple of initials on the bottom of it."

"What initials?" Sam asked.

Angus dumped the contents of the cradle out onto the floor. He turned the ornate piece of furniture upside down and Sam gasped when he saw "JH" carved on a corner of the cradle.

"It has to be John Hallett," Sam said. "It wouldn't be Jonathan. He was John's most bitter enemy. He would never have crafted such a beautiful thing, not for Maria. I heard rumors that it was him who had Maria accused of bein' a witch. Can you imagine? Her own uncle!"

Angus sat down on the sofa, the room now a mess from a combination of the books and magazines strewn about, as well as the pirate's costume.

"Wait a minute," he said, trying to fit the pieces of this puzzle together. "Are you trying to tell me that there were two brothers with the same name?"

"Nope," Sam replied. "They were as different as day and night. As varied as black and white. John, he was Maria's pa. Jonathan, he was a bit older than John. They fought over everything, from the time they were just young'uns, from what I heard tell when I was there those few days when I met Maria. They lived a ways apart. They said they fought over the land they were to inherit from their father. That would have been Andrew. Andrew Jr., that is. They both wanted the same parcel. Seems Andrew left the prime piece to Jonathan, but John was ready to fight him for it.

The will stated that if they couldn't agree in three years from the time Andrew died, one of the townsmen was supposed to make the decision of who got which part."

"Maria told you all of this?"

"Oh, Lord no! I got all that from askin' around at Crosby's Tavern while I was there. Maria and me, we didn't waste no time talkin' about silly family stuff. No, we had more than family matters to deal with. I took her up to my room at Widow Clark's Inn..."

Sam paused. This whole thing was becoming a blur in his mind. It was hard to tell what was real and what was imagined. His memory of the time he'd spent with Maria, and the lovers' tryst they'd shared, had been so clear to him when he was down at the bottom of the ocean. Now nothing made sense. At least he still knew who he was. Or did he?

Sam jumped up and said, "I've got to get dressed. It's getting dark enough that nobody will see us. Where can I get this garb on?"

Angus pointed to the bedroom. "Go on in there."

Sam disappeared, the clothes in his arms. In just a few minutes he came back out. "Well, how do I look?" he asked, turning around in a circle. Angus laughed. He had seen a number of models on TV walking the runway of a fashion show. He felt like Sam, instead, was about ready to walk the plank. If they got caught at their shenanigans, he just might end up that way.

"If I didn't know better," Angus admitted, "I'd swear you were Black Sam Bellamy."

Sam headed for the back door and letting loose with a loud "Argh, matey." Angus followed close behind. They got into the car and Angus was glad it was dark. He didn't particularly relish the idea of trying to explain his passenger to a policeman who thought he looked a bit strange. If it was closer to Halloween, perhaps he could have passed it off by saying they were on their way to a costume party, but it was still early spring, so that wouldn't wash.

"When we get there, park around back of the museum so we are not as apt to be spotted," Sam directed.

Now it was Angus's turn to laugh. "Can't do that," he said.

"Why not?"

"When you were looking at the computer for information you must have missed one important fact."

"And what's that?"

"The museum sits right at the end of the pier. The back door would lead right out into the water."

"You serious?" Sam asked.

"Dead."

"No, that's me," Sam said, chuckling. "Or at least so everybody thought. Seems I'm not as dead as they thought."

"The rumors of my death are greatly exaggerated," Angus said, quoting Mark Twain, one of his favorite authors.

Angus's mind went to a book he had read once. What was the name of it? Oh, *Waking Walt*. Apparently, Walt Disney had instructed that his body be quick-frozen. Cryogenics: a thing of the future. In the book, the author brought old Walt back from the dead, thawing him out just in time to prevent a takeover of all of the Disney holdings. Was such a thing possible? And then there was the old TV program, "The Second Hundred Years." A fellow had disappeared up in Alaska and eventually thawed out and showed up to live out the rest of his life.

"That's crazy," he said.

"What's crazy?" Sam asked.

"Nothing."

Oh, boy, here we go with the "nothing" thing again. I just don't understand it. If it's nothing, why do they bother to say it in the first place?

"It's the thing of science fiction," Angus said, like Sam would know what that was. Surely that was something outside his vocabulary. So many things had to be outside of his imagination, let alone his vocabulary.

When they got just a short distance from the museum, Angus parked the car and told Sam to get out. "I'll wait for you here. You can walk from here. There isn't much parking out on the pier. If anybody spots you, you had better make a run for it and hightail it back here so we can get out before you—we—get into too much trouble.

Sam reached down and removed his boots.

"I blew over two hundred bucks on those boots and you are going to make your big debut appearance as Black Sam Bellamy at the museum and you aren't going to wear them?" Angus was justifiably enraged.

"Sure anybody that's around would hear those blasted chains jangling."

"If they bother you," Angus suggested, "maybe you should just cut them off."

"And what? Throw away some perfectly good gold? No, I'll not do that, but I will choose where I will wear them."

Sam quietly got out of the car, shutting the door as softly as he could, then went up close to the buildings on the pier and walked where he hoped he wouldn't be seen.

Angus laughed as he watched him move stealthily along toward the museum. "Nobody would ever believe this," he said aloud. "I don't believe it myself. I swear, he must be a ghost. An imaginary being. No way can he be who and what he claims to be."

❋ ❋ ❋

Sam got to the front of the museum and peered in through the windows. He had a small flashlight he had taken from Blair, without asking her permission, of course. He shined it into the museum, where he could see coins, the *Whydah* bell, his pistol... He knew, instinctively, that many of the things he had seen on the computer were missing. He was horrified. He wanted to scream. Somebody had stolen part of the display in the museum. He, Black Sam Bellamy, had been robbed. Pillaged. Duped. It could not be. Maybe, he reasoned, they had some of the items under lock and key or in another room.

Sam was sure the door would be locked, so he pried at the window, trying to free it so he could crawl inside and investigate it for himself. The window was not meant to open, and the glass shattered. He jumped back quickly so he would not get cut. When it was safe, he carefully climbed inside. One of the items he noticed that was missing was the figure of Black Sam Bellamy. He knew he had seen it on the computer. Why would anybody steal the statue? The gold and silver and the jewels, yes, that made sense. But the figure of the pirate?

He shook his head in disbelief.

❈ ❈ ❈

Joan, the reporter from the local TV station, parked a couple of blocks from the Whydah Museum and walked up within a couple of buildings down to wait and see if the stranger showed up. She had a camera that she had borrowed from the station, just in case.

She sat, crouched in the shadows, and waited. She was just about ready to leave, deciding it must have been a prank call, when he saw the man, dressed like a pirate, making his way toward the museum.

She watched, putting the camera into action, and waited as the man broke the window and disappeared inside. Oh, this was going to be her pride and joy. She felt the excitement course through her veins, debating as to whether she should try to move closer, or if she was safer staying in the background and waiting for him to come back out, then follow him to see what he had taken and where he went.

❈ ❈ ❈

The alarms went off at the police station.

"Looks like we've got a live one," one of the officers called out. "Alert all the units down in the area of the pier. It's at the museum. This should be good."

In a matter of a few moments, squad car after squad car showed up. They didn't care that there was no parking on the pier. They were above the law—when they needed to be.

Sam heard the sirens and panicked. There was only one way out, and that was right into the arms of the police officers with their guns drawn. No, he couldn't risk that. What to do? His mind whirled like the eddy of old. He wished he was back there.

Suddenly, an idea hit him. He went to the spot where he had seen the statue standing in the pictures of the computer. He took the pose of the statue, and froze in place, not daring to breathe.

"Better get Kinkor on the phone," one of the policemen said. "He's the only one that will know what's missing."

❋ ❋ ❋

Angus sat in the car, not sure if he should wait to see if Sam got out and tried to make a run for it, or if he should leave before he was caught in a trap. The adrenaline was flowing, and he decided to wait it out. He didn't want to miss any of the excitement. He could talk his way out of most anything, so he was going to stick around. He was going to go see Blair in the morning though, and warn her to stay away from the pirate.

He opened the window in the car to see if he could hear what was going on. He thought about driving up closer, certain that with all of the police cars there his wouldn't even be noticed, but decided against it. He just sat in the car, waiting, wondering what they were doing inside the museum. None of the cops had come out yet.

A crouching figure moved closer to the museum. In the darkness it was hard to tell if it was a man or a woman. Whoever it was was wearing a hoodie, so he couldn't make out the face. The one thing he could see was that whoever it was was holding a camera up, catching all the action. A reporter from either the TV station or the newspaper, he guessed. Oh, this should make the headlines in the morning.

❋ ❋ ❋

The cops scooted around the museum, moving from one place to another, back to the storage unit, into the office, but there was no sign of anyone.

"Looks like whoever it was got away," one of the officers said, his gun still drawn.

"But how?" another one asked. "There's only one way out.

He had to go out through the front, either through the door or through that broken window."

"But the door was still locked when we got here," another cop said. "We had to break in. Remind me to have Kinkor leave an extra key with us so we won't have to break in if it happens again."

"You think this might be a regular occurrence? It's never happened before. Why do you think the perp might come back to finish up what he started?"

Ken Kinkor came into the museum, his eyes blazing as he quickly glanced around the main display room. "What'd he take? Did you catch him?"

"That's why we called you to come down," the chief said. "We figured you'd be able to notice if anything was missing, or even moved. You know this place better than anybody."

"Just at first sight, it doesn't look like it. Wonder what he wanted." He reached in his pocket and took out his cell phone. "Guess I'd better call Barry and let him know what's going on. He's supposed to be leaving to join the exhibit tomorrow, but I suspect he's going to want to come down here first to see for himself that everything is all right." Ken Kinkor looked at the broken window. "I'll grab some plywood to put up over the window for tonight. I'll give the insurance broker a call first thing in the morning and get them to put a new window in."

Barry Clifford's cell phone rang. He had just settled down to watch a bit of TV before he turned in for the night. He was going to be driving to Phoenix the next day and he wanted to get an early start. He had the new items he was going to add to the mobile display in the trailer out in the garage. He left his car outside. He knew what was important and what could be replaced.

He checked the Caller ID and saw that it was Ken. "Yeah? What's up?"

"Say what? What did they take? Did they ruin anything? Did they catch the guy?"

"I'm on my way. I will just hook the trailer of stuff I picked up earlier to the car and then I can leave right from there tomorrow."

"Not a lot of stuff," Barry answered when Ken asked him what he had taken.

"What time were you here?" Ken asked.

"About 7:30," Barry replied. "I took some of the Akan jewelry pieces. Oh, and the dummy."

Ken turned around and looked at the mannequin that was standing in the corner of the room, right where it always stood. It looked the same as always.

"You took the dummy?" Ken asked.

"Yup, he's out in the trailer. I actually thought about bringing him inside so he wouldn't get lonely out there." Barry laughed. "Then I realized that would make me a bigger dummy than he is."

"But...but...but the dummy's here," Ken insisted. "I'm staring at him."

Suddenly, Ken realized that this was not the same dummy. The clue? This dummy had no boots on. He was dressed in his regular costume, yet his feet were clad in just plain black socks.

Ken walked over towards the dummy. He had to be very careful to not let whoever this was didn't move—not until he wanted to break his stance. He'd heard about "living mannequins" in the big stores up in Boston, but he'd never seen one. Whoever this was, he was damn good at it. Was this some kind of a prank? Was this an actor that somebody had hired to... To what? If anybody wanted publicity for the museum, it would be him and Barry. He knew neither of them had done this.

Sam stood there, dead in his tracks, in the exact same pose the pirate had assumed, the one he'd seen on the computer. He knew he couldn't breathe. Even that would give him away.

Ken walked slowly, closer and closer. All of a sudden he reached into his pocket and pulled something out. He held it up and shot a spray of something into the air, aimed right at Sam.

No! I can't let that happen, Sam thought. He wanted to bite his lip, but he didn't dare even do that. He wanted to wiggle his nose, but no, they would see that too. Whatever it was in that thing he sprayed, it was going to make him...

"Ah...ah...ahchoo!"

"Amazing what a little pepper can do to a fellow, isn't it?" he said sarcastically to Sam.

Two of the policemen grabbed Sam and started for the door. One of the cops ran ahead and opened the back door of a squad car and held it while a third officer grabbed Sam's hands and pulled them behind him, locking them in handcuffs. They shoved him into the car, slammed the door shut and the chief and another cop got in.

"No way I'm letting somebody else have this one," the chief said. "I wonder what kind of a story he's going to come up with. I have a half a notion this must be the guy everybody is talking about. The one who claims to be the real Black Sam Bellamy."

❋ ❋ ❋

Angus watched as they hauled Sam away in the car. He reached for his cell phone, then set it down on the seat. Nope, this was one call he'd better make in person.

Angus headed for Blair's house. The reporter made her way back to her car and went to the TV station to get her big spot ready for airing on the ten o'clock news. She wouldn't be able to get the whole thing ready that fast, but she could give a short preview with the announcement that more would follow on tomorrow's news. The police had been so wrapped up with what was going on that they hadn't even noticed her.

Angus caught a glimpse of a kid, running, as he looked into the rearview mirror. He grumbled about kids that were out getting into trouble when it was dark out. He didn't look very big. Things sure weren't like they were when he was a kid. Nobody worried about kidnappings and junk like that. He was half tempted to go back and see if he could give him a ride, but when he looked up again, he was gone. Too late, he figured.

CHAPTER XXIV

Jenny and Blair were sitting at the kitchen table, drinking a cup of tea, when they heard the sirens going off. They went to the window to look out, but they couldn't see them so they went back to their conversation.

"You can't tell me you are falling for him," Jenny said. "Do you have any idea what that means? I mean, what if he is what he says he is—a three-hundred-year-old man? You can't be serious."

Blair laughed so hard the tears rolled down her face.

"What's so funny?" Jenny asked.

"Well, if you think about it, he was somewhere around thirty years old when his ship sank and he disappeared."

"So?" Jenny asked, not getting the connection at all.

"Well, he spent the next nearly three hundred years at the bottom of the ocean."

"So?" Jenny repeated.

"The water in the ocean is full of salt."

"So?" Jenny asked again, still in the dark as to what Blair was trying to get at.

"Silly! Don't you remember how our ancestors used to preserve food? It didn't matter if it was vegetables, meat, or what. They put it in salt. I'm willing to bet there's some of that stuff still down in the root cellar Sam found. It's probably still edible. By Sam going into the ocean, he obviously didn't get any older. He's still a young man. The salt preserved him. He's as fresh as a daisy."

"You don't really believe that, do you?" Jenny asked.

She shrugged her shoulders. "Oh, Jenny! I'm so confused! I don't know what I believe, but I do know that when I'm around him I feel like I've never felt about anybody before."

"Does he know how you feel?"

"Oh my God, no! I can't let him know!"

"Let me get this straight. You think you are falling in love with some crazy guy—some nut case—but you are afraid to tell him. I'm not so sure he's the one that's lost it."

"There are so many complications. For starters, my mom and dad would just totally freak out. They think he's a con man, but they don't know him. He really has a tender heart. He's told me about his crew and how much he cared for each one of them. And then there's Maria... I think he's still in love with her, but he has to know he can't have her."

"And he thinks you are Maria reincarnated, right? I heard him say you look just like her, except for the color of your hair."

Blair laughed. "Maybe I should dye my hair raven black and see what his reaction is."

Their conversation was interrupted when they heard a car pull up in front of the house. They both ran to the door to let Angus in. Seeing that he was alone, Blair asked nervously, "Where's Sam?"

"Probably behind bars, and I don't mean the kind from Crosby's Tavern."

"What happened?" Blair asked as she shut the door behind Angus. It was still cool in the evenings. She loved the springtime, but she felt as hot now as if it was the dog days of August.

"I'm not sure. I stayed in the car. I was his get-away guy." Angus grinned. He had never in his wildest imagination thought he'd be involved in aiding and abetting some old pirate, whether he was who he claimed to be or not, helping him escape from trying to break into a museum to see his own belongings. "I saw him break a window and crawl inside. In a few seconds the cops showed up. Probably a dozen cars. I'm sure there must be a silent alarm system set up in the museum that sounds at the police station if somebody is messing around down there. It was quite a while—maybe fifteen minutes or more—when they dragged him out and slapped the handcuffs on him and pushed him into the squad car and headed out."

Angus chuckled. "I think it was the chief himself that drove him off. I can just imagine how scared Sam must have been, back behind that wire divider that keeps the arrested guy away from the cops."

"Do you think the cops know who he is?" Jenny asked.

"How could they not?" Angus asked. "He's been in the news almost every day. I don't know how they are getting their information, but the TV station especially seems to have somebody following his every move."

Angus pointed at the TV. "There was a reporter there even before Sam showed up, like they knew he was coming. I'm pretty sure they caught the whole thing on film. There will no doubt be something on the ten o'clock news."

It was way too early, but Blair grabbed the remote from the coffee table and switched the TV on. "They might interrupt with a special announcement or something."

"Oh, and that guy from the museum showed up too," Angus said. "I suppose the police must have called him."

"Ken?" Blair asked. "I've got to call him and see what he can tell me."

※ ※ ※

"Yes, this is Ken. Is this Blair? Sorry, honey, but I have to call you back. I'm sort of in the middle of something." He laughed and hung up.

Blair hit redial and waited for Ken to answer again. Instead, she heard his voice mail, asking her to leave a message. Not to be deterred, she hit redial again and waited for his answer. It took five tries before he finally picked up.

"I told you I'm busy," he said, aggravated that she couldn't take a hint.

"I know," Blair said, "but listen a minute. Maybe I can help. If you can get them to set bail, I'll be glad to post it for him."

"You what?" Ken asked with disbelief. "Why?"

"It's a long story," Blair said. "Just let me know if that's possible. By the way, does he have an attorney?"

"He doesn't even know who he is," Ken said. "He really seems to believe that he is the original Black Sam Bellamy. I'm trying to wrap my mind around the whole thing." He paused, then added, laughingly, "And how to use this at the museum. Just think—if we could have a guy there who really believes he is Black Sam Bellamy! We could have the best museum in the country."

"You already do," Blair said.

"Thanks, but this could really make us a huge hit. Gotta run. I'll find out about the lawyer. If I need you, I'll call you back."

"What'd he say?" Angus asked.

"He's going to see about getting bail set and call me back. Meantime, I'm going to call Lyle. He'll know what to do to get him out. I haven't talked to him since we got the whole thing situated when I got my inheritance. He got plenty of money for that one. It's time I get some payback from him."

She dialed the number and waited for the answer. She didn't know what she'd interrupted, but Lyle was definitely not happy to hear from her, or anybody, probably.

"Lyle, have you heard about the fellow in town who claims to be Black Sam Bellamy?"

Lyle's attitude changed immediately. He was always looking for the high profile cases. He didn't usually snag them, but this could be his big break.

"Yeah, what about him?"

"He's been arrested."

"What's the charge? Impersonating a pirate?" Lyle laughed so hard both Jenny and Angus could hear him.

"It's serious," Blair said. "He went down to the museum to see the display of what he claims is rightfully his."

"The museum isn't open at night," Lyle reasoned.

"I know. That's the problem. I think he, um, he might have broken in."

"Let me guess. He got caught."

"Yeah, I guess so. I don't know the whole story, but he

doesn't have a lawyer. Could you go down there and see what's going on?"

"I wouldn't miss this one for the world," Lyle said, already getting his shirt buttoned up and his shoes on.

"I'll meet you at the station," Blair said.

"Why?"

"Because if you can get bail set I'll post the bond. See you in a few minutes."

Blair hung the phone up and asked Jenny and Angus, "Are you coming with me, or do you want to wait here? I have no clue how long this will take. It will probably depend on whether or not they can find a judge this late at night."

"We might as well tag along," Jenny said.

"We'll never get another chance to see something like this," Angus said as they all headed out the door.

"Did you lock it?" Angus asked. "I hear there's a pirate on the loose and there's nothing safe in this town anymore."

Blair checked to make sure the door was locked. She knew that everybody was safe from the likes of the pirate—*her* pirate, she thought, surprising herself at the idea.

❆ ❆ ❆

Blair, Jenny and Angus arrived at the police station before Lyle got there. Blair hollered, as she entered the main office, "Where is he?"

The female officer at the desk asked innocently, "Who, ma'am?"

"Sam!" Blair yelled back. "Sam Black."

"The pirate?"

"Yes, the pirate," Blair said, feeling exasperated at the woman laughing at her. *Yeah, right,* she thought. *Like she believes that.*

"He's in the interrogation room with the chief and a detective."

"Stop them," Blair ordered, causing a smirk to cross the lips of the desk officer.

"And why would I do that?"

"Because he has the right to an attorney. There's one on the way. Don't let him say another word until Lyle gets here."

"Lyle Carter?" the officer asked.

"Yes," Blair said, heading to the room where she could see Sam and the two officers inside.

"You can't go in there."

"Watch me," Blair challenged, opening the door and walking in.

Sam was spilling his guts to the chief and the detective. He was telling them the truth—or at least his version of it.

"I have no idea, sir," he said, looking square in the eyes of the chief. "I just know that one day I was in my ship, the *Whydah*, off the coast, when lightning hit it. Split it right in half, it did. Yes, sir. I stayed with me ship, like any good captain would do. I don't know what happened to the rest of them, but the next thing I knew I was at the bottom of the ocean. And that's where I stayed until that day last month when the ocean spit me up on dry land. I felt like ol' Jonah musta felt. You know Jonah, don't you, sir?"

Again with the Bible coming back to Sam. He guessed he learned more than he realized all those years on the ship when life got boring and he had nothing else to do but to read the Bible the lady who took him in gave him when he set sail from England when he was but a lad.

Sam suddenly clammed up. His mind went to the things he had seen in the museum, as well as the items he'd seen on the computer. Nobody mentioned the Bible. Maybe they never found it. The steel box it was in was supposed to be waterproof, but maybe it hadn't worked as well as it was supposed to. Or maybe there was a lot more loot down there that they hadn't found yet. He closed his eyes and tried to picture the things he had seen at the museum. There was only maybe a third of the things the computer had shown. What had happened to the rest of them?

"Don't say another word," Lyle ordered as he bounded into the room.

"And who do you think you might be?" Sam asked.

"He's a lawyer," Blair said, finally getting a chance to say something. "I called him when Angus told me they'd brought you down here."

"What's a lawyer?" Sam asked.

"It's what they call a barrister in England," Lyle interjected. He detected his English accent immediately, so no matter when he came from, he at least knew the *where*.

"I'm afraid, sir, I have no gold with which to pay you." Sam grinned, the gold in his teeth shining. "Unless you want to pull my teeth. Other than that, it appears that the museum has laid claim to all of my belongings."

"I need some time alone with my client," Lyle said, motioning toward the door and waiting for the chief and the detective to leave. Blair stood firm, not moving.

"You can leave too, Missy," he said, using the pet name Blair's father often used with her. She cringed. She didn't like Lyle. He was a slob. He drank too much. He had a beer belly as evidence. His receding hair line belied his age, making him look much older than he really was. Maybe the thing that aggravated her the most about him was the way he would get right up in your face and blow his stale breath at you. Still, he was the best attorney the Cape had to offer. If Sam had a chance at getting sprung, it was with Lyle as his legal counsel.

Blair stood her ground, not budging an inch. "I'm footing the bill for this one, so if you want your money you'll let me stay here."

"Whatever," Lyle said, shrugging his shoulders. He pulled a chair out from the table and turned it around and straddled it, putting his hands on the back of it and leaning his head on his hands. He was silent, studying Sam like he was a rat in a medical laboratory, just waiting for somebody to pounce on him.

"Well?" Blair finally asked. "What are you going to do to get him out of here?"

"For starters, let's hear your story, Sam, or whoever you are. That's quite the yarn you've been spinning for everybody. You think people are dumb enough to swallow your line?"

Sam tried to stand up, but he forgot about the handcuffs and he nearly lost his balance. Instead, he fell back onto the chair again, the chains rattling. "They make as much noise as the jangles on my new boots." He stared down at his feet. He was in his stockings. His boots were still in Angus's car, and he knew they would be way too big for Angus. He started to laugh. "Damn boots anyway. That's what gave me away, you know."

"What are you talking about?" Lyle asked him, getting more exasperated by the moment when he couldn't get a straight answer out of the imposter.

"Doc Angus bought me a new pair of boots because he wrecked my old ones."

Lyle shook his head. "Never mind. Let's just cut to the chase. So what is your name?"

"Sam Bellamy. Although when I came up out of the water, I told people I was Sam Black. You see, originally I was known as Black Sam Bellamy. But that was in another lifetime."

"Should be easy to get this one thrown out on the grounds of mental incompetence. Nobody would believe him for a second."

"What's that mean?" Sam asked, looking to Blair for an answer.

"It means he thinks you're crazy. A lunatic."

"What I've been through, who wouldn't be a bit mad?"

"Okay, just for the record," Lyle said, "let's hear your story. The whole thing." He pushed the button on the tape recorder.

"What's that thing?" Sam asked. It was clear that he didn't trust Lyle or anything he had to do or say.

"It's a tape recorder," Blair answered. "Show him what it does, Lyle."

Lyle spoke into the recorder, giving the date, the time, and the reason he was there. He hesitated when he said, "I am here to take a statement from...Sam Black, aka Sam Bellamy, aka Black Sam Bellamy."

He stopped the recorder and rewound it. He played it back so Sam could hear the same thing he had just listened to.

Sam rubbed his beard. "That's as bad as a television with all the little people running around inside a box."

"I've gotta hand it to him," Lyle said to Blair. "He's good. He could almost pass for the guy. Some stranger out of the past. But we know that's impossible. There is no such thing as time travel."

"That's what they used to say about putting a man on the moon," Blair reminded Lyle. This puzzled Sam even more. Next thing you know, Blair was going to try to convince him that they had actually done that too.

Sam started at the beginning, telling Lyle how he had been cast into the depths of the sea when his ship was split in two by lightning.

"And when was that?" Lyle asked.

"April 17, 1717," Sam answered matter-of-factly.

"This is unbelievable!" Lyle said, his eyes as wide as saucers. "Continue."

"I had no idea how long I was down there until one day I guess the sea got as tired of me as I was of it and it spit me up onto the dry land."

"And when was that?"

"April 17, but I learned that it was this year. I guess that's 2008."

"And you expect me to believe that you were in the ocean for almost three hundred years?"

"So it would seem. It's as odd to me as it is to you."

"Okay, let's move on. What happened last night? They said you broke into the Whydah Museum. Why?"

"I wasn't going to take anything, even though it all belongs to me. They stole it from me. Well, from the *Whydah*. I was just going to look at it. I tried to jimmy the door first, but it wouldn't move, so I tried the window. I was just going to pry it open, but before I knew it, the blasted thing busted into a million pieces. So, I picked the little slivers of glass out the best I could and I crawled in."

"And then?" Lyle asked.

"I started looking around to see what was there, and I realized somebody'd beat me to my own game. A lot of the things I saw on the computer were gone. Somebody'd already taken a bunch of the loot."

"You want me to believe that you had been buried in the ocean for all that time, but when you surfaced you just automatically knew how to use a computer."

"Of course not," Sam said. "Widow Clark, over at the Inn where I'm staying, she showed me how to use it. That's where I saw the things that were in the museum, but they weren't all there." He paused a bit. "Like the statue of me." He laughed, that deep throaty roar Blair had come to love. "They did a pretty good job of it, actually. Except I think I'm a mite taller than the statue, although I never did see it. Not really. Just in the pictures."

"So the statue was gone when you got to the museum? Blair, do you know what happened to it?"

"I don't rightly know, but I imagine Ken—that's Ken Kinkor from the museum—could tell you. I can't say for sure, but I sort of think he might have come down here. He might be out front."

Lyle went to the window and tapped on it. The detective came in.

"Is Ken Kinkor out there?" Lyle asked.

"Yup. Couldn't keep him away. I told him this might be a long night by the time we finished up with the guy."

"Could you ask him to step inside for a minute?" Lyle asked, his question followed by a huge burp. Blair felt like she was going to be sick.

Ken came into the room and Lyle told the detective he could leave. He knew this was going to hit the national headlines and he wasn't about to share the glory with some mere detective.

"You know this man?" Lyle asked Ken.

Ken grinned at Blair, then winked at Sam. "Sure. He's Black Sam Bellamy."

"You really believe that rubbish?" Lyle asked.

"His story sounds pretty credible to me." He motioned for Blair to follow him to a corner of the interrogation room so they could talk without being heard.

"I've got a plan, if you're willing to play along with me," he told Blair.

"What?" Blair asked, feeling the palms of her hands get sweaty from the mere anticipation of something fun.

"How well do you know this fellow?"

"Better than anybody else, I guess."

"Do you trust him?"

Blair hesitated. She honestly didn't know, but she was sure if she was going to get in on whatever Ken had up his sleeve, she needed to at least pretend that she did.

"I guess so. Why?"

"If Lyle what's-his-face can get him released, would you be willing to let it be to your recognizance? Would you be willing to assume responsibility for him?"

Blair could just imagine trying to tame a pirate. *The taming of a pirate,* she mused. *That could top Shakespeare's shrew any day.*

"Well, it would make life interesting," she admitted. "I guess so. I need to talk to him alone first to make sure he understands what's involved. But what's your plan? I can see those wheels turning up there." She pointed to his head.

"I won't know for sure if we can make this work or not. I'll have to run it by Barry first."

"What?"

"I think we could help Sam, or whoever he is, survive in today's world."

Blair waited for him to continue.

"I think we could use him at the museum. He does seem to be pretty well informed of everything about Black Sam, even if he isn't him. How cool would it be to have Black Sam conduct the tours at the museum?" Ken's eyes lit up like the Christmas tree in Rockefeller Center. "People might even start to believe him."

"Do you?" Blair asked pointedly.

"Don't know. Part of me—the sane part, if there is one—says no way is it possible. But the other part of me, I don't know, I just get this creepy feeling that it really is him. I know that doesn't make any sense, but most of life doesn't make any sense."

By the time they went back over to the table, Lyle was on the phone to a judge, trying to talk him into letting a crazy man loose on the streets. Ken motioned for him to hang up so he could talk to him.

"I have to go for right now," Lyle said, "but is it okay if I call you back in a few minutes?" He waited for an answer, then he said, "Thank you, sir." He heard the judge laughing as he hung up. He could just imagine what he was telling his wife.

"So what's up?" Lyle asked Ken.

"If you can get him released to Blair's custody, she's willing to keep an eye on him."

"You in for that?" he asked Blair, surprised that she would even consider it. If she was his daughter, there's no way he would trust that pirate with her. Not for an hour, and who knew how long it might be before they could get this thing sent to court. The longer it took, the more he could milk it for all the publicity he could get out of it. He could sell this one to a tabloid for mega bucks.

"I need to talk to Sam alone for a couple of minutes, then I can give you my answer."

Lyle and Ken left the room. Sam looked at her. He was shaking—but not in his boots, which made her snicker.

"Are you all right?" she asked.

"Yeah, but the last time I was in jail was the day I ended up being thrown in the ocean. And then the storm... Oh, nothing makes any sense."

"You weren't in jail," Blair said, trying to recall the accounts of the day of the demise of the *Whydah*. "You never made it onto shore."

"I remember being there," Sam argued. "I was at Crosby's Tavern, the place where I first met Maria. John and Jonathan—they must have been talking by then, and I don't know how that happened—grabbed me. Then something or somebody stuck me in the rear end with the sharpest bite I've ever felt in my life. All the mosquitoes in South America or the tsetse flies in Africa never packed a wallop like that."

❈ ❈ ❈

Martin was stretched out in his recliner, glancing at his watch, waiting for the last few minutes until the nightly news came on. He was a creature of habit. He watched the news every night, then immediately went to bed.

Maggie was out in the kitchen, setting the automatic coffeepot for the morning. She liked nothing better than to wake up to the smell of freshly brewed coffee.

"Maggie!" Martin let out a shrill yell. "Get in here. Now! You won't believe this."

She got in just as they showed a whole caravan of police cars pulling up in front of the Whydah Museum. "The man who claims to be Black Sam Bellamy allegedly broke a window of the museum and climbed inside, where the cops discovered him posing like the statue that is normally in the corner of the main display room."

"What?" Maggie said. "Why would he do that?"

"I told you you can't trust him," Martin said. "Hush! There is more."

"The man was taken in handcuffs to the police station. Before long the young woman who staged the whole festival to remember the sinking of his ship, the *Whydah*, came to the station, accompanied by another young woman and Dr. Angus MacPherson, a noted up-and-coming OB/GYN physician from Yarmouth, who also practices in Hyannis. Before long they were joined by attorney Lyle Carter. Please stay tuned, as we will bring you any breaking news as we learn more details."

"I've got to get to the police station," Martin said as he grabbed a sweatshirt and pulled it on over his head.

"What do you think you can do?" Maggie asked.

"I don't know, exactly, but I have to get Blair away from there. She's in too much trouble already. Everybody in town knows that she's befriended the rat."

He was already backing out of the driveway. It was too late for Maggie to catch him. She waved her arms in the air and called out to him, but he was oblivious to her. She listened to the rest of the news after he left.

"What's he going to do to her when he finds out the judge has sent Sam home with her? He's apt to kill the pirate." She shivered at the mere idea of what he might do. Would Sam be set free, released to Blair's care, while Martin ended up in jail for attempted murder? How would she ever survive without him?

CHAPTER XXV

Martin nearly broke the door at the police station when he swung it open.

"Where are they?" he shouted.

"Who?" the desk clerk asked him, although she was sure he knew who he was looking for. She had graduated from high school with Blair, and she knew Martin. She was pretty much a "nobody" in school, so it gave her a divine sense of superiority being able to keep him at bay, having to wait for her to fill him in on what was going on. Even so, she really didn't have to tell him anything. He had no rights to privileged information, not that it was all that secret after being on the news.

Hearing the commotion in the outer office, the chief went out.

"Evenin', Martin. I figured you'd show up sooner or later. Guess it's later."

"What do you mean?"

"They already left. You know, you ought to put a rein on that girl of yours."

"You know as well as I do," Martin said, "that's next to impossible. You didn't do so well with that girl of yours either, from what I hear."

The chief bristled. It was a well-known fact that she'd run off with a guy who was about as crooked as they came. Last Martin had heard they were on the run from the law after a bank robbery someplace in Virginia.

Port Call to the Future

"At least this varmint's behind bars," Martin said. "It's the only place the town's safe from the likes of him."

The chief grinned at the chance to get back at Martin. "Sorry, buddy, but he's free and clear. Well, almost."

"What do you mean?" Martin asked, the blood vessels in his face nearly popping.

"He left here with that doctor fellow and your girl. Seems the lawyer talked the judge into releasing him to your daughter."

"What?" Martin yelled, banging his fist on the desk, then rubbing his hand. "How could you let that happen?"

"You know as well as I do that a judge overrides my say-so on anything important."

Martin tore out of the police station and headed for Blair's house. How could this be happening? The guy had to be an imposter. Granted, he was one fine actor. At one point Sam almost had him convinced that he really was Black Sam Bellamy. *Magic*, Martin thought as he sped down the street. *Black magic! There's no way he could have survived for three hundred years. It's impossible.*

He saw Dr. MacPherson's car in the driveway, as well as Jenny's. *At least she's not alone with the scoundrel.*

Martin's heart was pounding like it would explode inside his chest. He didn't knock, as this was family. It was, he was convinced, a matter of life and death. There wasn't room to park in the driveway with all three cars already there, so he parked on the street in front of the house. He went to the front door and grumbled when he found it locked.

"Damn rat's already inside. No point in locking the door," he said as he made his way around to the back door. He could see the lights in the kitchen burning brightly, so he figured they must be there anyway.

As he entered, he found them all sitting at the kitchen table, drinking coffee and laughing. Laughing! This was no laughing matter.

Blair looked up at him and stood up to go get another cup and pour some coffee for her father. "Coffee, dad? It's not decaf, but you look like you could use a cup."

Martin didn't answer her, but headed straight for Sam. He grabbed him by the collar of the pirate's costume he was still wearing. He lifted him up off the chair and stepped on his toe, causing Sam to cry out in pain and agony. He should have stopped at Doc Angus's car and gotten his boots. It wouldn't have hurt nearly as bad if he'd had them on.

Martin drew his hand back, a fist heading straight for Sam's face, when Angus grabbed his arm and stopped him.

"Let me at him!" Martin shouted at Angus. "I'll have his head!"

"Dad," Blair said, "take it easy. He hasn't done anything that wrong. He just wanted to see his belongings. You know, the stuff that's at the museum."

"Yeah," Sam complained, "and somebody already beat me to my loot. Over half of it's missing. Somebody stole my booty right out from under the noses of those men running that museum. I intend to find out who's got it, and they'll rue the day they tried to outsmart Black Sam Bellamy. At least when it was in the museum I knew it was safe. Now, God only knows what's become of it."

Sam caught himself just in time before he blurted out that at least some things were safe in the root cellar. He vowed anew to get down there as soon as he could. He was sure his emeralds—the *piece de resistance*—was still there. Nobody knew about it. Suddenly he was hit with the thought that many years earlier Thomas and Sarah Hallett knew that he had hidden things there. What if they had taken it out when they heard that he was gone?

Martin wrestled with Angus, determined to beat Sam to a pulp. Angus chuckled slightly as he wished he had brought his medical bag in with him. He always carried a couple of ampules filled with a sedative in case of an emergency. A good swift stick in the butt might be the only way to get Martin to calm down. For a moment, he felt a strange tinge of regret for even thinking such a thing. He had sworn to uphold the Hipppocratic oath, and the thought of using his medical skills and equipment for such a matter were not part of his person. He was a good doctor. He would never do anything to endanger another person, not even if it was to protect another person. Or would he?

Martin finally sat down and shook his head. "What are you thinking?" he asked Blair. "Surely you can't keep the likes of this—this—this imposter here with you. I will take him back to the Inn. He'll be out of your hair, at least for now. We'll deal with long range plans tomorrow. By now I'm sure your mother is going out of her mind, wondering where I am and if you are okay."

"It's settled already, Dad," Blair said. "The judge only let him free on the condition of his staying where I can see him at all times."

"Which judge was it? I'll call him."

"It was Judge Berkins," Blair said.

"That shouldn't be a problem," Martin said, reaching for his cell phone. "We golf together. Have for years. I'm sure he'll understand the danger this puts you in."

"It was Judge *Penny* Berkins," Blair said, a smirk on her face. "The old judge retired over a year ago. How long has it been since you've seen him or golfed with him?"

"I guess longer than I thought," Martin said. He knew better than to try to tangle with Penelope Berkins. She was the head of the local chapter of the Women's Lib movement. He couldn't think of what they called themselves, but he knew she would take Blair's side in a second.

"Then I'm spending the night with you," Martin asserted.

"No need to do that," Jenny said. "I'll be glad to stay with them to see that they don't get into any..." She thought about saying "trouble," but decided "mischief" sounded better.

"I suppose that's all right," Martin conceded. "But if he gives you any trouble you promise you'll call me right away. Hear?"

"Yes, Dad," Blair assured him. "Now you'd better get home to Mom. Like you said, she's going to be worried."

Martin got up and headed for the door. As soon as he was gone, Sam leaned over and gave Blair a big kiss, surprising both of them. He wasn't quite sure what got into him. Was it a kiss of gratitude? A kiss of passion? A kiss of—wishing she was Maria? He honestly didn't know.

Blair was stunned, but both Jenny and Angus noticed that she didn't try to pull away from him. When they finally broke,

Jenny asked, "And just what was that for? I'm supposed to be here to monitor your behavior. I promised your dad I wouldn't let you get into any mischief. You sure don't make it easy to keep that promise."

Blair giggled. Sam blushed beneath his black beard. His eyes danced with delight. It felt good. It felt as good as the night he'd kissed Maria—and a whole lot more. He knew he had to be careful or he'd end up with a second notch in his belt for another conquest, but it wasn't one he wanted. Or did he? He could think of worse things.

"If you're sure you are going to be okay, I'm going to head home," Angus said.

"We'll be just fine," Jenny said. "I'll keep an eye on them. Go ahead."

Angus left, but he soon returned. He was holding Sam's boots out in front of him. "Need these?" he asked. "Seems like your boots carry bad karma with them wherever they go," he teased. "First you fall down the ladder in the root cellar and mess up your ankle and we have to cut them off. Then you leave them behind and get caught in the museum because you don't have them on. Maybe you should go back to the running shoes Blair got you."

"You forget, mate, the reason I got caught was because I *didn't* have them on. And don't forget that Mr. Smythe stepped mighty damn hard on my foot—and I wouldn't have even felt it if I'd had the blasted boots on. Methinks it's the lack of havin' me boots on that causes the problem." He flashed a grin at Angus, the gold in his teeth catching the light and setting forth a streak of brilliance. "Now git, will ya?"

"Aye, aye, cap'n," Angus said, giving him a salute and leaving—again.

After a few minutes, Sam said to Blair, "Maybe your father was right. Maybe I should go to the Inn for the night."

"No way," Blair said. "The cops are parked out front, just down the block a little ways. I'm sure they've been instructed to arrest you if you set foot out of my house or my yard. You have to stay right here, and that's final. I trust you."

But I don't trust myself, Sam thought.

Port Call to the Future

※ ※ ※

Blair debated about what to do about the sleeping arrangements. There was only one bedroom on the ground floor, and that was hers. She thought about letting Sam sleep there so she and Jenny could both be separated from him in one of the four upstairs bedrooms. She wasn't sure she wanted to leave Jenny up there alone with him, yet she knew, from watching them, that neither one of them was interested in the other one. Not in a million years. Oh, sure, Jenny was fascinated by his tales, but it didn't go beyond that. She could just imagine Sam in her bedroom, searching through all of her notebooks about him and Maria. No, that wouldn't work. Finally, she decided that the only way to deal with it was for all three of them to take one of the upstairs bedrooms.

It was getting late, and she was getting tired. It had been a crazy, busy day. She was glad that she always kept the extra beds all made up so she didn't have to mess with that.

"We are all going to sleep upstairs tonight," she announced.

Sam jerked and asked, "Are you serious? We are all going to sleep together? No! We can't do that!"

"Don't get your knickers in a knot," Blair said, laughing at such an old phrase. It was one of her Grandpa Hallett's favorites. "There are four bedrooms." She grinned and added, "And one of them has a lock on the outside. Sam, you will take that room, just in case you get any crazy ideas."

I could always go out the window, he thought. *They wouldn't know I was gone until the morning.*

"I thought you said you trusted me," he teased.

"I do, as long as I can either see or hear you."

"You could sleep in the same room as I'm in, just to make sure."

"Not on your life!" Jenny shouted. "Your dad would have my head if I let you do that."

"And such a pretty little head it is," Sam said, his eyes sparkling with the mischief Jenny had promised to keep at bay.

They all went upstairs and Blair pointed to Sam's room. Just as she had said, there was a lock on the outside.

"You weren't fooling, were you?"

"Never been more serious in my life," she said, grinning at him.

"Okay," he said, shrugging his shoulders, ready to face the doom of a strange, lonely room. He was not expecting the next thought to enter his mind. *It would be much more fun if we were in the same room. Whoa, boy! Look what trouble that kind of thinking got you into before. Leave it alone.*

Blair and Jenny headed for the other end of the hallway, where their rooms were across from each other.

"You tired?" Blair asked.

"Yeah, kind of. It's been a long day. Why?"

"I thought maybe we could talk a bit."

"I'm game," Jenny said, following Blair into her bedroom. As they plopped on the big old four-poster bed, she asked, "So what's up?"

"I don't know," Blair said. "I wish I did. I told you I can't help feeling what I'm feeling—for Sam."

"Are you serious? You've done some crazy things before, but that has to be the craziest thing you've ever done." She studied Blair carefully. "Your mom and dad would never stand for you to—um, get involved with somebody like Sam."

"Somebody like Sam," Blair repeated. "That's just it. There is nobody else like Sam."

"Well, you're sure right on that one. I've never heard of or met anybody else who claims to be over three hundred years old."

"Especially not one who looks like Sam," Blair said, grabbing her pillow and holding it close to her body. "You have to admit he's a hunk."

"I'll give you that. A mighty old hunk."

"But if his body is that of a thirty-year-old..." She rolled her eyes as an idea hit her. "What if we have him examined by a doctor?"

"And just what do you intend to tell the doctor? He'd have you locked up instead of Sam."

"What about if Angus examined him and did lab tests and stuff?" Blair asked.

Jenny laughed. "Are you forgetting that Angus is a baby doctor? What would he know about a pirate?"

"He's still a doctor. He had to study other things in med school before he could declare his specialty. I'm sure he could do it."

"I'm going to call him first thing in the morning," Blair said, "and see if he's game to try it. After all, it should be a rare treat for a doctor to examine such a specimen as Sam."

"Good luck," Jenny said, going toward the door. "I think we both need some sleep." She was shaking her head as she shut the door and went to her own room.

❈ ❈ ❈

Blair tossed and turned all night. When she did finally fall asleep, she dreamed about Sam. She saw him being washed up out of the ocean like he did on the day of the festival. She saw him standing at attention in the *Whydah*. She watched as he struggled to get his boots off, then saw Angus cutting the one off his twisted ankle. She saw him... She saw him holding her close to himself, kissing her, then...then she woke up.

"Darn it!" she whispered into her pillow. She couldn't help it. She wanted him to be there with her. She was tempted to go unlock his door and crawl in bed with him, but she knew better.

Maybe tomorrow we'll have some answers from Angus, she thought as she drifted back to sleep again, this time content in knowing that he was just down the hall from her. She would have to call Judge Penny Berkins tomorrow and thank her for letting him be in her charge. Oh, yes, she definitely owed the judge a big favor.

CHAPTER XXVI

The sun was already up when Blair heard Sam yelling at the top of his lungs. "Let me outa this bloody hold. I'm not a prisoner. They set me free. Now! I want to get out—now!"

There was silence for a few moments, then another outburst. "Let me out *now*! Damn it, I have to pee!"

Blair couldn't help it. She grabbed her bathrobe and pulled it on, zipping it up all the way to her neck, protecting herself from...what? He knew Jenny was there. No way would he attack her nor do anything improper. She had forgotten that there was only one bathroom upstairs. *Hmmm, wonder what a pirate does on the ship? Even on older ships, like the Whydah, were there "facilities"? They probably had thundermugs.*

"I'm coming," Blair called out to Sam. "Just keep your pants on."

"They'll be bloody wet ones if you don't hurry up."

Blair unchained the lock on the door and Sam sailed past her faster than any ship on the roiling seas with a high wind at its back. The door to the bathroom slammed shut and Jenny appeared in her doorway. She too was grinning.

"Did he make it?" she asked.

"I think so," Blair said. "Maybe I shouldn't have locked the door. I never thought about..."

"And let him run away? Who knows where he would have gone, or what he might have done. He was more than a little bit upset last night."

Sam joined them in the hallway. "Any grub on the burner yet? A man could starve to death around here."

Blair headed for the stairway and was followed by the other two. The smell of the coffee that had been pre-programmed to brew in the morning wafted through the air.

"Pancakes okay?" she asked, and Jenny and Sam nodded.

She poured some sort of a powdery stuff from a box marked Bisquick. Sam watched, fascinated, as she added a little milk and a couple of eggs to the dry stuff and stirred it up. Back on the *Whydah* the cook had taken flour and other raw materials to make pancakes. *More modern conveniences,* he thought. *I wonder if anybody today knows how to do anything the simple way?*

As they sat at the table, Sam asked, "So what do we do today? I guess I still can't go anywhere. How long is that going to last? I can't take being penned up like some common criminal."

"That's up to the court," Blair said. "In their eyes, that's exactly what you are. You broke the law when you broke and entered the museum."

Sam laughed. "I broke the window, that's what I did. If that's breakin' the law, then I broke the law too. I still don't see how that's so wrong, since it's all me own loot in there."

"But you can't prove that it is yours, or even that you are who you say you are," Blair said.

"Then find a way to prove it to them. I am what I am."

Jenny broke into some silly song as soon as he said that. "I yam what I yam and tha's all what I yam."

"That's just plain stupid," Sam snapped. "Of course everybody is that they am. I don't understand that at all."

"Actually, it was a sailor who said that," Jenny said. "Popeye the Sailor Man. Blair, can we get a tape of some of his stuff?"

"I'm sure we can find some somewhere," Blair said. "Or maybe we can find some on YouTube."

"What's your tube?" Sam asked.

"It's..." Blair threw her hands up in despair. "It's not *your* tube. It's *YouTube.*"

"Whatever," Sam said. Jenny chuckled. He was catching on to a lot of today's popular phrases. He sounded—almost modern!

Blair steered the conversation back to proving that Sam was—or wasn't—who and what he claimed to be. He was playing right into her hand and her plan, even though he didn't know it.

"I think there might be a way to prove that you are telling the truth," she said.

"Give him a lie detector test?" Jenny asked.

Blair shook her head.

"Give him some truth serum?" Jenny asked further.

"Nope," Blair said. "We will need Angus's help to do it." She looked Sam square in the eyes and asked, "Will you cooperate?"

"If it will prove I'm no lyin' viper, of course I will."

Blair reached behind her to the phone. She punched the number she had programmed that would reach Angus. He was proving to be a mighty handy person to have around.

The nurse at his office answered. She knew by now he would already be at the hospital making his early rounds for the day.

"I'd like to speak to Dr. McPherson."

"I'm sorry, but he hasn't come in yet. May I take a message? Or may I help you?"

Blair hated it when people who were underlings acted like they had all the power in a place. Oh, the nurse was pleasant enough. *Too pleasant*, Blair thought. She knew she was going to have trouble with this one.

"It's personal," Blair said, exasperation filling her voice. "Would you please tell him that Blair called and ask him to return the call as soon as possible. Tell him it's important."

"What is your last name, Blair?"

"He'll know who I am."

"I need a last name, Ms...."

"Fine. Just tell him 'the almost Blair' called. I told you, he'll know who it is."

"I said, I need a last name, Ms...."

Blair pushed the button on the phone to disconnect them. "Stupid people!" she grumbled.

❅ ❅ ❅

Blair jumped when the phone rang just a few minutes later. She figured it would be Angus, so she answered cheerfully, "Good morning, handsome. I need your help with Sam."

Her face reddened when another man's voice replied, "Well, that's the nicest greeting I've had in a good long spell. What did Sam do this time?"

"Who—who is this?" Blair asked.

"It's Ken. Ken Kinkor. I need to speak to Sam. I understand he's a guest at your home?"

"If that's what you call him," Blair said. "It's not like I had a lot of choice in the matter, and that's partly your doing."

"I'm truly sorry, Blair, but I have a mind to do something that could help everybody come out of this whole pirate charade smelling like a bunch of roses."

Blair glanced at Sam. "I don't think that's possible," she said, chuckling. "A rose by any other name might always be a rose, but I suspect that a pirate by any other name will always be a pirate."

"Probably right," Ken said. "Now, if it isn't too much trouble, could I stop over to talk to Sam—and you?"

"We will be home all day, as far as I know," Blair said. *Good thing Grandpa Smythe left me with the money he did so I don't have to go to a 9-5 job. What would I do with Sam while I worked?*

"Okay, see you in a few minutes," Ken said and hung up.

"Who was that?" Sam asked.

"Ken Kinkor," Blair answered. "The man who runs the museum. He's coming over to see you—us."

"I've got to make me escape," Sam said, getting up and heading for the door. He no sooner got onto the top step outside when two police officers charged at him.

"Going somewhere?" one of them asked.

"Just out to get some fresh air," Sam said, deciding it was a bad idea to try to make a run for it, especially when he noticed that one of the cops had his hand on his gun. "A fellow could get downright musty, never getting' outside. Spent most of my life outdoors, unless you count bein' holed up in a ship as bein' inside."

Sam stretched and then turned around and went back into the house. Blair was on the phone again. This time, he surmised that it was Doc Angus who had called her back. He shook his head, trying to clear the cobwebs out of his mind. He didn't know why, but he couldn't get away from that "Doc Angus" thing. It was still like he'd known him, back in that other world. Yet it seemed impossible. Of course his being here today was just as much of an impossibility. He couldn't blame people for not believing him. He wouldn't believe it either, if somebody tried to tell him the same fool story.

"Okay, whenever you can. You think it might be tonight before you can make it?"

"No, I worked all night. Late delivery, or maybe I should say early one. Little lady kept me up all night before she finally decided to put in an appearance about 5:30 this morning. I just finished my rounds and I'm heading home to catch a few winks before I start seeing patients. It shouldn't take long to get what I need. I'll stop on my way home."

"It's all set," Blair informed them. "He'll be here shortly. He can do some tests in the lab that might shed some light on your story, Sam, one way or the other."

Sam didn't utter a sound.

"Are you all right with this?" Blair asked.

"I guess I don't have a lot of choice. Either I can try to prove that I really am Black Sam Bellamy or they can lock me up in the brig and throw away the key if they can prove that I'm not." He rubbed his beard nervously. "Sometimes I'm not even sure I am who I am."

"Well, maybe we'll have some answers shortly, as soon as Angus gets here and does what he has to do."

"Will it hurt?" Sam asked, causing both of the women to laugh. It was hard to imagine that a big burly pirate who had sailed the seven seas, captured boats, and pillaged treasures from countless others, would be afraid of anything.

❋ ❋ ❋

Angus pulled into the driveway and knocked on the back door.

"Come on in," Blair hollered out to him.

"You know, you really shouldn't do that," Angus said, scolding her.

"Do what?" Blair asked innocently.

"Invite strangers into the house. You never know who might show up. Life isn't safe anymore." He tipped his head towards Sam. "You never know what the cat might drag in."

"You have a cat?" Sam asked.

"No," Blair said. "It's just an expression. Something we say."

"Oh, another one of those things that doesn't make any sense." Sam shivered as he thought of the black cats that seemed to cross his path on different occasions. For some reason, he detested the critters, and he had no idea why.

Angus set his medical bag up on the table. He took an empty syringe from it, putting surgical gloves on, then removing the plastic wrappings. Sam's usual brawny face turned ashen. He didn't know what that thing was, or what Angus intended to do with it, but it gave him an eerie feeling that he didn't like.

Angus took a little vial of alcohol and a cotton swab and ordered Sam, "Okay, roll up your sleeve so I can get some blood."

"You think you are going to draw blood? From me? You'd better think again. I've not shed one ounce of blood in all me battles, and I'll not start now."

"I gather you didn't tell him what we are going to do?" Angus asked Blair.

"No, I figured it would be easier for you to explain it."

"We are just going to take a little sample of your blood. This little needle will go into your vein and this tube will fill with the blood. That's all we'll need."

"And then what?" Sam asked.

"Then we will take it to the lab at the hospital and see what we can find out about you."

"And what exactly do you expect to find out from my blood?"

"If you have any diseases, if you are diabetic, if you are anemic, and with any luck we will be able to determine approximately how old you are."

"I don't like it," Sam said, clasping the cuff of his shirt to keep Angus from getting at a vein.

"I thought you wanted to prove that you are telling the truth," Blair said. "This is the first step in trying to do that."

"And how many more steps are there?" Sam asked. "I don't understand any of the things you said you can learn from my blood." He threw back his head and laughed, his long hair, for a change not tied back in a knot, flying like a tree in a strong wind as he moved his head back and forth. "Maybe you will find that my blood is blue. Wouldn't that be somethin'? Me, Black Sam Bellamy, a blue blood!"

"We'll never know until we try it," Angus said. "Now, roll up your sleeve."

Angus slowly complied, but he kept his hand over his arm as much as he could. He still wasn't comfortable with this whole thing, and he certainly didn't understand any of it. A lab? What was a lab, anyway?

Angus took the cotton swab with the alcohol on it and rubbed it on Sam's arm. He took the syringe and held it up, ready to insert it into one of Sam's veins. As soon as he stuck it in, Sam screamed and jumped up, causing the syringe to come out of the vein. Angus grabbed it, and Sam grabbed Angus. He fought with him, and it was obvious that Sam was going to be the winner in this battle. Sam was much stronger and bigger than Angus, but Angus did his best to fend him off.

Blair and Jenny both went to try to help, but Angus warned them to stay back and let him handle it. "I don't want either of you to get hurt," he warned.

Just in a nick of time, Ken showed up. He heard the ruckus inside so he charged in, not bothering to knock or ring the doorbell. He immediately went to Angus's aid and delivered a swift blow to Sam directly in the face, sending the pirate careening to the floor.

"What were you going to do to him?" Ken asked Angus. "Or do I want to know?"

Blair explained their plan and they all looked at Sam, lying helpless on the floor. Afraid that he would wake up and attack all of them again, Ken suggested, "Can you get what you need if I sit on him, just in case he comes to again?"

"Should be able to," Angus said, once again inserting the syringe into Sam's arm. He filled the tube quickly and easily. He held it up and grinned. "He didn't have to worry about that. His blood is as red as can be. No blue blood in the guy. I should get another vial just to be sure they have enough to run all the tests they need to."

As he prepared to insert the second syringe into Sam's arm, Sam began to rouse and he grabbed for Angus, prepared to attack him again.

"You got anything to calm him down?" Ken asked.

Angus reached into his medical bag and extracted a shot filled with a sedative. "This should do the trick," he said. "I never leave home without one. Never know when you'll meet up with something you can't control."

Angus took his foot and rolled Sam onto his side, aiming directly for his butt. Again, Angus screamed. This time, though, he was hurling accusations at Angus.

"You were there! I felt something hit me like the biggest mosquito that ever was. Then that was the last I remembered before they hauled me off to jail. It was you. You were there."

Angus shook his head in disbelief. He had no idea what Sam was talking about, but it certainly made no sense. He managed to stick the shot into Angus, and in a matter of a few seconds he was once again out cold.

"Get out of here," Ken said to Angus. "I'll deal with him when he wakes up. I don't know what that was all about, but there are certainly a lot more questions to find answers to." He looked at Angus, a puzzled look on his face, and said, "Maybe questions about more than just Black Sam. Go! Get out of here! He's likely to kill you if he sees you here when he comes to."

Angus put the two tubes of blood in his medical bag, closed it, then went to his car and steered it in the direction of the lab at his office. There was far too much at risk for him to go home and get any rest. There were too many questions to be answered. Too much truth to try to uncover. Sleep would have to wait.

CHAPTER XXVII

Ken sat down in a chair across the room from Sam once he was sure he was back among the living. *Boy, is that ironic,* he thought. *If there's any way in hell that he's who he says he is, that's truer than anybody can imagine.*

"I've got a proposition for you."

"What?" Sam asked, not sure he could trust this guy. He guessed he had better, since he was holding all of his booty. He did seem to be concerned about it. Last night, when he broke into the museum, he was pretty shook up when he thought the statue was gone.

"By the way," Sam asked, "what happened to that statue of me? I saw it on the computer, but when I got inside, it was nowhere to be found."

"Barry came and picked it up to take with him on the traveling exhibit across the country, along with all the other things he took to show off. I didn't know it was gone until I called him and told him you had somehow managed to get rid of it and that you had been impersonating the dummy. You could have fooled everybody if it hadn't been for your missing boots."

"Damn boots!" Sam sputtered.

Sam realized that must be what had happened to the other things that were missing too. He felt a sense of relief in knowing that the proper people had possession of them. *Ha! The proper people indeed. I am the rightful owner. How can I get them back in my hands? Back where they belong?*

He wondered how he would make any use of them. He couldn't sell them. People would know they were stolen, even if they were his. The police would surely throw him in jail if he tried to break in there again. He didn't see any choice but to trust this Ken, and Barry, whoever he was. He remembered Blair saying something about some Barry being the head of the group that found the *Whydah*. This must be that Barry.

"So what's your offer?" Sam asked Ken.

"How would you like a job at the museum?"

"Doing what?"

"You could dress up like you did last night and pretend to be Black Sam Bellamy."

"Pretend?" Sam bellowed. "What do you mean; 'pretend'? I *am* Black Sam Bellamy!"

"Guess we'll know soon enough, once the doc gets the results of your blood tests," Ken said. He turned to Blair. "Any idea how long that will take?"

"He said he would put a rush order on it. He said at the most a day or two."

"Still don't see what no blood has to do with who I am or where I'm from," Sam grumbled. "Me blood is as pure as the driven snow."

"And I'm Rumplestilskin," Ken said.

"Who?"

"Never mind. A made up character, just like you." Ken scratched his head, trying to formulate exactly how he thought it could work to have Sam at the museum.

Sam harrumphed but didn't argue. No point in it, he figured. Ken would think whatever he wanted to think, and nothing Sam said would change his mind, at least not until they had the results of whatever these tests were Doc Angus was running.

"If you are an imposter," Ken said, "you've done a mighty fine job of doing your homework. You seem to know more about Black Sam Bellamy, the Whydah, the treasure, and even Maria."

"Leave Maria out of this," Sam said, slamming his fist on the arm of the sofa he was sitting on. "She's got nothing to do with this. She's been dead and buried for years. Don't go castin' nasty things on..." He paused. He caught himself just before he said, "the witch." Instead, he said, "the dead."

Ken started to say something when they were interrupted by a knock on the front door. Ken got up and went to answer it. A deputy sheriff was standing there, a subpoena in his hand.

"I need to see the pirate," the deputy said, laughing. "Have to have him sign that he got this. That is, if he can write."

"I can read and write, thank you," Sam said, snarling at the officer.

Suddenly, an idea hit Sam. He knew exactly how he could prove to Ken, as well as to Blair, that he really was Black Sam Bellamy. If they could just find it... Nobody else knew about it. Even his crew didn't know he kept it there, well hidden so he could amuse himself in times of loneliness.

"What if I refuse to press charges?" Ken asked.

"Why would you do that?" the deputy asked.

"Because he didn't take anything."

"But he did damage the property."

"The insurance will cover a new window," Ken said, winking at Blair and Jenny. "Take your paper back to the sheriff and tell him we've worked it out."

"Can't be that he'll pay for the damages," the deputy said. "Don't appear as how he's got any money. Unless, of course, you believe his bunk about the loot over at the museum belonging to him."

The deputy shrugged his shoulders and left. They all watched through the window as he got into his car and drove away, slowly.

❊ ❊ ❊

"You really are serious about hiring me?" Sam asked in disbelief. "But why?"

"Like I said," Ken said, "it appears that you know more about the whole affair than anybody." He paused a moment, then added, "Either you're the real McCoy or you did your homework mighty good."

"McCoys?" Sam asked. "Who the devil are the McCoys?"

Blair laughed. The whole feud between the Hatfields and the McCoys happened long after Sam had lived, she was sure.

"Never mind," Ken said.

"Ah," Sam said, scratching his beard. "Another 'nothin' answer, eh?"

"Anyway, back to business," Ken said, directing the conversation. "You ready to tackle it?"

"Sure," Sam said, his voice dripping with enthusiasm. "As long as you let me tell it my way."

"What other way is there?" Ken asked.

"Well, some of the information on that blame computer wasn't exactly right."

Ken bristled. "Like what?"

"Like where I got certain things. You had some of the countries all wrong." He glared at Ken. "And then there's the emeralds..."

"Never did find any damn emeralds," Ken grumbled. "Don't believe there were no emeralds."

"Would you believe me if I could bring them to you?" Sam asked.

"Maybe," Ken said. "Maybe not."

"What if I could tell you about something else—something you haven't found yet—that would prove it?"

"Maybe, maybe not," Ken repeated. "Like what?" Ken was getting more intrigued by the minute.

"I'll tell you later, when we're alone," Sam confided. "It's something that nobody else on the *Whydah* ever knew I had."

"Whatever," Ken said, finding it hard to believe that he was swallowing this fellow's line more and more. It was preposterous.

"So do you want to come with me?" Ken invited Sam.

"Might as well. Not much to do around here."

The two men left, getting into Ken's car and heading towards the museum.

❈ ❈ ❈

"So what's your big secret?" Ken asked, eyeing Sam dubiously.

"It's...it's a Bible."

Ken threw his head back and laughed uproariously. "A Bible? Of all the damn things for a pirate to have—a Bible?"

"Yup," Sam said, studying Ken's reaction. "Not so dumb. I mean, if I was going to be stuck out in the middle of the ocean someplace, figured I might as well have had some decent reading. After all, St. Paul was shipwrecked off the coast of Malta. And Jonah, well, even ol' Jonah got spit out of the belly of the waters a hell of a lot sooner than I did."

"Seems to me," Ken said, "though it's been a whole lotta years since I was a lad in Sunday School, that Jonah was in more trouble than just bein' in the water. Way I remember the tale, he was swallowed by one of those big whales."

"Speakin' of tales and whales and such like," Sam said, "I have a question to ask you."

"Ask away."

"Blair showed me some book or somethin' sayin' that Maria used to go out and hang a lantern on the tail of a whale to warn the sailors if there was danger onshore."

Ken laughed again. "I've heard the tale of the tail of the whale before."

"Can't be," Sam said, shaking his head defiantly. "Just plain can't be."

"You don't think Maria could manage that?"

"Couldn't nobody manage that," Sam said.

"But if she was a witch..." Ken offered.

"She warn't no witch!" Sam shouted. "Though she mighty near bewitched me. Never met another woman like her. Nope, she was a one-of-a-kind."

Ken watched Sam intently. "You really did love her?"

"More than my life itself," Sam admitted. "I'd have done anything for her."

"But you knew she had the babe?" Ken asked. "And that he died?"

Sam looked puzzled. "That's what don't make no sense."

The two men got into Ken's jeep and headed for the museum. They rode in silence. There would be plenty of time to try to figure things out once they were inside, where Ken could watch the way Sam interacted with the objects on display. He would try to get him to tell him details about them that they didn't know from their research. Ah, yes, this would be an interesting voyage.

CHAPTER XXVIII

"Look!" Sam shouted. "Somebody's tryin' to break into the museum."

Ken pointed to the truck from the repair shop he had called to replace the plywood he had stuck in place of the window Sam had broken. "No need to panic. They are going to put a new window in. Thanks to you, it's necessary."

Sam felt a bit of remorse for his actions of the night before. *Strange. I've never been sorry for a thing I've done in me life. Don't understand it, not for the life of me.* His thoughts caused him to shiver. Yup, it was a conscience, sure as anything. He wondered how he could get rid of it? And where did it come from? And why now, after all the years he'd been missing?

Once inside, Sam began fingering the various coins.

"This one's from Jamaica," he said. "And this one's from Liberia."

Ken went to the computer and turned it on. He did a quick search for "ancient coins from Liberia." Sure enough. There they were. He and Barry had assumed they were also from one of the British West Indies, since the writing was in English. They had both thought it odd that there was no country marking on them.

"How did you know that?" Ken asked.

Sam laughed. "'Tis simple, my friend. 'Twas me what hoisted them."

"From Liberia?"

"No, from a ship. The name of the vessel escapes me at the moment." Sam laughed again, and that twinkle sparkled in his eyes like it did when it was impossible to tell if he was telling the truth or spinning a yarn. "Seems like it's been a far spot away since it happened."

Ken could not help but join in the laughter. *This guy is good,* he thought. *Whether he's a fraud or not, this is going to be one great education. Wish Barry could be here to share in the experience.*

❋ ❋ ❋

Sam continued to examine everything, mostly in silence. When he finished, he went and sat down so he was face-to-face with Ken.

"So do you want to know about the one thing you didn't find?"

Ken's ears itched in eager anticipation. "You said it's a Bible. Are you serious?"

"Dead," Sam said, sending them both into fits of laughter. "Or so everybody believed."

"Let me see, where do I begin?" Sam stroked his beard. He knew that the tale he was about to tell was incredible. A pirate, by very virtue of being a pirate, is often said to not have a soul. Where did he go wrong? He heard from the people in Yarmouth that Maria was accused of witchcraft because she had been "cavorting with the devil." He, of course, was the devil they referred to.

"Someplace back in England," he began, "when I was a lad, I went to church. There was an old lady who came to fetch me every Sunday. It was the Church of England, of course. There was no other choice, unless you were a Roman."

"Do you remember her name?"

"Of course I do. It was Susannah Wesley. Her husband was Samuel, but he was often gone."

"Gone?" Ken asked. Like almost everybody in Christendom, he knew the name of the Wesleys well. They were, after all, the founders of modern-day Methodism. He chuckled. If they were alive then, as they obviously were, Methodism could hardly be considered "modern-day." "Where did he go?"

"I think one time he left her and all those children alone. I think they must have had a dispute of some kind, but she never talked about it. Another time I believe he was in prison."

"In prison?" Ken asked. This was certainly a part of his education that had been neglected. "For what?"

"He never made a decent living, and they would throw him in jail every so often for debts he owed."

"So how did the family survive?" Ken asked.

"Oh, Mother Wesley, she was a brilliant woman. She spoke five or six languages. She educated all the children. Let's see...I think there were about a dozen of them. Maybe more. Seems to me that some of them died too. Yeah, I think she told me one time she birthed nineteen of them."

"Nineteen children?" Ken gasped. "All from one mother?"

"That's what I said," Sam said. "Anyway, she gave me a Bible. Most precious thing I ever had. When I set sail on the seven seas I took it with me. I had a special tin that kept it dry. If the tin worked like it was supposed to, it should still be there, at the bottom of the ocean, right where I left it. You didn't find it?"

"Nope," Ken said. "Where was the tin? We still have a lot of things to get. Barry says we're going back in a couple of months to try to salvage some more stuff. If I know where to look, I'll see if we can find it."

A tear trickled down Sam's cheek. Why on earth should a book make him feel such a sense of loss? It was just a book.

"It was in the trunk 'neath me bunk. There was a big chain wrapped around it. There was a lock to hold it tight. Me most precious belongings were in there."

Ken wanted to ask him what else the trunk contained, but he felt like he was invading Sam's privacy. It contained his innermost secrets. He wondered if there was anything from Maria that he might have taken with him. Did Sam lie in his cabin alone at night, fondling something special from the woman he loved, dreaming of the day when they might be together again?

"You'll surely have to cut the chain. No telling where the key might have gone to." Sam paused, studying Ken's expression carefully. Could he trust this man? He guessed he didn't have much choice in the matter. Other than Blair, he didn't have all that many friends. He was sure that he couldn't count on Doc Angus as being trustworthy. He shivered as he thought about the doctor. He didn't know what it was, but something sure registered strange about that one. He still felt like he had been back in Yarmouth that fateful day when he disappeared. If he could come forward in time, as he apparently had, why couldn't Doc Angus do the same thing, only in reverse? Could it be that they had crossed paths in time? Did he somehow know the secret to time travel? If so, why did he act so innocent about the whole thing? He seemed genuinely sincere when he said that he had never met Sam before the day he washed up on shore.

※ ※ ※

"You can't be serious," Jenny told Blair. "You hardly know him."

"I know," Blair admitted, "but it's like I've known him forever. I can't explain it, not even to myself. I have never felt like this about anybody before. I can't imagine spending the rest of my life without him. I think I'd just die if I couldn't have him."

"But what if he wandered down to the shore one day and disappeared the same way he appeared, just coming out of nowhere?"

"I don't know. I guess I would do like Maria did and go down to the water every day and watch for him to return."

"You're too much of a woman to do that," Jenny challenged. "You are full of life. Full of fun. I couldn't bear to watch you just mope your life away on some dream. Maybe he is really just a figment of our imagination."

"We might know more once Angus gets the lab results," Blair suggested.

As if on cue, the phone rang, startling Blair. She jumped, then went and grabbed the phone.

"Hello."

"Blair?" the man's voice said. "It's Angus. The lab was pretty interested in the blood samples I brought in. They ran the tests right away. I think I'd better come over and see you and explain it in person. I'm going to bring the lab tech with me so he can maybe answer some of your questions."

Angus didn't wait for an answer, but hung up and ran out the door to get to Blair's as soon as possible.

In almost no time at all, Angus and George, the lab tech, were running up to Blair's front door. The lab tech had a manila envelope, which Blair assumed held the results of the tests.

"Come on in," Blair said, opening the door.

They all sat down in the living room. George spread the papers out on the coffee table. Blair glanced at them, but they might as well have been written in Greek. Jenny shook her head. "What does it all mean?" she asked.

"It's a real puzzle," George said. "I've never seen anything like it in my life."

"What does it all mean?" Blair repeated. "What did you find out?"

"It's like he doesn't exist," George said. "I wouldn't think he was a person at all, except that Angus swears he has seen him and that he took the blood sample directly from his veins."

"I don't understand," Blair said.

"Neither do I," George said. "There is no DNA. He has no blood type. Normally, the blood is made up of different parts: red cells, white cells, hemoglobin, platelets and plasma. The red cells determine a person's blood type. This fellow has no red cells. Actually, he has no white cells, no hemoglobin, no platelets. All he has is a bunch of plasma. Plasma, by itself, is useless. It is like a yellow tinted water. It has a bit of sugar, fat, protein and salt. Its whole reason for being is to carry the red cells, the white cells, and the platelets. Since he has none of those things, he might as well not have any plasma either." George shook his head, bewildered. "It can't be. It's impossible."

"Is there any way a person could live with blood like that?" Blair asked.

"I don't know," George said. Angus sat silently, trying to absorb how this could be possible. "I haven't done any studies on cloning. Maybe he's a made up somebody that some scientist created in his test tube."

"That's impossible," Blair said. "He...he knows things..."

"What kind of things?" George asked.

"He knows all about the *Whydah*," Angus said. "And Maria, and life from back in the 1700s. He truly believes he is Black Sam Bellamy."

"That's just plain crazy!" George exclaimed. "There has to be some logical explanation."

The room was filled with a deathly silence. Finally, Blair broke the spell by saying, "I'm waiting for it."

"I don't have one," George said, "but I'd sure like to figure this one out."

Suddenly, Angus's face lit up. "I have another idea. I thought the blood tests would reveal something, but they obviously didn't."

"We're waiting," George said. "What's your idea?"

"What if we got Paul to examine him? You know, put him under and see what develops."

"The shrink?" George asked.

"You got a better idea?" Angus asked.

"No, but I want to be there when he does it."

"Me too," Blair said, the blood rushing through her body in anticipation of looking into Sam's subconscious mind.

"Count me in," Angus said. "I wouldn't miss this one for the world. I'm going to go over and see Paul now. I can just see him itching to get at this one. I'm sure by now he's heard about Sam."

"*Everybody's* heard about Sam," Jenny said. They all nodded in agreement.

George gathered his papers up and he and Angus left.

Blair and Jenny sat there, staring at one another.

"Where were we before we were so rudely interrupted?" Blair asked.

"You were telling me that you can't live without Sam in your life. The non-man. The man who isn't."

"But I can't," Blair insisted. "Even if he isn't really a man." Suddenly she began laughing. "I always wanted children. What if he doesn't have any... You know, what if he can't..."

"Then I guess you'll have to adopt," Jenny said. "Looking at him, though, I'm willing to bet he's good to go. He definitely looks like a man. A real man."

"Guess time will tell," Blair said.

Blair's face went wan. "What about Mom and Dad? If I were to marry Sam, they would so totally freak out. They'd never allow it."

"How old are you?" Jenny asked.

"Twenty-six," Blair said. She pondered Jenny's comment. "I'm old enough to do it anyway."

"Seems to me that's true," Jenny said. "Besides, if it meant you not being in their lives, I'm willing to bet they'd come around eventually. Especially if there were grandkids involved."

"You really think so?"

"Positive," Jenny said. "You're the apple of their eye, especially your dad. Yup, Daddy's little girl. Bryan might be your mom's best friend, but there's nobody like you where your dad is concerned."

"You noticed, huh?" Blair said, winking at her best friend. "I just have to figure how to wrap him around my little finger before I broach the subject with him."

"Aren't you forgetting something?" Jenny asked.

"What?"

"Um, you don't have any idea how Sam feels about you. Seems to me you are sort of jumping the gun here."

"Then I guess I'll just have to feel him out. He has dropped hints more than once though."

They were so intent in their conversation they didn't hear Ken and Sam drive up and come up to the house. Sam was making himself quite at home and never bothered to knock anymore.

"Feel who out?" Sam asked.

Blair blushed at getting caught in their private discussion. "Nothing," she said.

"Ah, yes," Sam said, "another 'nothing' answer. I should have known. Well, when you want to clue me in, I'll be available."

Blair snickered at how modern Sam's language was becoming. One day he would belong, sure as anything. Maybe sooner than any of them realized.

CHAPTER XXIX

Ken gave Blair a quizzical look. Suddenly he felt very protective of her. He was used to being in charge of a lot of things, but young susceptible women was not one of them. If she was up to skullduggery, so be it. Why should it concern him anyway?

He and Sam sat down, joining the two young women. It was Jenny who spoke first.

"What did you think of the museum?" she asked Sam.

"It is interesting, but there is so much more."

"More what?" Blair asked.

"Loot. Me booty was far greater than what they've found."

Blair looked pensive, then asked Ken, "Why don't you take Sam with you on your next dive?"

Ken watched Sam's face to see his reaction to the idea. Sam's face lit up like the Christmas tree in Rockefeller Plaza.

"Could I?" Sam asked.

"I'll have to ask Barry," Ken said, "but it's an interesting idea. You could show us where things are."

"Provided they haven't shifted over the years," Sam said. "It was quite a hit the *Whydah* took that day. Hard telling if anything is where it was the last time I set eyes on it." He laughed. "To be sure it didn't leave me standin' where I was."

"You'll get no argument from me on that one," Ken said. "All that time you were down there in the ocean, did you ever try to wander off to see if you could find the wreckage?"

"No. It was like I was trapped in that damn eddy. It kept spinnin' me 'round. I thought I'd never get free. I wondered if that's what hell was like. Then I remembered that hell is hot—you know, fire and brimstone—and that water was so cold. It's a wonder I didn't freeze to death. Don't know how that happened."

"So how did you get out?" Ken asked. "The day you showed up here, how..."

"Beats the devil out of me," Sam said. "I was whirlin' 'round, and the next thing I knew I was blowin' up on the shore. Felt just like Jonah, I did."

Ken took note of another reference to the Bible. It had been nigh unto three hundred years since he'd laid eyes on the Bible he claimed he had. Seemed like Susannah Wesley had done a fine job of teaching Sam, the same as she had done to her own offspring. Yup, the things she'd taught him, and his undying love for Maria, those were apparently the two things that kept him going all those years.

Abruptly, Ken said, "I think I'll be getting back to the museum. Are you ready to start work tomorrow?"

"More than ready," Sam said enthusiastically.

"I'll come and pick you up about 8 o'clock in the morning," Ken said.

"I'll meet you at the Inn," Sam said.

"You have to stay here," Blair quickly reminded them. "The judge said..."

"Ah, but I dropped the charges," Ken said. "Remember? He's a free man."

"I think I'll be going too," Jenny said. "I think Sam and Blair have some business to tend to."

"We do?" Sam asked, looking puzzled.

"They do," Jenny said, and she and Ken left.

❋ ❋ ❋

"What's our business?" Sam asked when they were alone.

"Let's go out in the kitchen and have some tea," Blair said, fidgeting nervously with her hair.

Sam followed her to the kitchen and sat at the table as Blair put the teakettle on to heat. She sat across the table from Sam, studying him carefully. Was she really about to do something that would change her life forever? Thoughts—crazy, mixed up ideas—screamed within her head. What if he left and went back in time again? Could she possibly go with him, or would she be left alone, stranded without the love of her life? Would she be condemned to a life of watching for him at the waterfront, like Maria did all of her life? Or would their love for each other be strong enough to keep him in the present day?

"I'm waiting," Sam said, rubbing his beard. "What's on your mind?"

"You," Blair said simply, not sure how to proceed.

Sam waited until she was ready to continue.

"I know you loved Maria," she finally said.

"Yes, I did. That is no secret. It seems that the entire world knows about my love for her." He waited, then said, "But that was another lifetime ago. A very long lifetime ago. I know that there is no chance of my ever seeing her again. She is dead and buried." Again, the big tough pirate allowed a tear to drop onto his cheek.

"Do you think you could ever love anyone again?" Blair asked, her voice almost in a whisper.

Sam looked at her. He didn't know if he dared hope that she was asking him what he thought she was implying. He had loved her from the moment he first espied her that day at the festival. It was like Maria had been resurrected, along with him. His waking hours were filled with images of her in his mind. His sleeping hours were filled with dreams of her. Or dreams of Maria. It was hard to separate the two. They were like identical twins, except for the color of their hair.

"Under the right circumstances, I could definitely love another."

"Under what circumstances?" Blair asked.

Sam fiddled with his beard so hard Blair was afraid he was going to pull it out by the roots. Had she gone beyond the boundaries of what was—what? It was daring, but she had never been afraid of facing anything. Now, she was filled with fear. What if he laughed at her? What if he didn't even like her? He had certainly acted like he cared, but...

"If it was the right person," Sam finally said.

"And do you have any idea who that might be?" Blair asked, afraid of the answer he might give.

"It would have to be someone...just like Maria. I have only met one other person who comes close to Maria. One woman who not only looks like her, but who acts the exact way she acted." He paused, weighing his words, waiting for them to sink in. "One woman who is like a reincarnation of the only woman I ever loved. One woman who is as bewitching as she was."

"And that woman is..."

"You silly woman. It is you! If I cannot have Maria, I have dreamt and prayed for you to come to me."

"But you have never said..."

"I dared not hope. I found love once. I spent an eternity waiting for that love to return to me. I thought I had been cast out into forever without knowing that love. And then you came..."

Blair jumped up and ran around the table and grabbed Sam around the neck, pulling his face to her and kissing him madly, passionately. There was no hesitation in his returning the kiss. When they finally released each other, Sam laughed and said, "It was harder to breathe through that than it was under the water."

Blair swatted him playfully on the arm. Was it possible? Did he truly love her as much as she loved him? All the questions she'd had about the what-ifs of a future with him vanished. She was his, and he was hers. Worry about what her parents would say was as far removed as east from west. Whatever their reaction was, she would handle it. *They* would handle it. Sam had come to her through the passage of time. They could conquer anything, as long as they were together.

❄ ❄ ❄

Blair remembered Angus's plan to hypnotize Sam. She felt like a traitor. Should she call Angus and plead with him to forsake the idea? Or would it put the whole issue of who and what he really was put things to rest for one final time? She decided to wait and talk to Angus about it and confide their feelings for one another to him. He had a good, solid head on his shoulders. He would know what to do. She would wait until Sam went back to the Inn, then she would call Angus. If they were going to go ahead with it, they might as well get it over with as soon as possible.

She wondered if he was exposed as a fraud if it would change the way she felt about him. Yes, the sooner the better. If he was legitimate, then all she had to do was convince her parents that he was on the level. That should be easy enough. Oh, who was she kidding?

CHAPTER XXX

She didn't want him to leave, but it was getting dark and she really did want to call Angus. As they sat and talked, their hands entwined, she knew exactly how Maria had felt so long ago. It was as hard for her to not succumb to his wiles as it must have been for Maria. She couldn't know that he was battling the urges within his body as much as she was.

"Do you want me to drive you back to the Inn?" she finally asked.

"No. I can walk. It will do me good. I can clear my head a bit. It's been a bit overwhelming tonight." He stood up and went to the window, looking off into the distance blankly.

"What are you thinking?" Blair asked.

"I'm thinking that no one man should be lucky enough to get two women to love in one lifetime. Actually, that's not quite right. No man should be lucky enough to love the same woman twice."

Blair giggled. "But I'm not Maria."

"You could be," he teased, "if you had different colored hair."

The wheels in Blair's head began to spin. She wondered if she could pull it off. She would get Jenny to help her. It wouldn't be hard to get a black wig and put it on to see his reaction.

❋ ❋ ❋

Sam ambled along to the Inn. He pinched himself to make sure he was really alive. He let out a yelp at the pain.

Jason put a hand over his mouth to stifle a laugh. If this guy was a real pirate, he wouldn't have even felt that. He ran from tree to tree, carefully staying hidden in the shadows.

"Yo ho ho and a bottle of rum," Sam bellowed out. Oh yes, a good stiff drink of rum was just what the doctor ordered.

A mental image of Doc Angus flashed in his mind. Why didn't he trust that man? And why couldn't he get rid of the idea that he did know him—from before?

❋ ❋ ❋

Blair dialed Angus's phone. He answered it on the first ring.

"Hello."

"Angus? I know it is late, but could you possibly come over here for a few minutes? I have to talk to you. I need your help."

"Is it Sam? Has he hurt you? I'll kill the bastard!"

"No, I'm fine. He's gone back to the Inn. I'm here alone."

"You trust me to be alone with you?" Angus teased.

"Completely."

"Okay, I'll be there in just a few minutes. Let me put Corky out first."

Blair pondered who or what Corky was. Angus had never mentioned him before. She assumed it must be a dog. People don't put cats out. Not usually, anyway.

"Bring Corky along," she invited. "I'd like to meet—him."

"You sure?"

"Yes. I'll put the outside light on for you."

❋ ❋ ❋

Blair turned the TV on while she waited for Angus. At least there didn't seem to be anything on the news tonight about Sam. He did make himself known around town.

She turned away from the set when the commercials came on. Suddenly, she recognized Ken's voice. He was standing beside

Sam, who was dressed in his official pirate garb. "You have no doubt heard that somehow Black Sam Bellamy has escaped from time and has returned to us. He has joined the staff at the Whydah Museum. Come and hear him spin the yarns of his life. It's a treat you won't want to miss."

Blair gasped. Surely Sam didn't know what Ken was up to. She knew he wanted him to be a guide at the museum, but he would never stand still for Ken exploiting him. He just wanted to keep an eye on what he believed rightfully belonged to him.

She turned the TV off and dialed Ken's number. Darn! All she got was his voice mail.

"What are you doing?" she screamed at the machine. "How could you do that to him? Call me! Immediately!"

She breathed a sigh of relief when Angus pulled into the driveway. She needed an ally, and Angus was as logical as anybody to fill the bill.

Corky went bounding across the yard and Angus whistled for him to stay with him. He wasn't in any mood to have to go chasing him. Corky obediently came and heeled, following Angus up to the front door. Blair was already there to greet them before Angus could knock.

"Come on in," she invited. She sat down on the floor, her legs crossed Indian style, and was soon making friends with Corky.

"He's so cute," Blair said. She winked at Angus. "You know what they say about people and their pets, don't you?"

"Not sure what you mean," Angus said.

"They say they look just like their owners."

"You think he looks like me?" Angus asked.

Blair tilted her head from side to side, closing one eye at a time to study both Corky and Angus. "Yup."

Angus laughed.

"Poor Corky," Angus remarked.

"Poor nothing," Blair said. "You're both pretty good looking fellows."

"Now, what was it you want my help with?" Angus asked.

"You know your idea to have Sam hypnotized?"

Angus nodded.

"How soon can your friend do it?"

"What's the hurry?"

"Nothing. Well, maybe a lot." Blair paused, twisting her hair in her fingers nervously. Angus sat silently, waiting for her to continue.

"I think—I think I'm falling in love," she finally said.

"With Sam?"

"Yes. I know that sounds crazy. We know so little about him, about who he really is. Do you think it is possible that he is telling the truth?"

"He seems to believe it himself," Angus admitted. "Either that or he's the best actor the world has ever seen. If it's all a made up story, he should get an Oscar for best performance."

"So how soon..." Blair repeated.

"So if he's who he claims to be, then what?"

"I don't know. Maybe it will be clearer if I know if he's telling the truth." Again, she paused. "What would you do if you fell in love with somebody from some other world, some other time? And is it even possible that he might have somehow crossed the boundaries of time?"

"I don't know how it is possible," Angus said, "but I have learned to never say never when it comes to matters of the heart. The parents of some of the babies I have delivered have stories of how they have met that have defied all odds of survival. I guess if it is meant to be for two people to be together, if it's part of fate or destiny, anything is possible."

"So if he has come across time somehow, you think it was for the two of us to be united?"

Angus just nodded his head.

"What would you do if you were in my shoes?" Blair repeated.

Angus laughed. "First of all, I would not be attracted to your pirate. I don't swing that way."

Blair laughed with him. "You know what I mean. What if you met a woman from some other time and you fell in love with her? Would you try to stay with her?"

"I guess I'll never know. I can't see it happening to both of us. If it did, I'd just have to cross that bridge when I got to it."

For some unexplained reason, a vision of a field of poverty grass flashed across Angus's mind. "Strange," he said, not making any sense to Blair at all, "there's no bridge in that field."

Angus reached into his jacket pocket and pulled out his cell phone. He dialed his friend Paul's number.

"Paul? It's Angus. If you are available, pick up. If not, please call me back ASAP." He waited for a few seconds, then heard Paul's voice.

"Yeah, buddy. What's up? You got an emergency with the pirate?"

"Actually, sort of," Angus said. "How soon can you schedule a session with him?"

"For this one, most any time he's available. This is one for the books. I can't wait to get to him. Can't you see this in the medical mags?"

"Tomorrow morning?" Angus asked.

"Sure. Just bring him in to the office. I'll put anything else on hold."

"Actually, if it's possible I think it would be better if we did it out at Blair's house. I've told you about her. She's the one that's been, um, the closest to him since he was resurrected. I'm not sure how he's going to take to this whole idea."

"You haven't told him what you plan to do to him?" Paul asked.

"Um, not exactly."

"How do you plan to get him to cooperate?"

"I figure I'll go up behind him when Blair is distracting him and give him a pop in the butt with a hypo needle full of a good stiff sedative. That's what I had to do to get his blood sample."

Angus shuddered. Why did this thought cause him such consternation? It was like *déjà vu*. He had given any number of prospective mothers a knock-out shot, or at least watched when an anesthetist administered such shots. But this was different. This was Black Sam Bellamy. It made no sense to him at all. He wondered if Black Sam was, as history recorded, truly "the devil incarnate."

"How are you going to get him there?" Paul asked. "I just heard on the news that he's going to be showing up at the museum to give some guided tours." Paul laughed. "Oh, yeah, I can't wait to get at this one."

"Can you bring a recorder along?" Angus asked. "I think we should keep this one for posterity, no matter what he has to say."

"Absolutely," Paul said, the palms of his hands getting sweaty at the mere anticipation of the morning's activities. "Are you going to let Blair and Ken know?"

"I'm at Blair's now," Angus said. "One of us will call Ken and let him know he needs to get him here in the morning. What time?"

"Let's say nine. That will give Blair time to get up and dressed."

Paul didn't realize that Angus had flipped his phone to the speaker, so Blair could hear the conversation.

"Hey, I'm nobody's slouch," Blair protested. "I get up before seven every morning."

"Oops. Sorry," Paul said. "I didn't realize you could hear us."

"No problem," Blair said. "I'll call Ken right away."

"He'll probably want to sit in on the session," Angus said. "Any objections?"

"No," Paul said. "Actually, the more witnesses we have the better it will probably be."

"Good. George, you know, the lab tech guy, he's the one who drew Sam's blood, he said he'd like to be in on it too."

Angus looked at Blair, an unframed question apparent.

"What are you thinking?" Blair asked him.

"What about your parents? Do you think you should include them?"

"No way!" Blair shouted. "If he's legit, we can let them hear the tape later. And if not..."

"We'll cross that bridge when we get to it," Angus said, and once again the image of that big field of poverty grass popped into his mind. He shook his head, trying to get rid of it. He'd seen fields like that many times, traveling along the Cape, but why did it haunt him now? What did it mean, and why did it make him feel so edgy?

"See you in the morning," Paul said and hung up.

"You want to call Ken, or you want me to do it?" Angus asked.

"I'll do it," Blair said, punching the number she had entered into her system so she didn't have to look it up all the time. She'd been using it a lot lately.

"You have reached the voice mailbox of Ken Kinkor, curator of the Whydah Museum."

"Do you ever answer your phone?" Blair snapped. "It's Blair, and I need to talk to you—now!"

"Ken here. What's up?"

"Can you bring Sam over here in the morning, about nine o'clock, instead of going into the museum right away?"

"I suppose so. What's up?"

"The shrink who's a friend of Angus's wants to try to hypnotize Sam tomorrow."

"What's the rush?" Ken asked.

"Nothing. Not really. It's just that we might as well get it over with so we know..."

"You really think this will work?"

"It better," Blair said. "If it doesn't..."

"What?"

"Nothing. Never mind. It's just that I—we—need to know what we are dealing with."

"I'll have him there with bells on."

"What will you tell him about coming over here instead of going to the museum?"

"Can't you come up with some kind of cookies or something you want to send over with us? You'll think of something, I'm sure."

"Yeah, right," Blair said. "I wonder if the bakery is still open."

Ken laughed. "You want me to stop in there before I pick Sam up and sneak them in?"

"Might be a good idea," Blair said. "I'm not exactly the domestic type."

"Okay. Will do. Any special kind?"

"Whatever you like. No sense getting something you can't stand."

"See you in the morning," Ken said. "Oh, is it all right if I sit in on it? I'd kill to see this one." He paused. "Figuratively speaking, of course."

"Paul said the more the merrier," Blair said. "Just come without any blinders on. No telling what this will produce."

"I can't wait," Ken said. "Too bad Barry's off on tour. I know he'd love to be here too."

"They're planning to tape it, so he can probably hear it, even if it's after-the-fact."

"Good. Bye."

❋ ❋ ❋

Blair turned the phone off and collapsed onto the recliner. "I don't know if I'm ready for this or not," she admitted.

"Little late to back out now, isn't it?" Angus asked. "What are you afraid of?"

"The truth, I guess. Or that it's all a lie and he's been playing us for fools." She buried her head in her hands and sobbed. "I don't know. Why ever did this have to happen to me? Why couldn't I fall in love with somebody—real? Somebody like you. Why am I such an idiot?"

Angus went over and stood beside her, putting his arm around her shoulder. "Maybe by tomorrow we'll know what it's all about and you can see things more clearly."

"Maybe," Blair said, pulling a tissue out of her pocket and blowing her nose loudly in a most unladylike manner. "And maybe not."

"I'm going to go home and get some rest," Angus said, "if you think you'll be all right here alone."

"I'll be fine," Blair said, trying to convince herself that she really would be. "Good night."

CHAPTER XXXI

"We have to make a stop over at Blair's before we go to the museum," Ken told Sam. "She called a little while ago and said we might as well have breakfast with her too."

"Widow Clark already fed me," Sam said, "but I guess I can manage to stuff a bit more down me gullet."

Ken took notice of his referring to the innkeeper as "Widow Clark." That was such an old-fashioned way of putting it. Maybe the guy really was from some time long ago. The more he saw of Sam, the more it seemed possible.

Ken pulled into the driveway and they went inside. Blair had made pancakes and put them into the oven to keep warm so she wouldn't be distracted once they arrived. Ha! Truth was, she was distracted every time Sam came near her. It was just a fact of life.

"Have a seat," Blair invited. "I'll get it on right away." She poured the coffee and set the plate of pancakes on the table, which already held the syrup and butter. She took some sausage patties out and took them out of the pan from the oven and placed them on a plate and added them to the table.

Ken was surprised when he saw Sam bow his head, obviously giving thanks for the food. *Not what you'd expect from a pirate,* he thought.

As they ate, the sound of another car pulling up in front of the house and stopping startled Sam.

"You expecting somebody else?" he asked Blair.

"Angus said something about stopping by on his way up to the hospital," she said. It was the truth, she tried to convince herself. Suddenly she felt awfully guilty about trying to trick Sam. She should trust him, but...

"Anybody home?" Angus called out as he opened the door and came in.

"Out in the kitchen," Blair called. "Come on out. Have you eaten? We have plenty of food here."

"Already stuffed," Angus said.

Sam shifted about on his chair. The more he saw of Doc Angus, the less he liked him. The less he trusted him. There was definitely something askew with the good doctor. If only he could remember what it was.

"You all know George."

Sam pulled his sleeves tight around his muscular arms. He knew better than to trust him. He'd gotten blood from him once, but it wasn't going to happen again. He'd make sure of that.

"This is my friend Paul," Angus said, introducing the man who was accompanying him. "He had to go on a medical trip too, so we figured we might as well car pool, the price of gas and all these days."

"Here in Hyannis?" Sam asked.

"Yup," Angus said, grinning far too widely, Sam reasoned. He felt sure that he was up to something. Probably something he didn't want any part of. Should he get up and leave? He looked at Blair, hoping she would give some indication of what was going on. He was way outnumbered. Whatever it was they were planning, he couldn't worm his way out of it, he was sure of that.

Paul bugged him something awful. He kept staring at Sam. Sam tried to look away, but it was if he was transfixed—involuntarily. Paul's eyes were like they were glued in one position. He didn't blink, no matter how much Sam blinked at him. Sam put his hand up in front of his eyes, then took it down. Paul was still staring at him. Sam tried to stand up, but it was if his feet were nailed to the floor.

"I think it's time," Paul said to Angus. Angus reached down into his medical bag and put something in his hand. Sam strained to see what it was, but he couldn't tell. He watched, unable to move, as Angus walked behind him. Then it hit.

Sam recognized the feeling immediately. It was the same big bug that had stung him back in Yarmouth. Way back in 1717. He knew it was the same thing, and he knew it was the same man who had been there when it stuck him. It was also the same thing that had stung him when Angus stole his blood. He knew Doc Angus was here, and he knew that he was there. And then he slumped over the table and that was the last he knew.

※ ※ ※

"Do you want us to move him into the living room so he's more comfortable?" Angus asked Paul.

"It might be easier if he's lying back in the recliner," Paul said. "Think we can manage him?"

Before they could answer, Ken had him by the feet and Paul and Angus each had a shoulder, and they deposited him into the chair like you would do with a corpse.

"We're ready," Paul said, pushing the start button on the tape recorder. "It is May 19, 2008. We are at the home of Blair Smythe in Hyannis, Massachusetts. Those present are myself, Dr. Paul Anderson, Dr. Angus McPherson, lab technician George Phelps, Blair Smythe, and Sam Bellamy, also known as Sam Black. Sam Bellamy is the subject of this study."

Blair watched Sam to see if there was any reaction. There did not appear to be any, but when Paul began to question him, Sam answered clearly.

"What is your name?"

"Sam Bellamy."

"Where were you born?"

"London, England."

"What do you do for a living?"

"I am a sailor. A man of the seas. Some would call me a pirate."

"What is the date of your birth?"

"February 23, 1689. I never liked that month. It is too hard to say."

Blair chuckled. Leave it to Sam to ad lib, even under hypnosis.

"How old are you?"

"I don't rightly know. I disappeared one day on Cape Cod, when I went back to claim Maria, and I don't know what happened after that."

"Who is Maria?"

"She is the woman I love. The only woman I will ever love. She bewitched me and beguiled me when I set on shore during a nor'easter. I have never been the same since then."

"You left her?"

"Aye. I set sail again, but I told her I would return for her when I had made my fortune."

"Did you ever see Maria again?"

"Only once."

"When was that?"

"I came back to bring her a token—a promise—that I intended to keep my word to return for her."

"What did you take her?"

"A basket. It had a hand embroidered handkerchief from France. Some pearls. Oh, and a fish. I knew she would know it was from me."

"And you saw her?"

"Aye. I heard at Crosby's Tavern that she had had a baby. They said it was my son. One man said the lad nearly died, but some stranger came to town and saved his life."

Sam paused, like he was trying to remember everything he'd heard.

"And you saw Maria?"

"I caught a glimpse of her through the window of the house where she lived. They said she was married to the man—a Doctor Angus McPherson—who had saved the baby's life."

Angus jumped up. He was just ready to shout something when Paul motioned for him to sit back down and be quiet. He was sure they were not at the end of this story yet.

"And then you left town?"

"Aye. I set sail again, but I vowed more than ever to return to her. I was going to claim her as me own, and no stranger was going to raise my son." He waited a few seconds, then added, "They said she named him Sam. They all called him 'Little Sam.'"

"What do you know about the doctor?"

"Not much, really. I left the Cape and set sail again. Then later, in April of 1717, I came back, my loot in tow, ready to take Maria and the lad away with me. I figured we would go back to England and make a life for us there."

"And what happened?"

"There was another terrible storm. We pulled the ship in and anchored it and we went back to Crosby's Tavern to wait it out. I asked about Maria, of course. They all told me to stay away from her. They said John—that was Maria's father—would kill me on the spot if he ever laid eyes on me again."

"So you just stayed in the Tavern?"

"Aye. But then John and Jonathan, that was Maria's uncle, they showed up. There was fire in their eyes. I knew they were aiming to kill me."

"Then what happened?"

"I don't know. Something bit me in the arse, and the next thing I knew I was in the jail."

They all watched, amazed by the tale Sam was spinning. This was nothing like the history books reported the events of the day. According to history, he never made it onto land before the ship sank.

"You don't know how you got there?" Paul asked.

"Nary a clue. I just know I was there. I managed to reach the keys and I got loose. I headed for the *Whydah*. It was the only place I felt like I would be safe."

"You got to the ship?"

"Aye. Most of me crew, not knowing what was happening, had also gone there. When I reached the ship, I thought that as soon as the weather cleared enough we would head back out to sea. I would have to wait for another time to claim Maria for me own."

"So you and your crew were all on the *Whydah*. Did you head back out to sea?"

"We had no chance to head anywhere. A bolt of lightning

struck the boat and split it right in two. Right down the middle, like it had been measured."

"And then?"

"And then nothing. It sank. We all sank. I had no clue what happened to anybody. I just know that when I woke up I was twirling around in an eddy at the bottom of the ocean. I stayed there for... I have no idea how long I stayed there. Then one day I was coughed up onto the seashore. They tell me I was under the water for nigh onto three hundred years. I cannot say if it is true or not. I just know that I was there, and then I was here."

"What did you feel like when you found yourself on the shore?"

"I can't tell you. I did not feel anything, except confused. But then I saw Maria—and I knew that I was safe."

"You saw Maria?"

"Aye, but she had flaxen hair. The last time I saw her she had hair as black as a raven's feathers."

"And what did you think of this Maria?"

"I knew it was the only other person I could ever love. I did not know if she was the same Maria or a different Maria, but I knew in an instant that I loved her, and I would never leave her again."

Blair wanted to run and grab him and hug him as hard as she could, but she had seen Paul instruct Angus to stay still, so she sat, her fingers twirling her hair. She would have to wait until he was out from under Paul's hypnotic spell before she could tell him that she loved him too. To tell him that she wanted to stay with him forever.

Suddenly, without any help from Paul to bring him out of the trance, Sam opened his eyes wide and looked around.

"What is everybody doing just sitting here? Why do I feel so strange? And what the devil was that that bit me? I haven't felt that since..."

"Since the last day you were alive in Yarmouth?" Angus asked. He was still befuddled by Sam's insistence that he had been there. It was completely impossible. There had to have been another Dr. Angus McPherson. He had his homework cut out for him. He was determined to find out who it was and if they were related.

"Then, and the day *he* stole me blood." He pointed an accusing finger at George.

"I think you will be interested in listening to this," Paul said, rewinding the tape. "I apologize, old boy, but I put you to sleep so we could find out if you really are Black Sam Bellamy or some imposter."

"And?" Sam asked.

"Seems like you're the real deal," Paul said. "Here, listen." He played the tape back as they all listened to it over again, but this time watching Sam's reaction to what he had said.

"I told you I am Black Sam Bellamy," Sam insisted.

"So you are," Paul said. "There's no doubt about it."

"I have to let Mom and Dad hear this," Blair said. "Angus, will you stay here with me when they hear it?"

"I'd love to," Angus said. "Still don't know why he thought I was there though. He might have traveled across time, but it's beyond me. It could never happen. At least not twice in one person's life."

CHAPTER XXXII

"Mom, you and Dad have to come over here tonight. I have something you need to hear."

"What have you gone and done now? Surely you and Sam…"

"No, Mom, I'm not pregnant. And we haven't." She wanted to add "not yet" just to see what her mother would say, but she decided against it. She had to play her cards right if she was going to get their blessing for her and Sam to be together. At least now she knew he loved her. There was no question in her mind as to whether or not she loved him. She'd known it from the beginning. Apparently, so had he.

"I'm not sure," Maggie said. "You know it's my bridge night."

"Mom, this is really important."

"I'll see if I can get Joyce to fill in for me. If she can, we'll come."

"Thanks," Blair said. She was irritated that her mother considered her bridge club more important than the biggest decision she would ever face.

❈ ❈ ❈

She sat for a few minutes, then called the museum.
"Whydah Museum. Ken Kinkor here."
"Ken? It's Blair. I, um, I need your help."

"For what? I know it can't be Sam. He's here with me. Oh, and the people love it. They are eating up his tales like a bear goes after honey. Can you believe it? Seems like he's the real deal."

"Thank you for being here when Paul did—you know, what he did."

"I wouldn't have missed it for the world. Now, what did you need?"

"Can you come over for supper tonight, and bring Sam along?"

"What's the occasion?"

"I am going to try to convince my mom and dad that he is who he says he is. It would help if I had a support system in place."

Ken laughed. "Of course I'll be there. I can just picture Martin."

"I'm going to ask Paul and Angus if they will come too."

"You really are calling out all the big guns, aren't you?"

"I need all the help I can get for this one."

"I suspect you're right. And then what do you intend to do?"

"About what?" Blair asked.

"About Sam, of course."

"I don't know. I guess it all depends."

"On what?"

"On Sam."

"You know, don't you, that he's madly in love with you? Only problem is he thinks he's fallen in love with Maria all over again."

"I know," Blair said. "I don't quite know what to do about that."

Ken hesitated, then asked, "Are you in love with him too?"

Blair stammered a bit. "I—I—I don't know. I think so." There was silence before she said, "Do you think I'm crazy?"

"Love makes people crazy," Ken replied. "Although in your case, it might be a bit over the top."

"So will you come? And bring Sam along?"

"Of course I will. What time?"

"Make it about six o'clock." Another pause. "No, make it 5:30. I want to talk to Sam before Mom and Dad get here."

"We'll be there with bells on." Ken laughed. "Or at least the chains on Sam's boots jingling."

"Thanks," Blair said, punching the "off" button on her phone.

❋ ❋ ❋

Next she called Angus.

"Hi, Doc. It's Blair."

"What's up?"

"I don't know yet. Maybe nothing. Maybe everything."

"Explain please. I'm not psychic, you know."

"I want you and Paul to come for supper tonight if you can. And can you ask Paul to bring the tape of Sam's session?"

"Sure. Any special reason? Maybe he can run off a copy of it so you'll have one of your own, just for future reference."

"That would be great, but I still need both of you here."

"You're up to something."

"You know me too well," Blair said, giggling nervously. "I've asked Mom and Dad to come too. And Sam and Ken. I want to have Paul play the tape for Mom and Dad. Try to convince them that he's not a fraud. That's he's really who he says he is. Who he thinks he is."

"Good luck on that one."

"That's why I need you here too—for luck."

"Don't know how much I can contribute, but it sounds like the most fun evening I've had in I can't remember when."

"Okay, I'll see you about six." She started to set the phone down, but picked it up again and said, "Thanks."

"Glad to be of help," Angus said. "And if you ever need a baby doctor, I'm your man."

"I'll remember that," Blair said.

❋ ❋ ❋

Blair made her final phone call—to Jenny. She needed her.

"Jen? Can you come over for a bit? Well, for all day? I need your help."

"Sure. What's up?"

"I have to go shopping and I want to know what you think of what I get."

"Sounds ominous."

"You have no idea. How soon can you get here?"

"Give me time to pull my hair back into a pony tail and I'll be on my way."

❋ ❋ ❋

Blair sat on the floor, her arms wrapped around her knees, pondering the events of the day ahead of her. Was Ken right? Was she crazy? Crazy in love, probably. Crazy to be in love. The thoughts danced around in her head like the fairies in the Nutcracker Suite.

What if he disappears one day, back to his other time, or into the ocean? Could I go with him? Is our love strong enough for us to travel through time together?

She slapped her cheek. *There is nothing certain—in life or in death. You could marry somebody perfectly normal, somebody like Doc Angus, and he could get hit by an oncoming ambulance and die on the spot.*

She laughed. If Angus was going to get hit by somebody, it would certainly be ironic if it was by an ambulance. *Probably on his way to deliver a baby and not paying attention to the road. What if he was going to deliver my baby?*

She remembered his offer to come at her beck and call if she ever needed a baby doctor. She tried to picture a little Sam. It brought a warm fuzzy feeling to her from the tip of her toes to the top of her head. Or if they had a daughter, would it look like her, but with black hair like Sam had? Black hair like Maria had? Or brown hair like she had when she was a little girl?

❋ ❋ ❋

The door swung open and Jenny came in and plopped on the sofa.

"So what are we going shopping for?"

"I need a wig."

"A wig? But you have a beautiful full head of hair. Whatever for?"

"I need a black wig."

Jenny tilted her head from side to side, studying Blair.

"Am I going to like this?" she asked.

"Doesn't matter. I have to know…"

"Know what?"

"If Sam loves me…or if he's still in love with Maria."

"You aren't making any sense at all," Jenny said, getting up and going out into the kitchen and pouring herself a cup of coffee.

"He says I look exactly like Maria, except for the color of our hair. If he looks at me differently when I have my blonde hair than when I have black hair—*Maria's hair*…"

"Then what?"

Suddenly Blair was in tears. "I don't know. He says he loves me. Even when he was under the spell, when Paul was questioning him, he said he loved me. But he said he loved Maria too. How will I know which one of us he loves? I mean, how will I *really* know? Know for sure?"

Jenny snorted into her coffee cup.

"What's so funny?" Blair asked.

"You are." Again, she studied Blair carefully. "If I didn't know better I'd think that maybe you are Maria. Maybe somehow you traveled across time too.'

"That's crazy," Blair said. "I have pictures of me as a baby. My mom has told me how hard her labor was. I know I'm from this time. I'm not a misfit!"

"Okay, let's get going. Where do you plan to get the wig? At Brenda's Salon?"

"No, silly!" Blair protested. "You know how gossip spreads from that place. It would be all over town in no time flat. We'll go a couple of towns over to make sure nobody knows."

"Ready when you are," Jenny said, pouring the last of her coffee into the sink and rinsing the cup out. "Maria Hallett, look out!"

"She's dead," Blair said. "Or at least I think she is."

"What do you mean?" Jenny asked as she got into the car.

Blair started the engine and rolled the window down. It was a beautiful morning, and the cool fresh air felt good blowing in her face.

"What if she somehow managed to cross time too? If Sam and I were together, would he leave me for her?"

"Like that's gonna happen," Jenny scoffed. "You should have been a playwright. That would make a great movie."

"They say that truth is stranger than fiction," Blair said. "After seeing Sam emerge from the ocean after almost three hundred years, I think anything is possible."

"I don't think you have to worry about competition from Maria any time soon."

"Thanks. I'm going to hold you to that."

"No problem," Jenny said, turning the radio on to some jazzy music and bouncing to the tune.

In no time at all Blair pulled up in front of a beauty salon and parked the car.

"Come on," she said, motioning to Jenny to go in with her. "I need your input on this one."

❆ ❆ ❆

"What do you think?" Blair asked, turning slightly so Jenny could get the full impact of her new look.

"It's...there's something spooky about it," Jenny said. "I don't know what it is, but it is like you really are her."

As they entered Provincetown, Blair steered the car towards the museum.

"What are you doing?" Jenny asked.

"I'm just going to see if I can catch a glimpse of Sam. He's working at the museum now, you know. Ken says it is wonderful. People are just gobbling up his tales."

They approached the museum, and Blair spotted Sam bending over in front of the museum. She honked the horn and waved and kept right on going.

※ ※ ※

"Ken! Come quick! Something is wrong with Sam! He's fainted—or died!"

Ken went running outside and there was Sam, lying on the boardwalk, passed out dead as a doornail and as white as if he'd just seen a ghost.

Ken sent somebody inside to get some cold water. He fanned Sam. He felt of his neck and found a good pulse. Thank God! At least he wasn't dead. How do you deal with a deceased three-hundred-year-old pirate anyway?

A few splatters of the cold water on Sam's face revived him.

"What...what happened?" he said, spitting the water back in Ken's face.

"I don't know," Ken said. "Why don't you tell me?"

Sam rubbed his eyes and stroked his beard.

"I...I...I saw Maria." He paused, shaking his head. "She...she was driving a car. A car just like Blair's."

"It must have been Blair and your eyes were playing tricks on you."

"No!" Sam insisted. "It was Maria. She had Maria's raven black hair."

Ken reached into the holster on his belt and pulled his cell phone out. He pushed the speed dial button for Blair.

"Hello?"

"What on earth are you doing?" Ken yelled into the phone. "You almost killed Sam!"

"What are you talking about?" Blair asked.

"He is sure he saw Maria driving your car. He said it couldn't have been you because she had black hair, just like Maria."

"Oh my God!" Blair shouted back. "I didn't mean to scare him. I just thought it would be fun to see what his reaction was if I had a black wig on."

"Well, you sure as the devil found out."

"What happened?"

"He passed out in front of the museum. I thought he was dead. Of course, he might already be dead. Maybe it's really a ghost we are dealing with. Maybe he's nothing more than a phantom. Maybe it's all a *spirit thing*."

"No, he's real," Blair said. "He's flesh and blood, just like you and me. Well, at least part of him is part blood. I still don't understand all of that medical stuff Angus did on him."

"Probably better if you don't question it," Ken suggested. "Just accept it. He's here. You're here. What more do you need?"

"Guess you're right. Anyway, you'd better go see if Sam's okay. Will you tell him what it was he saw?"

"And ruin all your fun?" Ken asked, chuckling.

"I guess it wasn't as much fun as I'd thought it would be. I'll get rid of it so he'll never see it again. Or me in it."

"Good idea," Ken said. "Okay, we'll see you about 5:30."

❋ ❋ ❋

"What was that all about?" Jenny asked. "Judging from the look on your face, I'd say you just saw a ghost—or something."

"No," Blair said, setting her cell phone on the seat and grasping the steering wheel firmly with both hands. "But Sam did. Or at least he thought he did."

"Huh?" Jenny asked.

"He saw me driving the car when we went past and I honked at him. With the black wig on he thought it was Maria come back to life."

"Oh my God!" Jenny gasped. "What happened?"

"I guess he fainted, or passed out, or something. Somebody went in and got Ken and he managed to bring him back around, but I'm going to get rid of this thing as soon as we get home." She grabbed the wig and flung it into the back seat. She ran her fingers through her own flaxen hair to let it blow freely in the wind. "Sometimes I can be really stupid."

"Sometimes?" Jenny joked.

"Yeah, sometimes," Blair said, glaring at her friend.

Changing the subject, Jenny asked, "So what are you fixing for supper?"

"No way am I going to take a chance on ruining everything. I called somebody to cater it in. In fact, maybe I'll have you run over and pick it up after Sam and Ken get there." She thumped her fingers on the steering wheel. "If you don't mind, I mean."

"No problem. Just tell me where to go to get it."

"Thanks." Blair was silent for a few moments. "Did I ever tell you that you are the bestest friend any gal could ever have?"

"Not recently," Jenny said, grinning. "But backatcha."

The exchanged a "high five" as they pulled into the driveway at Blair's house.

"So what are we going to do for the rest of the day until supper time?" Jenny asked. "That's hours away yet."

"I don't know," Blair said. Suddenly she exclaimed, "We can go on the Internet and look for wedding gowns."

"You're serious, aren't you?" Jenny asked.

"Dead serious," Blair replied.

"That's not funny!" Jenny shouted. "You are going to marry some three-hundred-year-old pirate who should be dead, only he's not, and you are joking about being dead?"

"Sorry," Blair said. "Bad joke."

"You got that right," Jenny said.

As they got out of the car, Blair opened the back door and grabbed the wig. As soon as they got into the house, she threw it into the sink and lit it on fire. They both watched as it sizzled. Despite the claims the hairdresser had made, it was definitely not made of human hair. They saw it melt and turn into a pool of ugly black tar-like goop.

"Goodbye, Maria," Blair said as she took a handful of paper towels and scooped it up. She carried it out to the trash can out in the back yard. As she came back in she said, "Whew! That is one nasty stink." She took a can of air freshener and sprayed it around. In a few minutes the smell was back again. She opened the windows and turned the ceiling fans on. It still didn't dissipate. "I hope that is gone by the time everybody gets here."

Jenny shook her head. "I can just hear your mom when you tell her what you plan to do. She's going to say 'Smells like something's rotten in Denmark.' But it will be rotten right here in Hyannis."

CHAPTER XXXIII

As they searched through thousands of wedding gowns on the computer, the time passed quickly for Blair and Jenny. There was one that Blair kept going back to, time after time.

"That's the one?" Jenny finally asked after the umpteenth time of looking at it.

"I think so," Blair said. She looked at it, taking in every little detail of the gown. "Yes, that's it."

"Did you look at the price?" Jenny asked.

"It's my wedding, and I have plenty of money to cover anything I want." She looked heavenward. "Thank you, Grandpa." She somehow felt that he was smiling down at her. He had told her, countless times, about Maria. It was because of him that she had such a fixation on the young lass of long ago. He could never have imagined that this day would ever come though. *No one could have foretold such an event*

Blair jumped when she heard a car pull up in front of the house. She glanced at the time on the computer.

"It's already 5:30," she exclaimed. "They're here."

"I'm outa here," Jenny said. "I've got the address of where to go to pick up the food. How long do you want me to stay away?"

"It won't take us long," Blair said. "We just have to get things settled."

"Okay," she said as she skipped out the door, whistling. She passed Sam and Ken on their way up to the house. "Go on in. She's waiting for you."

Blair was sitting on the sofa when the two men came in. Sam looked at her and asked, "Are you all right?"

"I think so. You will help me determine that."

"What?" he asked.

"Ken, would you mind our talking alone for a bit? There's coffee out in the kitchen. Make yourself at home."

"No problem," Ken said and headed out into the kitchen. He poured himself a cup of coffee, sat down at the table, then strained his ears for all he was worth to hear what was going on in the other room.

"What's the matter?" Sam asked, again showing concern for Blair.

"Nothing." Suddenly Blair was in tears. "Everything. I don't know. You tell me."

"How can I tell you when I don't have any idea what you are talking about?"

"Do you remember any of what you said to Paul?"

"I did listen to that tape thing afterwards. Remember? So yes, I know what I said."

"Do you remember saying that you loved me?"

Sam nodded.

"And you also said that you loved Maria."

Sam nodded again. He wasn't sure where she was headed with this.

"So do you love me or do you love Maria?"

"Yes."

Blair stared at him. "That doesn't help!" She slapped him on the arm.

"I don't know. There is a part of me that will always love Maria. But you know as well as I do that she's not here. She's dead and buried. You said so yourself."

Blair waited for him to continue.

"And you are here. And since I can't have Maria, yes, I would love to love you. I *do* love you. But I'm afraid."

"You're afraid? You? The big bad pirate Black Sam Bellamy is afraid? What are you afraid of?"

"I'm afraid that if I let myself truly love you..." He waited, trying to find the right words to tell her what he was afraid of.

"What if I go back in time? What if I end up back in Yarmouth, back when Maria was there. Or what if I get cast back into the ocean?"

He shivered at the thought of the cold water that he'd endured for the eternity he'd spent there. He would do anything to keep from facing that again.

"Maybe," Blair said hesitantly, "our love is strong enough to keep you here, in this time, with me."

"Do you think so?" Sam asked. He knew he would like to believe that. He was getting almost comfortable in his new surroundings. Granted, he still had a lot to learn about life in the twenty-first century, but he was willing to be a good student. And with Blair to teach him, he could handle it easily.

"Would you...would you want to stay here...with me?" she asked.

"I would like nothing better. But what are you saying?"

Sam could hardly believe his ears. Was it possible that Blair would consider spending her life with him? If he couldn't have Maria, could he have the next best thing? Could God be that good to him, especially after all he had endured?

"If you would have me, I would like to spend my life with you."

Sam lay back on the sofa, scratching his beard. Blair knew by now that meant that he was nervous. Had she jumped the gun? Had she assumed too much? Was she being too forward? After all, this *was* the twenty-first century, and women had rights too. Not that Sam had learned that lesson yet.

Blair got up on her knees and threw her arms around Sam's neck. She kissed him passionately. And that's how they were when Martin and Maggie came in.

"Get off my daughter!" Martin bellowed.

Blair jumped up and said, "Dad, once again, it was me who kissed Sam, not the other way around." She looked at her parents and said, as calmly as she could, "I think maybe you'd better sit down."

CHAPTER XXXIV

John King's Remains
This fibula, shoe and stocking were located inside of a concretion. It is believed to be the remains of John King, the young boy who demanded that Bellamy allow him to join his crew as a pirate.
Kenneth Garrett *National Geographic*

"You can't be serious!" Martin roared at Blair. "I forbid it! You can't marry that—con man. That imposter."

"Dad, in case you haven't noticed, I am a big girl now. I'm not Daddy's little girl any more. I can do what I want to, and I want to marry Sam. We love each other. I wanted you and Mom to be the first to know."

"But there's no way to know who—or what he is. A three-hundred-year-old pirate that just washes up out of the sea one day? That's preposterous!"

Right on cue, Angus and Paul walked in. They didn't bother to knock as they could hear the ruckus long before they got near the house.

"Oh, thank God you are here," Blair said. "Mom, Dad, you have met Dr. McPherson. This is a friend and colleague of his, Dr. Paul Anderson."

"What do you have to do with all of this?" Martin asked. "No baby doctor knows anything about any of this."

"Mr. Smythe," Angus said politely, "Paul is a psychiatrist, one of the top in his field. He has made a thorough examination of Sam. He has determined that he is exactly who and what he says he is." Angus waited for this to settle in before he continued. "In fact, Paul has brought proof with him that I think will satisfy your doubts and questions. Paul…"

Paul set the tape recorder on the coffee table, popped the tape in and began to play it. There was no mistaking Sam's voice.

"What kind of a hoax is this?" Martin asked.

"It is not a hoax, sir," Paul said. "I am a master of hypnotism. It is highly respected, as I'm sure you know, in the world of psychiatry. I hypnotized Sam and I would like you to listen—carefully—to what he had to say."

Martin sat quietly as the tape continued to roll. The sweat poured off him. This was too much. Were they all in on this together? He would call the hospital first thing in the morning to see if this shrink was on the level.

When the tape reached the end, Blair looked at her mom and dad and asked simply, "Well?"

"Well what?" Martin asked. "This could all be a big plot you all cooked up just to make us think it was real."

"I assure you," Sam said, "I did not rig any of this. I didn't even know they were going to do it."

"They did it against your will?" Martin asked. "You could sue them."

"You honestly want him to sue all of us for finding out the truth?" Blair asked. "I really thought…I hoped you would give us your blessing."

"Never!" Martin said. "I suppose we can't stop you, but we will never approve of such actions."

Maggie took Martin's hand in hers. "Marty," she said, "do you honestly want to lose our daughter over this? I couldn't bear the thought of her being out of our lives. I don't like it either, but if it means keeping our daughter, I think we should let them go ahead with the marriage. It seems to me that they are going to do it whether we approve or not."

"Thanks, Mom," Blair said, getting up and going over to give her mom a hug. "I really do love him. And you heard him say that he loves me too. And he said it when he was being completely honest about everything."

"But how..." Martin asked. "Nobody has ever traveled through time before."

"Not that we know of," Paul said. "There are a lot of things we don't understand. Remember when you were young and Buck Rogers said he was going to the moon?"

"But we all knew that was just a dream," Martin said.

"But you watched, like the rest of us, when man stepped off that first spaceship onto the surface of the moon. Who is to say this isn't possible too? Man has made huge strides in discovering things we all thought were impossible."

"This is just crazy," Martin insisted. "Maggie, how can you buy into this scheme?"

"Do you remember my folks when we told them we were going to get married?"

Martin's face flushed. "They had no right to say the things they did. Why, you'd have thought I was the worst person on the face of the earth." He paused. "And I even had a job, not like this gigolo."

"Oh, but he does have a job. A most respected one," Ken said, jumping to Ken's defense. "We have hired him at the museum. The people love him. He's only been there one day, but word has gotten out that the real Black Sam Bellamy is there, and we had a waiting line to get in all day long."

"You aren't serious, are you?" Martin asked.

"As much as I've ever been," Ken said. "He's the best thing that's ever happened to us."

"You see?" Maggie said, rubbing Martin's hand. "I think they will be just fine. Besides, as long as Sam is working here, they will be nearby." She grinned. "Especially if they have children, we would want them here."

"Oh, thank you, Mom," Blair said, jumping up and going to embrace her mother.

"Looks like I lost this battle," Martin grumbled, reaching over and shaking Sam's hand. "Welcome to the family. I know when I'm licked."

"Thank you, sir," Sam said. "I promise you that I will take good care of Maria—er, Blair."

Blair exchanged a quick glance at Angus. This was going to be harder than she had thought. Still, she knew she could do it. She would spend her entire lifetime making Sam forget about Maria and think only of her. It was like Jenny had said. It wasn't like Maria would ever show up and ruin everything.

Angus grinned like the cat that just swallowed the canary. He had gotten by the whole thing with Martin and Maggie listening to the tape but never catching on to the fact that Sam somehow was convinced that he had been back in the world of yesterday and that he had played a major part in Sam's demise. Angus was sure that if they had paid any attention to that they would have been sure that the whole thing was a fantasy. Somehow, he felt, for the first time, like maybe he was part of this whole scheme. He couldn't understand why that should make him feel good. He would never comprehend the whole idea that he had traveled through time, the same as Sam, but in the reverse direction.

Jenny walked up to the door and yelled out, "Anybody open the door for me? My hands are full."

Sam, Blair, Angus and Pete all jumped to go to her rescue.

"There's more in the car," she said. Sam held the door for her, and the others went to get the rest of the food.

Blair had the table all set in the dining room so it didn't take long to put the food into serving dishes and call them all to assemble.

Sam looked around a bit nervously. Blair started passing the first dishes around.

"You not goin' to bless the food?" Sam asked, much to everyone's surprise.

"You can do the honors," Martin said.

"Lord, bless this food, and thank you for this day. Thank you for Martin accepting me into the family. Amen."

As they all started to scoop the food onto their plates, Martin said, "Never figured a pirate knew much about praying."

"A pirate's got every right to pray, maybe more than most folks," Sam said. "If you remember Jonah, none of us want to take a chance on havin' somebody throw us overboard because of rough waters."

"You know a fair bit about the Bible, it seems," Martin said. "How is that?"

"Not much to do when you're out to sea for weeks on end sometimes. I had a Bible—a very special Bible—that Mother Wesley gave me," Sam explained.

"Mother Wesley?" Maggie asked, raising her eyebrow skeptically.

"Yep," Sam said. "She was like a mother to me back in the old country."

"You mean *the* Mother Wesley?" Maggie asked. "Susannah Wesley?"

"The same. Her kids, they was like brothers and sisters to me. When I left on me first voyage, she gave me the Bible and said she would pray that God would be present with me every step of the way."

"And He was?" Maggie asked.

"Yep. Right up till the day I perished. Still don't understand all that." Sam rubbed his beard. "I could swear *he* was in on it," he said, pointing to Angus. "But seems mighty unlikely." He shrugged his shoulders. "Anyway, don't matter no more. I'm here. He's here. All those other folks, they are long since dead, I'm sure. I've read all about what happened." He looked puzzled. "Ain't like I 'member it at all, but I guess history don't lie."

"Maybe your head got all messed up all those years you were under the water," Ken suggested. "I suspect it was enough to confuse anybody."

"Must be," Sam said.

❋❋❋

"So if you were a Methodist back in England," Maggie said, "that is wonderful. We have always gone to the Methodist Church here in Hyannis. The wedding, of course, will be there."

Blair smiled at her mother. Now this was more what she wanted. Still, she wasn't sure they should have a huge wedding.

Oh, sure, she had dreamed of a big bash like every young girl, but she knew it would make Sam nervous. No, the only thing that mattered was that she would be his bride, and that they would spend their lifetime together. *I wonder how long a lifetime with a three-hundred-year-old pirate might be,* she pondered. With a little bit of luck, they could make it last another three hundred years.

"I think we will keep it a small affair," Blair suggested. "Poor Sam, he's already had more than his share of attention in the news."

"I agree," Martin said. "We don't need the entire family to be made the laughing stock of the town."

"I think it should be just those of us who are here now," Blair said. "If that's all right with you, dear." She nodded towards Sam.

"I don't want no big show," Sam said. "But I do like the idea of having it at the church. Still, there wasn't no such thing as a Methodist Church back when I knew the Wesley's. I never heard tell of that till Ken told me about it."

"We hope to get back down to the *Whydah* in a month or so," Ken said. "Barry's itching to get back down to see what else we can find." He hesitated, then said, "We'd like to have Sam join us."

Blair began to twirl her hair like she always did when she was nervous. At first, when she had suggested it, she thought it was a great idea. Now, the thought of Sam going back down to the ruins of the *Whydah* terrified her. What if he ended up staying there? What if the shock of seeing it again killed him? They'd have to cross that bridge when they came to it. She guessed if a pirate could pray, she'd better try doing the same thing. She'd grown up in the church, but somehow Sam's faith seemed so much more real to him. She'd have to watch him closely and see if she could figure the whole thing out. Suddenly she felt like it was God who had brought Sam to her. They were in this thing together, for however long it would last.

"When do you plan on getting hitched?" Martin asked. "Any date in mind?"

"How about on May 19th," Maggie asked. "On our anniversary."

"That's only a little over a week off," Blair said.

"Well, if you are just going to have a simple little ceremony, it shouldn't take much planning."

"Is that okay with you, Sam?" Blair asked.

"The sooner the better," Sam said, grinning so widely even the gold teeth in the back shone brightly.

❈ ❈ ❈

Jason crept along close to the house so he wouldn't be seen, then he made a mad dash for home. He stopped along the way and took his cell phone out of his pocket. He was so glad his mother had insisted on his having one after she got out of the hospital.

He punched the button that was set to speed dial the TV station. As soon as the receptionist answered, he pulled the napkin out of his pocket and stretched it over the mouthpiece.

"I know you have been following the story about Black Sam Bellamy."

The receptionist quickly patched him through to the news room.

"Yes?"

"Do you want a scoop about Black Sam Bellamy?"

"Who's calling?"

"Do you want the story or not?" Jason said nervously.

"Of course we want the story. What's he up to now?"

"He's getting married. May 19th at the Methodist Church."

"Who is he marrying?" the reporter asked, but it was too late. Jason had already hung up.

The reporter went to the news director with the tip.

"You think it's legitimate?"

"All the other tips have been right on target," the reporter replied. "No reason to think this one isn't too."

"We keep getting these tips, but they must be coming from a cell phone. There's never a number that shows up on the Caller ID. What does the voice sound like?"

"Hard to tell," the reported said. "I thought on the first call it sounded like a kid. Now the voice is sort of muffled. Could be a woman. Or a kid. Not a man, though, I'm pretty sure."

"Wonder what they want out of it? Have they asked for anything?"

"You mean like money or something? Nope. They just drop the info, then they disappear. I didn't even get to find out who he's marrying."

"You suppose it's the Smythe gal? She seems to stick pretty close by his side."

"That'd be my guess. I will head over to the church and see if I can find anything out."

"Keep out of sight as much as you can. We don't want to blow this. This could be our ticket to the big time. This is bound to hit the AP, the UPI—hell, just about everybody in the world wants to know what's up with this guy."

"You've got it," the reporter said, grabbing her camera, her notebook and sticking a baseball cap on her mop of unruly brown hair.

CHAPTER XXXV

Jenny showed up at Blair's before seven. Blair was still lounging around in her pajamas. She was sitting at the table in the kitchen, sipping on a cup of coffee and paging through a bridal magazine.

"Where'd you get that this early?" Jenny asked.

"I went down last night after everybody'd left and picked it up at the drug store. Figured I wouldn't get much sleep, so I might as well do something constructive."

"I thought you'd already decided on the one you saw on the Net yesterday."

"Yeah," Blair said, "but I had to find something for you to wear."

"I've got plenty of things I can wear. I mean, how many times can you wear a prom dress? Might as well make use of one of them."

"No way are you going to use some old thing for my wedding. I have to give up having a big affair, so I'm going to make the most of it that I can." She took another slug of coffee, then asked, "You ready to head for Boston? I figure we can find something suitable on the rack for both of us. We don't have much time—less than a week."

"Looks to me like I'm a lot more ready than you are. You planning to go like that?"

Blair giggled. "Yeah, I'm all set. Here, finish my coffee while I go throw something on."

"Yuck! No way am I going to drink your coffee. I'll get a cup of my own, thank you very much."

Blair laughed as she went to get dressed. "Suit yourself. Be right back."

Shortly she was back, her hair pulled back in a pony tail, her purse slung over her shoulder. "Ready?"

"Can't wait," Jenny said. "We taking your car or mine?"

"Might as well take mine," Blair said. "The radio works better."

"Good," Jenny said. "That means I can take my coffee along to finish it on the way. It's hard to drive while you're drinking."

"Not supposed to do that anyway," Blair teased.

Missing the point, Jenny asked, "Do what?"

"Drink and drive."

"You spike the coffee or something?"

"I won't tell."

❈❈❈

They pulled up at a bridal boutique in Boston and Blair parked and jumped out. Jenny got out and Blair clicked the key to lock the doors.

"Here goes nothing," Jenny said.

"Here goes everything," Blair said, slugging Jenny playfully. "Just wait till your day comes."

"Yeah, in your dreams," Jenny said, pouting. "I doubt the ocean has any more of them guys hidden down there."

"I don't know," Blair said. Her mind went to Ken's invitation to take Sam with them on their next expedition. A shiver went through her whole body. It was as if fate, or the gods, or something was daring her to let him go, as if it was her ultimate test of their love. If they could survive that separation, with Sam going back to his original habitat... If he came back to her after that, she would know he was truly hers, for time and eternity.

"You okay?" Jenny asked.

"Yeah, just a little bit nervous, I guess."

Once inside the boutique, they were welcomed by a tall svelte young woman who asked them how she could help them.

"We—I need a wedding gown," Blair said. "Quickly."

"Aha. I understand," the clerk said, smirking.

"No, I don't think you do," Blair snapped at her. "You see, I have to get married before my husband-to-be goes back to sea."

"Oh, he's a sailor?" the clerk asked.

Too nosy for her own good, Blair thought.

"No," Jenny intercepted. "He's a pirate."

The clerk gasped. "You—you're the one who is going to marry Black Sam Bellamy?"

Blair cringed. How on earth did the news get out already? They had just decided on it last night.

"Where did you hear that?" Blair demanded.

"It's no big secret," the clerk said. "It was all over the news this morning. The wedding is going to be on May 19th at the Swift Memorial United Methodist Church in Hyannis."

"But it was supposed to be a secret," Blair said. "We didn't want a lot of fuss about it."

"Why on earth not?" the clerk questioned. "It's not every day a gal gets married, and certainly not to a guy that looks like *him*. You really lucked out, lady."

Blair got caught up in the moment and she said, "He is rather handsome, isn't he?"

"Yeah, and the story he's got cooked up. Heck, he's a better actor than Tom Cruise, Mel Gibson, or even Johnny Depp. You go, girl! Now, what kind of a gown were you looking for?"

Blair described the gown she and Jenny had seen on the computer. The clerk shook her head.

"No way. That's way too plain for an occasion like this. Let me show you a few gowns and see what you think."

Blair buried her head in her hands. "I thought this was going to be so simple. Seems like everybody knows what I want but me."

"You know exactly what you want," Jenny reminded her. "You want Sam. Nothing else really matters."

The clerk came back in a few minutes, her arms laden with frills and ruffles and glitter. Blair shook her head. "Those don't look like anything I'd wear to a circus," she said.

Soon they were nearly blinded by flashing lights. There were TV cameras clicking all around them. The manager of the boutique was there with a digital camera. "Best advertising we've ever had," she quipped.

"Wait a minute!" Blair shouted. "I didn't agree to all of this."

"Just think," the manager said. "It will be preserved in posterity for you. You can look back at this day and tell your children and your grandchildren about it."

"If I live that long," Blair said. "Or if you do. Now, get those people out of here."

The people all left, satisfied that they already had what they wanted anyway.

Blair hadn't noticed that Jenny had wandered off on her own and was looking through the dresses that were hanging on the rack. Suddenly she let out a yelp. "Blair! Come here!"

Blair went to see what she had found. There was the same dress they had seen on the computer yesterday.

"That's it!" Blair shrieked. "That's my dress." She took it off the rack and held it up in front of her. It was rather plain, yet elegant. It was fitted, with just a hint of a train, a draping neckline, and long tapered sleeves. It was of a soft jersey fabric that looked like it would cling to every curve in just the right way. "It's perfect. I'll take it."

The clerk could see that there was no point in arguing with her. "Try it on so we can see if it needs any alterations. Then we can order it in the right size."

"What size is this one?" Blair asked.

"It's a size eight," the clerk answered.

"Then it will fit," Blair said. "I'll take it."

"We don't sell things off the racks," the clerk said. "They have to be special ordered. These are just samples for people to choose from."

"I'll make it worth your while," Blair said. "How much does it cost?"

"I'll have to look it up to be sure." The clerk went behind a desk and put the code from the desk into the computer. "It's eight hundred dollars," she said, quickly closing the window so Blair couldn't see that she had added three hundred dollars onto the actual price.

"I'll pay you double," Blair said. "I don't care what you do with the extra money. If you want to keep it for yourself, I'll never tell. I just know that I want that dress, and I want it now."

"Sold," the clerk said. She hid a smile as she figured the profit she would make on this sale. That would be over a thousand dollars she could pocket and no one would be the wiser. "I'll get a box and wrap it up for you."

❈ ❈ ❈

As they drove back to Hyannis, the two friends chatted gaily about the upcoming wedding, their plans for the future, until suddenly Jenny got very quiet.

"A penny for your thoughts," Blair challenged.

"That's about all they're worth right now," Jenny replied. "I'm happy for you. I really am. I just wonder if it will ever be my turn." She sniffed a little as she added, "Always a bridesmaid, never a bride."

"I didn't know you'd been a bridesmaid before."

"I haven't," Jenny said, trying to laugh through her tears. "It's just a saying. You know that."

"You'll find your Mr. Right, I promise," Blair said, trying to assure her. "You just never know where they'll show up from."

"I guess you'd know about that one," Jenny said. She giggled as she said, "Who knew what all was under that algae hanging from his hair the day he washed up on shore."

"He was a sight for sore eyes, wasn't he?" Blair asked. "But he was so fascinating."

"You're right on that one too," Jenny said.

Blair pulled the car into the driveway, turned off the engine and jumped out, grabbing the box from the back seat that held her wedding gown.

"Want to come in and see how it looks?"

"Wouldn't miss it," Jenny said. Suddenly she realized that

they had forgotten all about getting a dress for Jenny. They would obviously have to take another trip back to Boston in the next couple of days. Blair always loved shopping, but it seemed like it was the last thing on her mind today.

As they walked into the house, Jenny said, "So you want me to wear one of my prom dresses after all?"

Blair gasped. "I forgot all about getting your dress. Oh, Jen, I'm so sorry. We'll go back this afternoon and get something for you to wear. Oh, I'm so glad you are here with me. You're the bestest." She gave her friend a big hug. "I'd be lost without you. You can't ever go up to New York and perform on Broadway. Whatever would I do if you weren't here?"

"Yeah, fat chance of that happening anyway," Jenny said. "I'll be lucky if I get onto the stage up in Boston."

"You have to believe in yourself," Blair challenged. "If you can dream it, it can happen."

Once inside the house, Blair opened the box and pulled the wedding gown out. She shed her jeans and sweatshirt and pulled it on. Like she suspected, it fit like it was made for her. There were no alterations needed. She walked into her bedroom and studied her image in the full length mirror. "Well? What do you think?"

To her surprise, she heard Sam's voice in reply. She had not heard him come in.

"No!" she screamed, slamming the door shut. "You can't see it. Not until the day of the wedding. It's bad luck."

"Little lady," Sam said through the closed door, "if I can come to you through the ocean and through the centuries of time itself, no bad luck is going to interfere with our being together."

"You're probably right," Blair said, trying hard not to cry. "But really, I don't want you to see it. No sense in taking chances."

"Fine. I'll leave. I just remembered that I forgot my hat when I was here with Ken last night. I came back to get it. He told me I needed it to make my costume look authentic."

"He brought you?" Blair asked.

"No," Sam said, jingling the keys in his hand. "He let me come by myself."

"You—you drove?" Blair asked.

"Yup. He's been teaching me. He said he knew I'd be fine because there isn't too much traffic this time of the morning."

"Get your hat and get out of here," Blair ordered, coming out of the bedroom with her jeans and sweatshirt on again. "I've got a wedding to get ready for."

"Yes, ma'am," Sam said and went out the door to go back to the museum. "Me too," he said.

CHAPTER XXXVI

Sam had decided to use Sam Black as his legal name, just to avoid any problems. Both Pete and Angus had gone with him to the court house to get a birth certificate. The Clerk of Courts was most skeptical about the whole thing, but Pete finally convinced her that Sam Bellamy was legally alive, despite what the news had said, but he had taken the necessary steps to change his name. He left with his certified birth certificate, and shortly thereafter he and Blair returned to get their marriage license. Angus had checked and made sure they didn't need a blood test, so that issue was not an issue.

"The only thing left," Sam said as they had departed, "is to get my drivers' license. Ken's been helping me a lot, so it shouldn't be hard to do."

Blair laughed. "Did you ever think, the first time you saw a car, that one day you would be driving one?"

"There are a whole lot of things I never thought I'd be doing," Sam said. "Getting married is one of them."

"Any regrets?"

"Not one," Sam assured her.

"Not even that I'm not Maria?"

"Who?" Sam asked, grinning at her. "I think that must have been in another lifetime."

They both laughed and Sam dropped Blair off at her house, then went back to the museum.

✼ ✼ ✼

The day before the wedding arrived and Sam and Blair met at the Methodist Church for the rehearsal. Jenny, the maid-of-honor, was with Blair, and Ken, the best man, was with Sam. Blair had tried to convince Sam to ask Angus to stand up with him, but Sam seemed awfully skittish about even being anywhere near Angus. Blair had made sure, however, that he would be at the wedding. She said to Jenny, "If Dad doesn't show up, I'll just ask Angus to give me away."

"You honestly think your dad might miss the wedding?" Jenny asked.

"He doesn't like my marrying Sam one bit. In fact, he had a long talk with Sam the other day. At the same time, Mom gave me a what-for about all the reasons why I shouldn't marry Sam."

"Did Sam tell you what your dad said?"

"No, he wouldn't say anything about it, other than that he knew he wasn't happy about it." Blair looked like she was on the verge of tears. "I really want Mom and Dad to like Sam."

"I don't think it's that they don't like him," Jenny said. "Not exactly. I think it's more that they don't trust him."

The bride and her maid-of-honor entered the church, where Sam, Ken and Rev. Perry, the minister, were waiting for them.

"We might have a problem," the minister said. "Nothing major, but it might make you re-think your plans."

"Whatever it is, I *am* marrying Sam tomorrow. I don't care what my father might have told you."

"It has nothing to do with your father," Rev. Perry said. "One of our parishioners called me and said that the news had leaked out to one of the TV reporters that you are getting married tomorrow, and that it was to be at two o'clock. She is planning to be there, photographers and all."

"How did they find out?" Blair exclaimed. "We've been so careful to keep it quiet. We haven't told anybody."

"My guess is that somebody is feeding them information," Ken said. "They seem to turn up every time there is anything going on with Sam."

"But who?" Blair asked.

"No idea," Ken said. "So what do you want to do about it? I know you wanted it to be a private ceremony."

"Can we move the time up?" Sam asked. "What if we get married at ten o'clock instead of at two? That way by the time they showed up it would be all over and done with."

"It's fine with me," Rev. Perry said. "Anybody have any objections?"

They all agreed, and the rehearsal was just about to get underway when Martin and Maggie showed up. Blair breathed a huge sigh of relief. Maggie smiled at her daughter, and Blair knew instinctively that it was her doings that Martin had agreed to come at all.

"Let's get started," Rev. Perry said. He told Ken and Jenny where to stand, then positioned Sam in the middle, between them, and instructed Blair to go to the end of the aisle to take her father's arm and come down the aisle together.

Blair leaned over to Martin and whispered, "Thank you for coming, Dad. I love you."

Despite his misgivings about Sam, Martin smiled at his daughter. "I love you too." He waited a moment, then said, "He better make you happy or he'll wish he'd never come up for air from that eddy."

Blair chuckled. "He will, Dad. I know he will. I love him so much."

The rehearsal went smoothly, with the vows being exchanged without a hitch, and the wedding party left.

"Should I come over to your house?" Sam asked Blair.

"No. I need a good night's rest. I have to get my beauty sleep tonight."

"You always look beautiful," Sam said, grinning at Blair, the gold in his teeth glistening from the streetlights.

"Okay, I'll see you in the morning," Sam said. "By this time tomorrow night we'll be Mr. and Mrs. Sam Black."

❈ ❈ ❈

Jason quietly slipped out the back door of the church, where he'd been listening to the entire process of the rehearsal. Once he was far enough away that he was sure nobody could hear him, he called the TV station and asked for the reporter by name. He had learned that there was one reporter he could trust after she had been assigned to all of the stories he had tipped them off about.

"There's been a change in plans," he said, holding the napkin over the phone as usual. "The wedding has been moved up to ten o'clock tomorrow morning. Don't tell anybody about it. Somebody at the station warned them that you were going to be there in the afternoon."

"What are you getting out of this?" the reporter asked the informant.

"Fun," Jason said and flipped the phone off.

❋ ❋ ❋

It was their wedding eve. Blair wondered if the night would ever pass. She was too restless to sleep, so she popped a movie into the TV to watch. She hadn't even looked at what she had chosen. Soon the town of Brigadoon was coming back to life after lying dormant for one hundred years. It sent cold chills up Blair's spine. She had watched this movie countless times. In fact, it was one of her favorites. Tonight, for some unexplainable reason, it cast an eerie mood over her. She ejected the movie, slipped it back into the case and turned the radio on to listen to some soft music. "Much better," she said to herself.

❋ ❋ ❋

The next morning, Jenny arrived bright and early. She had already donned the dress she and Blair had picked out on their return visit to the bridal boutique. Her hair was hanging loosely in curls, and she had flowers pinned in place. She looked beautiful.

Blair was still in her pajamas, drinking a cup of coffee and twisting her hair nervously.

"Come on and join me," Blair invited, pouring a cup of coffee for Jenny.

Jenny sat down at the table. Blair went over to the pantry and took out an apron and tied it around Jenny's neck.

"You think I need a bib?" Jenny mocked, sticking her thumb in her mouth and looking like a little child.

"I'm not taking any chances," Blair said. "That's why I didn't get dressed yet. Besides, I need your help with my hair. Yours looks perfect, by the way."

As soon as they finished drinking their coffee the long-time friends went into Blair's bedroom. She sat on the chair by her vanity and Jenny began twisting Blair's locks into curls on top of her head. Blair watched her every move, amazed at the transformation that was taking place.

"I look like somebody out of a fashion magazine," Blair said, turning her head slightly to get a different view of what Jenny was doing.

"Hold still," Jenny warned, "or you'll look like Godzilla."

"Yes, ma'am," Blair said, smiling.

"Well, what do you think?" Jenny asked as she put the last pin in place.

"I think you are a miracle worker. I've never looked like this."

Jenny laughed. "I didn't think a pony tail was quite appropriate for the occasion, although Sam is so in love with you he probably wouldn't have even noticed."

"As long as I didn't have that black wig on," Blair said, and they laughed together. "Oh, the memories that life is made from."

"I'll bet that's one you'll never repeat."

"You've got that right. I didn't think it would have quite the effect it had on him."

"Too bad we didn't stick around to see Ken try to revive him."

"I hope he doesn't pass out today," Blair said. She shivered slightly. "Or just disappear. What if his time travel thingy somehow gets reversed right in the middle of the ceremony?"

"I think your love for each other is so strong that it could overcome anything, even that."

"You really think so?"

"Positive," Jenny said, linking pinkies with Blair like they had done as little girls when they agreed on something.

"Pinkie, pinkie, we're not stinky," Blair said, quoting their old saying.

"Let's get your dress on," Jenny said. "You don't want to be late for your own wedding."

"Get me to the church on time..." Blair began singing as Jenny gathered the wedding gown into her arms and waited while Blair put on her undergarments. Soon she was sliding it, oh so carefully, over Blair's head and zipping the back up.

"Oh!" Blair exclaimed. "I have to wear these." She took a beautiful string of pearls out of a box and handed them to Jenny. "Sam gave me these. Aren't they just the prettiest thing you've ever seen? He said he got them from a Spanish ship he captured 'back in the day.' They were at the museum, but Ken agreed to let him have them back when he told him why he wanted them."

"Well, that sure qualifies as the something old," Jenny joked. "I'll bet it's the oldest thing any bride has ever worn. Now, do you have something blue?"

Blair reached into another little box and extracted the traditional blue garter. She slid it onto her leg.

"Perfect," Jenny said. "You dress is new. What about something borrowed?"

"I...I don't know," Blair said. "I guess I forgot about that."

Jenny took the high school class ring from her finger and slipped it onto Blair's. "This should work. I want it back, so that sure as the devil makes it borrowed."

"Thanks," Blair said, hugging her friend. "You're the best."

"I know," Jenny said, grinning. "But it's still always a bridesmaid, never a bride."

"Your turn will come," Blair said, trying to reassure her.

Jenny put the veil atop Blair's head, then stood back and admired her. "The way you look today would make anybody fall in love with you."

"Even a three-hundred-year-old pirate?"

"Even a three-hundred-year-old pirate would come to life at the sight of you."

"He already has," Blair said.

The two women went out to Jenny's car and headed for the

church. They could tell that the others were already there. Angus's car, Ken's truck, Martin and Maggie's car—they were all there.

"There's no car for Rev. Perry," Blair said, her voice filled with angst.

Jenny snickered. "Yeah, they need one, that's for sure. Did you forget that the parsonage is right behind the church?"

"Oh, yeah, I guess so," Blair said.

As they entered the church, they saw everybody already in their place. Mrs. Perry was seated at the organ, and as soon as Martin was beside Blair, she began playing the wedding march. Sam's grin was as big as all outdoors. He had never seen anything more beautiful in his life than his lovely bride. For just a fleeting moment, he thought he saw Maria coming towards him instead of Blair, then he snapped back to reality. *How do I know what's real,* he wondered. *I don't even know if I'm real.*

None of them had seen the TV van that was parked about a block away. As soon as Rev. Perry said, "We are gathered here to unite these two in..." the reporter and the photographer burst through the door, the camera already rolling.

Furious, Sam, dressed in his finest pirate costume, ran towards the reporter. He didn't care that it was a woman. He would not let anyone spoil today.

Angus tackled Sam, casting him onto the floor. He sat on top of him, trying to keep him from doing something that would land him in jail instead of at the altar.

A weird sense of *déjà vu* crept through Angus. For some reason, he felt like he had done this before, but that made no sense to him. Was it Sam's hypnotized account of what had happened the day he disappeared, when he insisted that he had been thrown in jail? He said he had felt that "sting" Angus administered when he gave him the sedative in the butt before. How Angus wished he had his medical bag now so he could sedate him again. He knew Sam was probably capable of killing both the reporter and the photographer with his bare hands.

Ken escorted the reporter and the photographer outside, with a warning that if they returned he would call the police and have them arrested.

"For breaking and entering a church?" the reporter scoffed. "Now that would make a great story for the evening news."

"Get out of here!" Ken threatened. He re-entered the church, securely locking the doors behind him.

"Now, where were we?" Rev. Perry said, and resumed the ceremony like nothing had happened.

Jason peered through the crack in the door of the small office to the side of the platform to watch the whole scene. He wondered if things would go back to being boring once they were happily married. He'd follow them, from afar, just in case. He couldn't imagine any life with Black Sam Bellamy, or Sam Black, being either boring or normal.

"I now pronounce you man and wife," Rev. Perry said, and Jason hid his head when he said, "Sam Black, you may kiss your bride."

"Yuck!" Jason mumbled, then he slid out the side door of the office to get home. He was glad they had decided to get married on a Saturday. He knew he'd be in trouble if he skipped school. He didn't want to miss this event. He was sure it would be a day that would go down in history.

CHAPTER XXXVII

August, 2008

"I don't want you to go," Blair protested as she clung to Sam.

"I won't be gone long," Sam said, running his fingers through her hair. "It's the one sure way I have of proving that I am who I am."

"I'm Popeye the Sailor Man," Blair sang. "I yam who I yam..."

"Do you have a song for everything?" Sam asked. "Some of them don't make any sense."

"When you get back I'll get a movie of Popeye and we'll watch it."

"Okay. At least you said *when* I get back. Last night you said *if* I get back."

Blair broke out in sobs, burying her face in Sam's chest. "Oh, Sam! That's the problem. I'm so afraid that if you get back in the ocean, back where you came from, that it will keep you there. I couldn't bear to lose you."

"I promise I'll come back," he said, holding her tightly.

"But you promised Maria that you would go back for her too..."

"But I did go back. I still don't understand it, but she was married and Little Sam—that's what she called the baby, *our* baby—was there with her. I swear I saw them. I don't care what the history books say. I saw it with my own eyes. And she was living in a nice house in Yarmouth, not out in some shanty by the bay."

"I don't understand it either," Blair said. "That doesn't matter. All that matters is that you come to me. You were supposed to come to me, and you did. At least now we can check the computer for the weather conditions so you won't go diving with Ken and Barry and the crew if there's going to be another nor'easter."

"I promise if they say bad weather is coming, I won't go. Does that make you feel better?"

"I guess so," she said, pulling away from him and drying her tears on his sleeve. "I will be a lot happier when you get back." She was silent for a few minutes, then asked Sam for the umpteenth time, "What is it that you think you can find on the ship that will prove everything?"

"If I find it, you will be the first one I show it to. I promise. Then I will show Ken and Barry. I have told them about it so they would believe me."

"You told them but you didn't tell me? I'm your wife! You have to tell me."

"I'm afraid, after all these years, it might not be any good. It might be ruined. It is in a box that is supposed to keep it safe from the water. Then that box is inside a big trunk. I just hope and pray it has been preserved through all these years."

Blair looked Sam straight in the eyes and asked him, "How is it that you so often talk about God and prayer and the Bible and religious things? That just doesn't seem like something a pirate would do."

"What I bring up, if I can find it, will answer your questions. Then I'll tell you the rest of the story."

"Just like Paul Harvey," Blair said.

"Who?"

"Paul Harvey. He is—was—an old man that told the news every day on the radio. My dad wouldn't miss him for anything. And nobody better say a word, not even in a whisper, when Paul Harvey was on."

"He sounds like a powerful man," Sam said.

"He was. I doubt that he ever really knew how many people listened to his every word. And they believed him. I think he could have said the sky was falling and people would have gone and hid to make sure they were safe."

"I wish people believed me like that," Sam said softly. "I wonder if they ever will, even if I find the proof on the *Whydah*."

"I believe you," Blair said, squeezing his hand. "What else matters?"

"Your dad. It would make me feel so much better if he believed me."

"It doesn't matter," Blair insisted.

"It does matter. It matters to you. I can see it in your eyes when he questions the whole thing. And you matter to me, more than I can ever tell you. No matter what happens, I will always love you."

Blair cringed. "*No matter what happens?* You are afraid, too, that you might not come back to me."

"No," Sam insisted. "I know in my heart of hearts that I will come back. But there is something else. Something I can't explain. Something that I think could change our lives forever."

"Like what?"

"I don't know," Sam said, shaking his head. "I can't explain it. It's just a feeling. I guess when it happens we'll know what it was."

"You sound like we are on Jeopardy," Blair said. She and Sam had watched the TV program together many times. It was one way of trying to help him learn about many things. Things that were new to him, things that were in the ancient history on the game show. "If we get the answer, we will know what the question was."

"Something like that," Sam said.

"You are leaving in the morning?" Blair asked cautiously, still hoping he might change his mind.

"Yes. It is something I have to do. Ken is going to stop by here early in the morning to pick me up. They already have all the gear ready so we can leave as soon as we get to the site where we'll be diving."

Port Call to the Future

"I want to go watch you," Blair said.

"I think you should stay home," Sam said. "We will say our goodbyes in the morning. I promise, I'll be safe."

❈ ❈ ❈

Blair tossed and turned in the bed, snuggled against Sam. Not only was she nervous about him leaving, but she wondered if she played her trump card if he would reconsider and abort his part of the expedition. Was that playing dirty pool? She felt almost like it would be blackmail. If he knew that she was pregnant...that might be the only way to stop him. But if she told him, would he always regret not being able to go back to the *Whydah* to get whatever the proof was that would settle the question once and for all that he truly was Black Sam Bellamy?

Sam lay there, awake, waiting to make sure Blair was deep in sleep. He knew she had been taking some medications lately to help her sleep. He knew he was to blame for her sleeplessness. He had made sure she took one of the tablets tonight. He couldn't risk her awakening and finding him gone, even if it was just for a short period of time. She was so afraid. He prayed silently that he would be able to fulfill his promise to her to return after the dive. He also prayed that he would find the proof he so desperately sought. It was the most valuable treasure on the entire ship.

Finally, certain that she was asleep, he pulled his clothes on and looked at the clock. The red numbers flashed 1:23. He tiptoed out of the bedroom, trying to make sure the chains on his boots didn't jingle.

He went out through the kitchen and opened the door to the basement, flipping on the light switch. He still marveled at all the things he had learned about in this new world. People seemed to take them for granted, but they were novelties to him. He wondered if he would ever get used to them.

Once he was in the basement, he got a claw hammer, a big flashlight, and a rope. He climbed the stairs, turned the light off, closed the basement door, and went outside. He made sure the back door wasn't locked. He didn't want to lock himself outside.

Sam went over to a tree near the root door cellar. He fastened the rope securely around it. He didn't want to take a chance on falling on another breaking run on the ladder that led to his hiding place. There was plenty of light from the streetlights, so he didn't have to turn the flashlight on. He didn't want to attract any attention. He would turn it on when he got down into the hole. He had seen the police prowling on their street on a regular basis. He was sure they were watching for him to do something—anything—illegal.

Sam stood still for a few moments, waiting for his eyes to adjust to the near darkness. He reflected on what the people from his other life would have thought of such an invention as a flashlight instead of their oil-filled lanterns.

He inched his way along, feeling the wall as he went. He could still remember the night he had hid them there, almost three hundred years ago. He counted his steps—one, two, three... twelve, thirteen—then he stopped. He had made it a point of choosing thirteen paces, just to prove, to whom he had no idea, that he was not superstitious. He shone the flashlight on the wall and easily found the "x" he had placed there to mark the spot.

He took the hammer and began to pull the mud blocks free. Before long he could see that it was still there. He jumped up in the air, let out a huge "Aargh!" and carefully pulled the wool sack from the hiding place. It fell into shreds, just from sheer age, and the jewels tumbled onto the ground, surrounding his feet. He carefully bent over and grabbed them, stuffing them into his pockets. He ran his hands over the ground to make sure he had not missed any of them. He ambled slowly back to the opening and the rope, pulling himself up to the fresh air. His mind went back to his days on the *Whydah* when he would shinny up the ropes to get to the sails to secure them after they had loosened from high winds at sea. He was suddenly homesick for his days of yore. Still, he could not deny that he had more here with Blair than he had ever dreamed possible.

He went and untied the rope and returned to the house. He went down to the basement and returned the hammer, the flashlight and the rope. He ascended the stairway, turned the basement light off, then stopped to remove his boots. He left them sitting by the back door.

As he sat on the edge of the bed, he was glad to see that Blair was sleeping much more peacefully than she had been earlier. He credited the sleeping pill for doing its job. He removed his clothes and reached into his pants pocket and gently withdrew the emeralds.

Sam grinned. For all of the years since he'd been missing, people far and wide had speculated about the claimed emeralds he was supposed to have had on board. He guessed they had heard about them from the two survivors of the ship. Still, the Expedition Whydah crew had not found any evidence that they existed. No one, not even his crew, knew that he had taken them on that last fateful day and hid them in Thomas Hallett's root cellar, just waiting for the proper time to present them to Maria. In the morning he would give them to Blair.

Sam slid in between the cool sheets. Blair rolled over and subconsciously wrapped her arm over his chest. He grinned in the darkness. Oh, yes, life was good!

He soon fell asleep, dreaming of his trip down to the *Whydah* in the morning. His final trip, he knew, back to the depths of the ocean. Back to a life that used to be, and that never would be again.

CHAPTER XXXVIII

Maria awoke in the morning and stretched. She turned towards the other side of the bed to discover that Sam was already up—and gone? She hoped not. She had to tell him goodbye before he left. She shivered, afraid that she would never see him again, yet he had promised to come back to her.

She got up and raced out to the kitchen. He was sitting at the table, drinking a cup of coffee. He looked up at her and smiled. He reached for his boots and put them on.

"Good morning, Sleepyhead," he said.

Blair went over to him, wrapped her arms around him and kissed him like there was no tomorrow. Perhaps, she feared, there would not be, not for the two of them.

"You slept hard," Sam said.

"I shouldn't have taken that sleeping pill," Blair said. "I wanted to stay awake all night."

"Why?"

"I just wanted to watch you, in case..."

"Hush!" Sam cautioned, placing his hand over her mouth. "None of that talk! It's a day to celebrate."

"I hope you are right," Blair said.

"Have I ever lied to you?"

"Not that I know of," Blair teased. "Of course how could I know if you did or not?"

"If I find what I'm going after, I can prove it to everybody once and for all."

"I still don't know what could be that valuable," Blair said.

"Well, it isn't these," Sam said, reaching into his pocket and letting the emeralds fall onto the table from his hand.

Blair gasped. "What are they?"

"They are emeralds. Of course they aren't all shaped and polished yet, but those are the emeralds Ken and Barry looked for when they found the *Whydah*. The ones everybody for centuries has claimed I brought back for Maria. I did bring them back, but I hid them until the time was right to give them to her." He took her tender hands in his big, rough ruddy ones. "I think the time is right. You are not Maria. We both know that. But you are *my* Maria. You are the one I love. The only one I will ever love."

"Where were they hidden?"

Sam grinned. "They were practically under your nose the whole time. I hid them in the root cellar. I went down there last night to see if they had survived, and they were right where I had hidden them, placed behind one of the mud blocks."

"You went into the root cellar with no one with you?" Blair asked. "What if the ladder had broken again? You couldn't have gone with the crew today if you had sprained you ankle again." How she wished that had happened. She longed to find some way to keep him with her. Why couldn't the men from Barry's crew find whatever it was he wanted so badly and bring it up? Why did he have to be there to recover it?

"I didn't use the ladder. I tied a rope around a tree and lowered myself down by it."

"But how did you get back up?"

"It was easy. I had gone up and down ropes tied to the masts on the *Whydah* many times. Some things you never forget."

❋ ❋ ❋

Blair pleaded with Sam to let her go along to see them off as they dove into the waters off the coast. She finally agreed to stay home, but she knew she would go down there to welcome them back, when—*if*...

She knew they would only be gone a few hours at the most. Their air supply came from hoses on the boat they dove from. She was confident that Barry and Ken would watch out for him. After all, he was their most prized treasure. If he should disappear from the museum, they would lose a big part of their appeal. Their business had definitely picked up since he'd started doing the tours there. No, they couldn't afford to lose him. Still, what if fate decided he should stay down there another three hundred years? How would she—how would *they*—survive without him?

Blair rubbed her stomach. She wondered if Maria had the same fears and "what-ifs" she felt now. Would Sam ever know his child? Should she have told him? Her mind whirled with a million questions. One thing was certain: as soon as he came up, she was going to tell him. He had lost one child. She was not going to make him lose another one.

She pondered the things he had said when he was under the hypnotic spell. They still didn't make any sense. How could he have seen Maria with a husband and a baby—*his* baby? She had heard all her life that history doesn't lie. But it seemed as if it had. Why had the history books all said that Maria's baby died the night he was born? And they all had her as an outcast, an accused witch, that was banned from the town. How did they allow her to live in a nice house with her husband and baby?

Blair felt her head start to spin. She reclined on the sofa and was soon asleep. Her questions plagued her in her dreams. She saw Maria and the baby—*and Angus McPherson*!

She awoke with a start, jumping up and rubbing her eyes and massaging her forehead. She had a nasty headache. What did any of this mean? She had dreamed the same things Sam had related when he was hypnotized. It had to be her mind playing tricks on her, yet it seemed so real.

She grabbed for her phone and punched the number that would reach Angus. Perhaps he would have some answers for her, yet he had seemed as stymied by Sam's declarations as the rest of them.

"Dr. McPherson's office," the receptionist answered.

"I need to speak to Angus," Blair said. "Immediately."

"I'm sorry but he is in with a patient."

"Then have him call me as soon as he's finished. It is urgent."

"Are you in labor, ma'am?"

"No, I'm not in labor! I'm just barely pregnant! I am Blair Smythe...Blair *Smythe-Black*," she said emphatically, as if that would give her special privileges.

"Your phone number?" the receptionist asked coldly. "Are you a patient of Dr. McPherson?"

"He has my phone number," Blair said and turned the phone off. There was nothing to do now but to wait.

❊ ❊ ❊

It was only twenty minutes until Angus called, but to Blair it seemed like a lifetime.

"Blair? It's Angus. What's the matter, honey?"

Blair burst into tears. "I don't know. It's Sam. It's me. It's us."

"Calm down," Angus said, trying to use his most soothing voice, the one he always used when a woman was having a particularly difficult labor. "I have one more patient I have to see before lunch. As soon as I'm done with her I'll come over." He hesitated, and didn't know why he added, "Don't do anything stupid."

"Don't worry," Blair assured him. "I'm not going to kill myself or anything. I have everything in the world to live for. At least if Sam comes back, I will."

Angus didn't bother to ask her where he was or what she was talking about. He would find out when he got there.

❊ ❊ ❊

Blair ran to Angus and threw her arms around him, sobbing against his chest.

"Wow! I don't know what has you spooked, but it must be something huge. Come on and sit down and let's figure it out."

Blair told him about the dream and about Sam going with the Expedition Whydah crew and how scared she was that he would get stuck in the ocean again. She rambled on so fast Angus had to strain to catch everything she was saying.

"When are they supposed to be back?" he asked her.

"Just a few hours, he said. It's only been two hours, but I think I will go down to the docks and wait for them. I want to be there to greet him." The fear showed in her eyes. Her hands were as cold as clams.

"I'll go with you," Angus said. "Just let me call and cancel my afternoon appointments."

"Oh! I didn't mean to take you away from your patients. They need you more than I do. At least so far."

"And what is that supposed to mean?" Angus asked. "Right now you are my top priority."

Blair blushed a bit. "I think I'm pregnant." She waited for Angus's reaction.

"Have you seen anybody yet? You should be checked out to make sure. We don't want anything to happen to that little one."

"Of course I haven't seen anybody," Blair said, surprised by his asking such a question. "I would never go to any doctor except you." She hesitated, then asked, "It wouldn't be a conflict of interest, would it? I mean, since we are good friends and all."

"Only if you are a family member," Angus said. "The medical field sort of frowns on that. How do you know you are pregnant?"

"Well, the obvious lack of my period, and then I got a home pregnancy test." Blair laughed. "Actually, I bought six of them, just to make sure."

"And they were all positive?"

"Yup. All six of them. I got rid of them before Sam got home from the museum. Not that he would have known what they were anyway."

"Don't be too surprised. He's a pretty sharp fellow," Angus warned. "In fact, Ken reminded me just the other day, when we were talking about the night he broke into the museum, that he's pretty sneaky. That was really pretty ingenious for him to pose as his own statue."

Blair laughed again. "Oh, he's creative in a lot of ways." She didn't explain any further, but left Angus to his own imagination as to what she was talking about. He had more than proved his expertise in the bedroom on many occasions. It was no wonder she was already pregnant.

Angus studied Blair carefully. He had done a very unscientific study in his practice as an OB/GYN doctor. So far, the tests had proven rather impressive. *Oh, heck, what do you have to lose? Just go ahead and ask her.*

"I don't mean to embarrass you, but I've been doing a study and I would like you to participate, if you don't mind."

"I doubt that there's much you could do that would embarrass me. Go ahead, what do you want to know?"

"Have you and Sam made love in the morning, or just at night?"

"Morning, noon, night... He'll do it whenever he gets a chance," Blair said, again turning a bit red. "He's pretty good, for an old guy."

They both laughed. Angus had to admit that Sam was definitely the oldest father he'd had as a patient. Well, technically, Blair was—would be—his patient, but he always liked to have both prospective parents in on the exams. He thought about what life must have been like back in the early 1700s, delivering a baby. So much knowledge that they had now that had never been heard of back then. He wondered if he had been there, knowing what he knew now, if he could possibly have saved Maria's baby's life. *What an absurd thought*, he mused. No way to know what could have been. That was long ago and far away.

He reached into his pocket and took out a business card. He wrote a time down for her first pre-natal exam. "That makes it official," he announced.

"Now, do you want to wander down to the waterfront and see if there is any sign of them coming back up?" Angus asked.

It didn't take much more than a minute for Blair to jump up, run to the bathroom, lock the kitchen door and come back to head to the shore. She prayed as she got in Angus's car, that Sam would soon come back to her.

CHAPTER XXXIX

Ken had given Sam instructions on how to communicate if he found what he was looking for. There was no way, of course, for them to talk to one another, but they had a signaling system set up using their air hoses so they could send a message up to the men on the boat that was waiting for them.

Sam was swimming around, feeling like he had come back home, as he made his way from one end of the *Whydah* to the other. He found the remains of his bed. He tried to take a deep breath and nearly drowned in his oxygen supply. He went over beside it and groped for the bed's leg. Yes! It was there! The lock was still in place.

Sam hurried to send a message up to have either Barry or Ken find him. He knew they were well supplied and he had told them he might need a metal cutter to get the chain free.

In a matter of mere moments, Ken was beside him. Sam pointed to the lock and the chain. Ken took the metal cutter he had and made one hard snip. The chain fell to the bottom of the ship and Sam struggled to pull the trunk out from under the bed. It was not nearly as big as Ken thought it would be, but they would still have to have someone send the winch down to raise it.

Ken tried to open it, but Sam shook his head no. He knew that if the proof he was looking for was exposed to the water it would be ruined. It might well already be of no use to them. Still, he hoped.

Before long the winch was lowered and they fastened the trunk onto it so it could be hoisted up to the waiting boat.

They had been down there long enough, Ken knew, for them all to head up. The water, even in their gear, was incredibly cold. Hypothermia could set in at any time. He motioned for Sam to follow him. They soon found the other members of the crew, and they all headed towards the top of the ocean, all of them with bits and pieces of treasures they had found.

When they reached the top, the men on the boat helped them climb aboard. They each took off their breathing apparatus and Barry asked Sam, "Is that it?"

"Yes," Sam said, "but you can't open it yet. I promised Blair I would let her see it before anybody else."

"Whatever," Barry said, his hands itching to get inside to see if the verification Sam had promised them was still intact. "Home, Jeeves," he directed the captain of the boat.

Shortly they were in sight of the shoreline. Sam could see Blair and Angus there, waiting for them. For him. As soon as he was on shore, Blair ran to him and hugged him tightly.

"You came back to me," she said.

"I told you I would."

"Did you find what you were looking for?"

"Yes, but we won't know until we get to the museum if it survived or not."

"Now will you tell me what it is?"

"Soon. It will only be a few minutes to get it hauled over there. Then we'll all open it together."

Blair and Sam walked, hand in hand, to the museum. The others all followed. Barry and Ken struggled to get the trunk into Ken's vehicle, and when it was loaded, Barry got in with him and they pulled up in front of the museum, then unloaded it.

Inside, Sam looked as nervous as a mouse being eyed by a hungry cat. Ken cut the lock on the trunk itself, and waited for Sam to open it. When it was opened, piles of pearls, gold coins, silver, all sorts of other jewels were visible. Sam seemed to ignore them as he dug to the bottom of the stash. He pulled out a tin box, sealed with wax. He cut the wax and took the top off the box. Inside, as good as new, was a Bible. The Bible Mother Wesley had given him when he was but a lad. He opened it, carefully in case it was fragile from time, and turned to John 3:16. "For God so loved the world that He gave His only begotten Son, that whosoever believeth on Him should not perish but have everlasting life," he read. "It's the same as always," he said, laughing.

"It was a Bible?" Blair asked, disbelief in her voice. "That's what you said would prove you really are Black Sam Bellamy? But how..."

"Here, look," Sam said, turning to the frontispiece. "Mother Wesley signed it before she gave it to me." There, still legible, was the inscription Mother Wesley had written in it in the early 1700s. She promised to pray for Sam as long as she should live, and asked that he find a true faith in God.

"That's what kept me going many times when we were out at sea," Sam said. "I spent hours alone in my cabin, memorizing it. When I was in that eddy, all those years, it was almost like I had it with me."

Ken and Barry looked at one another. It was incredible. The box that was supposed to be waterproof obviously was. Nobody but the real Black Sam Bellamy could possibly have known about the Bible. It was not the type of a thing that a pirate was apt to broadcast. Yes, they had their proof. Sam Black was Black Sam Bellamy. Far and above the proof of the tale he spun when he was hypnotized, this removed any shadow of doubt there might have been. Now all they had to do was to figure out if they should announce their findings to the world or to keep it secret. Somehow, it seemed to be almost a holy thing. Like Moses in the wilderness with the Ark of the Covenant. It was a finding bigger than the Shroud of Turen or the Dead Sea Scrolls. *All in good time*, Barry thought.

Ken still tried to make sense out of the whole story Sam had told about Maria being married to a doctor and the baby surviving. *It's just one of those mysteries of life that will never be explained*, he thought. He wished he had a penny for every one of them he'd encountered in his life.

❋ ❋ ❋

Blair and Sam climbed into Ken's jeep and he headed towards Hyannis, where he would let Sam and Blair go in and discuss what Sam had felt when he had been back in the *Whydah*. Again, it seemed almost like invading something holy to ask Sam about it. He would share his feelings with him when he was ready. For now, it was between the two of them.

As they pulled up in front of the house, Sam got out. He had gotten out of his gear and had his usual pirate costume on. Ken chuckled as he tried to envision Sam in a pair of blue jeans and a t-shirt some day. He had been wearing a jogging suit the first time they had met. He was sure it was something Blair had bought for him. Since his insistence that he was indeed Black Sam Bellamy, they had seen to it that he had several changes of his pirate garb.

❋ ❋ ❋

"I'm so glad you are back," Blair said, clinging to him like the barnacles on the bottom of the *Whydah*. "Promise me you will never go back there again."

Sam winked at her. "Can you give me one good reason why I shouldn't? It felt—oddly comfortable down there."

"Oh, I can give you at least two good reasons why you should stay here."

"Two?"

"Yes. Because I love you so much I would go crazy if I lost you."

"That's one," Sam said.

"The other one is because your son or daughter needs you as much as I do."

Sam's mouth dropped open. "What are you saying?"

"I'm saying that I am pregnant. We are going to have a baby." She paused to study his reaction. "I know it isn't the baby you lost, the one Maria had, whether he died or not, but I can give you your very own baby. *Our* baby."

Sam embraced Blair and kissed her warmly. "Oh, Blair, you have made me the happiest man alive." He chuckled. "This is worth waiting three hundred years for!"

"I'm glad," she said.

"Have you told anybody yet?"

"I told Angus. I mean, since he's a baby doctor..."

"A baby doctor," Sam said, staring up at the ceiling. "That's who they said had come and saved Little Sam's life, back then." He shook his head. None of it still made any sense. He guessed it didn't matter. That was then and this was now.

CHAPTER XXXX

April, 2009

The time passed quickly for Sam and Blair as they awaited the arrival of their baby. They had not really talked about having children before they were married, but Blair knew how much Sam regretted not being a part of his son's—his other son's—life. Blair was glad she was able to give him what he had never had before. Almost daily she learned new things about Sam. Almost daily she felt her girth expand.

"Give me your hand," she said to Sam as they sat on the couch, watching TV.

Sam held his hand out and Blair placed it on her stomach. The little bundle was bouncing like a basketball being dribbled.

"Does that hurt you?" he asked.

"No," Blair said, smiling at him, grateful for his concern. "It feels good. It means that the baby is healthy and getting anxious to get out of there."

"Do you mean it's time?" Sam said, jumping up and running to the bedroom to grab the suitcase Blair had packed and ready to go.

"No, silly," Blair said. "I don't think it will be long though. The baby is getting very restless. I have to go see Angus in a couple of days. He said he would decide then if he should induce labor if he or she is getting too big."

Sam stared at Blair. He hated the thought of her going through labor. He had heard horrible stories about how painful it was. He also could not get over the loss of the baby Maria had borne him. Angus and Blair had both tried to reassure him that their baby was in no danger. The medical field had progressed so much since Maria had lost their baby.

The idea that somehow the baby had survived, despite what everyone said and seemed to believe, still plagued him. He wondered if somebody with Doc Angus's expertise had been there, would things have been different? He would never know. Surely if Doc Angus had been there, as he reported in his hypnotic state, he would remember it. It seemed impossible, yet if he could travel through time, why couldn't other people do the same thing? Especially if it was for a very special reason, like saving the life of a baby. *His baby.*

Sam and Blair had purposely decided not to find out the sex of the baby. They would be thrilled with whatever God sent them. They had settled on a name. If it was a boy, of course he would be named Samuel. If it was a girl, it would be Samantha. When Blair had suggested that, Sam's face lit up like the Christmas tree in Rockefeller Center. "So either way, we could call him or her Sam?" he asked Blair.

"Yes, he or she will be our own little version of Sam." She beamed at how much her idea had affected him.

Sam and Blair's love had grown during their first year. Much to Blair's relief, Sam had not mentioned going back to the ocean again, even if Barry and Ken and the crew made other trips. He seemed perfectly satisfied and content once he recovered the Bible.

Ah, yes, the Bible. It was in a vacuum unit at the museum. He wished he could take it out and read it sometimes, but Blair had gotten him a new one. She assured him that it was the same exact words, as she had made sure it was the King James Version. They often read it together. And they attended church at the Methodist Church in Hyannis, where they were married, regularly. Once the Bible was authenticated, everybody—even the biggest skeptics, like Martin Smythe—accepted Sam as Black Sam Bellamy. Nobody could explain it, but neither could they dispute it.

※ ※ ※

The sky grew dark and the wind howled. Sam threw his head back and laughed his throaty growl that Blair loved so much.

"It's sure to be a nor'easter tonight," he remarked.

The idea made Blair extremely nervous. She knew his luck with nor'easters. The night he had first made love with Maria, the night her baby was conceived, was because he had come ashore to survive a nor'easter. The night the *Whydah* sank was during a nor'easter. The only important day in his life that hadn't been affected by one of the nasty storms seemed to be the day he washed up on shore, like Jonah of old, the luckiest day in Blair's life. The day both of their lives had changed forever. She wondered if Mother Nature would be so cruel. Would tonight be the night? She patted her stomach, willing the baby to hang on for a few more days.

Suddenly, for some unexplainable reason, Sam announced, "I have to go down to the water."

"No," Blair protested. "Not tonight." Panic registered on her face. "You can't go there in a storm."

"I'll be okay," Sam assured her. "I just have to go..."

Blair couldn't explain her feelings or her fears. It was as if he thought if he went there he could make some contact with Maria. *That's crazy*, she thought. *Maria has been dead for years. For centuries. You don't have to worry about her any more. Sam is yours, completely and willingly.*

"If you insist," she said, "but I don't like it. Just promise me that you won't be gone long."

"I promise," Sam said, grabbing his rain slicker and hat and heading out the door. He turned around and walked back to her, kissing her warmly, then patting her tummy. "You take good care of your mother, you hear?" And with that, he fastened the door securely so it wouldn't be caught by the wicked wind.

※ ※ ※

Blair paced back and forth. She wasn't sure how long Sam had been gone, but it seemed like hours. She checked her watch.

Less than half an hour had passed. The pains were getting stronger and stronger and closer together. She thought about getting in the car and going down to the coast to see if she could spot Sam.

As another pain, much fiercer than before, consumed her, she decided instead to call Angus. He would have to go to the hospital and meet her there. She prayed that the baby would hold off until she got there.

"Angus?" she said into the phone. "I think it's time. The pains are—aiyee!—they are terrible. And they are coming really fast. I thought a first baby was supposed to take a long time."

"I'll head for the hospital right away. With the weather like it is, it will probably take me longer than usual. If I don't get there in time, the ER doctors can handle it."

"No!" Blair shouted. "You have to deliver the baby. I won't push until you get there."

"Have Sam drive," Angus said. "You don't want to have an accident if you get a pain while you're on the way."

"I—I can't," Blair said. "He's gone."

There was a dead silence. Angus's imagination spun into high gear. Of all times for him to leave her alone. He knew how close it was to the baby's coming. Or was she saying... Was it possible that Sam had somehow been cast back in time, back into the ocean, back into wherever he came from? No, it could not be. This baby meant everything to Sam. Angus knew that. It was like God had granted him a second chance at living his dream.

❃ ❃ ❃

Blair practically crawled past the museum, looking inside through the window to see if there were any lights on or any sign of Sam. She watched along the coast, but she saw no sign of him.

Fear filled her entire being. Had he left her? Had he gone to the ocean and returned to the sea? Was he once again swirling in an eddy?

She knew she didn't have time to stop and look for him. She opened the window, the wind blowing her hair wildly about, and called to him as she drove along.

Feeling another bitter pain, she closed the window and went toward the hospital. At least she had left a note for him in case he came home. She knew he would come to her, if he could. He had to! He couldn't desert her, not now.

She turned into the parking lot. She was sure Angus wouldn't be there yet, but she looked around for his car, just on the off chance that he had made better time than he had estimated.

She parked the car by the emergency entrance and got out. Suddenly she felt her knees buckle. She grabbed onto the car just as her water broke. Fortunately, an orderly was on his way in to work and spotted her. He ran to her and helped her lean against the car. He grabbed his cell phone and called inside and told them to bring a wheelchair out for her.

The rest of it seemed like a blur. She felt pain. She was wet—and embarrassed. She felt fear, mainly because Sam wasn't there. She felt anxiety because Angus wasn't there. She felt anticipation because the baby was on its way. She felt every emotion she had ever felt in her entire lifetime.

An ER doctor came in to examine her, then he got a nurse to get her up to the labor unit to wait it out.

She was determined to try to hold out as long as she could. She really wanted Angus to deliver the baby. And she wanted—no, she yearned like she had never yearned before—for Sam to show up. Why did there have to be a nor'easter today of all days? Was it fate? Was their baby doomed, as Maria's had been? She remembered reading, in all of her study of Maria, that there had also been an awful storm the night her baby was born. The night her baby died.

No! She would not allow herself to go there. She was not Maria! Her baby, hers and Sam's, would be just fine. She would smile when she heard that first cry. She would count its toes and fingers to make sure it was normal.

She smiled in spite of herself. Funny, how for centuries that seemed to have been the measuring stick for a child to be born with no defects. She knew her baby would be perfect. It had to be.

She had just gotten into the bed when Sam showed up.

He raced to her side and took her hand. They had been through the birthing classes together, much against his will, and she needed him now like she had never needed him before. She was determined to stake her claim on him. The sea be damned! It couldn't have him. He had been its prisoner for centuries. Now it was her turn to have him as her own.

They waited, the pains continuing on but seemingly not getting any closer together. She began to get worried. A fill-in doctor came in periodically to check on her.

"Where is Dr. McPherson?" Blair asked a nurse.

"I don't know," the nurse answered. "Maybe he got caught in the storm. I have been trying to reach him on his cell phone, but he hasn't answered. The system is probably down."

The labor continued for several hours. There was still no sign of Angus. The doctor on call checked and she was dilating at a normal rate for a first baby. He didn't seem concerned in the least. The fleeting thought that she might need a C-section passed through Blair's mind. She asked the doctor about it, and he said it didn't look like it would be necessary but he would keep a close eye on her.

"I wouldn't dare let anything go wrong," he told her. "I hear you are Doc Angus's prize patient."

At the sound of someone else calling him "Doc Angus," Sam shuddered. He still couldn't shake the feeling that something was wrong, or that somehow this life and his past life were entwined, and Doc Angus was a big part of that.

❈ ❈ ❈

Angus came running into the room, a woman by his side. She was odd-looking, Blair thought, like somebody out of the past. If she had not been so tired from the long labor, she might have put two and two together. Little did she know just how odd this whole night would turn out.

Sam took one look at the woman and the woman looked at her.

"Sam?" the woman asked.

"Maria?" came Sam's response. And then the woman fainted dead away.

The little boy who had been clinging to the woman nearly fell, but Sam reached for him and rescued him. As soon as he touched the lad, he felt like he had been hit by lightning. He knew, in a flash, that this was Little Sam. *His son*, Little Sam. He didn't understand it at all, but neither did he understand his own resurrection.

CHAPTER XXXXI

Two nurses lifted the woman onto a gurney and wheeled her off so they could tend to her. Sam was as white as a ghost, but the baby began to pop its head out so nobody had time to worry about him. A nurse stood beside Angus and asked him, "Should we wheel her down to the delivery room?"

"No time," Angus said, then instructed Blair, "Push."

Angus looked at Sam, who was holding Little Sam in his arms.

"Sam, take the boy and get him outside. Sorry you can't stay to see this, but the lad should not have to witness this."

Sam obediently left, the boy still in his arms. He wanted to be there for Blair, but he wanted to protect his son too. He wondered if he could find where they had taken *her*—the mysterious woman whom he knew was Maria.

After about three good pushes, the baby was far enough out so Angus could help her make her dramatic entrance into the world.

"Congratulations," he said to the new mother. "You have a perfect little daughter."

Blair beamed. For the moment, the strange woman was as far away as if she had been...

In her own time and her own place, Blair thought. It was as impossible for Maria to be here, now, as...as it was for Sam to be here. Was that why it had taken Doc Angus so long to get there? Had he gone back to rescue Maria and bring her here with him?

The whole idea was absurd. Still, Sam being there, giving her his baby—*their baby*—was completely crazy too.

"I have to go find Sam," Angus said abruptly, *before he finds Maria*, his mind warned him. There was no telling what might happen if they were left alone together. How would she explain what had happened to Sam? How would Sam explain to her how he got here? How was he going to explain to either of them—*both of them*—what had happened on the way to...

"A funny thing happened on the way to the Forum," he recited as he walked through the hallway, looking for any sign of either of them.

"Ah, yes, you see, I was coming to deliver a baby, Sam's baby, when I was flagged down by another man, John Hallett, to go deliver another baby, Sam's baby..." He was trying to frame the words he would tell Sam when he found him.

"Oh, yes, piece of cake," he mumbled.

An orderly walked past him, then turned around and asked, "You okay, Doc?"

"Just hunky dory," Angus said, continuing on his way to look for the two lost, misplaced souls he had to deal with.

He spotted Little Sam sitting on a bench outside one of the ER holding rooms. A nurses' aide was with him. She was showing him a coloring book. Of course she had no idea that he had never seen such a thing before. She took a color crayon and showed him how to hold it, then began to fill in the picture. Little Sam caught on quickly, and Angus beamed as he watched his son, or Sam's son, scribble, not staying inside the lines at all. He looked up at Angus and beamed.

"I did it, Papa," he said, pointing to the picture.

"You sure did," Angus said. "Which room is his mother in?" he asked the aide.

"Room 142."

Angus went inside. Maria was being examined by one of the ER doctors.

"I'll take over," Angus said, pushing his way in front of the ER doctor.

"Sure thing, Doc," he said. "She seems a bit disoriented. I'm not sure what happened, but she keeps talking about crossing some field…"

"Best thing, or worst thing she's ever done," Angus said. "It remains to be seen which it was."

The ER doctor shook his head and walked away. "Good luck on this one. You're going to need it."

❈ ❈ ❈

Angus took Maria's hand. "It's going to be okay," he said, trying to reassure her.

"But—but I thought I saw Sam."

"You did," Angus said. "I don't know how to explain this to you, but life has a funny way of doing things sometimes."

And in the simplest terms he could find, Angus let the story unfold of how Sam had washed up on the shore just a little over a year ago. He had tried to explain to Maria on the way to the hospital how they had gone back to the future, back to his time. They had left the old world behind them. He had told her many times during the days—or was it years—he had spent with her in Yarmouth, protecting her and Little Sam, how her father had brought him through time to save her life. He had told her on their trip to the hospital after they crossed the field of time that she had to trust him.

"You told me to trust you," she said, looking up at him with eyes as wide as saucers. "I do, Angus. I truly do. But why did you bring me back to Sam? He is…he is nothing to me anymore. It is you I love. But if I tell him that, he may just kill you, like he was going to do—back there. He is ruthless. I know that now."

"Not to worry," Angus said, rubbing her hand with his. "I think Sam will be glad to know you are all right and that you did not have to endure the fate the history books declared you had to face. Somehow I was able to change history. Why? I have no idea why. How? By the power of God, I would guess. I have no other explanation."

"But where did Sam go?" Maria asked.

"I am not sure. My guess is that he went to look for you. He had Little Sam with him."

"No!" Maria shouted, trying to sit up but still dizzy from the shock of seeing him. "He must not have Little Sam. He will take him and run away with him. I know he will. That was what he tried to do that day..."

"Little Sam is fine," Angus said. "He is just outside your room here with a nurses' aide. She works at the hospital. I told her to keep him safe, and she will."

"But does Sam know that Little Sam is his son?"

"I doubt it," Angus said. "At least I haven't told him—yet."

"You can't tell him," Maria insisted. "We have to keep him safe with us."

"We will," Angus said. "We are going to have to all sit down together and try to explain this whole mess."

"All?" Maria asked. "Who is 'all'?"

"You, me, Sam—and Blair."

"Blair?"

"Blair is Sam's wife," Angus said, watching Maria closely for her reaction. She did not appear angry, simply puzzled, and perhaps a bit betrayed. She had moved on with her life with Angus and Little Sam, and now she was expecting another baby.

In the hallway, Sam walked up and stared at Little Sam. He reached his hand out and mussed with his hair, as black and curly as his own.

"What is your name?" Sam asked the lad.

"Sam, but everybody calls me Little Sam."

Sam didn't need the answer. He knew, instinctively, that was who he was. But how did he get here? And why?

"Where are you from?" Sam asked.

"Yarmouth," Little Sam replied.

"What is your mother's name?"

Little Sam looked puzzled for a moment, then answered, "Mama."

Sam laughed. He was so confused. He wanted to hug his son, but he didn't want to frighten him.

"And who is your father?"

"Papa," came the quick response. "He's a doctor." He paused, then asked, "Is he going to fix my mama? When she fell..."

"I'm sure he will take good care of her," Sam said, trying to believe his own words. "Stay here with the lady. I will go inside and make sure your mama is doing okay."

Sam looked at the nurse, and she pointed to the room where Maria and Angus were. He quickly entered the room. Maria looked at him, her eyes filled with wonder.

"Sam? Is that really you? But how..."

"Yes, it is me. And you are truly Maria? I don't understand this at all. Doc Angus, can you help us?"

"I think, if you feel up to it, we should go back to Blair and figure this whole thing out together."

Angus went out into the hallway and found a wheelchair to take Maria back to Blair's room. Sam followed along behind them. Angus asked the nurses' aide if she could entertain Little Sam a while longer.

"No problem," she said, smiling at the boy. "We are getting along just fine. He seems a little confused, but I suppose, since it is probably his first visit to a hospital..."

"His first visit to our world," Angus said, reaching down to embrace his son. "I will be back before long. Be a good boy for Helena."

"I will, Papa."

Sam felt like he had been stabbed in his heart. How could his son call another man, especially *that man*, "Papa"?

❋ ❋ ❋

Blair was lying in the bed, her daughter lying in her arms.

"Looks like you two have already gotten acquainted," Angus said, smiling at the picture of mother and daughter.

"She's perfect," Blair said, pulling the blanket down a little so they could all get a better look at her.

She turned to Sam and said, "Sam, meet your daughter. *Our* daughter. Samantha."

Maria grasped Angus's hand. "I don't understand," she said.

"Remember when I told you that your father took me across

the field of poverty grass, and across time so I could save you and Little Sam?"

Maria nodded. She hadn't understood it then, and she didn't understand it now.

"We have entered the twenty-first century. When you crossed the field with me, in the other direction, we came forward in time. I have no idea how it works, but your father apparently did."

Angus looked at Sam, who had finally begun to comprehend that he had been under the ocean for almost three hundred years. He was certain he would never see Maria again. Yet here she was, as alive and current as he was.

Angus began to unravel the tale of how he had been on the way to the hospital in Hyannis to deliver Blair's baby, but he had been waved down by a man in that field of poverty grass. He had followed him, feeling like he was compelled to help him, and had somehow ended up in Yarmouth in 1713, where he was able to keep Little Sam from dying.

"And that is how history was changed," Angus said, almost matter-of-factly.

"But Sam?" Maria asked. "I know you told me we would enter another time when we crossed the field. You told me to trust you—and I did. How did he get here?"

"I had nothing to do with that," Angus said. "When the *Whydah* sank, that day in April in 1717, his body was the only one that was never found."

"I know," Maria said. "They looked for him for years. Somebody thought they saw him up in Maine once, but it turned out to be somebody else." She looked at Sam and asked, "Are you all right? Are you really alive?" She looked at Blair, then said to Sam, "Angus said she is your wife."

"Yes," Sam said, reaching over and kissing his wife and his daughter.

Angus continued answering questions. He could not possibly expect them to take everything in that had happened in the past twenty-four hours—or three hundred years—in one sitting.

"I will try to explain the rest of it to you once Blair gets home, but for now, Maria, I think I should take you and Little Sam home."

"Home? Where is home?"

"To my home, in Brewster. You will live with me there." He put his arm around Maria. "We are a family. Nothing can change that."

"But Little Sam? How will we keep him safe from Sam?"

"I will not harm my son," Sam said. "I vow that I will not try to take him from you. A child is meant to be with his mother. Besides, I have my own family now too. I love Blair."

Sam began to laugh. Blair smiled at him. She loved his deep, throaty laugh.

"When I first saw Blair I thought it was you, except that her hair was like flax instead of black like a raven, as yours is. One day she bought a wig, black as coal, and when I saw her I fainted dead away, as you did today when you first saw me. I thought sure you had come back to haunt me."

"And here I am," Maria said. Angus and Sam both stared at the two women. Maria had wheeled her chair up beside Blair and was rubbing her hand gently across Samantha's little hand. "Are you disappointed?"

"Never," Sam said. "I could not be happier. I dreamed of you for three hundred years. Then God brought me Blair—today's version of you. I don't know how I can love two women, but you seem happy with Angus. And he does seem to be a good papa to Little Sam."

"He is the best with him," Maria said. "Angus loves him like he was his own son. And Little Sam adores Angus."

Sam rubbed his beard. "So you are saying, Doc Angus, that the things I saw when Paul messed with my head really happened?"

"So it would seem," Angus said. "And now that it has happened and I spent nearly three years in Yarmouth, miraculously all in the space of about five minutes, I can fill in the blanks for you too." He grinned devilishly at Sam. "And yes, it was me that bit you in the butt with a hypodermic needle."

Sam rubbed his rear. He could almost feel it again.

"I'll get even with you for that one day."

Port Call to the Future

❄ ❄ ❄

"Paul?" Angus asked as he spoke into the phone. Maria just sat and stared at him. Who was he talking to? That little tiny thing he held in his hand. Had her husband gone mad? Perhaps they would lock him up like they wanted to do to her before he rescued her.

"I think we might need your help," Angus said. "There is someone here I think you should meet."

Maria sat, open-mouthed, clinging to Little Sam like she was afraid he would disappear.

"Yes, at my house. You know where it is, right? How soon can you come?"

In less than half an hour, Paul was sounding the knocker on Angus's front door.

"Come on in," Angus called out. "We're all in here."

Paul came in and saw Maria, dressed like a vision out of the past, and Angus, with Little Sam sitting on his lap as the boy tweaked his nose. Angus would honk like a goose each time he pinched it, making Little Sam laugh.

"And just who do we have here?" Paul asked.

"Paul—Dr. Anderson—I would like you to meet my wife."

Paul looked at Angus in disbelief. There must be some logical explanation why Angus would marry a woman so suddenly. Perhaps it was another one of Angus's "rescue missions" he was so well known for. The woman obviously had a child from another man.

"And this is my son, Little Sam," Angus said, causing Paul to be even more confused.

"I think maybe you'd better sit down," Angus suggested.

"I think you are right. Do you want to start from the beginning? Where did you find her, and why did you marry her?"

"Well," Angus began, "once upon a time…"

Paul rolled his eyes. *He'd better make this one great fairy tale for me to swallow it*, he thought.

"I was on my way in this awful storm, the one we are still in tonight, headed toward the hospital in Hyannis to deliver Blair's baby."

"She had the baby?" Paul asked excitedly.

"Yes, a little girl. Her name is Samantha."

"After her daddy?" Paul asked.

"Yes, after Sam Black. Or Black Sam Bellamy."

At the mere mention of his name the woman Angus had introduced as his wife shivered. She thought, after the day Angus had exorcised Black Sam's ghost from their lives, she was rid of him forever. But now...

"But who is she?" Paul asked.

"Like I started to say, as I was struggling to see through the rain to get to the hospital, a man was standing out in a field of poverty grass. He seemed desperate to get my attention. I had no choice in the matter, having taken the Hippocratic oath and all, but to stop to try to help him."

Angus paused for this much to sink in for Paul.

"He told me his daughter was having a baby, but the baby and his daughter were both in trouble. He said he knew I could help them. So I followed him. Corky and I went running through the field, in the rain, and when we got to his home it was 1713, and we were in Yarmouth."

Paul scratched his head, trying to make sense of this whole thing.

"I don't understand it any more than I can figure out the whole thing of Sam coming forward in time. Somehow—I know it defies all scientific reason—I crossed time and went backwards, just as he came forward."

"So what happened while you were there?" Paul asked.

"Just like history recorded, Maria was having Black Sam's baby, and the baby was about to die. I did what I could to revive the baby, and it worked. The baby did not die, thus Maria was not a witch."

Paul sat in silence, trying to take this whole tale in.

"And then what happened?"

"Well, they were still upset with Maria. She was not a witch, but ah, she was bewitching." Angus reached over and drew Maria close to him. "The only way I could redeem her was to marry her. So I did."

"You married Maria Hallett? In 1713? In Yarmouth?"

"Indeed I did, and it was quite a romp. At first they thought I must be a witch or something too, to be able to breathe life into a dead child. But they soon began to accept me. They helped me build a house for Maria and Little Sam and me. They put a medical office on the side of it."

"I know this sounds like a silly question, but how long were you there?"

"Almost four years," Angus said, like it was perfectly normal. "Until Black Sam returned and we—a group of men at Crosby's Tavern and I—hauled him off to jail. He managed to escape, but we caught up with him and threw him into the ocean."

"And that's where he made it aboard his ship, and it sank, just like Sam said when he was hypnotized?"

"Exactly," Angus said, thrilled that Paul seemed to grasp that the things Sam had seen happened, even though they were totally unexplainable.

"So now what?" Paul asked. "Has Sam seen...her?"

"Yes."

"And?"

"And he is in love with Blair. He is still trying to make sense out of all of it, but he figures if he can come forward in time, why can't Maria do the same, only in reverse?"

Paul looked at Maria. She was listening to every word Angus was saying, trying to understand it. "If she needs help, I'm available," he said. "There are bound to be some big adjustments ahead."

"That's an understatement!" Angus said. "It complicates things a bit that she is pregnant again."

"With Sam's baby?"

"No way!" Maria shouted. "This baby belongs to my husband and me. This baby is mine and Angus's."

"You say you were gone four years?" Paul asked.

"That's the way it works out. Somehow, though, when we got back to my car, after we crossed that same field again, the clock had only move five minutes.

"Boy, you work fast," Paul said, winking at Angus.

"You don't know the half of it."

"No, but I'm looking forward to hearing the rest of it. I'll leave you alone. Good luck with this one, pal. I think you're going to need it."

"Not as long as we have each other, and Little Sam, and our love."

"Love conquers all," Paul said as he got up and left. "At least that's what they say."

EPILOGUE

July 2012

The foursome had become the best of friends. They seldom spoke of "other times." There were some things that were better left unspoken. Sam loved Blair with all his heart, and Maria could not imagine her life with anyone other than Angus.

On a lovely sunny Sunday afternoon, the whole gang had gathered at Sam and Blair's home. They were sitting on the wraparound porch, reminiscing of the events in the last—what? Was it almost four years ago when they had first all assembled in Hyannis? Or should they start counting time from the early 1700s, when Sam and Maria had their first tryst? The group consisted of Sam and Blair, their two youngsters—three-year old Samantha and baby Jeremy, Doc Angus and Maria, with their two children—Little Sam, now nearly seven, and three-and-a-half-year-old Annabelle. And of course Doc Angus's faithful dog, Corky, was running about, chasing the kids like his life depended on it.

Suddenly, Corky growled and turned to face the hedge that surrounded the yard. In no time flat he was off like a speeding bullet. He charged into the bushes like a herd of buffalo on the western plains. Fearing for its life, a black cat darted out from the bushes and ran across the road, barely missing an oncoming car.

"Nine lives," Sam remarked. "I swear, if I see one more black cat I'll let out a yell."

A look of glee crossed between Doc Angus and Maria. They'd had more than their share of black cats too. The first one had been that awful day when Doc Angus swore to be rid of Black Sam's ghost haunting Maria, so he performed a fake exorcism and a black cat went screaming into the woods. They laughed, shook their heads, and refused to share their private joke.

Since that fateful day when Doc Angus had returned to Cape Cod, and once they swallowed the fact that Sam Black was indeed Black Sam Bellamy, they had discussed at length what they would tell Little Sam when he was old enough to understand things about who his father was. Sam had a real problem letting go of the fact that Little Sam was truly his child, and the adults all acknowledged him as such, but Doc Angus was the only father he had ever known, so Sam became the most devoted "Uncle Sam" anyone had ever seen. The fact that he was the spitting image of Sam was not lost on any of them. And he had the same wonderful dry sense of humor his father possessed. You just never knew what kind of a comment he would come up with next.

Little Sam was, well, a conundrum, to say the least. He and his sister, Annabelle, were as opposite as day and night. Even as a tiny tyke, Annabelle always seemed to have a somber demeanor, while Little Sam was never serious about anything. He would often surprise them with something from their "past lives," when he would mention something. The talk of the cat was all it took.

"Mama," he said, hopping up the steps and crouching down in front of her. "Do you like cats?"

"I can take them or leave them," Maria said. "Why?"

"Because Gramma Mary didn't like them. I 'member her telling me one time that the only reason God made cats was to keep too many mice from bein' 'round."

"Quite a memory the lad's got there," Doc Angus quipped. "Let's see. That was about two hundred and ninety-eight years ago, give or take a couple of years."

Sam threw his head back and laughed. "I'll not be havin' ye fill the lad's head with impossibilities," he cautioned Doc Angus.

"You think that cat was somethin' else?" Little Sam asked.

"What do you mean?" Maria asked.

"Well, like Uncle Sam. He told me once that he used to be a pirate, but that now he's not. So he was somethin', then he wasn't, and maybe the cat was somethin' else and now it's not."

"Serious thinking for such a little fellow," Doc Angus said. "Who or what do you think the cat might have been before?"

Doc Angus had never really thought much about reincarnation, and he didn't buy into the concept. He knew for certain that at Little Sam's age his mind was full of playing marbles and what he could find to eat.

"I don't know," Little Sam said, shrugging his shoulders. "One thing's certain though. It can't be Gramma Mary. Sure and be'gory she'd not come back as a cat!"

They all laughed at the very idea of Gramma Mary coming back to life after nearly three hundred years as a cat, the thing she hated even more than mice! Or pigs! Ah, yes, the pigs that laid the pearls in the yard. But that was another story too. One they would tell Little Sam about one day.

※ ※ ※

Doc Angus shook his head, trying to imagine the tales Little Sam would spin when he got to school in the fall. Show-and-tell would be more than his teacher ever bargained for. He could just picture their parent-teacher conferences.

※ ※ ※

After the kids went back to playing again, Maria and Blair went inside to get some lemonade and cookies. Alone, Doc Angus asked Sam, "Did you ever think you'd see the day that we'd be sitting here together, actually enjoying each other's company?"

"You mean after you tried to kill me?" Sam asked.

"It's a mighty good thing you ended up in the ocean, or you'd have been done for for sure. At the time, I wouldn't have been sad to see your body float up to the top of the water and know that you were dead and gone forever."

"Fooled ya, didn't I?" Sam asked.

"Yup. I really thought I'd seen the last of you. Especially when that crew found the *Whydah*. I was sure they'd find your rattling bones down there. I knew you'd never give up the ship without a fight."

Neither of the men was aware that Little Sam was huddled up close to the base of the porch, listening to the "grown up talk," as he liked to call it. He jumped up and stomped his foot hard on the ground and bellowed, "Well, shiver me timbers!"

Doc Angus and Sam both roared with laughter. Little Sam joined them, rolling on the ground as he repeated the phrase over and over again. "Well, shiver me timbers! Shiver me timbers! Yup, me timbers are shiverin' all over the place!"

Doc Angus looked at Sam and asked, too softly for Little Sam to hear, "And just whose son is he?"

"Shiver me timbers, beats me," Sam answered, grabbing Doc Angus by the hand. "Maybe we'll one day forget and it'll be anybody's guess."

A NOTE FROM THE AUTHOR

Which came first, the chicken or the egg? It's an age old question. For me, the question is more aptly, "Which came first, writing or genealogy?" One thing led to the other. While my late husband, Ivan, had the rich and famous ancestry, mine had the fun ones—the witches and pirates, among others. And that discovery is what led to the story of Maria Hallett and Black Sam Bellamy, true historic characters from Cape Cod in the early 1700s.

As fate (or God) would have it, about the time I started writing the first book, told from Maria's point-of-view, *House Call to the Past*, a crew actually discovered the shipwrecked *Whydah*, Black Sam's ship. Eventually, they established a museum in Provincetown, Massachusetts.

I owe a great debt to Ken Kinkor, a member of the crew who devotes his time to running the Whydah Museum. He was very helpful in answering questions from a "land lubber." While there was some input needed for *House Call to the Past*, it became even more important for *Port Call to the Future*, as that was Black Sam's tale, and there are no better experts on the couple than the crew from Expedition Whydah. In one phone conversation, Ken reminded me, "Remember, Sam was very clever." I felt like he was giving me his permission to have Sam do—well, whatever Sam wanted to do. I asked Ken if it was okay to include the museum itself in the book, and he graciously agreed. (I'm not sure what I would have done with the story had he said they would rather that I not mention it.) The only request Ken had was, "I would appreciate it if you don't kill me off." Rest easy, Ken. You survived quite well.

I hope you have half as much fun reading the rest of the story as I had writing it. Sam had definite ideas of his own as to where the story should go, and I felt like I had no control over him. For that, it is probably a better story than it started out to be. I've learned long ago not to argue with my characters, nor do I outline ahead of time. It is a complete waste of time.

So, to my 13th great-aunt Maria Hallett, thank you for your story. And to Sam, I'm really glad they never found you or your remains. It makes for one magnificent tale!

I love to hear from readers. You can contact me at janetelainesmith@yahoo.com or through my website at http://www.janetelainesmith.com or by snail mail at Janet Elaine Smith, W7969 Vine St., Amberg WI 54102.

Janet Elaine Smith